Also by Robert Boswell

LIVING TO BE A HUNDRED
MYSTERY RIDE
THE GEOGRAPHY OF DESIRE
CROOKED HEARTS
DANCING IN THE MOVIES

AMERICAN OWNED LOVE

American Owned Love

ROBERT BOSWELL

Alfred A. Knopf   New York

1997

This Is a Borzoi Book
Published by Alfred A. Knopf, Inc.

Copyright © 1997 by Robert Boswell

Library of Congress Cataloging-in-Publication Data
Boswell, Robert.
American owned love / by Robert Boswell.—1st ed.
    p.   cm.
    ISBN 0-679-43251-5 (alk. paper)
    I. Title.
PS3552.O8126A8   1997
813´.54—dc20   96-20731
                                                    CIP

Manufactured in the United States of America
First Edition

For Antonya Nelson,
Jade
&
Noah

The author wishes to thank the National Endowment for the Arts, New Mexico State University, and Warren Wilson College for their support. Thanks also to the following individuals:

Ashbel Green

Antonya Nelson

Kim Witherspoon

and Steven Schwartz, Kevin McIlvoy, Christopher McIlroy, Margot Livesey, David Schweidel, Susan Nelson, Julie Nelson, Stuart Brown, Gretchen Mazur, Don Kurtz, Nicole Nelson, and Jennifer Bernstein.

PART I

1993

River

1

Even asleep, Rita Schaefer heard her mother advancing. She would remember nothing of her dream except the way her mother entered it—as a black swan gliding inches above Rita's head, larger than any living swan, the curve of her long neck a hieroglyphic of elegance, the expanse of her wings blotting out the sun, wind rushing through her dark feathers.

Her mother's actual approach was less poetic. This time of year the door to Rita's bedroom stuck, and her mother threw herself against it, knocking a pile of T-shirts from the top of the dresser as she burst in. She collided with Rita's old dollhouse, tipping it over, miniature family abruptly evicted, flying out onto the hardwood floor. "Hurry," she called to her sleeping daughter. She leapt onto the mattress, taking Rita by the shoulders, shaking her, lifting her head from the pillow.

By the time Rita opened her eyes, her mother straddled her, leaning so close that her hair touched Rita's cheeks. A breeze from the window lifted a gauze curtain, which fluttered between them. Behind the gauze, her mother's face hovered like the afterimage of a dream.

"Hurry," her mother said again, flinging aside the curtain, pulling Rita up by the arm but letting her head drop back to the feather pillow, "and wait here until I get Heart."

Her mother's black dress murmured as she climbed from the bed, an extravagant gown with puffed sleeves and a draped neckline, making a noise that spoke of underthings, of skirts and garters and camisoles—a noise like the rush of wind through feathers. She again sprinted across the floor, the black gown flying out behind her as she ran through the doorway.

Rita sat up in the dim and suddenly hushed room, her heart racing. She touched her white petticoat to be certain what she was wearing. Should she change? Did her mother want her to hurry and get dressed? She had not inherited her mother's slender body and did not have the same interest in clothing. She didn't know how to dress for disaster.

She crawled from the bed and immediately bumped into the upended dollhouse, bruising her shin. She rubbed the soreness. A cobweb attached itself to her fingers, and she tried to flick it off. She was fifteen and couldn't remember when she had last played with the dollhouse. In the morning she would start high school—if she could get up. If this weren't a catastrophe her mother was waking her to embrace.

The closet door stood ajar. Should she put on her best clothes like her mother? Was there a storm? During the season of desert monsoon the weather could be unpredictable. She glanced back at the gauze curtain, which floated lazily on the air.

"Don't bother with clothes." Her mother, at the door again, extended her arm, a long black sleeve. She wore lacy, fingerless gloves, and Rita tried again to flick away the spider's web. "You don't need clothes," her mother said. "Come on. Hurry."

Beside her mother appeared Heart, who lived in their attic. She was roughly the same age as Rita's mother, but her flatfooted and tilting stance, as well as the homemade white smock she slept in, made her look like a child—hair ruffled from bed, eyes made enormous by thick, round glasses. Rita felt a measure of relief just seeing her there, equally bewildered.

Her mother wiggled the extended hand impatiently. Rita picked her way across the floor. When she gripped the hand, it tugged her into the hall, Heart trailing, barefoot like Rita, her alarm magnified by the lenses covering her eyes.

The living room smelled of liquor. Two tumblers of melting ice shared the coffee table, the neck of the reading lamp craned low as if to illuminate the weave of the rug. Something about the couch was wrong, but there was no time to name it. Rita stepped on the abandoned cap of a rum bottle, which skidded across the floor, entering the mouth of an overturned shoe, one of her mother's high heels.

They rushed into the kitchen, the wooden floor cool against Rita's feet, ice trays in a puddle beside the sink, a green ribbon curling next to the trays, one end of it darkened by the water. Before they passed through the back door, her mother switched off the yellow light that lit the concrete stoop. "Hurry," she said a final time, and swung open the door. She gripped Rita by one hand and Heart by the other, pulling them awkwardly through the narrow portal and into the tall grass, still damp from the afternoon shower. They stepped barefoot and blind into the yard.

Rita's mother released her grip on them, running ahead in the light of a brilliant moon, the black dress swinging behind her like a loosened shadow, her feet shimmering in their stockings, then disappearing beneath the black skirt. Shapes coalesced about the river—the crowd of trees arching over the banks, shadowy branches shifting, leaves pulsing in the mild wind. Rita felt herself slow. On the grass near the water lay a white blanket, square and un-rumpled. It almost made her stop running, that white square against the dark ground like an object from another world.

Her mother did not slow, not even at the riverbank. She planted a foot on the grassy ledge and leapt into the water. It thrilled Rita to see her mother fly like that, her legs still churning beneath the skirt. Spray from the splash misted Rita's face, and she stopped at the river's edge to watch her mother gallop through the shallow water, the black dress trailing her, roil-ing on the water's surface. "Don't be cowards," her mother called without turning.

Rita glanced at Heart, who stood beside her in the damp grass. "I think we're supposed to go in," Rita said.

Heart lifted her narrow shoulders uncertainly, looking from the river to the blanket and then to Rita's mother. She adjusted her glasses. Her mouth opened crookedly. "It's a nice night for a swim, I suppose."

Rita nodded in agreement, then took a tentative step into the water—warmer than she'd expected and more shallow, barely above the knee. She heard, somewhere in the distance, a sound lower than her mother's splash, the rumble of a tractor making a turn in a field, a farmer working unspeak-ably late. It calmed her to hear it, to picture his dust-laden face, the brilliant headlamps shining on a field of chiles or cotton or onions.

Heart followed Rita into the water, lifting her smock high so that her white underwear showed. "I was baptized in the Ohio River," she said, "but it didn't really take." She knotted the tails of her smock in her fist. "The preacher wore hip waders."

Rita scarcely heard her, walking now in pursuit of her mother, the muddy river bottom squeezing in between her toes, a sensation that made her feel like a little girl. She took a dozen steps before stopping. Up to her thighs in the river, she suddenly saw what her mother had called them from sleep to witness. She glanced back at Heart to see if she'd noticed it, too, but Heart was concentrating on keeping her clothes dry, the smock up above her bellybutton, as if her pale skin and old-fashioned underwear were the point of this adventure.

"Look at the water," Rita said.

The river was running black. Black water in the light of a blue moon.

Heart's magnified eyes grew wider. "It's as black as coal," she said. "What in the—"

Rita stumbled, throwing out her arms as if to catch herself on the water. She sank beneath the surface, the black river closing about her, swallowing her whole. But she instantly rose, flinging her hair back with a shake of her head, wiping her face with her hands.

"You all right?" Heart asked.

Rita nodded and blew water from her lips. The dunking, in fact, had calmed her.

"We can't all be as agile as your mother," Heart said. She pulled her smock even higher. With her free hand, she dipped fingers experimentally into the water. "I've never seen anything like it. Does it feel oily to you? What do you suppose caused this?"

Rita had seen the river run muddy brown in the spring, and a rust brown one November from tannin in the leaves. She had seen it blue many summer days, and most often green, a green like her mother's eyes, but she had never seen it black.

"This could be toxic," Heart said. "But it doesn't have that chemical odor. Can you smell anything?"

It occurred to Rita that she would remember this night for the rest of her life—the river flowing darkly between her legs, her petticoat heavy with black water, water darker than the dark around it, a charred black, as if it had been burned by the desert sun.

Rita's mother made a noise in her throat, a wet shudder of breath. "I knew you'd see it," her mother said, and she began to weep, touching her face with her fingertips. "Isn't it amazing?" Her face became contorted by the crying. "I knew you'd get it," she said hoarsely. "I knew you wouldn't let me down."

Rita nodded. "I see it."

Her mother dropped to her knees in the riverbed, dark water circling her waist, her hair lit by the moon. "Anything is possible," she said, her arms opening as if to embrace the flow. "Anything can happen."

They lingered in the river, the dark flow swift and insistent, Rita in her wet petticoat, Heart with her white smock bunched above her pale thighs, Rita's mother kneeling in black, the elaborate dress invisible now, the same color as the water, as if they were one and the same, as if she were wearing the river.

2

The semitrailer bearing the insignia and slogan of Tyson Farms heaved past the Fairlane with such noise and at such speed that the car's windows shook, and Enrique Calzado woke. His head had slipped off the seat, and he looked up from the dead space above the floorboard. He could see only a moving wall of metal, the bold red letters appearing singly, framed by his father's window—a huge red *S–O–N*. "Whoa," Enrique said, banging his head against the armrest as he jerked himself up.

The semi roared ahead, already signaling its intention to reclaim their lane. Enrique's father, usually a vocal driver, said nothing. He slumped against his door, one hand on the steering wheel, the other propping up his head.

Enrique said, "That guy's flying."

"You've got school," his father said, his voice almost a whisper. "Sleep."

Enrique leaned close to his father to check the speedometer. The indicator dipped below forty. No wonder the big truck flew by. Pulling back, he knocked his head against the rearview mirror, leaving a white smear. He touched his hair. His finger came away with a streak of white cream. "Something's coming out of my head?" he said, sniffing the finger: his mother's Swiss Formula Collagen lotion, a dollar ninety-nine if he rode his bike all the way out to the Safeway, or three dollars at Arzate's grocery downtown. He used to augment his allowance by secretly riding out to the Safeway on errands and pocketing the savings, until his sister Cecilia pointed out that it was dishonest. "Clever, though," she had added, which had pleased him.

The bottle of lotion lay on the floorboard, having slipped from its hidden spot beneath the seat. His mother liked to wring her hands and this lotion gave her an excuse, or so his father claimed. From the back, beneath the same seat, Enrique had hidden a magazine. He wondered if everyone in his family had hidden things in the Fairlane, but before he could consider what his father might have stashed, he stuck his head in front of the rearview mirror again. He wanted to see the white stuff in his hair. How did he look as a blonde?

"Sit down," his father said. "I can't drive with you all over . . . " He let the sentence fade out.

Enrique's hair had a single dab of white lotion, the hair around it greased down and dirty but not blond. He tried to adjust the mirror back to its previous position. "How's that?" he asked.

"Yes," his father said without examining it. The headlights of another car rushed up from behind them and zoomed past, the car's body blue and sleek, its windows dark. The indicator on the Fairlane's speedometer sank closer to thirty.

"Maybe I'll climb in the back," Enrique said. His father didn't respond. From his knees, Enrique bent over the seatback, careful not to bump his father, his feet coming up and striking the ceiling as he tumbled into the rear of the Fairlane. For the past week, he had been living in the car, sleeping in the backseat every night. It smelled familiar now, like his bedroom at home.

His mother had covered the seat with a striped sheet, his pillow at one end, a stain on the pillowcase from opening his mouth while he slept, a drooling habit that made him think girls wouldn't want to spend the night once he was old enough to ask. Did they check the pillows before they agreed to stay over?

He felt under the seat for the magazine. His sister had left it in the car, *New Woman*, a title that had to mean something, but Enrique couldn't figure out what. At fourteen and about to start his final year of junior high, he had entered that gray area where terms like *New Woman* called to mind wildly different images. He pictured a naked, somewhat shiny woman touching his shoulder and saying that sex with him had made her feel like a New Woman. Her teeth shone especially brightly in Enrique's imagined scene, but the shoulder she had touched was still clothed. Evidently he hadn't taken his shirt off, which was probably rude. Wouldn't it be uncomfortable for her? He imagined the buttons of his shirt pressing into her skin, the perfectly round indentations in her belly, which led him to picture the woman as a creature who had been assembled Frankenstein-style, ending with the buttoning up of the front—hidden buttons, of course, beneath a flap of skin, but he would feel them whenever he lay on top of her, like the buttons on some mattresses that you could feel right through the sheets.

His thoughts kept jumping about between what he considered mature thoughts—his concern about the shiny woman's comfort—and what he considered kid stuff—*New Woman* meaning a Frankenstein monster, only beautiful and with bright teeth and who liked him.

His favorite page featured a woman in a brassiere and panties, *lingerie—*

one of those words that made Enrique's stomach jump like a dip on a bad road. He let the magazine slip from his hands. As if by magic, it fell open to the ad, a photograph he had all but memorized over the past week, the pages creased and shiny from his handling. The woman was skinny and Anglo with a funny look on her face, like maybe she was hungry and had traded her clothes for food, and now if she wanted to eat she had to trade her underwear. Enrique turned the page, knowing there was no sequel but checking to make sure. He paged back to the woman—just an ad, and for lingerie, but somehow it made him hungry, which reminded him that there was a slice of pizza in the car somewhere. Under the seat?

He began groping, sticking his arms far into the dark crack between floorboard and seat springs, touching, finally, a plastic bag. Had he wrapped the slice? He tugged it through, but it was only his father's pills, round ones and oblong ones, all trapped in brown plastic bottles with big white lids.

He shoved the sack of pills and the magazine both under the seat, figuring he must have eaten the leftover slice after all. He sat up just enough to peek at the back of his father's head. "You awake, Dad?" he said.

"Fine," his father said softly, a voice barely related to his real voice. "You sleep." His father, the custodian at the elementary school that Enrique and his siblings had attended, had to return to work in the morning after spending a week of his vacation in Tucson, Arizona. Enrique had to start school, too, which pleased him—friends to see, things to do. He had been the only family member invited to go with his father, which had also pleased him, although neither his sister nor his mother would have liked sleeping in the car. So maybe it wasn't such an honor, but it still pleased him, and one night he had seen River Phoenix in *My Own Private Idaho*. The movie had changed his life. He was almost certain it had.

He had accompanied his father to the University Cancer Center, which had turned out to be a hospital, and his father had undergone tests, a biopsy, other things that his father assured him he did not need to understand, although he had come to help make sense of the forms. His father could not read English, which embarrassed him, and he would admit this to virtually no one, especially not to Anglo doctors. As it turned out, the forms were all written in English on one side and Spanish on the other. Although his father would not speak Spanish and would not permit it to be spoken in their house, he evidently could read it. He studied the questions on one side of the form and checked the boxes on the other side. Except to help his father write the paragraph describing his symptoms, Enrique had not been needed.

Nights, Enrique had slept in the Fairlane parked in the hospital lot. Days, he watched television in his father's room, wandered down to the campus of the university, ate in the hospital cafeteria or the McDonald's a few blocks away. One day, standing in the shadow of a curving campus sculpture he could not comprehend, a girl with blond hair woven into dozens of braids cropping out like electrodes all over her head, asked him for directions to the Modern Languages Building.

"My Summer Mod Civ one-oh-one got bumped out of the old library," she explained, "but I don't know where Modern Languages is."

He smiled at her grandly, thinking that it was his proximity to the sculpture that had made him, a middle school student, pass for a college guy, the sort of college guy who knew his way around campus. "It's right over that way," he said, not wanting to be rude, pointing down the grassy mall toward a cluster of buildings.

"The one before the Union or the one before that?"

"The one before that," he said.

"Got it," she said, her fingers rising one at a time from her notebook to wave good-bye.

He had watched her walk away, her ragged denim shorts barely covering her bottom, watched her duck into one of the buildings, and felt, for the moment, that this sort of life was available to him. Then he decided he should leave before she came charging out of whatever building he had sent her to.

That evening at the hospital he found his father sleepy and cross, unwilling to eat, his face gray and sunken like a wooden mask left to weather outdoors. "Take some money from my wallet," his father instructed. "See a movie—not a dirty show." Then his father added, "Hurry. Go."

As Enrique left the room, his father added, "It's these tests. Wear you out. Don't you worry. They can't find nothing wrong with me. I'm a bull, that's what they tell me." He spoke another few words, but too feebly for Enrique to hear. Enrique did not question whether his father was telling the truth. It was what he wanted to believe, and he could not imagine his father genuinely ill.

The only theater within walking distance offered several choices, but Enrique had taken time to eat before coming, and most of the movies were already in progress. He selected *My Own Private Idaho* for its strange title and convenient starting time: midnight. The movie made almost no sense to him, not sense in the way he expected movies to make sense. He didn't know why River Phoenix kept waking up in the road, or why the other guy wanted to run through warehouses, or whether he was supposed to think the boys actually liked kissing men, but the movie had a quality of sexual energy and confusion that spoke to him so profoundly it was as if the filmmaker had read not his mind but his soul. The scenes of the Idaho landscape, the images that came to River Phoenix whenever he passed out, seemed somehow pure, elemental, so pure that they became for Enrique *his* landscape, although his home—Persimmon, New Mexico—looked not at all like the Idaho depicted, which made the film seem more like a dream than a movie—personal and strange, yet also familiar.

Sitting in the dark theater, Enrique longed to be River Phoenix, wind blowing through his shaggy blond hair one minute, and then the next minute in seizure, completely gone, partly in the past but not a past he—or anyone—had ever lived, rather a past that conveyed in an image what the real past denied—the liquid, magic slur of the senses against the backdrop of circumstance.

Enrique did not exactly understand all of this, but he felt the pull of the movie as powerfully as if it had been called *Enrique Calzado's Secret Life*, a life secret even to himself, but one which now and again left traces on the life he lived.

Upon leaving the theater, he discovered that the world had changed, that the attributes of darkness had altered, that city lights had a different sheen, that creosote and sage—plants he had seen and smelled all his life—had become infinitely strange. He walked through the university neighborhood, gaping at cars and asphalt, the bizarre aluminum television antennae—just like at his home—the impossibly tall palm trees. On a street called Mabel, he stared through a lighted window and saw a family sitting around a table eating sandwiches and talking, gesturing with their bottles of soda—a family no different from his, really, but made exotic by the window he had to view them through, and by the strange property that inhabited the night. As he watched, they one by one came outside to a station wagon and removed luggage. In their yard, they looked like ordinary people, but through the window they seemed extraordinary. "Are you lost?" one of them—the mother—asked him. "No, thank you," he had said and begun walking again. The night had proved to be the most profound of his life.

He sat up again to peer over his father's shoulder at the dash. His father had been discharged only this afternoon. The drive, which had taken four hours going, had already taken eight coming back, and they weren't yet to the Rio Grande, where they would leave the interstate and follow the two-lane highway to Persimmon. They had stopped numerous times, his father claiming that the medications made him need to pee, but he would not let Enrique come into the bathrooms, and he stayed as long as forty minutes.

Now they were doing only twenty-five miles an hour, as if the car itself had taken on his father's exhaustion, as if machines might be sympathetic to the people who operated them—a thought that let Enrique's mind drift again toward sleep, a murky sleep lit by the passing lights of speeding vehicles, punctuated irregularly by the growl of tires on the gravel shoulder. His dream took him back to the front seat, red block letters appearing once again in his father's window, but too large to read, overfilling the frame. Part of a curved line appeared—a D perhaps—then long and short horizontal lines—an E or F—then the peak of an A. The truck was passing too quickly for Enrique to puzzle out all the shapes, paint bleeding down the metal wall, his father's face a silhouette in one corner.

He woke because the Fairlane had all but stopped. Lifting his head, he expected to see their slump block house, concrete driveway, and their small square of grass. Instead, he stared beyond the Fairlane's hood at the curving exit ramp they were inching down. The ramp would take them to the two-lane highway, still miles above Persimmon. People called the highway "River Road" because it followed the Rio Grande down the state and into Texas. The Rio Grande divided New Mexico almost exactly in the center, then turned upon leaving the state, angling east as well as south, becoming the national border between Mexico and the United States all along the west side of Texas.

As soon as the Fairlane left the exit ramp, the river appeared. Enrique could not say immediately what was different, but he sensed a change, a disturbance in the familiar landscape. Then he perceived the unnatural darkness of the water. "It's black," he said, rolling down his window to stick his head out. "The river's all black." On his knees in the backseat directly behind his father, he leaned out into the night air and stared at the black water, a black like the asphalt that lay in front of the Fairlane. He pulled his head in, touched his father's shoulder. "The water's black," he said.

"I'm just a little tired," his father replied. "Nothing to worry about."

Enrique leaned out the window again. His mother would have said he was riding like a dog, and he felt a corresponding urge to yowl. The river ran as black as the night sky in the movie that had changed his life. He glanced up at the real night sky, which was lit by a bright moon, more blue than black, an uncooperative sky. The black river spoke to Enrique of the world's strangeness, a strangeness that he now felt specially privy to, a strangeness that must always have been there. How had he missed it?

"Those doctors took all my blood," his father said softly, but Enrique, his head out the window, could not hear.

At two-forty in the morning they arrived home. Enrique had to wake his mother to help guide his father inside, one of them under each arm, his father saying, "Just worn down. Medicine makes you tired."

Lost in his own science of self-discovery, Enrique did not worry about his father. He even felt superior to his mother's instant concern, until they lowered his father onto the bed, and his father said, *"No te preocupes."*

In his fourteen years of life, Enrique had never before heard his father speak Spanish. "He's dying," Enrique said. He dropped to his knees beside the bed, taking his father's hand, but his father had already fallen asleep.

"He's just tuckered out," his mother said decisively, patting her kneeling son on the head. "Driving all night like a teenager." She had become calm in the face of Enrique's anguish. "You're tired, too, Mr. Big Boy. Gone traipsing off with your father like some kind of I don't know what. You're tired, too."

Enrique suddenly felt the truth of this. He let his mother lead him to his bed. A quick, heavy sleep overcame him and returned him to his dreams, taking him this time to the Idaho of the movie, but no longer Idaho at all, Persimmon, and not Persimmon, the river not black but luminous, so bright with the sun that it seemed a source of light, the branches of the trees arching unsteadily over the banks, lifting and falling, but the sky dark and speckled with stars. Enrique found himself among the trees but at the same time in his house looking out the window at the moving water, the undulating branches—things that could not be seen from his real house. The dream of the truck had frightened him, but this dream filled him with joy.

His mother let him sleep an extra thirty minutes. When he woke, he ran immediately to his father's bed. He found it empty and neatly made, as if no one had ever slept there. He looked to the spot on the carpet where he had fallen to his knees certain that his father was dying, but the carpet retained nothing of the moment.

"It's seven thirty," his mother said, startling him. She stood in the doorway to the bedroom, holding a stack of folded clothing—his clothes for the first day of school. "Your father's eating his breakfast. Get your sleepy self in there before he leaves for work."

This was not real life, Enrique thought, looking again to the unperturbed carpet, the perfectly made bed. Even his pajamas, his regular pajamas that he was wearing—when had he put them on the night before? He knew he was not dreaming, but he could not believe he was in the real world.

In the kitchen, everything returned to normal, even his father. " 'Strong as a bull cow.' That's what those fancy doctors said," his father bragged. "But they got it wrong. I'm strong as two bulls."

Enrique and his sister—Cecilia, his only sibling still at home—laughed at this, but Enrique now believed his father had his own private place. Not Idaho, not Persimmon. Someplace unspeakably strange, belonging to no one but him.

His mother began picking at Enrique's hair, the grease spot at the top of his head. "Get your fancy self washed," she said. "You have to get to school." She took his head and aimed it toward her nose. "That's not for hair. That's to keep my skin from drying out like a lizard's."

"Let the boy alone," his father said. "He's been to Tucson now, seen all the latest fashions."

"Ooh," his sister said.

And on it went, the normal teasing and talk, like any other morning of his life. His father kissed his mother good-bye, as he always did, then patted each of his children on the shoulder as he swung around the table to the door. His mother took her position at the kitchen window to watch until her husband was in their car. She whistled the same familiar nameless tune that Enrique had heard all his life. Even the cereal in his bowl, the little circles of oats, floated, same as always, in the milk's shallow scrim.

3

Seven hours before the river ran black, Gay Schaefer kicked her neighbor's security door. It was a satisfying act, like being the only person to address an impostor by his real name. In one hand she held a bowl filled with fruit salad, while the other knotted her hair and lifted it up off her neck. The sun had only nominally begun its descent, the dark still hours away, the temperature climbing after the brief rain.

Gay booted the door again just as Margaret Lamb began to push it open. Margaret frowned, smoke trailing from her mouth, but Gay didn't let her speak. "Don't you feel the slightest bit rude not inviting Heart?"

"It's grownups only," Margaret said.

"Heart is older than I am," Gay said.

"Are we looking for honesty?" Margaret raised her cigarette to permit Gay entry, an inadvertent parody of the Statue of Liberty, Gay thought, the burning torch an imported cigarette—from France, no less—with a snaky smell that reminded her of the odor of new shoes. "Heart doesn't like me," Margaret said.

"That's not true," Gay said, although it was true. Heart considered Margaret Lamb a snob. Accurate, Gay conceded, but everyone had flaws. "I made fruit salad," Gay said. "The bananas are already turning." She shouldn't have come without Heart, but Margaret had talked her into it. She had to be home by eleven in any case. Sander was driving down from Albuquerque to see her. It was their fifteenth wedding anniversary. She might have felt guilty going to this dinner party before he arrived, but she had the day off from work tomorrow to spend with him. Their daughter did not know that she and Sander were still married. Rita thought they were divorced, like all the other parents. She thought them largely normal. Gay wiped her feet on a straw mat. "You didn't tell me what to bring."

"Get in before the house is full of flies," Margaret said. "You look radiant."

Gay maneuvered past the cigarette. She had worn a green two-piece floral rayon thing. Nice enough, but Margaret was wearing a tight scarlet dress that made her shimmer when she moved, and matching scarlet lipstick. "You didn't tell me you were dressing up," Gay said. Then she added, "That lipstick looks ridiculous."

"Oh, hush and get in here."

Unlike virtually every other house in town, the Lambs' had central air conditioning. The cool air struck Gay so forcefully she thought she might get a headache. Most houses in Persimmon had evaporative coolers, which used a fraction of the electricity but relied on dry desert air and failed to do anything during the rainy season. The Lambs entertained almost nightly during the monsoon, as if to share their good fortune or to brag.

Margaret snatched the bowl from Gay and led her to the living room, where Randall Lamb sat watching television—a big screen Mitsubishi that dominated the room. Pictures of a smoking urban landscape jerked across the screen from a handheld camera held aloft in a Jeep. Superimposed lettering spelled out "Sarajevo." Randall Lamb rose and shook Gay's hand formally. "I hope you don't mind if we see the end of the news?" He had the modulated voice and lofty manner of a newscaster himself.

"Not at all," Gay said, becoming instantly more formal, which made her feel like a child pretending. She didn't know Randall well. He was superintendent of public schools, and they usually discussed Rita's teachers. Tall and probably handsome at one time, he had become beefy in middle age and had a slight discoloring of the skin at the cheekbone.

"I asked her to come early," Margaret said to Randall, an explanation by the tone of it. She set the bowl of fruit salad on the coffee table and settled beside her husband on the couch, tapping the ash of her cigarette into a clay pot that held a leafy, root-bound ficus. At forty-five, Margaret was twelve years older than Gay, thin and pretty in a severe way. "I would have invited Heart, too," Margaret went on, never glancing from the set, "but it's going to be dinner and chatter and she'd have been out of her element. Besides, you'd have no one to stay with Rita."

"Rita is fifteen. She doesn't require a sitter."

They fell into the silence that television engendered. Gay had never owned a TV. There had been a Motorola console in her parents' living room, and her husband had possessed a black-and-white Zenith, but she had never owned one herself. She had been tempted a few times to purchase one, but years ago, when she had decided to reclaim her life, stashing the Zenith in the closet had been her first act of emancipation.

"Can you believe this war, Gay?" Randall asked her. "Ethnic cleansing. I can't believe it."

"I know," Gay said, feeling herself stiffen and begin acting the schoolgirl again. "I can't believe it either." The tentative strain in her voice annoyed her, an ingratiating jiggle in the vowels that suggested too much respect for his opinion.

"Watch the news and you'll believe it," Randall said, reversing himself. "You have to believe it. I believe it."

On screen now, children wept and clung to haggard adults, who were watching the cameraman, a wariness in their eyes as if they might be asked to do something indecent. "I don't have a television," Gay said, trying not to sound defensive. "But I listen to NPR."

"The newspaper here is a joke," Margaret said. Randall cast a disapproving look in her direction. "I wish I didn't know what was going on in the world," she continued. "The rest of the planet is in flames, that's what Hubby says—"

"Margaret."

"Oh, I can call you whatever I like in front of Gay. He doesn't want school people to hear me call him anything but 'Your Honor.' "

"'Randall' would do fine."

Margaret made a face at him. "One of our guests tonight is the editor of the local rag. Hubby's afraid I'm going to make the papers. I've had to promise to hold my tongue and keep fully clothed."

"How dull," Gay said.

"You're exempt," Margaret told her. "You can peel and squeal all you want." She smiled, impressed with her own turn of phrase. "What good is a party without a little peeling and squealing?"

"Just give me a signal," Gay said.

A car suddenly appeared on the screen, a beautiful silver Lexus driven by an equally beautiful black woman. Gay didn't own a car, either. This, too, had been a conscious decision on her part, but lately she was at a loss to explain it. She had felt she was taking a stand, but now it simply meant she was forever borrowing Heart's Nissan. Randall lifted the remote control and muted. "Ethnic conflict," he said, "and how it's dealt with, will determine the merit of this administration. Clinton will sink or swim on this one issue."

"Hubby and I support the president," Margaret said, "even if he did ask the occasional odd woman for a blow job."

Randall bowed his head and put his hand to his face. "That's not precisely how I'd phrase it."

"It's just Gay. If we can't have fun in front of Gay, then we're genuinely fuddy-duddies and not just pretending."

Randall pointed the remote again. The sound resumed, although the commercial had not ended. Randall was a frump, but Gay preferred him to the husbands who tried to show off physically, lifting things, their veins bulging from exertion. Physical flirting, harmless or serious, put her off. Flirting required wit. Television seemed to dull the wits the way hacking through cardboard dulled a good knife. Now and again friends had invited her to watch a specific program. But like a blind person suddenly given vision, she had been incapable of accommodating the images, unable to make sense of *Married . . . With Children* or *N.Y.P.D. Blue* or *Northern Exposure.* They all seemed stupid, gratuitous, and conspicuously without wit.

When the news ended, Randall immediately rose. "You women look terrific," he said, clapping his meaty hands. "I'd better go change."

Margaret screwed her cigarette into the ficus soil. Once he was gone, she said, "He isn't going to change. He's just going to hole up in our room until the last minute." She swept potting soil over the twisted butt and dusted her fingers. "He's a functionary. He needs to *preside*. Give him a podium, or give him death. Want to help me set some things out?" She got up, grabbed the bowl of fruit salad, and headed for the kitchen.

Gay rinsed cauliflower and broccoli while Margaret chopped the stalks to dipping size. Each had a glass of dry white wine. Natalie Cole sang a duet with her long-dead father on the CD player.

The Lambs' kitchen, like Gay's, had a view of the river, although the fence the Lambs had built blocked out the closest water. Most of the people on Calle Blanca referred to Margaret as "that lady with the fence." During the construction, Gay had thought they were building the fence to keep out the river, that the proximity of moving water frightened them. But it had turned out to be a beautiful redwood fence, which gave their backyard order and limits. Gay's place, with its unkempt and limitless backyard, was just two doors away. She glanced in that direction now, but didn't have the angle to see it. Across the river, between locust trees and overgrown with weeds, sat a charred Volkswagen Beetle, nothing but a hull. "I saw an owl on that VW skeleton early this morning," Gay said. "A tiny gray owl."

Margaret stopped chopping and stepped beside her, looking out the window at the car shell. "I know. Hubby was going to haul the thing away, but he found a nest in it. 'Think of it as an atrium,' he said to me. He meant 'aviary,' of course."

"That doesn't sound like a functionary."

"Oh, he's not a functionary with me. He won't be with you, either, if you come over often enough. He lets a few people in."

"And then what's he like?"

Margaret looked up at the ceiling, musing. "Once you get to know him, he's actually several people," she said. "Just like everybody else."

The Brownlees arrived shortly after the vegetables were chopped. Dick Brownlee, a bald man in his fifties, was a detective on the Persimmon police force. "*The* detective, unfortunately," he said, the only comment he made all night that seemed to affect him. Claire Brownlee looked to be thirty years younger than her husband, a blonde with a layered seventies hairstyle, who smiled broadly and too often. A carefully practiced bovine quality to her, Gay thought, as if she had studied the humdrum in order to hide some worse quality. She taught third grade.

"That *hair*," Margaret whispered to Gay. "Sort of a Farrah-come-lately, wouldn't you say?"

"She'll hear you," Gay whispered with an urgency that made Claire turn her head. She stood across the room inspecting a painting of a child in artistic shadows. She spoke then, which made Gay think she had overheard. "Is this an original?" she asked.

Margaret told her that it was. "In Scottsdale we lived up the street from a wonderful artist. Now we live up the street from Gay."

"How can I make it up to you?" Gay said.

"We'll figure out something," Margaret assured her.

Gay had tried to think of herself as an artist, designing her life as one might a canvas, trying to make it original, graceful, adventurous. An ongoing piece of performance art. A long running installation in a little-known gallery. But she could not honestly think herself an artist. All she had done was question certain conventions, attitudes others took for granted. She wanted to possess her life. Things that intruded upon that self-possession, she pushed aside.

A few minutes later the Morrisons arrived. Ron Morrison edited *The Persimmon Sun*. In his forties, Gay guessed, thin and dark with sharp features, like a burrowing animal. Ana Morrison, an exotic-looking Hispanic, wore a sleeveless jumper featuring Disney creatures. Her dark tan suggested a lifetime spent on a lawn recliner. They didn't look like they belonged together.

The guests arrived separately because Margaret had suggested different arrival times. "It's more entertaining that way," she confided to Gay. Each of the women was attractive, Gay noted, including herself in the appraisal, and if you could excuse the cavorting of Snow White and the Little Mermaid on Ana's jumper, they were all well dressed. Margaret liked to associate with attractive women, which would explain why Heart had not been invited. Heart was plain, homely, unadorned; Gay couldn't think of other euphemisms for *ugly*. Short and skinny, with a pasty complexion, a big nose, and a toothy, lopsided smile, Heart wore wire-rimmed glasses and her bangs angled oddly across her forehead (she cut her hair herself). Her entire wardrobe consisted of short hand-sewn dresses that hung like drapery from her shoulders, revealing her bony knees and white, pimply legs. She was Gay's cousin, and like Gay, she lived a life of her own fashion. It was petty of Margaret to omit her, but Gay understood the desire to associate with people one found attractive.

Randall made an appearance with each new arrival, then excused himself to finish dressing, to shave, to tidy up. That he still remained in hiding suggested to Gay that they were short a guest. She understood the appeal of predictable men, but it wore thin on her quickly. Men were like books: if they didn't surprise her now and again, she'd put them down.

When the doorbell rang this time, Margaret patted Gay on the shoulder. "Pay attention now," she said. She swung open the door and ushered in a man. "This is Denny, everyone. He's been in Persimmon all of three days. Our new basketball coach."

"I teach a little, too," he said.

A handsome man, Gay decided immediately, in the manner of the young Paul Newman or Marlon Brando—not so much in the features as in his overall presence. It occurred to her that her daughter had likely never seen a movie featuring the young Paul Newman or Marlon Brando. Maybe she should get a television, after all.

Denny's shirt was not ironed, she noted. He wore no belt or socks, but he had shaved and his hair was combed. One of his pants pockets was inside out, the white cloth peeking up like an emissary from his groin.

As soon as the handshakes ended, Randall emerged from the bedroom. He had put on a gray jacket, but wore the same shirt and slacks he had earlier. "Well, Denny," he said and clapped him on the back, "so glad you could join the fray."

Margaret clutched Gay's elbow and leaned in close, her nails digging into Gay's flesh like talons. She said, "He's all but gift-wrapped."

"The newspaper editor has to choose the steep moral path," Ron Morrison said. He had been talking about himself all night. They were drinking, slouched about the living room furniture after dinner. Randall had made curried chicken sometime before the news began, warming the sliced breasts and dousing them dramatically with yellow curry before serving. Men only liked to cook when they could make a show of it, Gay had thought, but the curry had been hot and delicious. Margaret had supplied spicy lentils and a salad with mixed greens, but the conversation had been enough to induce catatonia. Gay's bowl of fruit had not been a hit, the brownish banana wheels staring out like bruised eyes.

Ron continued, "The same, I imagine, is true for the police officer, the coach, the administrator." He gestured with his gin and tonic at each of the men in turn.

Margaret laughed, touching the corners of her scarlet mouth with a paper napkin. "Since you only addressed the men, I guess we gals are free to give morality the boot." She lit a new cigarette and inhaled with great pleasure.

Ron cocked his head slightly and squinted one eye. "Women—I think it's fair to say—have higher spiritual planes than men, but—let's face it—they have fewer natural defenses."

Denny cut him off. "Even *you* don't believe that." The others stared at him a moment, and then glanced about at one another. They came to a tacit agreement to pretend this comment was not rude. Gay found herself participating in this, although she liked rudeness in the face of idiocy. Margaret smiled openly at Gay. She mouthed, "A live one." Claire Brownlee saw her do it and laughed.

Denny had not made any effort to talk to Gay, although it was obvious they were meant to be thrown together. Except for answering direct questions, he had said almost nothing, but he had taken a portion of the fruit salad and eaten it, which endeared him to her. She had made one attempt to engage him in conversation, mentioning the single basketball game she had seen during her twelve years in Persimmon.

She had accompanied her daughter and her daughter's best friend, Cecilia Calzado, to watch Cecilia's older brother play. Normally the girls went with Cecilia's parents, but her father had been sick. The students, led by a group of loud shirtless boys, called the team "the Farts," despite the tiger logo on their uniforms. With hands in armpits, they flapped their arms to make noises. They transformed the classic chorus of "Go, team, fight, fight, fight!" in a predictable fashion.

"They're not a particularly sophisticated group," Gay had said to Rita, dismayed to find none of these Neanderthals even vaguely interested in her daughter. However, one did make a pass at her. She had just stepped from the women's room into the lobby when a boy, a cute kid with dark bristles on his chin and a ratty leather jacket that hung to his knees, said, "Wanna smoke some joy in the parking lot?"

Immediately she looked through the open metal doors to be certain Rita had not witnessed the come-on. Gay did not want competition between them, especially the ugly sexual kind. It was part of the reason she would not let Rita see her and Sander together. Let Rita think her father was all hers. "No, thanks," she said to the boy.

" 'Kay, chica." He glanced at his friends who watched glassy-eyed from the water fountain. "How 'bout we just *park* in the parking lot?"

Gay declined, returning to the bleachers to study her daughter. She had always considered Rita beautiful. It resided in her face despite a slightly unfinished quality, which meant she had begun the transition from girl to woman, and despite the chubbiness, which had always seemed a sign of good health.

Boys liked the gaudy stuff. Racks of waist-length hair, cleavage so deep they could store whole cartons of Marlboros. Gay suddenly felt awful for Rita, recalling the miserable fretting and pain of loving boys.

"What's wrong?" Rita asked her.

"Nothing," she said. "Thinking how I hated high school."

"You went to a creepy place," Rita explained, then turned back to the game. The Farts continued to play poorly, and Cecilia's brother had his nose broken by a teammate. Gay could not imagine why someone like Denny would want to coach high school anything. He was still trying to get the editor of the newspaper to act like a human. "You are *joking*, aren't you?" he said to Ron.

Randall leapt in to forestall argument. "Generalizations are arguable, but it's certainly true that there are differences between men and women."

"I'll say," Margaret said. "You boys talked for half an hour about drainage and sewers. Hah!"

"We were talking about the *colonias*," Ron Morrison said. "I'm working on an editorial about them."

"Is that what we were talking about?" Denny said.

Gay smiled at him. She appreciated a degree of sarcasm in men. She wondered why he wasn't flirting with her.

"There are now ninety-two in the state," Ron continued. *Colonias*—rural, unincorporated communities near the Mexico border without electricity or running water—had existed in the state for decades, he explained, but the number of them had recently tripled, largely the result of real-estate scams. "Our local *colonia* is the largest. We ought to plow it under."

Gay wanted to argue with him but didn't want to extend the conversation. The local *colonia* was just across the river from Persimmon, and she liked to think that everyone in it was like her—determined to make a life outside the normal boundaries of the culture.

Dick Brownlee offered the police perspective. "They have trouble, it better be big." These were the first words he had spoken in an hour. "Otherwise the sheriff says, 'I have no available officers.' "

Ana Morrison perked up at this. "I got stuck out west of town just the other day, down by that oil well. I pulled onto the shoulder to get a bee out of the car, and the tires sank in the sand."

"It's a bitumen pump," Ron Morrison said, "not an oil well."

"My daughter used to ride horses down there," Gay said.

"At that ranch?" Ana asked. "I walked over there to get help, and this nice man pulled me out with his pickup."

"Was he cute?" Margaret asked.

"Does he let just anyone ride?" Claire asked Gay. "I love to ride horses."

"He didn't say two words the whole time," Ana said.

"But was he cute?" Margaret asked again.

"I don't know who he lets ride," Gay said. "My cousin arranged it. She dates him."

"Heart?" Margaret said. "Heart *dates* someone? A *man*?"

"He was cute," Ana said. "Although not my type." She tried to take Ron's hand, but his arms were crossed, so gave his elbow a squeeze.

"Something about riding horses really relaxes you, doesn't it?" Claire said.

"Well," said Margaret, but Randall gave her a look. "You're awfully quiet," she said to Dick Brownlee.

He rocked his head back and forth as if to crack his neck, then ran his hand over his bald pate. "Get to know people better listening," he said.

"But we don't get to know you," Margaret said.

He rocked his head again. "What's to know?"

Margaret pivoted in her chair to avoid Randall's gaze. "How'd you wind up with such a young wife?"

Claire laughed at this, a little gleeful shout.

"We met in an official capacity," Dick said.

Claire laughed again, slapping his leg. "He says that so people will think I was a hooker."

Dick tilted his head to one side and held it there. "Claire's folks had some family trouble, which I was asked to look into. Officially."

"My dad beat up my mom," Claire said, smiling and rolling her eyes as if she were reporting a prank.

"I could do nothing about the situation, but Claire came to my office to see what options she had. We worked together and became acquainted— *well* acquainted."

"He never *would* arrest my dad." She punched him in the arm. "But I fell for him anyway."

Ron made a snorting noise. "The acorn doesn't fall far from the tree."

"What does that mean?" Denny said.

"It's an aphorism that—"

"It's not an aphorism," Denny said. "Not anymore. It used to be one, somewhere back in the fourteenth century. Now it's a cliché." He got up from the couch quickly and headed toward the kitchen. "Anybody else want a drink?" he asked without pausing for replies.

"I'll have a gin and tonic," Ron called to his back, "if you're serving."

"Go help him." Margaret gave Gay a nudge. Claire also got up, asking directions to the bathroom.

In the dining room, Claire took Gay's arm and tugged her aside. "You're the only single woman I know in this town," she whispered. "Oh," she amended, rolling her eyes as she had all evening, "not the only one, but the only one I could talk to."

Gay considered telling her that she was married, but she could not imagine Claire understanding. She nodded, offering a polite and phony smile.

"Dick can't stay up past ten-thirty," Claire went on. "But I can. Just between you and me and the wall, I *like* to stay up late." She put her open palm on the dining room wall, as if this were the wall in question. "Dick will let me stay to help Margaret clean up, and maybe we could talk. Girl to girl?"

She wore such an earnest, quizzical look that Gay said, "Certainly. Sure."

Claire patted her arm, glanced back at the living room, and mouthed *Thanks*, before returning to the others.

Gay found Denny in a dramatic pose, leaning stiff-armed against the kitchen counter, staring into the aluminum sink. He lifted his head slightly to watch her enter, then reached past her and closed the door, his face whisking by hers. "So tell me," he said, "do those people make you fucking crazy?"

Gay considered the question. She leaned away from him, the small of her back against the kitchen counter. "I like Margaret, and she says Randall is okay once you get to know him. And the others . . . the others are just stupid."

He squinted at this, as if her answer caused him pain. "Stupid people don't make you crazy?"

"I like to think nothing makes me *crazy*," she said. "I'm not even sure Claire's stupid. She has that ridiculous hair that I associate with stupidity, so I can't tell for sure. Ana may not be stupid either, although she's wearing a dress with cartoon characters on it. Dick *is* stupid. And patronizing. And dull. Ron is a turd, so whether he's stupid or not is moot."

Denny smiled at this, a toothy, charming smile. He said, "I'm leaving. Want to come with me?"

She said, "There's a back door."

Denny's old Buick sedan was parked halfway into the street, the back tire in the gutter while the front angled out into the driving lane. Gay couldn't tell the color in the near dark, but she guessed blue. The air still felt wet but not cool, the horizon light despite the late hour.

Denny opened the passenger door for her. "It may be a mess," he said, not so much an apology as a warning.

"That's where I live." She pointed to her dark, tree-infested yard. "So you'll know."

"Okay," he said, staring. "Looks haunted—the yard anyway." He ducked down to peer through the wall of leafy limbs. "The house looks sort of . . . pink." He straightened and turned to her. "Bad light," he said.

"No, it's pink," she said. "I always wanted a pink house."

"Hmm," he said, rounding the car. "What else have you always wanted?"

A good question, she thought, and one she had no intention of answering. The front seat had been badly reupholstered in white vinyl and was darkening from human wear. She thought for a moment of her failed bananas. Gum wrappers littered the floorboard, and wads of silver filled the open ashtray.

"I chew gum," he said, climbing in, "especially when I drive." He started the Buick and shifted into gear, easing out into the street. "What is there to do in Persimmon besides—"

"I can't stay out late," she said. "I have to see someone at eleven. I'll need to be home by ten-thirty."

"Okay." He glanced at his watch as he drove. "We've got an hour or so." He had shoved his sleeves up and rested an elbow out the window. "I don't know my way around yet. What—"

"Let's go swimming," she said.

He eyed her suspiciously and slowed the car as they approached the intersection. A huge yellow bulldozer was stationed on the corner like a sentry. "Swimming?"

"I know a good place," she said. "Nearby."

He pursed his lips and nodded, staring out the windshield at the highway. "Okay," he said. "Show me." He flicked a finger in either direction. "Which way?"

"You're not a mindless jock, are you?" she asked him.

"No," he said. "Although I had ambitions for a while. Which way do I turn?"

She pointed left, and he hit the turn signal. "Have you got anything in here that could pass for bobby pins?" she asked him. "I don't want to get my hair wet." The glove box held a bundle of maps, a jumbo pack of sugarless gum, and a pocket knife. She took a rubber band from the stack of maps.

"Help yourself." He edged the car forward to see past the giant bulldozer.

"You want your gum?" she asked him.

"Not this second."

"Quit smoking?"

He shook his head. "I just like gum."

The river's deepest spot, about a mile downriver from her house, was at the Apuro ledge, halfway through town. A man had taken Gay swimming there one drunken night a decade ago, and she had been back every year since then.

"We're still in the city," Denny pointed out, slowing the Buick as he surveyed the area. "It's not entirely dark yet, and I don't have a bathing suit."

"Trust me," she said. "Park in front of that brown house."

"I hardly know you," he added with annoyance, but he parked the Buick as she directed, the front bumper grazing the ugly paneled wall of the cheap frame house. He's a lousy parker, she thought, and wondered how that would show itself in bed. She had discovered that driving habits often revealed sexual traits. There were times that the life she had constructed made her feel merely sleazy. She felt almost obligated to be promiscuous. But she liked the idea of seeing another man just before she and her husband celebrated their wedding anniversary. Her husband would appreciate it, too— the spirited defiance of convention.

She circled the Buick and opened his door. His dubious expression reminded her of the limits of cynical men. "Just don't get me fired before my first day," he said, but he climbed from the car willingly and took her hand before she could tell him to.

A stand of mulberry trees bordered the opposite side of the two-lane highway. "It'll be dark in another five minutes," she said, although in the shade of the trees it was already dark. A wall of high cane separated the trees from the river, and she pulled him into the green, leafy thicket, pushing the pliant cane to one side and then the other, working their way to the water. "See," she said, tugging him onto a secluded spit of sand. The river, still brown from the rain, rolled leisurely past. It would not turn black for another three hours.

Gay stepped out of her skirt. "We're completely protected." She hung the skirt on a cane stalk.

"So," Denny said, slipping off his shoes while he watched her undress. "What is it you do here? For a living?"

"I work at a company that transports cars to dealers," she told him, unsnapping her bra. She stepped out of her panties, and hung her underwear beside her skirt and blouse. She folded her arms but didn't try to hide her breasts. She liked the way he looked at her. She wished she had a cigarette to pose as a nude Statue of Liberty. Real liberties often required nudity. "*Apuro* means 'deep water,'" she said. "You swim, don't you?"

He nodded. "Yeah, I swim."

"Don't dive. It's too shallow on this side to dive." She stepped off the short ledge into the water, waded in a few feet, then crouched down. "There's a space here where cars on the road can spot us." She turned from the road to look at him. "Wait until there aren't any headlights."

He had a nice body and wore boxer shorts, which she preferred. His stomach was not so firm that he might be a bodybuilder. She didn't like bodybuilders. He snapped the elastic band of his shorts. "You're going to watch these come off?" he asked.

"You watched me," she said.

"That I did," he said, slipping them down. He was partially erect, which pleased her, although she had no intention of having sex with him tonight. It waggled when he walked.

"No laughing," he said.

They crouched together in the murky water, watching headlights approach. A spray of light illuminated the water, coming so near them that Denny leaned away from it.

"We're safe here," Gay said. "We just have to be patient." Her chest was so inflated with the hilarity of the situation, she felt she could float across the river, cutting through the water like the ornamental prow of a ship. Two more cars came and went before she pushed off and began swimming. Denny followed, splashing a good deal more than she. "You come here a lot?" he asked, the strain of the swim in his voice, almost a bleat.

"Not that often," she said. "I like to swim."

"I can see that," he said.

"It gets deep here," she warned as they neared the far side of the river. She swam ahead to the bank and stopped there, treading water.

He collided with her. "Where we going?"

"We're here," she said. "Look."

Peering through the limbs of the scrubby bushes that lined the bank, they could make out several adobe houses built at odd angles to one another, a peculiar quality of light in their windows, the mud nest of wasps beneath the eaves of the nearest dwelling.

"Is this some kind of suburb?" Denny asked.

"You're breathing awfully heavy," Gay said. "Is it from swimming or bumping into me?"

"I said I could swim, I didn't say I was a good swimmer."

"Here." She reached for the branch of a gray tree whose limbs fanned out across the river. "Hold on."

He dangled by one arm from the branch, wiping water from his face with his free hand. "I feel like a monkey." He nodded toward the houses. "Why are the lights so weird?"

"No electricity. I don't know whether they're gas lamps or—"

"What is this we're looking at? This isn't Mexico, is it? We're not on the border."

"Not Mexico," she said. "The Rio Grande doesn't become the border for another thirty miles. This is Apuro. The local *colonia*. Weren't you listening during dinner? The boonies. The shantytown. The wrong side of the tracks—only the tracks, in this case, is the river."

"They don't look like shanties. They look like pretty solid houses."

"Adobe shanties. No running water, no electricity, no sewer."

"No sewer?"

"I don't know," she said, inhaling through her nose, the water brackish but not really foul. "That's what I've heard, but I don't smell anything."

"They must have some kind of pipes, then," he said. "So this swim was inspired by that clown Morrison?" He paused, waiting, she could tell, for her to disagree. "Hate the thought of that," he went on. "There must be sewer pipes. You're romanticizing the place."

"Maybe, but—" A voice came from inside the nearest house. Another voice answered in Spanish. She put her lips close to his ear and whispered, "Could you understand that?"

He shook his head, water flying from his hair, his cheek brushing against hers. "Why are we spying on these people?"

"Because I like to," she said. "Because they're across the river and there's no bridge. Because they speak another language. Because we're naked and they're lit by fire."

He put his free hand on the small of her back and then ran it over her bottom, pulling her close to him. She straddled his hip and put her lips to his ear again, while his hand caressed and explored her butt. "Did you wear your watch?"

The hand lifted. "Oh, hell, I did."

"What time is it?"

"It was ten after ten whenever my watch stopped." He put the watch to his mouth and pulled it off, then spat it into the dark water. The hand returned to her bottom.

She lowered her hand to his butt, then raised her foot to his crotch, gripping him with her toes. "I have to go," she said, and pushed off against him.

He had to wait for two cars to pass. She had on her panties and bra by the time he got out of the water. He had an erection, but he was no longer embarrassed. "You sure you can't put this engagement off for a while?"

"Positive."

"What did you dry off with?"

"Your shirt. Here." She tossed it to him.

"Thanks," he said. "Mighty hospitable of you."

"You seem to be in a friendly mood yourself." Then she added, "I'm meeting my husband." She wanted to see if his erection would immediately deflate.

"Gonna take him swimming?" He seemed unaffected, which disappointed her. She watched him step into his boxers and pull them up, tucking himself down awkwardly.

"He drove from Albuquerque," she said. "We haven't lived together for a dozen years."

He continued dressing without looking up. "Why don't you get divorced?"

"We don't want to. If you ever meet my daughter, she doesn't know we're not divorced."

"Mum's the word," he said.

"It's too complicated to explain to her."

"Or to me either, I guess."

"I just did explain it to you. I'm going to see my husband for our anniversary." She pinched at the wet rayon sticking to her stomach and flapped it back and forth. "I'm going to change out of these wet things and talk to my daughter before she goes to bed—she starts high school tomorrow."

"So do I."

"Then I'm going to get dressed up and see my husband. If he wears a suit, I'm going to let him into my house. He's never set foot in my house." She paused, then added, "When we're apart, we're free to do whatever we want."

Denny buckled his belt and then slipped the wet shirt over his arms. "So are you a . . . " He paused and craned his head around as if looking for words in the dark. "I don't even know what to call you."

"Gay. My name, not my persuasion. I'm not an anything. People seem to think I'm a hippie, as if that were the newest craze and I was right on the cutting edge. Hippies tend to be boring and they dress badly. I was never a hippie. I'm a nothing, really."

"You're something, I'm certain of that." He began buttoning the wet shirt, the sopping collar standing up on one side of his neck, lying flat on the other.

Men sometimes admired her arrangement with her husband, but they often acted jealous even if they respected it. Heart was the only woman who not only understood the arrangement but wished to embrace it herself. Others talked generically about security and safety, about the dailiness of commitment, but Gay believed it was dailiness that made love predictable, and predictability that made it warp and turn on itself. As for safety and security, reliance on anyone other than oneself for these seemed both unfair and stupid.

"You're buttoning it crooked," she said.

Denny pulled at the sopping shirttails. "Does it matter?" he said, but he immediately began fixing it. "Don't want to look like a slob."

Gay considered making her pitch, her justification for the way she and Sander lived. She could not name one genuinely happy married couple, and yet every year another million couples agreed to try the same formula for misery, each believing their union would be the exception. When it inevitably went sour, they looked to faults in their partners, in themselves, their children. None questioned the nature of the agreement. Free of one spouse, they began the search for a new one, possessed by the idea of marriage, in chains to a concept, blind to reality.

Gay and Sander saw each other one weekend a month. During their nights together, they made love like teenagers, had adventures, caroused. If not for Rita, Gay would have lived in this manner openly, but she did not want her daughter to suffer for her parents' unconventional life.

She took Denny's hand again. They climbed through the cane and wove through the stand of trees. She said, "Why don't you call me next week?"

Denny carried his shoes and socks in one hand, stepping gingerly across the tree roots. "What's your number?"

"Come by. I showed you my house."

"That you did," he said. "Big place." He took a couple of steps to come up even with her, then he kissed her on the lips. A sweet kiss that lingered just long enough. The kiss brought back the giddy feeling she'd had earlier, although they were dressed now and out of the water.

"I have a teenage daughter," she said to him, catching her breath. "And a cousin who lives with us."

"And a husband," he said, striding past her now to the edge of the highway.

They rolled down the car windows. Their damp clothes stuck to the Buick's reupholstered vinyl. Denny had the radio tuned to the oldies station. Thirty years later and Otis Redding was still sittin' on the dock of the bay. "That's my husband's favorite song in the world," Gay said.

"That right?" Denny smiled at her and switched the radio off. The click registered in her chest. In the silence that followed, Gay could hear the heavy thump of her own heart, so loud to her ears that she switched the radio back on to cover the noise. She changed the station to lose Otis Redding, spinning the knob so that voices squeaked incoherently in the radio's speaker, a clamor much like the pandemonium in her chest. The reaction surprised her, but she would not deny it—her body would not let her deny it. Running off with him, which she'd done as a lark, now felt like something else, something she preferred not to define. She glanced at Denny again, then swiftly turned away.

In another hour, dressed in the outfit Sander had ordered from Victoria's Secret, his anniversary present of a year ago, Gay led her husband into her house, showed him the kitchen and living room, let him gaze at his sleeping daughter, let him see her own bed, even led him up the stairs to look at Heart's garret. They settled on the couch and drank Jamaican rum. Heart had a drink and reminisced with them about the time they all lived together. When she finished her rum, she said good night and climbed the stairs to her room.

Gay found herself incapable of making love in the house. What if Rita woke? How would they explain? She had made love to plenty of men in this house, but she could not this night. She took a blanket from the oak chest at the foot of her bed.

The grass had not been cut all summer and still held a dampness from the afternoon shower. She considered getting another blanket—more protection against the wet, more padding against the hard ground—but Sander settled beside her, his shoes already off, tie already loose, moonlight painting his face. He began rolling a joint. He always got high before sex.

She found herself thinking of Denny, which disturbed her. She had planned to tell Sander about their getaway from the dinner party, but she hadn't, and now it felt like a betrayal to picture Denny while sitting with Sander.

"That dress suits you," Sander said, then he began describing a driver who had passed him on the freeway, how he'd had a keyboard on the dash of his car and was typing as he drove. "Poor guy got a phone call right as he was whizzing by me. I don't know how he could manage it all."

It was while he spoke that she noticed the river. The black water stood out in the dark, a distinct and defining black. "Something's funny," she said, rising to her knees to see it better. "Look at the water. It's . . . unreal." The river's movement, or the way the black made her see its movement, changed her perception of its form. It occurred to her that water floated on the earth's surface, that water floated better on some substances than others, that water—like any floating thing—was always in danger of going under, of slipping down beneath the surface and disappearing.

Sander hardly looked up from his rolling papers. He slipped one hand beneath her hair, along her neck, while the other expertly finished the cigarette, lifting it to his tongue for a final lick. "You're what's funny," he said.

She took this wrong, as a reference to some things in their past. Her breakdowns. She knew he didn't mean it that way, but she took it to convey as much. Her umbrage felt willed, but nonetheless real. "Look at it," she said, making her voice calm. "Open your eyes, and look at it. The river is black as death."

He pulled his socked feet under him, sat up in a crouch. His eyes widened, but they still looked sleepy, as they always did. "Color," he said, "is a trick of light. Things don't possess color, they just borrow it. Rent it. On a night like this—"

"I'm *not* imagining," she said. "I'm not." Even she heard the wavering note in her voice, the manner in which she gave herself away. Nothing he could say now would satisfy her. She no longer had control over it. He might eventually agree with her, but it would feel patronizing. Or he could continue to argue, which—she could not help thinking this—would be his way of suggesting she was not quite sane. "I'm leaving," Denny had said, and just like that they had escaped the dinner party. Now, fairly or unfairly, she wished to escape her husband.

He had heard the note, too, knew her well enough to stare at the river for a long time without speaking, then to settle back on the blanket and reach for his shoes. He slipped them on before saying, "I can't see it."

4

If Rudy Salazar knew nothing else, he knew Apuro. He walked the paths among the houses every morning and every evening, looking for difference, looking for sameness. He paced between the outhouses, all of them new and lined up in a single row—charity from asses across river in Persimmon. The old holes from the previous wooden shitbooths, in all their random places, had been filled in, now just vague squares of depression glittering from the afternoon rain. Rudy preferred the new outhouses, even took some pride in them, but he didn't like the people who had donated them, their mock-serious smiles, their condescending self-congratulations, didn't like their Porta Potties—as if Apuro were populated by children needing potties. He could not name all his reasons for disliking those people, but they lived inside him, like the fish in the Rio Grande, only occasionally coming to the surface, rarely identified, but always down there swimming around, churning up the muddy depths.

He walked beyond the plastic outhouses, checked on the plants on the Ramirez doorstep: red flowers in an orange Mexican pot, blue flowers in a rusting bucket. The specific names of the flowers he did not know, had been surprised as a boy to discover that such things had names, and even then he'd thought it childish. He stuck his head in the window of the sole trailer in Apuro, an aluminum hut, its tires long gone, enlarged with walls made of packing crates, sleeping seven now, the old woman Maria de la O taking in more relatives from Ciudad Juárez for the new school year. Rudy counted them up by the evening's frail light, having to pull his head out of the narrow window, turn in the opposite direction, and then insert it again: five on the floor in their underwear ready for sleep, the old woman in her separate room, invisible to him, with at least one more child. The children shyly looked away or stared back in respectful silence. A framed picture of the Virgin Mary faced Rudy, as did a poster of Janet Jackson dressed in military garb. He moved on, walking down the familiar path.

Coleman lanterns lit most of the homes. Like the outhouses, the lanterns had been donated. A church youth group had waded across river one evening carrying the lit lanterns and singing "We Shall Overcome." They hadn't had sense enough to walk upstream to the shallow water, and they'd had to lift the lanterns high, the shorter ones passing off their lamps to keep from burning their arms. They had emerged from the river soaked to their chests, some of them embarrassed, others animated and laughing. One girl in particular he remembered, how her white dress, drenched by the river water, had taken on a muddy transparence, how by the light of her own lantern she revealed her small breasts and pointing nipples. The memory of the evening produced in him a specific rage, and Rudy upended a lawn chair, then kicked it across the path.

Earlier in the evening, men and women had sat outside their front doors chatting with their neighbors, enjoying the respite from the heat that followed the rain, battery-powered radios tuned to a Juárez station playing Mexican songs with a polka rhythm. Concha Obregon had brought ice over from Persimmon, and she had set the chest on her brick stoop, inviting people to help themselves. Her little boy had a Dallas Cowboys poster that he had carried from person to person, unrolling it each time to the length of his short arms. Rudy's mother had sat among them. She claimed that, at times, she forgot Apuro was a part of the United States and thirty miles north of the border.

The state of New Mexico also seemed to forget that Apuro was within its borders. It had come into being several decades ago when the Rio Grande had changed course, creating a spur of land between the far end of some cottonfields and the river. The first houses had been built by men who worked those fields, and Apuro had evolved into a community of undocumented workers. Even now, virtually everyone in Apuro lived in the United States illegally.

Rudy opened the door to inspect the Obregon house. He stood in the entry, examining the interior. The house had only a single room with one wide bed, where Concha and her husband now feigned sleep. Their boy, wedged between his parents, did not pretend. He sat up, the rolled poster still in his arms. He searched for the poster's edge, then pulled it down like a curtain, revealing to Rudy an upside-down helmet. Rudy stepped back and closed the door.

He hooded his eyes and stared through the windows of one adobe house and then another. He pushed open the doors of the plywood shanties. The people not yet in bed nodded at him, some of the children somberly waved, one couple knelt before a crude shrine, their faces spooky in the candlelight.

Everyone knew the routine, and no one complained, not for two years, not since one of the shacks had burned down, the *culero* who'd lived there, who'd told Rudy to stay the fuck out of his place, saved from smoke inhalation by none other than Rudy Salazar, who had taken it upon himself, after all, to keep an eye on things.

Some people he treated differently. Nita Sandoval lived with a girlfriend in one adobe, and he always walked quietly to the side window and sneaked a look, hoping to catch them, as he had once before, in their underwear. Others he didn't mess with at all, although he would admit as much to no one, not even to himself, thinking instead that he was letting them stew, that he was playing a trick on them by staying away, but knowing, too, in that alternate kind of thought, that wordless tug of the insides—not the organs, but the other insides, the body's version of the mind—that he was afraid of them.

He had made these rounds for eleven years, since he was eight, a little boy, a joke among people back then, but he was no longer a joke. As a boy, he did it to be out of the house before his father woke in the morning and before his father slept at night—dangerous times—but now he walked twice a day to inspect his domain, his place, his *sitio*, his turf—but *turf* sounded like a rap word, and Rudy hated rap. In truth, he didn't much like any music, but rap he especially hated, because of the rappers' insipid names, like Ice T, like Snoop Doggy Dogg. He hated, too, the jowly sound of their black voices—kid stuff, boys pretending to be tough. To hell with them and that crap.

He shifted his inspection to the automobiles of Apuro. There were only a few, and he started with the old Dodge Dart that no longer ran. As he opened the door, someone called his name. Tito Tafoya churned through the dirt, raising his hand to wave as he ran, a skinny boy, two or three years younger than Rudy. "Hey," he called out, "you know that *hay una* good-looking *mujer en su casa*?"

Rudy slammed the door to the Dart. "What's she want?"

Tito's brows rose, and his face seemed to open. "You." He shook his head and shrugged simultaneously. "I don't know why, but you could maybe ask her, no?"

"Maybe," Rudy said, rounding the car's bumper, stepping over a puddle. Tito joined him. He wore no shoes. "What's with your feet?" Rudy asked.

Tito instantly stared down at them. "I don't see nothing. Is there?"

"Where your shoes, *payaso*?"

"Oh. *Pues*, my dad's sewing on them. Fixing them, you know."

The woman stood on the Salazar doorstep talking to Rudy's mother, who had just returned from Persimmon, still in the short black skirt she wore as a barmaid. Normally she changed before speaking to anyone. Her work was irregular and paid poorly, but what she hated most about it was that short black skirt. She tugged at the hem while conversing with the woman.

The stranger was an Anglo with blond hair, not pretty but with a sheen like lacquer, like the covers of magazines, that made her pass for pretty with other Anglos, but which made Rudy despise her. Before she had spoken a word to him, he hated her.

"My son," Rudy's mother said, pointing vaguely in Rudy's direction. She stepped inside to change, leaving the door open.

"Him," Tito said, pointing at Rudy. "Not me. I'm Tito."

Rudy charged past the woman without acknowledging her smile or extended hand, stepping into his house. Tito lunged for the door and held it open for the woman, but Rudy pivoted, blocking their entry. The woman did not even hesitate. She started talking as if nothing were the matter, slipping one hand up to hold the door so that Tito could back out of the narrow portal. Rudy crossed his arms and glared at her while she spoke.

She was from "the Bay Area," she said, like anyone would know what that meant, like already he was dirt. *People like you wipe my ass*, she was saying, but she didn't think he was capable of understanding. "I have journalistic contacts in El Paso," she explained, talking to Rudy but glancing at his mother, who had emerged from the back partition wearing sweatpants and smoking a cigarette. Rudy wanted to take the woman's jaw, turn it to face him every time she looked away, but not yet. He didn't want to commit to anything yet. First he wanted to see what he could get from her, what there was to take.

"They told me about this place—how you don't have water or lights," she said, her face imitating surprise, indignation. A single trail of sweat emerged from her hair and trickled down to her eyebrow. "They said the city council in Persimmon won't permit a bridge to be built across the river. I find it an outrage."

Fuck you, Rudy thought, but his expression didn't change, his eyes piercing hers, which were blue like the toilet water at the Conoco station.

"I arrived in Apuro just this afternoon," she said, "and I was advised to talk to you, Señor Salazar. I was told—" She stopped to watch as his mother returned to her room in the back of the house. His mother did not say, "Señor Salazar is not home. Señor Salazar has not been home for years. This is my boy, my boy who drove Señor Salazar away," but Rudy could hear her slippers saying as much as they shuffled into the bedroom, hear it in their resigned, sniveling slide. This hearing was his gift. He could sink through a muck of words, could sift through calculation or logic, could *hear* the heart of the matter, recognize it, make use of it. His gift.

As soon as his mother shut the door to her room, the woman said, "I understand you're the *patrón* around here."

Rudy laughed at her. "Wrong word." *Stupid bitch*, he thought, showing off how stupid she is, but he didn't say that, not yet. He spotted Tito's head bobbing just beyond her shoulder.

"You want to be famous?" she asked suddenly, the tone of her voice shifting. "This story has a decent shot at syndication. Take a look at these." She had magazines. "I've written about gangs in Oakland. Got on the inside. I—"

"You a writer?"

She paused a moment too long, looking away before she spoke. "That's what I've been saying."

"You haven't said that yet."

She paused again, looking at him now, just looking, but also thinking, trying to figure. She said, "I'm a writer. A correspondent for—"

He nodded. "You want to write about Apuro?"

"Yes, Apuro and the other *colonias*. I know they're not all like Apuro, less settled, worse living conditions, but I think I can use Apuro—"

"You think I'm going to help you?"

"Maybe," she said. "At least I thought I'd talk to you before I did anything. Respect your . . . knowledge of the place."

She was kissing his ass, but he didn't like his ass kissed. "No gangs here," he said, glancing at the magazines. "*Ni colores*. Across river, in town, some stuff maybe. Not much. Here, *no hay nada*. You speak *español*?"

"*Un poco*," she said. "*Estud*—"

"Keep it out of your mouth. You make it stupid. *Entiendes*?"

"I understand," she said. "Read these." She shoved the magazines into his hands.

He lifted them briefly to look at their glossy faces, but then he let them fall to the floor. She quickly knelt, scooped them up, and backed through the door, looking up at him, trying to make him think she wasn't scared. "You can change things around here if you want. *You*. You help me with this, and we can *force* them to recognize Apuro. Put in sewers, water, lights. A bridge."

"Know a lot about sewers?"

"My name is Rhonda Hassinger." She extended her hand, a pale trembling thing like some kind of fish.

Rudy looked at the hand, studied it without moving his head, thinking that if he looked closely enough he would find scales. Then he examined her face, her pretend look of exasperation, of courage. He decided he liked her make-up after all, the dark lift of her lashes.

"I'm going to wander around," she said. "I'm going to look over this place right now before it gets too dark. If you want to come with me, I'm sure your comments would be helpful. I'll be here only a few days. I could meet you tomorrow, or—"

"You talk too much." He stepped through the doorway, bumping into her, wedging one of her legs against the deep adobe doorjamb while he shut the door. She was wearing white pants, and now there would be a streak of brown down her butt from the adobe wall. He kept the leg pinned another moment after shutting the door. She wore a look of impatience, a look you give some little trouble, an expression of resignation and annoyance. Finally she pulled her leg free and dusted off her pants, but as she took her first step, talking again, a high singsong tone that meant she would make believe nothing had happened, he saw the brown streak down the seat of her pants. Apuro would leave its mark on her, Rudy thought, staring at the smudge, at the churning of her ass in the tight jeans.

Tito ran up next to her, chattering, but Rudy purposely slowed his pace. They strolled through the intense evening heat, the woman's face quickly turning pink. Two other boys joined them. She needed to sit, she said. "How can you manage this weather?" she asked Rudy cheerfully. "I was fine after the rain, but now I'm boiling."

Tito scampered to his house and retrieved a blanket, which he spread over the hood of the immobile Dodge Dart, permitting her to sit without dirtying her dirty pants or burning her fair skin. The boys smiled hopelessly at her, eager to become her servants. They thought they were doing this because she was a woman and a visitor, or because she was pretty, but Rudy understood better than they did. It was because she was Anglo. She was no better looking than a lot of women in Apuro, but she was white, skin the color of dead grass, hair the phony blond of chrome. There was something more to it, something Rudy could see but didn't have the language to name, a condescension in her tone and a gloss of wealth to her appearance that suggested both her place in the world and theirs. Rudy detested her.

She wiped the sweat from her forehead with the tips of her fingers. When she leaned back on her elbows and spread herself across the hood of the Dart, the boys stepped closer, hovering over her in their eagerness. They told her about Apuro, and she acted like she was listening, but Rudy could tell her attention was on him.

For his part, he had other things to consider. School started in the morning, which brought with it obligations and opportunities. He had played basketball on and off during his years in school. As a junior he had been a starter on the varsity squad, not a scorer much, but a good rebounder, until, after five games, he gave Arturo Calzado an elbow across the face during a game—his own teammate, but they called a technical, threw him out.

The coach kicked him off the team. "That boy had done nothing to you," the coach had said, ignorant Anglo clown that he was. "I can put up with a lot, but not deliberate, malicious . . ." He had tried to come up with a word, but failing that had said, "To your own teammate, for Christsakes." He had turned his back on Rudy's glare and said, under his breath, "Thank God you're both Mexican."

The Calzado family had once lived in Apuro, their house a safe haven when Rudy's father came looking for him. Señora Calzado had once hidden Rudy under a bed and swiped at Rudy's father with a broom to make him go away. Rudy could still picture that, the woman swinging the broom not like a baseball bat but like a mallet, as if she were pounding on a spike, his father raising his hands and arms to cover his face.

Then the Calzados left Apuro, taking away his safe place. For that he could forgive them. But by moving to Persimmon, they showed that they felt themselves too good for Apuro, too good for the red and blue flowers of the Ramirez doorstep, too good for the gas lanterns, too good for Rudy Salazar. For this he could not forgive them.

He had paid back the basketball coach, taking a gun that he kept hidden in the Dart and shooting out the windows of the coach's car—a silver Chrysler with cartoon stickers of Aladdin and the great blue Genie on a rear window, a gray child safety seat in the back that filled with broken glass. The police never even asked Rudy a question. The coach had not called them. Instead, he had moved his family that very month to Arizona, where he had joined them at the end of the semester.

But the Calzado fuck, Rudy still owed. Arturo had graduated and moved to Las Cruces to attend the university—just thirty miles away, but without a car, it might as well have been a thousand. However, Rudy knew that Calzado's little sister would be starting high school this year. Cecilia. He remembered her name, remembered all the Calzados, the older girls who were grown and gone, Arturo, and the youngest, Enrique. Rudy could see them sitting around the table at dinner, their heads bowed in prayer, the little ones sneaking looks at the grownups to see if they were doing it right.

Rudy had one year of school remaining. He would find Cecilia at school the first day. He would let her know that he had business with her. That would be enough for now, to let her know there was an obligation. She would pay for her brother, for her parents. The pain Rudy carried was a debt that could never be fully reimbursed. From time to time he was forced to make others offer installments. Cecilia Calzado would be next.

Rhonda Hassinger shifted on the blanket, making the hood of the Dart bend, causing a noise like a metal burp. She asked about their pantlegs, the mark left from wading the Rio Grande, the residual darkness to the knee.

"Just water," Rudy said, silencing the others. "Want to see the outhouses? Want to smell our shit?"

"I've heard about the portable rest rooms," she said. "I met with the environmental organization that donated them. They were concerned about the groundwater, afraid of being sullied by the excrement of Apuro. I don't think there was any goodwill involved. All self-interest." She made a face for Rudy's benefit, still trying to kiss his ass.

He pointed to a tire of the Dart, which rested in a muddy rut where one of the old outhouses had been. "Before we got the outhouses *plasticas*, this whole place smelled like shit," he said. Then he reversed himself. "But not so bad. Not like that place stinks." He nodded in the direction of Persimmon, the crooked line of cane and tall trees that masked the city beyond.

"You don't like Persimmon," she said.

"What's to like?" he said. "They got electricity. You sell your soul for electricity?" He shoved one of the boys out of his way and moved his face close to hers, stared hard into her eyes. "Maybe you already have."

She sat up quickly, as if she thought Rudy might crawl on top of her. She slid off the hood, failing to catch the blanket before it dropped to the bumper and the ground. She asked to see the shallow spot on the riverbank where they crossed daily to school. "That's not a secret place or anything, is it?"

Rudy didn't answer, merely pointed, then began walking, the other boys trailing.

"Hasn't a gang ever tried to move in on you?" she asked.

"They don't like Apuro," Rudy said. "No roads here much. No roads, no drive-bys."

A large boulder marked the crossing point, the river phlegmatic and wide, the banks weedy and wet. A trail led to the boulder, where people took off their shoes and socks before leaving, or put them back on upon returning. Rudy waved the other boys back, then led the reporter past the boulder to the water's edge. He extended his arm and aimed a finger at a dark and leafy tree across the river. "*Mira*," he said. "Take a good look," he insisted.

She raised a hand to shade her eyes, although the sun had almost set and no longer reflected in the river. Rudy stepped closer to her, bending, his shoulder brushing hers, still pointing. Then he wrapped one hand around her waist and jerked her next to his body. "Shut up," he commanded, although she had said nothing. His other hand slipped inside the back of her pants and felt her ass, the plane of his hand running circles around her cheeks. "Flat-ass bitch," he said. He yanked his hand free. "Fuck you," he said. *"No entiendes nada."* You understand nothing.

She began running as soon as he released her, swinging her arms awkwardly like a child. Her ass had felt like rubber.

Later, deep in the night, Rudy heard tapping at his window. He took a metal baseball bat from beneath the couch where he slept. Waited. The tapping came again, someone whispering his name. "Tito?" Rudy said. He stepped to the open window, the screen loose and baggy but untorn. Tito Tafoya's face appeared on the other side.

"I got to show you something," Tito said.

"What? That writer bitch back?"

"No, the river. *Tienes que verlo."* You have to see this.

"It's a flood?" he said, his heart suddenly alive within him.

"No, it's black."

"Black?" He tried to look into Tito's eyes, but the screen and the dark made it impossible to see much. "So what?"

"It's wild," Tito said. "I want to show you it."

"You waking me up to see the *pinche* river I look at every day of my life?"

"It's all black."

Rudy hesitated, feeling in himself a desire—not to see the river, but to go along with Tito. "I'm going back to bed, *pendejo,"* he said. "Don't wake me up about no fucking black river." Tito's face now pressed close enough to the screen window that Rudy flicked the wire with his fingers and tapped Tito's nose.

Tito laughed, touched his nose. "Rudy," he said. "You seen it black before? Why's it black?"

"The fuck I care," he said.

"Could be it's important, no?"

"Important?"

"Like when the stars start falling. Or the moon goes in front of the sun."

"Eclipse," Rudy said. "That's only important if you're a farmer or something."

"A farmer?"

"It's when to plant."

"What about a black river?"

Rudy thought for a moment. "It's when to sleep. I'm going to sleep." He said this, but he didn't move, the screen between them like the blind in a confessional booth. Neither spoke for several seconds.

Tito said, "You still there?"

"That magazine bitch," Rudy said, "I grabbed her ass."

"I didn't see that."

"You don't pay attention, *cabrón*."

"I liked her."

"You what?"

"I liked her. She was . . . okay, I thought. Hey, what I was getting at—you think maybe it's a cure? The black river?"

"Cure for what?"

"I don't know. For when you're sick or got an *ataque* or something."

"Don't get stupid on me."

"Oh," Tito said. "I won't."

"Now, go away."

"*Bueno*, okay. So. Pleasant dreams."

Rudy shook his head. *Pleasant dreams* you said when you were a child. "How old are you, motherfucker?" he said, but no one answered. Tito had gone, and Rudy felt a tiny slide of disappointment that his friend had obeyed him and left. He returned to the couch, laying the baseball bat on the floor.

But he couldn't sleep, his mind agitated. Just beyond his window flowed the ebony river, a black division in the dark ground, spilling down the continent like upended wine over an uneven floor, like a current of blood cutting its own wound, like a stream of ink staining a map.

Rain

5

Four years earlier, through a living room window, Rita had spotted a taxi at their curb. The driver opened his door before the car rocked to a full stop, then scrambled out and yanked open the car's back door, removing a huge suitcase. He took three smaller suitcases from the trunk, each of his movements sudden and forceful, as if the taxi did not want to give up its contents. Rita decided she did not like this man.

Her mother stepped beside her and placed a hand on the small of her back. "Someone is moving in with us," she said.

Rita's first thought was that the taxi driver was her mother's new boyfriend. "I don't want him living here," she said angrily, which made her mother laugh.

"Not him," her mother said, stepping closer to the window to examine the man. "He . . . sweats."

She had almost said, "He's fat," Rita thought, although the man was not fat, just big, like Rita. "Big-boned," Gay would sometimes say, but Rita found that term as ugly as *fat*, and she knew there was no truth to it. Her bones were the same size as everyone else's.

"The person moving in is a woman," her mother explained. "A boarder. A cousin of mine—of ours. We have so much room here, it's criminal not to share it with somebody." The taxi driver tucked the smallest suitcase under an arm, then lifted two other bags, leaving the huge thing on the sidewalk. He trudged awkwardly over the buckling walk. "Let that poor man in," Gay said. Rita ran to open the door for him.

He didn't speak to Rita, just lifted his head slightly and stepped past her, sweat running down his nose and the back of his hairy neck. When he saw

Gay, he straightened, as if the luggage had suddenly grown lighter. "Hi there," he said and began explaining the obvious, that he had baggage to deliver. Behind his back, Rita put her hand to her nose and made a face. He didn't actually smell, but she wished to remind her mother that neither of them liked him. He placed the bags in a neat line on the living room floor before returning for the huge one.

"This should be fun," Gay said, stepping again to the window to watch. The man tucked in his shirt, then heaved the bag to his shoulder, stumbling slightly, then steadying himself. He managed the sidewalk without falling and planted the bag beside the others. " 'At's a big 'un," he said, smiling at Gay, even thinking to glance at Rita. "A lot of single people are renting out rooms nowadays," he added hopefully. "Hard to make ends meet."

Rita didn't listen to her mother's reply. She knew her mother would flirt with him, but she also knew this man had no chance. She studied the suitcases, which were blond and made of leather, with buckles on the top like belts.

"You'll like our cousin," Gay said after the taxi driver had given up and departed. "She's about your size. But she's a lot flimsier than you. You'll hardly notice her around the house. It'll be more like having a haunting than having a guest."

"Where's she going to sleep?" Rita worried that she might lose her room.

Gay pointed to the ceiling. "Up there." She wagged her finger at the attic. "Let's hope she doesn't snore."

They laughed at that. As long as she didn't have to give up her room, the prospect of a boarder excited Rita. She settled herself on a throw pillow in front of one of the low windows to watch for her cousin's arrival. She wanted to see her first from a distance and then study her approach in order to have several impressions of her. Gay made a glass of iced tea for them to share.

"Is she incredibly pretty?" Rita asked.

"No," her mother said and drank from the glass. Her mother had a long, slender neck, and Rita liked to watch her tip her head back and drink, the muscles in her throat moving up and down. She handed the glass over to Rita and said, "She's not pretty at all. Not in the way we typically look at people. But she has a secret prettiness not everyone can see. I'm not sure you'll be able to see it."

"Of course I will," Rita said, instantly affronted. "I'm eleven," she reminded her mother.

Gay nodded. "Don't you want to know her name?"

"Not yet," Rita said. "Not until I see her."

The New Mexico town in which they lived bordered the Rio Grande River, thirty miles north of Mexico. Long ago a Chinese immigrant and his American wife had planted a persimmon grove there. The trees had disappeared, but the town was still known as Persimmon. Rita liked to imagine the Chinese man and his Anglo wife standing in a grove of the exotic trees. In her fantasy they wore the handsome work shirts and faded chinos sold in J. Crew catalogs. He had beautiful eyes and skin, while she was thin like Rita's mother and so pale that after even a moment in direct sunlight her flesh would blister. Rita imagined they had lived in the house that she and her mother now shared, an adobe house across the highway from town, in a leafy cul-de-sac, although no one, including them, called it that. Gay would say, "We live on Calle Blanca, at the very end of the big dead end."

Their house had mud walls two feet thick. Unlike most adobe structures, it had a steeply pitched roof, covered with rotting cedar shingles. The outside walls, layered in crinkled stucco, her mother had painted pink with a green trim. A garret bedroom with dormer windows filled the attic. Downstairs, the windows began just inches above the floor and rose higher than the doors, tall and narrow, deeply inset in the thick walls. "Like the entrance to heaven," her mother liked to say, standing before them in the indelible desert sunlight. When they went on trips together, as they rarely did, Gay inevitably would say, "It's nice here, but we miss our pink and green house in the valley, don't we?"

In the front yard grew pecan trees, mulberries, pines, blue spruce, honey locusts, and one giant ginkgo. They made for treacherous terrain, the earth rippling with heavy dark roots and always covered with something—the dark splatter of mulberries, pecans in their tart-smelling husks, miniature pinecones, the lacy puffs of fallen nests, dry broken branches, tiny pastel eggs, an amazing assortment of leaves. A buckling concrete walk divided the yard, and on moonlit nights it shone a luminescent gray, like a bridge over a deep ravine. Rita and her friend Cecilia imagined questions the ogre of such a bridge might ask, and imagined, too, their own clever and resourceful replies.

One of their neighbors, Mr. Perez, a full-grown man with a family, came once or twice a month with a push mower and clippers to cut the few stray patches of grass in the front yard. Gay made him iced tea so sour with lemon that he could barely hide the grimace when he drank it. She didn't like him and had not asked for his help. "He thinks if he keeps cutting my grass, I'll go to bed with him," she had confided to Rita one day while they watched him through the living room window. "If he really wanted to make points with me," she added, raising her brows as she contradicted herself, "he'd do 'round back." She opened her eyes wide and looked in Rita's direction, then began laughing, throwing her brown hair from shoulder to shoulder.

The backyard was enormous and unfenced, a rarely mown stretch of grass that ran right down to the river ledge. A big palo verde shaded one corner of the house, and a skinny mesquite stood alone out near the water, but the remainder of the yard was strictly grass, coarse fescue and high Bermuda that tickled the backs of their legs. Beyond their yard, the riverbanks were crowded with trees.

During the winter months, the Rio Grande constricted to a meandering stream, eddying apathetically in its sandy bed, but in the spring it filled to its borders, sometimes riding up into the yard, shimmering just below the tallest blades, then flattening the grass when it receded. The flow was controlled more by irrigation gates and reservoir levels than by the weather or the season. Rain had not yet come under the dominion of men, but the tide of the river could be governed. Most of the year there was a little drop-off from the yard to the water.

Like her luggage, their cousin arrived by taxi, which in itself made her exotic. She appeared at the edge of the rippling sidewalk, behind and beneath a network of tree limbs, pale legs beneath a pale skirt, clunky dark shoes meant for a man to wear. She walked hesitantly, her arms bent and lifted, slightly spread. The sidewalk tripped her twice, the second time forcing her to one knee. When she straightened, a square of blood appeared on her shin. She spotted Rita and waved, unaware she was bleeding.

Gay leaned close. "Her name is Heart."

"Heart," Rita repeated, smiling, waving back to her, watching her tentative approach—a shapeless woman in a shapeless beige dress. If there really were an ogre lurking about, Heart would be no match. Rita could tell that much.

When her mother and Heart finally stood side by side, Rita burst out laughing. She wouldn't tell them why. Eventually they joined her, giggling as they lugged the suitcases up the stairs. No two women on earth resembled each other less, Rita thought. Heart was no taller than a sixth-grader, with gawky, crooked features. But she was thin. They were both thin, Rita acknowledged. They had that much in common. Saying that Heart had a secret beauty was her mother's way of telling her they would like Heart even though she was ugly. Rita understood her mother's euphemisms.

Heart moved into the attic and took over for Gay the task of getting Rita to go to bed. "It's part of my rent payment," Heart told Rita that first week. "Skidoodle. You get to bed by ten o'clock every night, and I don't have to do any lawn work."

Rita almost revealed that they did no lawn work, but she liked having Heart's attention. Heart even promised a bedtime story, something Gay had given up on years ago. Her mother had told meandering tales, full of backtracking and meaningless details, red herrings, fabulous events, sudden betrayals, and fantastic secrets. They often ended in natural disaster, a single tornado wiping out an entire city racked with plot. But Heart turned out to be incapable of telling a story. Much as she loved to read, she could not relate a coherent narrative. She might begin with a girl searching for her parents, but something would hang her up.

"The path the girl chose was muddy with a lot of puddles," she said one night, her eyes darting to Rita's for approval. She sat cross-legged on the bed, while Rita lay with her head on the pillow, studying Heart's face, amazed at its imbalance. Not the face of someone deformed or scarred, just an unattractive one. How did certain shapes come to be thought desirable, while others remained hopelessly unacceptable? "Now she had to jump over these puddles because . . . " Heart's forehead creased and her eyes rolled upward while she tried to imagine. Rita had thought that once she knew and liked Heart, she would no longer think of her as ugly, but that wasn't the case. Heart's features lacked symmetry, as if carelessly molded by distracted hands. "She had to jump," Heart repeated, nodding, her mouth sagging on one side while she tried to think.

"Because she had just one pair of shoes," Rita offered.

"It's all anybody needs," Heart said. "They're not like underwear. You don't need a pair for every day of the week."

"Don't you have sneakers?" Rita asked her.

"I'm not much of an athlete." Heart's brows lifted, as if this news might be a surprise. "Wouldn't mind some riding boots, but it would be wrong to say that I *need* them. No matter what you hear, people only *need* just a few things: family, food, seven pairs of underwear, five dresses, a pair of shoes, and a stick so you can scratch places down your spine that you can't reach with your hands." She smiled, toothy and lopsided, proud of her list, then glanced about the room, thinking. Several seconds passed before she looked again to Rita.

"Puddles," Rita said.

"The path was full of them," Heart agreed.

Eventually she gave up all pretense of telling stories. Instead, she let Rita in on her plans. "Your mother has the right idea about raising kids. Do it without a man in the house. I'm going to do the same," she promised.

It intrigued Rita to think that her mother might have planned to live separate from her father in order to "raise" her. She didn't believe it, but it was interesting to consider. She tried to picture the man who would want to live with Heart. Supposedly, somewhere out in the world, for every person, no matter what she looked like, there was a perfect mate, but Rita couldn't imagine who that would be for Heart. When this conversation took place, Rita had not yet begun riding horses at Mr. Gene's ranch, had not yet witnessed Heart kissing him on the cheek. Free to imagine any sort of man, she couldn't formulate one that would do. They were either too handsome for Heart or too ugly. Rita was not yet twelve, and had trouble believing a man could love Heart as she and her mother did, that a woman's looks might not be the most important thing.

One night Heart revealed that she had given up smoking in preparation for motherhood. Her shapeless dresses each had a single pocket in the center where she kept plastic drinking straws cut to cigarette length, which she would occasionally hold between her fingers and put to her mouth, as if to smoke. "It's foolish but it works," she explained, puffing on the plastic straw. "You want one?"

"I'll try yours," Rita said.

Heart passed her the straw. "I'll have a man around to help, but not in the house," she told Rita. "Just me and the baby in the house." She volunteered to make dresses for Rita, and Rita accepted. "In some ways I've had it easier than your mom," Heart said. "Beauty makes you susceptible to things—certain kinds of men, for example. And fashion. The more you think about clothes, the less free you are."

Later still, Heart began telling Rita things about Gay—the men she dated, the way other adults thought of her. "Most of the men are terrified. They think she'll eat them alive."

"They all think she's pretty," Rita said.

"She *is* pretty," Heart said, and then, a second too late, added, "just like you." Which made Rita wonder whether she belonged more to the category of women that included Heart, or the one headed by her mother. Rita liked Heart better, but she preferred to be classified with Gay.

Rita had questions for Heart about the men her mother saw. While her questions were specific, Heart's answers tended to be metaphorical. "About half think she's some wild horse they need to lasso, and your mother isn't about to let herself be lassoed. The other half are mostly taken. At least officially."

Rita had stayed up most of the night thinking about that one. On the morning of her first day of high school, she wanted to ask Heart about her mother's elaborate dress, about the couch and the liquor, about the green ribbon on the kitchen counter and the white blanket on the grass. The mystery of the black river interested her less than the mystery of her mother.

She waited in her room. If she stalled long enough, Heart would volunteer to drive her to school, but she didn't have the patience for it. She had already dressed and straightened her room. Even the dollhouse she never used was once again upright and peopled with its plastic family.

She tiptoed into the hall, thinking that her mother might still be asleep but knowing that Heart would be up, waiting for her, ready to gossip and advise. She peeked into the living room, which was empty but had been cleaned—more evidence that Heart was awake. Through the arched doorway that led to the kitchen, Rita spotted Heart at the table, eating toast. One pale leg, crossed over the other, rocked rhythmically, her homemade flannel gown revealing a purple bruise on her white thigh and the stubble of black hair on her chalky legs. Beside her plate of dry toast, a cup of milk rested on the table and rocked with the movement of her leg. Even the wood floor, Rita thought, seemed to give under the sway of that leg.

Gay stood before the kitchen sink in her speckled robe, brushing her teeth. Just as Rita gave up her hiding spot and stepped into the hall, she heard the back door creak open. Both of the women in the kitchen turned their heads.

"I wish you'd knock," Gay said through the foam of toothpaste.

Mrs. Lamb appeared in the kitchen bearing a thermos of coffee, the ceramic bowl Rita's mother had filled the night before with fruit salad, and a lit cigarette. Rita slipped back into the hall. She didn't like Margaret Lamb. "That robe makes you look like an amphibian," Margaret Lamb said, her voice sharp and piercing, like the cry of a bird. Then she added, "Hi, Heart. You look like death warmed over."

"I didn't sleep well," Heart said. The faucet came on. Rita pictured her mother rinsing her toothbrush. Then came the sound of shoe movement, followed by Margaret Lamb's voice. "Goddamn mud."

Rita covered her smiling mouth, although there was no one in the hallway to see her. Margaret Lamb would never say "goddamn" in front of Rita. A hypocrite, she thought, but her mother liked the woman.

The faucet went off. Rita could hear her mother spitting into the sink.

Margaret Lamb spoke again. "Isn't that girl up yet?" A shiver ran through Rita. Now they would talk about her.

"I'll get her up in a few minutes," Gay said. "Let me have some of that coffee." Her mother felt guilty, Rita understood, about waking her in the night. The river water had been a silky black, and lustrous, like beautiful hair. Coffee slurped out of the thermos. That's what the river had looked like, she thought, like a current of black coffee.

"You're not going to believe this," Margaret Lamb said, then paused—to smoke, Rita imagined. She smoked fancy cigarettes that stank. The cigarette was thin and stylish, but Margaret Lamb would wedge it between the base of her fingers so that she had to put her whole palm to her face to smoke, and then she puffed out of just one side of her mouth, a combination of the elegant and the ugly that reminded Rita of a dog show where an elaborately groomed poodle, upon receiving its ribbon, had defecated on the platform.

Heart spoke. "You shouldn't have gotten Rita up on a school night."

Rita held her breath to ensure hearing her mother's reply.

"I wanted her to see it."

"See what?" Margaret Lamb asked.

"You wanted to know if *you* were really seeing it," Heart said.

"See what?" Margaret Lamb asked again.

"The river," Gay said. "Last night, it looked so strange."

"I don't mind getting up," Heart went on. "I can go back to sleep on a dime."

"On a dime?" Margaret Lamb said.

"In a second. At the drop of a hat."

"You should go into show business," Margaret said, and from her tone Rita could tell that she was defending Gay. "We'll get a man in a turban to work with you onstage. He'll throw a velvet hat into the air. By the time it hits the floor, you'll be in a deep slumber. We'll have to rig up some wires and machines to prove you're sleeping. Would you mind shaving your head?"

The silence that followed was easy for Rita to interpret. Heart, long ago, had lost all her hair to radiation therapy. According to Rita's mother, it had taken years to grow back.

"The river was black," Gay said. "I wanted her to see."

Margaret said, "They won't have anything for her to do the first day, anyway."

The conversation again stalled. Rita considered making her entrance. She wanted to side with Heart in this argument, but she was glad that her mother had awakened her. The black river on the eve of her starting high school had to portend something. Black things usually meant something bad, but miraculous things typically predicted good events. It didn't matter what the river promised, only that it suggested the extraordinary.

"So what am I not going to believe?" Gay asked. "You said I wasn't going to believe something."

"Last night—after you . . . left—Hubby told us one of the new junior high teachers is living in Apuro. She's part Mexican and all of twenty-three, so she probably doesn't know any better."

"How is she going to come to school?" Gay asked. "Is she going to wade across like the kids?"

"What she's going to do is *move*. Hubby can't have a teacher without electricity. It's bad enough he has so many without sense."

Gay said, "Is there anything in this house that I can put in a lunch box?"

"I brought home some pears yesterday," Heart said, "but they bruise easy. Will she eat a bruised pear?"

"I won't let it bruise," Gay said. "Speaking of which, how'd you get that?"

"Riding," Heart said.

Margaret said, "Metaphorical riding or literal riding?"

"Horse riding," Heart said.

"Metaphorical horse or literal horse?"

"A horse horse. One that neighs and has hooves. How was your dinner party?"

"Dull as dishwater. Gay didn't even stick around."

"Good," Heart said.

"It was a couples thing," Margaret said. "I didn't know you had a boyfriend, or I would have invited you."

" 'Boyfriend' is not the right word," Heart said.

"Oh, we're all so progressive these days," Margaret said. "Your romantic associate, then, the cute rancher."

"He is a rancher." Heart sighed. "You want me to get Rita up?"

Margaret said, "Let's all get her."

Rita started to duck back into her room, but she heard someone whisper. She couldn't make out the words, although she thought she heard "Prince Charming."

"I don't know," her mother said. "Maybe."

"Are we talking about who I think we're talking about?" Margaret asked.

Again Rita held her breath, but no reply came. Her mother must have nodded or shook her head. Rita waited another moment, but she heard someone rise from the table. She tiptoed back to her room, pulling the door shut behind her. Her mother kept secrets about men. About doing things with them. Secrets about the secret things that women did with men, and that men did with women. Rita sat on her bed and waited for one of them to come for her.

This morning Rudy paid special attention to the vehicles. There were six, three of them pickups—a rusted-out Toyota that Fred Chavez had driven from L.A. and a banged-up Ford with that old-fashioned step bed that belonged not to Luís Magana but to his wife, who was from Guatemala and spoke Spanish like she had tree bark in her mouth, and an Isuzu, just five years old, loaned to the Obregon family by the Persimmon people whose house they cleaned and yard they mowed.

Of the three cars, the ugliest belonged to Humberto Douglas, a '79 Chevy station wagon with peeling paneling that Humberto took once a week to El Paso to see his brother. The ancient Dodge Dart—thirty years old—with pitted paint and pushbutton transmission but undented and handsome in its own way, had not run now for three years. It had once belonged to Rudy's father, but no longer belonged to anyone. The Dart had become something like a community bench or statue, Apuro's only work of public art. The silver Yugo, looking almost new, piece of *caca* that it was, Antonio Nieves had stolen from a girl he'd met in Mazatlán, having to fly with her to San Diego (she paid for his ticket) to steal it, so that she could force her father to buy her a Miata. Antonio hated the car so much that one drunken night he had stood on the roof and peed on the windshield. "She wouldn't kiss me in the U.S.," he had said, pissing. "We crossed the border, and she crossed her legs." When Tito Tafoya got ready to pee on it, Antonio had threatened him. "Get your dick away from my car."

For Rudy, knowing these things meant something. When the Persimmon kids at the high school he attended flaunted their clothes, their lunches, their digital fucking watches, he thought of the Dodge Dart, where at various times he had stashed amphetamines, pot, downers, several different guns, where they—not one of them—could ever show their faces without answering to *him*, without eating *his* shit. When they talked their television, their stupid rap lyrics, their secret fucking codes of who was and who wasn't worth the air they breathed, when they came to school in ridiculous baggy pants turned backwards or fancy jeans ironed stiff to look like steel, he could think of Antonio driving from California in the stolen Yugo, how Antonio had taken panties from the girl's suitcase and kept them in the glovebox, used them to blow his nose. Let them have their ugly stork Seinfeld on their stupid television, their moronic T-shirts. Blaze in hell, Seinfeld, whoever the fuck you are. When he heard somebody talking about Bart Simpson, he wanted to pound the idiot in the gut. He hated television not just because he was denied it, but because it made you a child. He could see it in their faces, those wretched, soft faces.

He hated the ones who spoke only English, but despised, too, the ones who spoke only Spanish. All he knew of Mexico was Ciudad Juárez, and he hated that choking, exhaust-filled crowd, the rumble of horns and sweating limbs, but he hated Persimmon as well, which was practically all he knew of the United States, the houses all facing the street like traffic was the real focus of life, so if you didn't have a car you were nothing.

Only in Apuro did he find peace, speaking English, some Spanish, living in the *casita* his grandfather had built, no television, no toilet, light from a lantern, heat from a fireplace, cool air—if there was any—from a wet towel draped over an open window. The houses turned this way and that, so anyone with feet could feel he belonged.

The Yugo, this morning, had one door ajar, a dim light illuminating the interior. Rudy stepped closer to examine. Antonio was one of the people he treated with care. He did not stare in the window of Antonio's house, and unless he was certain of his actions, he would not touch Antonio's car. Fear kept him from doing it, but he told himself it was his regard for Antonio, for the stolen panties, for the pissing on the windshield. He eased himself closer to the open door of the Yugo, looking about, pretending—to himself—that he had to be sure it wasn't an ambush, but really looking to be certain that no one noticed the hesitant way he approached the car.

The door simply wasn't entirely closed, no mystery: Antonio, home from drinking after work, fails to shut the door. On the floorboard were coins, and Rudy immediately checked Antonio's house. Antonio would be asleep, weary from the swing shift at the diner where he washed dishes, hefted racks of filthy plates. Rudy eased the car door open just enough to slip in his hand and take the coins. Almost a dollar in change.

The Chevy he eyed from a distance, a glimpse of the interior sufficient for his purposes. Humberto was another man he did not taunt or challenge. Rudy had once hidden in the backseat of this Chevy years ago and had not revealed himself until they were almost in El Paso. He had been ten or eleven and often hid from his father. Humberto had been surprised but not annoyed. They drove to a park on Franklin Mountain, a dirt lot with a view of the dirty city and the other dirty city beyond the river—although this was not how Rudy had thought of the view at the time. He had never seen so much civilization at one glance, had never enjoyed quite this perspective on how people lived. He looked out with a kind of awe at El Paso, at Ciudad Juárez, at the slender bandage of water that united and divided the cities, the countries.

Rudy had been born in Mexico, south of Juárez, in a ranch house belonging to the owners, the rancher's wife serving as midwife, Rudy's father fetching sheets, a blanket, water—the story was one Rudy's mother loved to tell. Rudy's father had been a *caballero*, a gentleman, not a drinker back then, a few after dinner with the other men, a nightcap with the rancher if invited, but a good worker, good with the horses, good with the dogs, could change the oil and plugs in the Dodge—his mother always included this detail about spark plugs. When Rudy heard it, he knew that the story was almost over. The lament would begin. They should have stayed on the ranch, should never have left Mexico to come live in Apuro in the house her father had built, should have had more children while it was possible, should should should. Now, the list would end in a rant about her job and the short skirt she was forced to wear, how the men at the bar would brush up against her. But even back then, when Rudy was eleven, he had hated her sad stories of Mexico. He had no desire to live *al otro lado*, on the other side. Coming to Apuro was the one thing his father had ever gotten right.

The polluted cloud that smothered Ciudad Juárez had seemed to justify Rudy's belief. While he stood beside Humberto Douglas on the Franklin Mountain lookout, he imagined all that he had escaped—starting with the manure of horses and cows, the sweat-stained sombreros, the silly attachment to animals. He longed for none of it.

Eventually they were joined by Humberto's brother, who looked nothing like Humberto. Where Humberto's face was pocked and slack, this man was handsome, his skin tight and clear. *"Mi hermano,"* Humberto said. My brother. The other man nodded theatrically. Later, Rudy spotted them holding hands. At the time he had thought it was something that brothers did in cities as large as El Paso, one more bit of evidence that he had no grasp of the world, that Humberto had a kind of sophistication Rudy had to respect and be wary of.

Now, years later, what had stayed with him was his fear that Humberto could somehow sully him, either by making him look stupid, or by telling the others that Rudy had become involved somehow in this business, this *joto* business. Rudy couldn't entirely articulate his fear, but he left Humberto alone.

Besides, everyone liked Humberto. Which made no sense to Rudy because he suspected that they too knew Humberto was *un joto*, a faggot. But no one would say as much, and as long as it could remain unsaid, they would pretend it was unthought. They gave themselves permission to like him. Even Rudy liked him, or he had, back when he'd hidden in his car, thinking that a day with Humberto, who smiled easily, bought him a Whopper, and expected nothing in return, would spare him a day with his father, who seemed to smile only at another's pain. Rudy often thought about his father when he, Rudy, smiled at another's pain. He knew that he was emulating his father, whom he loathed, and yet he could not alter it. Seeing another in pain *did* bring him pleasure, and to deny it would be to deny something essential in himself.

When he finished his tour, he walked to the crossing point to meet the other boys. The first day of his final year of school, and he was ready for the semester to begin. The school provided diversion and the opportunity for the exercise of his fierce and indomitable will. He looked forward to it.

"Enrique." He announced his name as if conceding a sin. He might as well have been saying *Adultery* or *Avarice*. He might as well have been saying, "I masturbate," or "I wet the bed."

Enrique reddened under the scrutiny of his teacher, a slender Hispanic woman with great brown eyes, who merely nodded at his confession, and said, "Do you have a last name, Enrique? *Su apellido?*"

"I speak English perfectly well," he told her, and gave her his surname.

"I don't have any Enrique Calzado on my class list," she said. "That wouldn't be an alias, would it?"

He could tell that she meant it to be funny, but no one else in the class seemed to understand as much. He felt the urge to rescue her with humor, but nothing would come to mind. "I have my schedule—" he began, but she cut him off with a wave of her hand.

"You're here," she announced. "But they list you as 'Calzado, Erin.' You don't have a sister, do you?"

Now the class tittered, which embarrassed him. He attempted to hide it. "Four of them," he said, forcing a smile. "But no Erin. Most of them are grown up. One lives in El Paso and has a baby. One—"

"I'm going to go out on a limb and count you as present." She extended her hand to him, and he surprised her by rising from his desk to accept it. "It's a pleasure, Mr. Enrique Calzado," she said.

She moved to the desk in front of him. He sat again and studied her, the way she bent slightly, the amusement in her eyes. He thought of the woman in the lingerie ad, but his teacher looked nothing like her. Despite his ongoing work on maturity, despite his status as eighth-grader—the dominant class at the middle school—he could not always decide the simplest of things, such as whether his teacher was pretty or not. It seemed to him that this should be the first thing he decided about her, but he realized that he had already decided something else, that he liked her. This shoved the other question into the background.

He was no good at deciding such difficult things anyway. That actress Winona Ryder, who everyone knew was stunning, looked to him like a scarecrow. Not her face, which was nice enough, but she was so skinny it looked dangerous just to be around her. Like if you made some sweeping movement with your hand—say you were describing the size of Einstein's brain—you could accidentally chop her with the side of your hand, and with her being so light—wham!—there'd she'd be at your feet, unconscious, and you'd have to take her to the hospital and try to explain about Einstein's brain, and they'd say, "This is Winona Ryder, can't you be a little careful?" and you'd feel terrible. Enrique couldn't even watch her in the movies without thinking, "Look out . . . Be careful!" So he wouldn't particularly want to date her, although he wouldn't say no to her, of course, but he'd prefer it if she ate something first.

Which made him picture himself as Winona Ryder's personal nurse, only not like real nurses, who can get AIDS from poking themselves with infected needles, but just somebody who got her to eat—"The Pizza Nurse"—or something like that, although "nurse" made you think of a woman, even though he knew that there were a lot of male nurses, including one cousin of his who lived in Los Angeles but who the family hadn't talked to in months. Maybe *he* knew Winona Ryder.

When he glanced back at his teacher, she was somehow already two rows away, talking to Monica Gutierrez, who last spring had told Enrique that she couldn't dance with him—they had been at the seventh-grade Easter Ball in the gym—because he reminded her too much of her little brother who never washed his feet. "I washed my feet this morning," he told her, but she still wouldn't dance with him, and he'd hardly said a word to her since then. *She* was pretty. That was already established all over school, which simplified things for him, but he wasn't about to risk any more hygiene questions, even though he definitely felt it was time he had a girlfriend. His parents even thought it was time, mainly because he didn't play sports. If he played sports, they wouldn't worry about how he spent his time or whether he liked girls—which he did—which they didn't seem to be all that sure about. Had he washed his feet this morning? He'd showered and some of the soap and water must have dribbled down, but he wasn't going to risk talking to Monica, anyway.

The teacher's name was still on the board: Ms. Anna Ordaz. He was bad with names and liked to make up memory tricks so he'd remember them. Anna Ordaz; *An order as* . . . he pictured a menu, but he'd used that one for a girl in his English class last year—her name was Anita Sandwich, or something like that. He couldn't think of anything good for Anna Ordaz. Probably he needed something with a *z* in it, and the only thing he could think of was pizza, which made him think he must be hungry to keep thinking about pizza and how skinny people like Winona Ryder were. An-na Or-daz; *an odor as* . . . bad as stinking feet. Which brought him right back around to Monica Gutierrez, her established beauty, her not wanting to dance with him. Funny how everything was tied to everything else.

Ms. Ordaz was talking with an Anglo boy who lived on a farm upriver. She didn't seem to smile over Anglos any more than she did over Chicanos, or maybe she was just eager to get away from this particular boy, whose front teeth, Enrique recalled, were ruined and black around the edges— which had something to do with the memory trick he used to remember this guy's name, although he couldn't figure just what it was unless his name was Robert, maybe, because the black was *robbing* his smile. Ms. Ordaz said, "Thank you, Kevin," and Enrique remembered: Kevin/Cave-in. His mouth was a black hole.

Suddenly, while watching Ms. Ordaz walk to the front of the class, he felt an erection coming on. He tried to think immediately of vegetables, which was one of those rare topics free of sexual content—except for asparagus and certain heads of lettuce—although right now it was doing no good. Steamed cauliflower, he thought, shredded cabbage. Then he thought, if his parents could see him, crossing his legs to hide his hard-on just because his teacher walked in a way that was really just walking but sent some message to his brain about, well, *movement,* and how it got him up like that, then they wouldn't have the worries they won't admit having but he can tell they do have by the way they suggest girls he might want to talk to or take to a dance. Did the message go to his brain or directly to his penis? Einstein's *brain* wouldn't be any bigger than anyone else's. It had to fit in his head, didn't it? It was his *mind* that was big, not his brain, and you wouldn't throw your arms out to show how big a mind was because you couldn't even see a mind, so maybe it wasn't that dangerous to be around Winona Ryder after all.

He sighed and smiled, feeling for a second that he'd cleared the way to love Winona Ryder and she might well be in his arms by nightfall. It suddenly seemed infinitely possible. Ms. Ordaz said, "Why should we bother studying history, anyway?" which was evidently what she taught, and Enrique remembered seeing HIS on his schedule. He raised his hand.

"Let's see." She glanced at her roll card. "Enrique—aka Erin—Calzado."

"We study history to avoid getting dizzy," he said.

She paused, expecting him to go on. "I like it so far," she said. "Can you explain your answer?"

"Well, ants, they go in a line from their anthills to look for some, I don't know, crumbs or something, and for them history is the back of the line and if they don't remember it, then maybe they think, 'I'll go left here,' when they've already been to the left, and before long they're just going in circles and all dizzy." He took a breath. "So that's why we need to study history. And besides, it's required, unless you take, what? Geology?"

"Geography," someone corrected.

"Yeah, I get those confused like astrology and that other one, but Mr. Davis teaches that, and everyone knows he's a hard"—he started to say *hardass*—"a hardnose."

"Mr. Davis teaches astrology?" Ms. Ordaz asked.

"Geology."

"Geography," the same someone corrected.

"Yeah, they don't teach astrology here," Enrique explained. "We don't have a telescope."

"Back to the first part of your answer—the ants—I like that reason for studying history. To avoid dizziness." She raised her gaze from his eyes and looked over the classroom. "Can you think of any examples of dizziness you see in our culture?"

"River Phoenix in *My Own Private Idaho*," Enrique said, but Monica Gutierrez had said, "The way everybody is getting a divorce," and no one seemed to hear him, which reminded him of why he didn't like to say his name—not that it explained to himself why he didn't like to say his name, but suddenly he was reminded that he didn't like to say his name, and that was probably why the teacher thought he didn't know English. It was something like giving an answer that nobody listened to because Monica Gutierrez, who everyone agreed was pretty, and who wouldn't dance with you no matter how clean your feet were, had beat you to the punch.

At the end of the class, as Enrique walked out the door, his erection long gone, Ms. Ordaz said, "I liked *My Own Private Idaho*, too."

Enrique nodded, permitting himself only a glance at her face, but it was beautiful—he didn't need to ask anyone what they thought. She was gorgeous.

6

Her mother had packed the lunch box with little marshmallows to cushion the sandwich and pear. The marshmallows expanded when Rita opened the lid, rising up in a way that made them look vaguely fungal. A few tumbled onto the cafeteria table.

"That's a lot of marshmallows," Cecilia noted.

Rita agreed, tilting her torso to partially hide the spectacle. She had just been telling Cecilia about seeing the river run black. Although she had been up for two hours in the middle of the night, she felt alert and not at all tired. She hunched forward and with the back of her hand pushed the escaped marshmallows toward her friend. "Have some," she said. Two more leaped out and fell to the floor as she removed her sandwich. It was the first time she had ever eaten in this cafeteria, and she didn't want to call attention to herself.

Cecilia corralled the liberated marshmallows with her palms. "What kind of black was it?" she asked. "Black like my shoes?" She placed the toe of her patent leather shoe on the cafeteria bench. She was overdressed for the first day of school in T-strap heels and a Sunday school dress, the formality of the outfit tempered by modifications she and Rita had made. Cecilia's mother didn't believe in throwing out clothes that still fit, and Cecilia had hardly grown since seventh grade. Originally pink with ruffles, the dress was now free of flounce and dyed the flat black of automobile tires.

"Yeah," Rita said, examining the shoe and dress at the same time, "that black." An exaggeration, she knew, but she and Cecilia had been friends long enough to know how to compensate for embellishments.

Cecilia slid her shoe off the bench, crossing one leg beneath the other. "We can't see the river from my house. Papa grew up in Apuro and doesn't like the water." She suddenly shifted closer and whispered in Rita's ear. "I'm not supposed to tell anyone he grew up in Apuro."

She neglected to mention, although Rita knew, that she, Cecilia, had lived there as a child. Good storytellers, Rita had noticed, always left things out. "Why is it a secret?" Rita asked.

Cecilia nibbled on a marshmallow. "He's ashamed, I think. Mostly."

Rita said, "My mother is ashamed of my dad." She had not thought this until this very moment, but now it seemed obviously true. She often made discoveries about her life while talking to Cecilia. They had become best friends in the fifth grade when none of the other girls in their class had cared for either of them. Rita, that year, had wanted braces for her perfectly straight teeth. It seemed to her that all the girls she wanted to be like had them. After fashioning braces for herself made of tinfoil and paper clips, Cecilia alone had told her they looked good. The other girls, in fact, had ridiculed Rita. She had worn the braces for two months, staining every blouse she owned with the blood of her ravaged gums. "She was wearing a fancy black dress when she jumped into the river, did I tell you that?"

Cecilia touched the skirt of her own once-abundant dress. "So does your mother still sleep with your papa, or is that what makes her feel shame?"

Rita removed her sandwich from its plastic bag—sharp cheddar cheese and honey on white bread. Her mother had evidently forgotten to shop. The marshmallows, Rita understood, were supposed to distract her from this failure. "My parents don't even look at each other," she said. "When my dad comes to visit, my mom makes me walk to the motel, or if she borrows Heart's car, she drops me off in the parking lot. They never get close enough to do anything."

Cecilia perked up at this. "Do you get to stay with him at the motel? I like motels but I've never stayed in one. I have an aunt in Mexico City, but I've never been there."

"Do they have motels in Mexico City?"

"They have *everything* in Mexico City. They have taxis waiting on the street so you can just wave your hand like this"—she raised her index finger and jiggled it—"and they pull over and take you anywhere you want to go."

"Heart came to our house in a taxi, when she moved in," Rita said, picturing Heart on a busy street in some place like Mexico City, jiggling her finger. Rita couldn't quite see it. "She even had her suitcases come over by themselves in a taxi."

"Did they leave a tip?" Cecilia laughed, a soft and inviting sound that Rita never resisted. They laughed together for a while before Cecilia picked up the thread of the conversation. "My aunt says tipping is an art like macrame or painting or being a priest."

"My parents don't even shake hands," Rita said. "I've *never* seen them together." She had told this to Cecilia before, but each time it struck her as strange and sad. "Except when I was a baby," she added, to be honest, "which I don't remember, so even if I have seen them together, I can't remember it."

Cecilia considered this. "Babies can't focus on anything when they're just born," Cecilia said, "so you probably *never* saw them together. How old were you when they split up?"

"Three," Rita said.

"Your eyes are focused by then, but maybe they had already started living in different parts of the house. Did they have a big house?"

Rita pictured the ranch-style house on Bloom Street where her father still lived, a simple place with a well-manicured lawn, but in Rita's memory it always appeared slightly shabby. "It's a little bit big, but there's only one bathroom."

Cecilia leaned close again. She whispered, "My mother will sit down on the toilet and pee while my dad is standing right there shaving."

"Gross. Then why is he ashamed of being from Apuro?"

"I think because one time he told me he waded across the river to go to a job, so he took extra pants and walked across barefooted and changed in the men's room at the Conoco and forgot socks, but he still got the job even with no socks, and worked all day, but somebody stole his wet pants, so he lost money because the pants cost more than what he made working."

"That makes sense," Rita said. Cecilia pushed her pile of marshmallows to one side and opened a paper sack, removing a slice of pressed turkey wrapped in a buttered flour tortilla. They ate for a few moments in companionable silence.

Persimmon High was a single-story concrete block edifice layered with brown stucco to look like adobe. The grounds had been covered with asphalt to keep down the dust. Because the asphalt absorbed heat, covered walkways made of steel girders and topped with corrugated metal had been erected. These metal "breezeways" and the stark walls gave the compound the look of a prison. A high mesh fence topped with barbed wire contributed to the effect.

Students had first labeled the school "Fort Persimmon," which, according to the whim of the week, became "Fort Failure," "Fort Wagging Tongue," or "Fort in Your Face." Now even teachers called it "the Fort," and students "the Fart."

Rita's first day at the Fart had begun with two confrontations. She had worn a beige dress that Heart had made for her, and the vice-principal took her aside to suggest that it was in violation of the Persimmon High dress code, the hem being significantly shorter than the two-inches-above-the-knee rule. Heart had only one design for the dresses and made them all one size. She sewed them in her bedroom on an ancient sewing machine with a treadle.

"You're going to have to go home and change," the vice-principal told her.

"My cousin, who is our boarder, makes these for me," she said. "All my dresses are like this." A lie, as she had a closet full of dresses, but she wore almost none of the others, and so she did not think of it as a lie.

"I can tell that it's . . . homemade," he said, his voice softening. He was a Hispanic man with a narrow mustache, who now seemed slightly disoriented, as if he suddenly had to reinvent everything he saw. "I don't doubt your—what's your name?" he asked, and Rita told him. "Who are your parents?"

"My father doesn't live here," Rita said. "My mom works downtown. She gives truckdrivers carrying cars directions. Her name is Gay."

"Your dress is too short. I won't make you go home this time, but I'd appreciate it if you'd tell your cousin that we have a dress code here."

"I'll tell her that," Rita said.

"If you get here early, you know, there's a breakfast provided to eligible students. There are some forms you have to fill out, but I'll help you with them."

"I don't really eat breakfast," she said.

"Lunch, too," he said. "Free hot lunch."

"I brought my lunch," she said. "My mom made it for me."

He nodded. "I'm sure it's good. You have a good day. You need anything, you have any problems—" He pointed to the name tag on his shirt: Mr. Padilla. "Just ask for me." He smiled then, having forgotten, it seemed, about the dress.

The second confrontation had ended in a less friendly manner. Her second period class began with a boy's desk falling apart. He sat down and put his arms on the writing surface, which immediately gave way and fell into his lap. While the kids around him laughed, he stared at the desk, first surprised and then amused.

"I suppose you think that's funny," the teacher said, and his tone made the laughter stop. A balding man with dark-rimmed glasses and jowls, he walked quickly over to the broken desk and pointed at the boy. "School property is not for you to capriciously destroy," he began, but Rita cut him off.

"It just fell apart, Mr. Harrelson," she said, and all of the heads turned toward her. "I was watching. All he did was sit down."

"And who are you? Tito's girlfriend?" The tone of this question gave the students permission to laugh, and they did. "Well?"

"A witness," Rita replied.

"I see-e-e," Mr. Harrelson said, teasing the last vowel, bringing on more laughter.

"No," said Rita. "*I* saw." She collected her books and left the room.

"Are you leaving—" The door closed on his question. She had wanted to be in the same civics class as Cecilia, anyway. Cutting across the asphalt breezeway, she stepped into the room where she and Cecilia had parted only moments before. The teacher, a young woman with a bow in her hair, said, "Yes?"

"I've been sent over to this class," Rita said, which, she thought, was more or less true. She introduced herself. "I should be on the next roll list."

"Very well," the teacher said.

Was this a good way to start her high school career, or a conspicuously bad one? Her mother had told her that no one got to step on her. "Do what you think is right," Gay had told her, "and I'll come in and help clean up." Rita felt both righteous and worried, and hoped she'd be able to finesse the paperwork so her mother wouldn't have to know. If she had it to do over again, she'd sit in the bad desk herself. Mr. Harrelson never would have accused her of breaking it, she was quite certain—and this certainty had made her like him even less.

Cecilia took a miniature marshmallow and stuffed it in her tortilla along with the pressed turkey. "Papa doesn't even like to look at Apuro," she said while she ate. "Although I guess he didn't actually grow up there, but he and my mom moved there when they just got married. Enrique is teaching him how to read English."

"My dad cleans swimming pools in Albuquerque," Rita said.

"You told me," Cecilia said. "I don't remember when."

"It's a cool job. You get to be around water and look in people's yards."

"Yeah," Cecilia agreed, "but I'd rather be a nurse and marry a doctor and not have to worry about anything ever again." She shifted her focus to her hands on the cafeteria table, her posture suddenly tense. Rita followed suit. They were being nonchalant. "That boy is watching us," Cecilia said. "Don't look."

Rita touched her hair and looked sideways at the boy. "He's not looking at us," Rita said. "He's just looking for someone to beat up." She whispered, "That's Rudy Salazar."

Cecilia inhaled audibly. "He's the one who broke Arturo's nose." Then she added, "He's big enough to be a man."

"My mother says not to worry about bullies. She says she'll make mince-meat of anybody who messes with me." Rita could hear her mother's confident tone. "Her name is Gay, so she's used to fighting."

"I wish my parents were like that," Cecilia said. Then she whispered urgently. "He's staring right at us. He's grinning and staring right at us."

Rita turned and looked directly at him. He *was* staring. She stared back, refusing to look away when he sneered. In another moment, he discovered his food and began eating.

"Is he still looking at us?" Cecilia asked.

"No." Then she said, "Do you think he saw the river last night?" He was a *rodilla negra*, and so he had to live close to the river. Any kid from Apuro was a *rodilla negra*, a "black knee," because their jeans were wet to the knee and the dark line would remain all day, even after the pants dried. They were called *negras* for short. "Do you think anybody else has ever seen the river go completely black like that?"

Cecilia folded the empty brown paper bag she had carried her lunch in. She tucked it inside a textbook. "I'll ask my dad for you."

When they rose to leave, Rita eyed Rudy Salazar once more. Now he gave her a malevolent gaze. "That guy gives me the creeps," she said.

Cecilia, careful not to look in his direction, agreed, adding, "He's a senior."

Gay had been meeting Sander at the Desert Oasis Motel one or two nights a month for twelve years. However, she rarely came during the daylight, and the motel looked decidedly better in the dark. Dead flowers, little more than burnt stems, blemished an otherwise bare brick planter before the manager's big window, which held a greasy film of dust. A red windsock with a black, oriental-style fish pattern waved wearily above the planter like an advertisement for condoms.

Except for Sander's truck, the vehicles matched the sleaziness of the establishment. They had all been turned into jokes. An old Corolla featured the bottom half of a stuffed cat sticking out of the trunk, while a pale gray Mercedes had the personalized license plate RU EZ. A Jeep with Colorado plates had the most offensive messages, bearing bumper stickers on either side of a huge trailer hitch. One read UGLY GIRLS, the words circled and slashed in red. The sticker on the opposite side was even worse: COLORADO: FAG FREE IN 93. Even the manager's otherwise innocuous K car bore the message MY KID BEAT UP YOUR HONOR ROLL STUDENT. The Banality Conference must be in town, Gay thought. And she had complimentary tickets.

She opened the door to Sander's room without knocking and surprised him. The sun cast a harsh light on the dingy room, his clothes spread about a corner of the floor in folded piles. Barefoot and bare-chested, he stood before the dresser mirror studying himself, his hair pulled back in a short pony tail, knotted with a shoestring.

"Like what you see?" she asked him.

He glanced at her, then looked back to the mirror. "I'm getting a gut."

"Again," she said.

"Close the door." It was his habit to speak softly, as if his voice might do others damage. He raised his arms and stretched self-consciously. He would admit to vanity, but he preferred not to be caught indulging in it. He yanked the string from his hair. Just seeing him made Gay feel instantly better. She stepped in and shut the door, a painted metal monstrosity that transferred heat from the outside with remarkable efficiency and clanked like a prison gate.

Nothing in the room's decor charmed her. Early American Ugly chairs, glued and reglued amateurishly, slumped in the corners. A matching dresser had drawers that came out crookedly and didn't want to go back in, leading Sander to pile his clothes on the floor. The mattress sagged in the middle like the butt of an old man, while the foam pillows had the shape and elasticity of bullets. Cheap without the allure of the genuinely seedy, the room featured generic prints of the desert and several framed needlepoint Bible quotations.

"I didn't think I was coming," she said. She ran her hands over the waist of the sun dress that he had given her the night before. That she had dressed in it seemed to contradict what she was saying. "I just started walking and found myself heading out here." A partial truth. She was sufficiently upset with Sander to avoid seeing him, but she came because of Denny. If she refused to see Sander right after meeting Denny, it lent too much gravity to their fugitive swim. She made it a practice to do nothing that threatened the unique conventions of her marriage.

"I could have picked you up," Sander said. He lifted the canvas flap of his suitcase with his foot, then bent over and grabbed a purple T-shirt, pausing as if to count his possessions. He held the shirt out for her to read: POOL MEN DO IT IN THE DEEP END.

"Don't tell me you've become one of them," she said. "What does that mean?"

He shrugged and studied the shirt, his hooded eyes almost shut. "One of my clients gave it to me. I can't seem to get around to wearing it. Thought you might want it. A bonus anniversary gift."

"What you really mean," she said, "is that one of the clients you're screwing gave it to you."

He shook his head in slow motion, still scrutinizing the shirt's message. "Mrs. Kallecky. Middle-aged—"

"Like you."

"Heavyset—"

"Like you."

"Hey, now," he said, "I'm sorry about last night."

"I know," she said. "I am too. I shouldn't have . . . " She didn't know what it was precisely that she regretted, but she knew it had to do with Denny. Somehow she had let the elation of her night with him interfere with her wedding anniversary, and she felt bad about it. At the same time, Sander's behavior had disappointed her. "It *was* black," she said. Then she added, "I'm not seventeen. I don't *imagine* things." It seemed to her that Sander was both the most difficult and the easiest person she knew to be with. It all had to do with their history, with having a history.

Sander tossed the T-shirt back to the suitcase. It landed on one edge and slid to the floor in a purple puddle. He wasn't fat, but he had filled out in predictable ways, his middle thickening, the skin below his jaws starting to sag. She still found him attractive, but she couldn't help comparing his body to the one that had climbed dripping from the river, athletic without being muscled, a flat stomach and square shoulders. At the same time, she knew it was not Denny's body that had excited her. Half the boys in the high school where Denny taught had bodies like his, but she had no interest in boys.

"You see the new edict on the sign?" Sander asked her.

Embarrassed to be picturing Denny's naked body, she smiled at him, her lips spreading and continuing to move, an exaggeration of her normal smile.

Sander loved when she smiled this way. She would be especially kind to him today, she thought. "Let's go out and look at it," she said, pausing to show him the smile again. "We have about twenty minutes before the day becomes unbearable, and I don't want to spend it inside."

Sander studied her for a moment, waiting for her to give him the real reason she wanted to go out in the heat. He knew her too well, she thought. Bending to avoid his scrutiny, she began picking through the pile of clothing on the floor to find him a suitable shirt, but he retrieved the purple T-shirt with the stupid message and slipped it on before she could object.

In the sunlight, Sander's appearance changed. He had an air of competence, his sun-damaged complexion suggesting experience, his disheveled hair the recognizable trademark of a certain kind of man, one who worked with his hands and took pleasure in it. Sometimes she thought she had moved away from him—without leaving him—because of this sure sense of himself. She had wanted to find the same for herself, and it had seemed impossible while living with him.

She took his hand, heat from the blacktop lot already causing her thighs to sweat, and they headed for the sign. During the years they had been coming to the Oasis, the motel had changed hands twice. The original owner had used the marquee below the neon palms to advertise special rates, 20% DISCOUNT FOR VETERANS, or KIDS STAY FREE, and always, AIR CONDITIONED, capitalizing every letter in the manner preferred by motel owners across the country. The next owner had used the top line to assert that the establishment was AMERICAN OWNED, and the present owners maintained the practice, adding short spiritual messages below. Adhering to marquee etiquette, they used no punctuation. Last month the sign had read,

AMERICAN OWNED

GOD BE

WITH YOU

COUPLES $20

"I figured it was just a matter of time before He started charging," Sander had said. "Once I heard Pete Rose and those guys were charging money for autographs—and getting away with it—I figured God would get wise. American Owned God would have to be a capitalist, no?"

"How does it work to your advantage to have God be with you?" Gay had asked.

"Improves your odds, I guess," Sander said. "Of course, He has been known to be petty. There are times I'd rather not have Him looking over my shoulder. If He's American owned, you can be certain He's got a terrible, swift sword."

The new message on the marquee was no less entertaining.

AMERICAN OWNED
LOVE COVERS
ALL SINS
COUPLES $20

"That's a lot of sins to cover for twenty bills," Sander said.

"Considering our history," Gay replied, "twenty dollars is a steal. But I don't want my sins covered."

"Sorry," Sander said, "but I already paid. Your sins are forgotten. You're sinless in the eyes of God and strangers."

"Let's walk." She tugged him toward River Road. They strolled north, away from town, walking on the sandy shoulder. Trees along the riverbank hid most of the water, but it glinted through in patches, while on their side of the road a field of chiles stretched in parallel grooves to a distant irrigation canal, the gray-green plants, already picked through once, scantily spotted with pointed red peppers that dangled obscenely. The heat exaggerated the chile odor, which was a burning smell anyway, but a gratifying one, Gay thought, like a good memory from a bad time.

"Only fitting and proper that America should own love," Sander said. "What commodity is more universally sought after than love? There must be an army of executives in New York trying to corner the market on it as we speak."

Gay decided to agree with him. "American Owned Love is that feeling you get in those huge department stores like Marshall Field's or Bloomingdale's—"

"That's not the half of it," Sander said. He showed her a wide, brief smile, a signal she recognized. He was about to connect the motel sign to whatever his latest passion was. Maybe if he had gone to college he would have found a single direction for his intellectual interests, but left to his own devices, he dipped into one and then another haphazardly. Gay liked this about her husband. It amused and moved her at the same time. It permitted her to let Denny and her dazzled libido slip into the background where it belonged. Long-standing loves fed you in ways that affairs could not.

"If our concepts of love and beauty and truth are merely cultural constructions," Sander began, "as a lot of people think, then the only love we can know is American Owned Love."

Gay pulled up short. "Do you believe that?"

His shaggy head slanted in a thoughtful way. "No. I mean it *is* mostly true, but that's the powerful thing about love and beauty and so on, that sometimes you can get past the concepts we take for granted and touch on something, I don't know, *bigger*."

It occurred to her then that lovemaking in shabby motels did seem specifically American, at least in places like this one, complete with religious messages on the walls, so that shame was an integral part of the loving, so that America really did own part of it. She and Sander—their love—she wished to exclude from this assessment, but she understood that each couple in each tacky room would think themselves exempt. Even the man sitting in his underwear watching cable movies would exclude himself, his desire for soft porn merely a curiosity in his character. They were none of them immune, each possessing and possessed by a love greater than the boundaries of any human body. American Owned Love. No wonder their cars had ridiculous stickers and mangled stuffed animals. If they could not mock their feelings, they might be too tender to bear.

"It's too hot to walk," she said suddenly, interrupting him. "Tell me more," she added, embracing his arm, turning him in the opposite direction before she let him continue.

On her third wedding anniversary, in August of 1981—the year she had turned twenty-one—Gay had climbed into her husband's Chevy LUV pickup and driven south from Albuquerque, following the Rio Grande two hundred sixty miles to Persimmon. She had gone looking for a house to purchase, preferably one close to the river and surrounded by trees. It also had to be cheap. And at least four hours' drive from Albuquerque—too far for Sander to commute from her bedroom.

The place on Calle Blanca met all her criteria, an attractive house gone to ruin. Vacant for five years and boarded up for the past three, it featured a leaky roof and stucco wall covering that undulated weirdly—presumably from the intense desert heat. The wiring upstairs was believed to be faulty, the realtor reported, although there had been no electricity to the house since it was shut up. Otherwise, it was merely filthy.

But it had been very cheap, and Gay bought it.

The repair to the roof was estimated at three thousand dollars. She returned to Albuquerque to pack while it was completed. A new hookup and fuse box solved the electrical problem. The stucco, the contractor assured her, was meant to look that way and merely needed paint. "Pink," she told him by phone, "with a green trim."

During the years of her marriage she had worked at a day-care center— the only job she could find that permitted her to be with her daughter and get paid for it. Sander had encouraged her to save the money she earned for something she really wanted.

"I was thinking more like a hot tub," he said to her. "Or maybe a trip to Hawaii."

"I've saved thirty thousand dollars," she told him.

"Paris, then," he said. "With thirty grand you could buy a Mercedes. We could use another car."

Instead, she rented a U-Haul truck, loaded it with the few things she needed, and strapped her daughter's safety seat into the cab. It had become important for her to take control of her life, to shape it as she pleased.

He had trailed her to the rented truck and leaned heavily against the door. "Going to live there by yourself without a car?"

"I won't be by myself." She patted her daughter's head. "You can visit us in exactly one month." She held up her index finger, and he leaned into the cab to plant a kiss on its tip. "Between now and then"—she paused until the kissing stopped—"have fun. Hasn't what's-her-name with the high dive been trying to seduce you?"

"Maybe," he said. "But maybe she just wants a tan."

"I'm all right," Gay assured him. "This will be good for me. Good for all of us."

"I'm not so sure," he said.

Twice, years earlier, Gay had suffered breakdowns. She knew that he could stop her from taking their daughter. He could hire a lawyer and stop her. Officially speaking, she had a history of mental illness. But she also knew that he would not do this. He would see it as a kind of betrayal.

He said, "What if we just took separate vacations?"

Gay kissed him on the lips, buckled Rita in, and drove away.

The kitchen floor of the pink and green house had been covered with a dotty sort of brown linoleum that Gay hated. She planned to rip it up the same week she moved in. But first she had to find a job. After a week of looking, she accepted a position with a flower nursery. The owner, a red-faced woman in her fifties, let Gay bring Rita to work. "Nothing better for a child than living plants," the woman had said. "Just get your work done, and don't let the girl eat manure."

Rita had just turned three—her birthday preceded her parents' wedding by a week—and with her at work, it often took Gay ten hours to complete an eight-hour day. After a few weeks of this, Rosa Perez, their next-door neighbor, volunteered to keep Rita. Four years passed before Gay got around to pulling up the linoleum in the kitchen. She discovered that the floor was not made of oak as the floors were elsewhere in the house. The pine boards were wide and soft, chipped in places.

Gay sanded the boards by hand on weekends and in the evenings after Rita was asleep, her work uneven but satisfying. Another year passed before she painted the floor—a pale blue, initially, the pastel of swimming pools. She had given it two new coats since then, each time using a darker shade in order to better hide the pits and scars. Now, twelve years hers, the floor was the blue of deep water. But dust showed, and either Rita or Heart was forever sweeping it. There was no keeping floors clean in the desert.

The original wallpaper in the kitchen had featured sunflowers, and some child or adult had drawn faces in their yellow centers—several smiling, many scowling, a few in tears. Gay stripped the kitchen walls a couple of months after moving in, but she left them exposed, glue-stained, and discolored until Rita was in second grade. Finally, Gay and her boyfriend of the moment cleaned and painted them—a light gray like the belly of a bird. The boyfriend, a bartender who raced motorcycles, disliked the choice. "You're going to wish it was all white," he told her, offering a resigned smirk and a shake of the head. "And I'm going to have to come do it all over again." He'd said it pleasantly enough, but the presumption that he'd still be around doing chores in the near future annoyed Gay. She dumped him before the paint dried. "A tacky breakup," she liked to say, but no one ever got the joke.

Against the east wall, surrounding the window and wrapping around the corners, wooden cabinets reached from floor to ceiling. The top doors were squat and long, like the overhead bins in airplanes. Standing on the counter to reach them, Gay had not been able to get them open, finally deciding they were merely decorative. Nine years later, when she and Heart stripped and refinished the cabinets, she discovered that the top doors had only been painted shut.

Two of the cupboards were empty but for dust and the remains of a few cockroaches. The third held wineglasses, and two bottles of Merlot from Chile. The fourth contained darkroom equipment—a huge cracked bulb, warped metal trays, corked canisters. Also a homemade leather wallet, a dancing Indian with an oddly cocked head hammered into the wallet's crease, a flock of crude birds rising all about him. By turning the wallet upside down, the Indian's dancing legs became the lips of a vagina, the birds became wisps of coarse hair, while the Indian's head now kissed the lips in the wallet's fold.

"That," Heart had said, pointing to the wallet's sexual crease, "is by far the *strangest* pornography I've ever seen."

In the fifth cupboard they found a tackle box with fishing gear and a roll of bills bundled in copper wire, four hundred dollars in silver certificates. Beneath the tray, in the bottom of the tackle box, was a pile of black-and-white photographs divided by tissues into sets.

The first photograph in the first set showed a man and a woman standing together naked in the woods. It was autumn, and they were holding hands. In the second photo, the naked man, by himself now, urinated into the fallen leaves, his expression steady, as if he were daily photographed peeing nude in the woods, his penis held in the V of his first two fingers like a cigar. The third featured the naked woman, squatting, peeing onto a bed of moss, a rivulet of urine curling between her bare feet and trickling out of the frame, she with her hands back on her buttocks, her head lifted, staring at the camera, her face illuminated by her smile.

In the second set, the same naked woman, a little older and with a new hairstyle, stood naked on a ladder-back chair in Gay's kitchen. The photograph mainly featured her round bottom and her smiling face. A man joined her in the next photo, a different man with strange eyebrows and a slightly lopsided nose, naked, standing beside her on the kitchen counter. The two photographs that followed showed each separately peeing into the kitchen sink.

The box held two more sets of photographs. The woman continued to age, while each featured a new man. In the third set, the naked couple peed in the desert—it might have been at White Sands Monument, which was about an hour's drive. In the final group, the woman stood with a very short man in the Rio Grande, the water just above their knees. She looked to be in her late forties now, still thin, still handsome, her face still lit by some perverse glee. In separate photographs, each peed into the river.

A final photo belonged to no set. It showed the woman, fully dressed in creased pants and workshirt, pointing to the leafy ground while beside her stood the first naked man, his head slightly blurred, as if nodding.

Gay's initial response to the photographs had been to scour her sink. But while steam rose from the hot water, she felt a deep longing for her husband and the little depravities of their early years. An unexpected result of their marital arrangement had been the simplifying of their sexual lives together. After a month apart, neither particularly wanted to experiment. Once, though, not long after finding the photographs, Gay had talked Sander into lying in the motel tub while she squatted over him, a foot perilously perched on either rim, and peed on his stomach.

He hadn't liked it. "I'm going to shower, Madame X." Later, he'd said, "My turn," and tried to talk her into reclining in the tub.

"Forget it," she had said. "We're no good at funny stuff anymore."

"To tell the truth, I don't really feel much desire to pee on you," he had said. "Not *sexual* desire, anyway. Maybe some get-even desire."

Gay kept the photos in her room, in the bottom of a Kleenex box beneath an array of old postcards, loose change, paper clips, and ballpoint pens. Her favorite was the one that showed the woman clothed and directing the naked man, indicating where to pee, which meant she thought of herself as an artist.

The final kitchen cupboard was nailed shut. There were at least a dozen nails, and Gay could see no way to open it without damaging the door and frame. She tried to pry it free with a crowbar, but the wood chipped, a big piece dropping onto the counter. She decided to glue the chip back into place and leave the cupboard alone.

"It's probably a lot more interesting nailed shut," Heart said to her, sitting in a kitchen chair, staring up at Gay, who stood on the countertop.

"Maybe," Gay said. She slathered glue onto the broken piece. "But the others were more interesting once we opened them."

"What would you put away in a cupboard that you nailed shut?" Heart asked.

"Evidence," Gay said without hesitation.

"No," Heart said. "Evidence, you destroy."

"Something that can't be destroyed, or that you can't destroy."

Heart eyed the cupboard, reconsidering. "Maybe there's more money in there."

"Enough to repair the cupboard after we pry the door off?"

"I doubt it," Heart said. "Probably the damn door kept falling open, and somebody was drunk and nailed it shut."

"Some naked guy with a hammer who needed to pee," Gay said. She pushed the chip into place and held it there until the glue dried. "Can you tell it's banged up?"

"Well," Heart said.

"It'll have to do," Gay said.

The refrigerator, an old white and chrome Kelvinator, Gay had found in a secondhand store. The white stove—an ornate gas model with eight top burners, three of them functional—had come with the house. The large oak table, round and supported by a single center column, Gay had stolen from an abandoned farmhouse. Sander, during one of his weekend visits, had assisted in the theft.

"How'd you find this place?" he had asked as he pushed open the decrepit front door. The farmhouse was fifteen miles south of Persimmon, across the river and out in the desert. The road to it, washed out and covered with rocks, required fording the Rio Grande.

"A man took me here," Gay said.

"That's what I figured," he said. "Why didn't you get him to lug this thing away?"

"I didn't like him that much."

This answer pleased Sander. "Larceny *is* best with intimates," he said, and they wrestled the table into his truck.

He had to drive slowly down the rutted road. The river was all but dry, but the bed was muddy and he worried about getting stuck. "No wonder Mexico is so pissed off," he said, sticking his head out the window to study the riverbed in the spray of the headlights. "By the time the river gets to them, there's no water left in it." It was almost midnight when they finally arrived at her house. Together they unloaded the table and carried it to the stoop by the back door. "We're going to have to take it apart to get it through here," Sander told her.

"Heart and I can do that," Gay said. "We shouldn't waste the time we have left." He was leaving for Albuquerque in the morning, but also she didn't want him to come into the house. He had not yet set foot in her house.

Sander did not miss the slight. "I'd rather make love than dismantle a table," he said to her, "but I'm insulted nonetheless."

The following morning Heart helped her take the table apart. Together they maneuvered it through the narrow back door—a solid wooden door with a round window. This door, on the very day that she and Rita took possession of the house, Gay had painted turquoise in order to hide a swastika and the word FUCK. It had taken four coats, and every few years the shadow of the word or the shadow of the symbol would return, and Gay would have to work once again to cover them up.

7

Rita walked with Cecilia after school. She had planned to walk only as far as Cinco de Mayo Street, and then veer toward home, but Rudy Salazar was following them. They stuck together another two blocks, until he disappeared.

"If he keeps following you," Cecilia advised, "walk in the middle of the street. Then he can't do something without everyone seeing."

"I'm not afraid of him," Rita said, but immediately felt hot in the face. She had, after all, just walked two blocks out of her way because of him.

"I *am* scared of him," Cecilia said. "He's the kind of guy who could do anything. I've got to go." She turned and began walking away, her fancy dress bouncing as she stepped, looking back to wave after she had crossed the street.

The detour had taken Rita downtown, and she decided to go to Heart's bookstore, as if that had been her destination all along. Heart had opened the bookstore six months earlier. She had purchased the stock of a store that had failed in El Paso, but the selection had not entirely suited her. There were boxes of unopened books in the back room, and Heart had ordered hundreds of titles that the defunct store had not carried. One whole wall was devoted to "Classics," and two big ceiling-to-floor shelves to "Metaphysical Awareness, Philosophy, and Holistic Healing."

The store had the uninventive title of "Persimmon Books," and had opened in an adobe building downtown between Arzate's Grocery and Turnball Liquor. Rita decided to take the alley to the bookstore's back door. She did it to prove that she was not afraid of Rudy Salazar.

No sooner had she entered the alley than she regretted the decision. She kept peeking over her shoulder, half expecting to see him charging after her. The last dozen yards, she ran, stopping at the door and looking in both directions down the alley. Nobody. She caught her breath. It was far too hot to run. She calmed herself. She didn't want Heart asking questions.

The back door entered into the storeroom. Rita could hear Heart talking and pausing to listen—probably on the phone—and she cracked open the door to the store an inch to eavesdrop.

"—seeing him today like nothing happened," Heart was saying. "It's the arrangement they have. She doesn't need to hold a grudge." She paused and something in the quality of the hesitation let Rita know that she was not on the phone but talking to someone in the store. "Maybe," Heart said in response to what must have been a whisper, "but you tend to be more conservative than me."

Rita tried to peek through the door, but it made such a noise opening that she had to pretend to be marching in.

"Oh," Heart said, turning to Rita, "you scared me." She stood behind the sales counter in the little cubby of space that held the cash register, the telephone, a home-model espresso machine, and the doorway that Rita now stepped through. There was a second counter by the front door, but the phone was in the back, and the front desk was hardly ever manned.

Heart's partner in conversation made a quick retreat into the tall aisles of books, a young man in a cowboy hat now holding an oversized picture book to his face, *Ancient Ruins of the Southwest*. Rita didn't need to see his face to know it was Mr. Gene, Heart's boyfriend—romantic associate, Margaret Lamb had called him. Rita should have guessed. He was the only person she knew too shy to speak loudly enough to be heard.

For a year or so, Heart had taken Rita twice a week to Mr. Gene's ranch outside of Persimmon, where they'd both saddle up and lunge around a field, or trot up and down the dirt roads connecting pecan groves. Once Rita saw Heart kiss Mr. Gene on the cheek as they were ready to leave. He was handsome and thin, with red, rough hands and eyes that kept flitting away from your gaze. Rita had been introduced to him at the ranch, but all he'd done was tip his cowboy hat and smile timidly, then disappear inside the house. "Mr. Gene is the shyest person you'll ever want to meet," Heart had told her proudly.

Rita headed down the aisle to talk to him, but Heart called to her. "How was your first day of high school?"

"Fine," she said.

"Don't tell me you've come to do the inventory," Heart said, but Rita would not be deterred. "I thought Cecilia was going to help you with it."

"Okay," Rita said, without slowing. As she reached Mr. Gene's row, he slipped around the shelf of books. Rita had to backtrack to stop him. "You remember me?" she said. "Heart used to take me riding at your ranch."

He offered her the shy smile and touched his hat with his hand. Dirt traced the lines in his face, embellishing them, giving him a look of exaggerated sadness, but it made him no less handsome in her eyes. His fingertips left marks on his dusty hat as if something had alighted there. "Pleasure," he said softly, already moving away from her, his single utterance lingering before Rita like a balloon losing its helium—pliant, underfilled, and imperceptibly sinking. *Pleasure*.

"How are your horses?" she called to his back, immediately embarrassed by the question. She needed to work on her small talk.

He may have tilted his head in response, but he did not slow his gait, walking quickly to the door, tossing *Ancient Ruins of the Southwest* onto the front counter, the book's binding thudding against the wooden countertop, causing the book to splay open, hesitate, and then begin to shut, the pages turning themselves, the book ultimately closing. Mr. Gene and Heart had not even exchanged a departing glance.

"What's with him?" Rita asked. "Do I stink or something?"

"He's a bashful man," Heart said, her voice just above a whisper. "Your mother doesn't like bashful men, but I think they can be nice. Besides, seeing you out of school must have reminded him of the time. He has chores."

Rita had no interest in this explanation. "He remembered me," she said, trying to imagine Heart in his arms. All she could see was the kiss, Heart rising to her tiptoes and leaning close, her lips on his cheek less than a second. "I could see that fizzy look in his eyes people get when they know they know you." A kiss should last longer, she thought, should involve embracing, should be on the lips. Heart did not seem equal to this task, or a fair match for the man.

"Do you know what *inventory* means?" Heart asked her.

"Of course," Rita said. "It means seeing if you've got everything you think you've got."

"Well," Heart said, looking around the store, touching the bridge of her glasses, then removing them, wiping the lenses with her sleeve. Her bare face and unfocused stare made Rita turn away, as if removing the glasses had made Heart naked. "I think I've got a losing proposition, but I won't know for sure until we count everything up."

"How about tomorrow?" Rita asked, walking now to retrieve *Ancient Ruins of the Southwest*. "I don't think Cecilia's doing anything tomorrow. She didn't mention anything, anyway."

Heart said, "Your father is coming to see you tomorrow."

"Then he can help, too, right?" She glanced back at Heart as she lifted the book. Just pictures of tumbled-down houses built on plateaus, glued pots with swirling designs. "You're not prejudiced against my father, are you?"

"Heavens, no," Heart said. "I'll even trust him with a mop if he shows. But there's not *that* much rush."

Rita nodded and shut the book. "I thought this guy from school was following me home, so that's why I came in through the back door."

"Oh, I see," Heart said, as if this made sense. "You ought to get on home now. Your mom wants to hear about your day. She told me she was taking off early from work to be there for you."

"It's stuffy in here," Rita said, already turning to leave, feeling suddenly short of breath. She waved to Heart without saying good-bye.

Half a block up the street from the bookstore, Rita paused next to a brown truck. She wasn't certain that Mr. Gene drove a brown pickup, but she remembered it being some ugly color. The seat was dusty, as his would be, and clumps of dried mud covered the floorboard. A long, wrinkled red scarf lay on the seat, a tiny spiral notebook on the dash. She wasn't certain that the truck was his, but decided to examine the notebook, just in case.

The truck window was open. Up the street, a woman tried one key after another on a faded green station wagon, and down the street, a Hispanic couple emerged from Arzate's Grocery, turning their backs to Rita, strolling arm in arm despite the heat. No one else ventured out in the afternoon swelter. The notebook fit snugly in her hand. As she pulled away, she saw there were two red scarves. *Presents*, she thought, although both needed ironing.

She folded her arms and strolled toward home. The spiral ring, hot from the dashboard, burned her palm. She would file the notebook in her memento chest—a metal tackle box with a combination lock that her mother had found in a cupboard. Rita kept her earring collection in it. She'd had her ears pierced when she was seven. Gay had given her two pairs of earrings that first day, which had started her collection. One pair had a blue stone surrounded by fake pearls, but the other was the pair Rita loved—a woman's face in profile, an African woman, whose hair was a perfect oval of jade. "They were the gift of a friend," Gay told her, "but it's okay for me to give them to you." The earrings did not have studs but long, sturdy wires with pointed ends that Rita slid through the holes in her lobes. The wire would poke sharply against her neck if she ran.

She carried the notebook discreetly in her palm until she turned off Main Street. The first page was blank, which made her worry that it all might be bare. But on the second page there were numbers and the letters MPG. His gas mileage. *Trés* dull. And no proof that it belonged to Mr. Gene. A notebook that belonged to just anyone wasn't worth stealing.

A few pages had been torn out, she could tell, by the scraps remaining about the spiral. On the last page she found a list, printed in pencil—definitely a man's writing.

Buy oats
Get coffee, Kix, Tabasco, ice cream, fig newts
Fix spare
Drop off purse
Hope for double figures before meeting

Scribbled in ink just below the pencil list, she found this:

Ask Q if he's ever seen it black

Rita felt a rush of excitement. The notebook belonged to Mr. Gene. Heart had told him about the river running black. Rita found a pencil in her backpack and added a line to the list.

Make love to R

Reading it made her laugh. The next time she saw the truck, she would slip the notebook back onto the dash and leave him to wonder. She pictured him finding the message, the look of surprise on his face, which, in her imagined scene, had already grown more handsome.

With his hands in his pockets, his eyes shaded by sunglasses he had taken from a freshman, Rudy Salazar followed the two girls, not pretending to do otherwise, letting them know he was there, and yet staying far enough back so that they would not be tempted to turn and talk to him, not that Cecilia Calzado ever would do that, but the Anglo girl—Tito said her name was Shaffer, and Rudy couldn't help but turn it into "Shopper," which seemed like the perfect name for a rich white girl—she might do it, might turn and say, "What do you want?" or "Quit following us!" He remembered the stare she had given him during lunch. He didn't want any verbal business in the streets, didn't want to call attention to his actions—except to let the Calzado girl know he was there. "Bitch," he wanted to call her, but the word had been ruined for him by the mug-faced rappers. "*Puta*," he might say, but he knew that Cecilia Calzado was neither a bitch nor a *puta*, and that was the point after all. If she were, it wouldn't be half as good trailing her, scaring her. She was a good girl, too fucking good for Apuro, or so her parents thought, and he wished to correct this. He hadn't decided how.

What had made breaking her big brother's nose special was that he'd done it in front of a crowd, during a home game. Perfect, except he hadn't disguised it enough, and so he'd gotten thrown out of the game and off the team. But there was a new coach now, from out of town, and Rudy could find his way back onto the team. He had no intention of breaking Cecilia's nose. What he wanted from her he didn't yet know, would need time to discover.

The girls stopped at the streetcorner just before the little strip of downtown buildings. Rudy stepped back behind a truck, easing his head around the cab to watch the girls without being seen. They were splitting up, which relieved him. The Shopper was trouble, and maybe he'd have to find a way to make her less trouble, but for now he preferred to follow the Calzado girl, and he would no longer have to hang back. He watched where Cecilia turned, then waited for the Shopper to disappear. He despised her, not simply for being an Anglo—he was ready enough to like Anglos if they had sense, the kind of sense that he could use. He hated her for her hair, which was perfectly combed still, almost four in the afternoon, and for her ugly fucking dress, so short it looked like her ass would show with each step but it didn't ever, not a trace, and he knew this was no accident, that she had stood with some tailor in a big store, and the tailor had raised the hem one inch and another inch until finally her white butt began showing, and then she told the tailor to put back one inch or maybe only half an inch, so that she could have the shortest possible dress without her *culo* hanging out. Rudy hated her for this, and for the way the dress was supposed to be so ugly it was cool, this fashion stuff that he had no comprehension of except as yet another way to divide the world into those who know and who have, versus those who don't know and can't have.

The Calzado girl wore a frilly thing, not too short, the kind of thing a girl might wear to her sister's wedding, the kind of thing even he could have picked out for a special occasion, the kind of dress that showed respect for the first day of school. Cecilia's dress made him loathe the Anglo girl, the Shopper, even more.

But he had certain rules he followed, and one was to stick to a plan. Don't get distracted. His plans were always open at the end—even now he didn't know what he'd do when he reached the Calzado girl's yard—but he wasn't going to chase after the Shopper girl just because at this moment he hated her with all his heart. He had his business to conduct, the business of obedience to the wild and demanding arguments of his soul, that powerful steel band strung tight up and down his spine that must be obeyed. Nobody, anymore, made it knot up. Nobody scarred its shiny surface. Sometimes things made it shimmer, made his chest shudder with the ache of desire or the startled tremor of love. But not often. This steel band was his code, his integrity, his *corazón*, his truest self. He would let no one mess with it, no one laugh at it, no one touch it. If people fucked with him, they would be made to salute it.

Without it—he could not imagine living without it. He would have no idea how to behave.

The middle school Enrique attended lay on the far west side of town facing the desert, a ten-minute walk from his home in the heart of the town. Which gave him time to imagine himself dating Ms. Anna Ordaz. "Some people will say it's wrong," he could hear her saying, her voice all soft and friendly. "Some people will try and stop our love," she said, and it sounded to him like a rock-and-roll song, with him and his teacher the main guys in the video. He imagined himself pushing his face into her bosom, her breasts, which were still clothed regardless of how hard he imagined, and although he rubbed his face around the soft fabric and the greater softness beyond, he could not imagine himself pulling the shirt over her head. In fact, he could not picture her breasts and his head in the same frame. This was annoying. Couldn't he at least be the master of his own fantasy? The director of his own internal video?

He exhaled loudly and in disgust. The miserably hot afternoon seemed to settle in his hair, heat radiating about his head. Wasn't there a science-fiction character whose head put out heat? Didn't people use to believe in spontaneous combustion? He remembered something about meat and maggots and spontaneous combustion. In a history class, probably. What had led a woman as beautiful as Ms. Anna Ordaz into teaching history? She could have been an actress. Or a singer, if she could sing, which you couldn't really tell from looking. Who would guess that Aaron Neville could sing, just looking at him?

Whoa, he thought, his mind was getting overheated from this hot-hair thing, and just bouncing around all over the place. He needed a Coke. Even if spontaneous combustion had been disproved scientifically, why risk it and have your head suddenly in flames? He checked his pocket: sixty-three cents. Enough for a twelve-ouncer. Not that he really believed his hair would catch on fire, unless there was some kind of giant magnifying glass floating in the sky, pivoting to keep the sun's rays focused on his hair. Not that such things could really happen, but it would make a good story. This kid, who hasn't even had sex yet, although he thinks about it all the time, is walking along in the desert, which is already so hot the air above the streets is all wavy like the air filling a hot-air balloon, and the magnifying glass is floating along in the sky with some kind of antigravity machine holding it up, which the Army probably already has a prototype of hidden somewhere in a warehouse, and it's shining a sharp beam of light on his hair, so that people passing him think, "Wow, what kind of shampoo does he use?" Until suddenly, whoosh, his whole head is in flames and his face starts melting and dribbling down his white shirt.

Enrique looked down at his white shirt as he thought this, and a drop of sweat from his nose hit the fabric, making him jump and stumble off the sidewalk into a yard, twisting his ankle a little bit, but not quite falling down.

I've got to stop scaring myself, he thought, looking around to see if anybody had noticed. One woman across the street was sweeping cobwebs off her wall, and she seemed to be intentionally not looking at him, but she wasn't laughing or anything. Enrique began smiling then at the pure pleasure of being so lost in his thoughts that even the sidewalk was a hindrance and a poor reminder of the world outside the world inside his head. He detoured down Main Street.

Narrow, dim, and crowded with little boxes of everything, Arzate's Grocery smelled of laundry detergent and bubble gum, a combination Enrique liked, although sometimes the detergent made his nose burn. Mr. Arzate was ringing up Pampers for a woman and trying to get her little kid to say, "No way, Jose." The kid kept turning her/his (who could tell?) head whenever Mr. Arzate spoke. "Shy one, eh?" Mr. Arzate said, but Enrique knew that the grocer ate cream cheese and onion burritos and had breath that smelled like burning hair. How'd he get back to that? Why did his mind keep going in such weird circles even when he was inside and his hair wasn't so hot anymore? What did he come here to buy, anyway? He dug out his change: sixty-three cents. A twelve-ouncer, of course. He was thirsty.

"Enrique, my boy," Mr. Arzate said as he approached with the Coke. "You start school today, son? What are you in now, fourth grade?"

"Eighth," Enrique said, smiling because he knew Mr. Arzate was teasing, and knew it was supposed to be funny. He set the plastic Coke bottle on the counter.

"Eighth!" Mr. Arzate threw his age-freckled hand over his heart. "*Dios!* You'll be getting married any day now, no? You don't want to spend all your *dinero por otra Coca.* You got to start saving for the *niños!*" He rang up the total on his adding machine, pulling the lever down as he squinted at the white roll of paper. "Fifty-three cents. Got to pay the governor his three cents on every Coke, you know. He's a *cabrón* can't hold his behind with both hands, won't give the southern half of the state nothing but grief, but he has to have his three cents, and we have to give it to him, hmmm, *mijo?*"

"Yes, sir," Enrique said, backing off a little, the man's breath starting to create an invisible cloud of onion and cream cheese odor all around them, which made Enrique imagine a time when everybody would have to wear gas masks, but when he pictured it the people were all naked except for the gas masks, only how would they kiss? He'd never seen any movie where the people had sex without kissing, although it had to be optional, he reasoned. It couldn't be required, like the way you had to take English 1a before you could take 1b, could it?

"Hey, there," Mr. Arzate said, "you take a vacation there for a moment? Thinking about your *novia?*"

"No way," Enrique said, imagining Ms. Ordaz in a gas mask, putting the Coke all the way to his mouth before he realized he hadn't opened the bottle.

"They last longer that way," Mr. Arzate said, laughing long enough for Enrique to smile and get out the door. Luckily he didn't have a hard-on, and as long as he didn't think about it too much, he probably could get home without getting one. Who would have thought that gas masks were sexy? And what had he done with his notebook? He'd left it at school, so he didn't have any of his assignments, and if he did get a hard-on, he wouldn't even be able to hold his notebook down low to hide it.

He headed up his street, staying on the shady side, which wasn't all that shady because the sun seemed to be directly overhead, even though it was almost four in the afternoon. Why did people want to live in the desert anyway? His father and mother had crossed the Rio Grande into El Paso from Ciudad Juárez, and they had come up to Apuro from El Paso, and then crossed the Rio Grande again into Persimmon from Apuro, but why had they stopped here in a desert so hot a boy could light his hair on fire just by thinking about his history teacher? Why not move to someplace not so hot, like Wyoming or Philadelphia?

Contemplating Philadelphia, he did not see the person sitting in his yard until he was almost home.

Rita's mother stood at the kitchen counter working a large spoon around a mixing bowl. She had twisted her hair into a ponytail, then clipped the end of the tail to the top of her head—she called it her funny bun. Her hair was beetle brown and held a slight wave from a fading permanent.

"I planned on doing this together," Gay said. "You must have stopped at the money sink."

"One customer, no business," Rita said. Then she added, "I'll make my own lunch for tomorrow."

"They were a joke," Gay said. "Don't you have a sense of humor?"

It took Rita a moment to realize she was talking about the miniature marshmallows that had padded her sandwich. "Nobody carries a lunch box but me," she said. "Cecilia had a paper bag, but most kids buy lunch. I wouldn't mind a paper bag, but Cecilia had to fold hers and take it home, which is kind of squirrely, don't you think?"

Gay displayed the cookie batter to her. "Peanut butter."

"Your favorite," Rita said.

"You like it, too."

Rita climbed onto the counter and leaned over the sink to look out the window at the approaching clouds. "So you decided the kitchen wasn't hot enough and you ought to bake cookies?"

"Something like that," Gay said. "I decided that I'd be home when my girl returned from her first day of high school, so she could cry on my shoulder if she wanted to. That's why I picked this Peter Pan collar. Just lift the flap and dry your eyes."

"I'll pass on the tears," Rita said. "School was school, except in a bigger place." There was plenty to tell her, but Rita was not certain how to begin or what to include. She might mention the trouble with her Heart dress, but jumping out of her first-period class and being followed by Rudy Salazar were not things she wanted to discuss with her mother.

"If my timing is right," Gay said, "the cookies should be ready right when it rains."

Each afternoon during monsoon season, while the temperature rose above one hundred degrees, the intensity of the humidity rose, too, making the wooden doors swell and the evaporative cooler worthless. A corresponding pressure would build in Rita's ears and in her chest as the rain drew near. She could actually see it approaching from the southeast every day around four, the sky low and dark, riddled with lightning. When the rain finally arrived, there would be a sudden release of pressure, and a cooling, soothing, pounding downpour. Then it would be gone. It streamed over them in a rush and moved on across the desert. The daily rains lasted all of ten minutes, but the three weeks of monsoon season were her favorite time of year.

Rita sat on the kitchen counter, glancing out at the still distant clouds, the occasional far-off shard of lightning. In the wire basket that hung from the ceiling, bananas were ripening. Faintly green the day before, they had become fully yellow, carrying that slight banana odor. Her mother could smell them, too, and opened a drawer, removed a paper sack of avocados she had left there to mature. She dipped into the bag and squeezed one gently. "Perfect," she said, and emptied them onto the counter beside Rita: three black avocados, their nubbly skin pliant to the touch. She said, "We can have guacamole tonight. Let's talk Heart into making it."

Gay pulled from a drawer clover-shaped fans they had taken from the Methodist church on one of their rare visits. She liked to go to different churches and see what went on. "Tourists in the Holy Land," she liked to say. The fans bore the body of Jesus, painted in colors too rich and soft to be real. Jesus wore a brown vest much like the kind that were once again popular. Rita pointed this out.

"No fringe," Gay said, rubbing her finger over the miniature figure on the fan. "If he wants to be totally cool, he needs fringe." She preferred his robe, although all they could see were the billowy sleeves, which were a brilliant yellow, as if lit by his holy skin. "It's the color of the bug light," she said, tilting her head toward the back door, which made Rita look, although the bare yellow bulb that lorded over that entrance was on the outside wall and impossible to see.

"Cecilia called," her mother said. "I told her you'd return her call after dinner."

"I just saw her ten minutes ago," Rita said. "It must be important."

"It can wait."

Cut flowers sat in a mason jar on the window ledge, and Rita tried to fan their fragrance toward her. The blooms had fully opened only this afternoon: pink and yellow carnations, three peach-colored daisies. But the flowers' smell was too sweet, making it even harder for her to breathe.

She slipped off her shoes and let them clatter to the floor, swung her bare feet over the countertop and into the sink, and ran cool water over them. She flapped her skirt and leaned toward the window. Black clouds took up a little more of the sky than before, roiling like smoke from a great fire. She waited for another flash of lightning, but what she saw was not among the clouds but in the high grass near the river. A blur of movement at the edge of her perception. She had to assure herself that she had really seen it, that she was not imagining. But she had no reason to mistrust her vision. She fumbled for the faucet handle without moving her gaze, stopping the water in order to concentrate.

Down by the river, at the edge of their yard, a man had stood and stared at their window. When he thought she'd spotted him, he'd ducked and disappeared. But she had not seen him until he'd moved. If he had remained still, she might never have noticed. She hadn't seen *him*, only his movement, his dip behind the single mesquite tree, his drop among the tall grass, his vanishing below the riverbank.

Gay opened the oven door to check the cookies. Their sweet odor filled the kitchen. The summer before, they had seen a coyote out this same window, a skinny gray gent, his mouth open in a wincing smile, loping through the moonlit grass, stepping lightly, as if the soft ground hurt his paws. "Are the cats in?" her mother had asked.

"We don't have cats," Rita had said.

"This one's come to take something from us," Gay had insisted. In the morning they found garbage cans askew and a sheet, left overnight on the line, with a long and ragged tear.

It was not an animal this time. Rita had seen a blur of shoulders dropping, the quick slicing of legs as a man fell to the grass, his agile roll into the riverbed.

If she said to her mother, "I saw a man," they might look together, Rita thought. They might leave the house and step into the heavy afternoon air to seek him out. Or maybe Gay would find the binoculars, and they would study the riverbank, laughing at their good luck, their little adventure in the kitchen. Or Gay would stare at the manless landscape and say, "Rita, you must be a woman now. You're imagining men." Her mother was never at a loss for words; no ogre on earth could make her do more than pause on her journey.

Rita did not tell her what she had seen. Instead, she asked why her mother had left her father. She hadn't intended to ask, but the disappearing man had made the question suddenly urgent.

Gay kept busy with the oven for a few moments, adjusting the temperature, wiping her hands on the lavender dishtowel that hung from a cabinet hook. Even when she began talking, she kept moving, wiping flour from the counter, spooning leftover batter from the mixing bowl. She said, "Did I ever tell you, Rita, that your father wanted to name you Evelyn?" She offered Rita the wooden mixing spoon streaked with cookie batter.

Rita had heard this many times, and said again that she was happy with Rita. She licked the cookie batter from the spoon, which tasted more delicious, she thought, than the cookies would.

Gay put the mixing bowl in the sink beside Rita's wet feet, then looked out the window at the approaching storm. Drops of sweat appeared on her forehead, a line of tiny, identical pools across her brow. Seeing them, Rita wiped her own forehead on the short sleeve of her blouse and waited for her mother to speak.

Finally Gay said, "Men and women are not really compatible."

"That's not an answer." Rita scanned the riverbank, then quit focusing, letting her eyes feel the full range of their vision, waiting—like a cat—for movement.

Gay nodded grudgingly, her funny bun bouncing. Rita could see her mother's faint reflection in the window, and it broke her concentration. Rita fluttered the clover-shaped fan about her hair—a darker brown than her mother's—and turned to face her.

"I've always known you'd ask about this one day," her mother said.

"I've asked about it lots of times."

"Have you?" Thunder sounded dully in the distance. Gay touched her dress just beneath her shoulders. "Well, I've known that one day I would have to actually answer you." She was damp about the armpits, along the Peter Pan collar, and between her breasts—a tiny wet spot in the center of her chest, which, it seemed to Rita, was in the shape of a heart.

The first three years of her life—time Rita had forgotten—they had lived with her father in Albuquerque. Gay had always been tight-lipped about those days. "I was so young when I married your father, I still had a tail and gills."

When Rita's father visited her every month, he brought her something: a book, a new dress, underwear, Barbie accessories. As Rita grew older, he worked hard to keep up, making sure he had the right size, the newest style. Although Rita would sleep in the pink and green house at the very end of the big dead end, he and Rita would spend all Saturday and Sunday together, often leaving New Mexico to drive to El Paso or Ciudad Juárez. They went to the zoo, the dog track, the *mercado*, the mountains, whatever museums he could locate. Once he took her to El Paso General Hospital, where he had arranged for them to sit in a glassed-in booth and watch surgery. Rita had been nine years old at the time.

Rita spent two or three weeks every July with her father in Albuquerque. He'd take her all over town, pool to pool. Rita would swim while he vacuumed, showing him flips, waving at him with her feet. He'd throw coins onto the bottom, which Rita would retrieve, hurrying to get them as his long vacuum hose moved perilously close to a shiny quarter, a sparkling dime—this was how Rita got her allowance.

Eventually, Rita would climb out of the pool and load the truck while he dosed the water with chlorine. Driving from place to place, they'd talk about the pool he would buy for her if only Gay would let him. He had a deep but gentle voice, like the somber men who read the news over the radio. "Certainly not a kidney," he'd say, shaking his woolly head. He had long auburn hair that covered the collar of his blue workshirt. "A kidney encourages pretension," he said. Rita agreed. She wanted a perfect square. "Squares, for some reason, they don't come in," he told her sadly, shrugging his shoulders at the stupidity of the real world. Something in that shrug made her think of a deer, the languid movements of a deer. Then he suggested a pool in the shape of a pumpkin or a heart or, her favorite, a star. "I could ask about a square, if you're set on it," he said to her, "but there's a lot of prejudice against squares from people of my generation, and I don't think it's a battle we could win."

Later, back in Persimmon, Rita mentioned the pools to Gay. She laughed and said, "The Rio Grande is fifty-three feet from your bedroom window. We need a pool like we need a financial adviser."

Even that very afternoon, while she and her mother waited in the kitchen for rain, her father might be in his truck, driving through volatile weather to see her. Or perhaps he had already checked into his room at the Desert Oasis Motor Inn to wait for morning, when Heart would drop her off.

Again she asked her mother why she had left Sander.

Gay sighed dramatically. "When we got that house on Bloom Street, we bought beautiful new garbage cans," she began. Rita knew the Bloom house; her father still lived in it. "They were silver like little space capsules. Sander painted our address on the sides, but he painted 2345 East Bloom and we lived at 2435. It's the kind of mistake men always make. I thought it was funny. But when I pointed it out to him that afternoon, he became furious and went outside and drove around town for an hour."

"That's why you left Daddy?" Rita asked.

"Not exactly that, but not exactly not that. Do you remember Heart talking about her cancer?"

"When they cut off her . . . "

"They removed a lump from her breast."

"She lost her hair and wore a hat?"

"No more hair than a coconut," Gay admitted sadly. She ran a single finger over her cheeks and beneath her eyes, then flung the sweat onto the tile floor. "Heart wore that same green felt hat and chin strap, summer and winter, waking and sleeping, for months." Gay leaned close to her and whispered, "We had decided that if she died we would bury her with that hat on her head." She straightened and nodded, as if Rita wouldn't believe it otherwise. "We're cousins, but we didn't know each other growing up. We were strangers when I moved into the commune with her."

Rita had heard all of this before. "What does Heart's hat have to do with Daddy?" Rita asked her.

"She was the one who suggested Rita. For your name. She used to say, 'Give her a chance to be a great woman.' Heart was sure you were marked for greatness even before you were born. She's always been foolish about you. She was also fond of Sander back then. And he liked her. We all lived together on the farm the year I was pregnant with you."

"I know, I know. You lived in a commune, but you were *not* hippies."

"*I* wasn't. Heart was. Your father, too, more or less. *I* was just there to be with Heart." Thunder sounded again. Gay leaned over the kitchen sink to the window, and stared out at the sky. "Another five minutes, tops," she announced.

"So?" Rita said, glancing from the great dark clouds to the river.

"Heart wasn't wearing the hat yet. She wore a wig, a pretty blond thing." She shook her own hair just once, and Rita mirrored the gesture. "I had penciled in eyebrows for her—a woman might have noticed them, but not a man—and she had dates. Not dates, exactly, but there were men at the commune interested in her. One man, anyway. She liked this guy Miguel Delgado. He wasn't especially handsome, but he was smart and kind. Heart had cancer, but her outlook was bright."

"Keep going," Rita said.

"Your father and I had been married, oh, a while, and he had just started up the yard service, which later became the pool service. Heart and I taught the men to play bridge, and three or four nights a week we'd play cards, maybe betting a penny a point. One night your father is playing with Miguel as his partner, and he says rather than money he wants a bet about Heart's wig."

Gay opened the oven door. The room filled again with the smell of baking. She wrapped her hand in the lavender dish towel and removed the sheet of cookies. "If they won, your father wanted Heart to take off her wig and let him see her head. He thought this was fun, teasing. Your father is not by nature a cruel man," she said. "Just a typical man. It was a manly sort of thing to do." She slid the dozen cookies onto a piece of waxed paper to cool.

"And what if the women won?" Rita asked.

Gay paused with the cookie sheet, and then put it in the sink. "That's hot," she warned. She ran water. Steam rose from the shiny aluminum and heated her face.

Rita had to ask her again. "What if the women won?"

"Oh," she said, "I can't really remember, let's say." She picked up the mixing bowl, ran her finger over a remaining streak of batter, then let Rita lick the finger clean. "Miguel thought this was terribly funny, this bet," she went on, "but I knew Heart didn't want anyone to see her bald head. I'd seen it. Like a man's bald head, but with wisps and scraps of brown hair."

"Like a coconut," Rita said.

"Right. Well, Heart has already looked at her cards and she has a big hand, a fabulous hand, so she makes the bet, saying it is your father's only chance to see her bald head. As soon as I pick up my cards, I know there's trouble. I don't have a single point. Not even a Jack. In all my life, I'd never had such a bad hand. I suppose you could say I let Heart down. We went under. Badly. Then, oh, your father struts around the table and lifts the wig from Heart's head. She just shuffles the cards and plays the remaining hands bald. Poor Heart. Never wore that wig again. Put a scarf on her head and drove into town the next day. Bought that hat with a chin strap that could not be tugged or blown from her head. Made of green felt. Pretty enough for the right occasion, but she'd wear it to the movies or the Laundromat just the same. Got ratty after a few months. Some of the felt rubbed off, and there were raised and bald spots, little islands and big continents of felt, like a relief map."

"Why didn't she get another hat?" Rita asked.

Gay looked at the ceiling, thinking, chin pointing past her to the window. "Stubbornness, I'd say. Maybe something else, too. Something there isn't a word for. Not a decent word for it." She lowered her chin and eyed Rita again. "She and Miguel never worked things out. Maybe it's unfair of me to blame it all on that bet, but everything started falling apart for her after that night. She and I . . . grew apart for a while, until time did its work, and we became friends again, and she moved down here. This isn't something you can talk to her about, understand?" She waited until Rita nodded. "No point in dredging up painful memories."

Rita watched her mother soap a sponge and wash the mixing bowl and cookie sheet. She had turned off the oven burner but left the door open, and the residual heat cooked them. "And that's why you left Daddy?"

Gay sighed again and studied the high ceiling once more. "I thought I could forgive him," she said, finally wiping the drops of sweat from her forehead. Rain began to patter lightly against the shingles. "But there was always some garbage can making him angry or some other nonsense, and I never did find it in my heart to forgive him." She tapped her chest with a damp finger, as if the problem were there.

Thunder exploded above, which made them both jump and then laugh. In another moment, rain filled the yard and "hounded the roof like a bill collector," as Gay liked to say. The pressure and heat lifted, permitting them to breathe.

Gay had let the cookies get dark on the bottom, but neither of them cared. The cookies were warm, thick, sweet, and delicious. While they ate, the cool air from the open window drifted over them, and they watched the thousand silver needles of rainwater.

Through the rain, behind the mesquite tree, the dark form of a man again wavered before Rita's eyes. She held herself perfectly still, studying, suddenly certain that it was her father. She looked hard into the downpour, but the figure was moving, and she could only catch his disappearance.

Once more, Rita considered pointing out the man—now only an absence—to Gay, but she kept it to herself, and by doing so began the mercurial movement into her own life.

"Don't you love the smell of the rain?" Gay said. She cranked the window even farther open. They leaned across the sink, letting their foreheads rest against the screen's metal net. "Breathe," she said. Rita's cheek resting on Gay's, rainwater pushing against their faces, they breathed in the wet, dreamy air.

8

When the Shopper girl finally disappeared, Rudy bounded across the asphalt and through the front yard of a red brick house, swinging open a wooden gate and tromping through a brown backyard into an alley. Lifting his foot to the top rail of the opposing fence, he vaulted into another backyard, landing in a garden, crippling a tomato plant. He didn't bother to walk in the rows, but stomped on the plants, kicked at the puny stakes.

There was no guard dog, but he understood that if there had been, he would have grabbed one of the stakes and shoved it down the dog's throat. The muscles in his arms jerked, feeling the pleasure of the thrust.

He headed for the front gate, hardly giving the yard a look, and as he stepped through the gate he spotted Cecilia Calzado walking down the sidewalk, gazing uneasily behind herself, *looking for me*, he thought victoriously. He waited for her to get a little ahead so that he could be suddenly just behind her the next time she looked, as if he were an apparition.

He also realized that there had been something strange in the yard, the yard whose tomatoes he had smashed. Something he had recognized out of the corner of his eye, what had it been? He watched the Calzado girl and tried to make a picture of it in his head—a silver thing, moving, lifting itself up like a fountain of chrome, molten chrome rising into the sky.

He couldn't have seen this and yet he had. He had seen it, and he hadn't even stopped.

His shoulders turned as if he might go back to look again, but the Calzado girl was at the end of the yard now. The moment was ripe.

He rushed quietly across the yard, stepping in just behind her, speaking to hide his step onto the concrete. "Nik-nik-nik," he said, letting his tongue make a liquid click. She whirled around. He fingered the fine lace of her dress and began whispering, the words suddenly coming to him, just appearing on his lips. "Was the dyke wearing a dress like this when the boy put his finger in it?" Her eyes widened in fear, and she turned her head quickly, yanking the cloth from his fingers, staring straight ahead now, walking stiffly. "Nik-nik-nik," Rudy whispered. "This one fine day for watching ass. *Verdad*?"

She scurried out into the street, not to cross it, as he first thought, but to walk down the middle, which made him laugh and linger a moment in the shade of a big mulberry. It was a hot fucking day, and he had been close enough to her to hear the swing of her skirt, that little rustle of fabric, the satiny swish that covered her satiny swish. "Swish, swish," he said. "Nik-nik-nik." Although she was too far ahead now to hear his low whisper, he said it just for himself. "Nik-nik-nik."

He didn't want her to run, so he watched her for a while, let her get ahead before moving to the next shady spot and then the next, until at last he saw her disappear into a house, an ordinary slump-block house, nothing special except for the yard, which had been made all fancy, divided up so that there could be one little green square of grass, the green of the bitter-smelling leaves from the trees that bordered the river.

This son of a bitch Calzado and his son of a bitch wife think they can deny they ever knew Apuro by that patch of grass, Rudy understood, understood so clearly and powerfully that he didn't even need to sound it out, didn't need to turn the feeling into words that he could hear in his skull. He saw the grass and felt the rage, and he *knew*.

He tramped across the street and onto the grass. He seated himself in the middle of it. He wasn't sure what he would do next. Maybe nothing. Maybe he'd just sit for a while and then leave. She'd gotten his message, although, really, he wasn't sure what that message was. That he had singled her out? Something like that. Better not to be too specific. Let her fill in her own terror.

Then the boy came up the street, walking like such a dreamy stupid kid that Rudy didn't think he could be old enough to be the other Calzado brother, the one little more than a toddler when they fled Apuro. Enrique, whom Rudy himself had defended once, way back when, against some other boys—he couldn't remember the circumstances, but he was certain it had happened. *We could have been friends.* He was surprised by the thought, but believed it, even though he was five or six years older. But no, this boy's parents could not face who they were, wanted to pretend to belong elsewhere, and by doing so slandered the people left behind.

He let the boy get in the first words.

"Hey, you can't sit there," Enrique said. His father permitted no one to walk on the small square where he cultivated grass. "My piece of heaven," his father called it. "My amber waves of green grass," he liked to say. The guy on the grass did not move. From his posture, Enrique could tell he was a high school student and not an adult, despite his size. "That's my dad's yard," Enrique explained. The guy made no effort to move, just eyed Enrique indifferently from the grass, and Enrique knew he knew the boy, knew that the boy was a bully, was some specific trouble.

"I can't sit here?" Rudy said. "*¿Estás seguro?*" Are you certain?

Enrique immediately wanted to back off, to be friendly. "My dad doesn't even want us casting a shadow over it," he revealed. Then he thought he might be behaving rudely and added, "My name's Enrique."

"I remember," Rudy said.

Each boy assessed the other. Enrique noted Rudy's size and tried to place him, to identify him. How did this guy know his name? Rudy, meanwhile, looked Enrique up and down, seeing the baby in the boy, which was a kind of remembering. He could see little Enrique at that table in the Calzado house all those years ago. Rudy felt something like compassion for him. Enrique himself had not chosen to leave Apuro. The decision had been forced upon him.

Rudy got up because suddenly he felt strange, a weird softness inside, as if the band within him were melting in a spot. To cover, he said, "I got a secret to tell you. Come here." He didn't know what he might say, had no idea what would come out, but he would be true to whatever it was. *I'm gonna fuck you up*, he might say, and then he would, he'd have to. Otherwise, it would be a betrayal of himself, of that steel ribbon that was his truest self.

"Not on the *grass*!" Enrique said, his father's love for the lawn overcoming his immediate fear. He still could not name this boy, but he knew enough to be scared. "You want a drink of water?" he added. The boy looked thirsty. He was taller than Enrique's father.

The smile Rudy offered wasn't entirely a friendly smile. It started as a genuine one—he liked this kid—but he twisted it, made it snide. "Don't want ruin this *pinche* grass of yours," he said and spat, but the kid didn't see him spit, and Rudy didn't want some fight over the grass, so he walked over to the driveway, still wondering what he was going to say, how he would reveal himself to himself.

"It's not my grass. My dad's," Enrique told him, looking at the footprints in the flattened grass. He began to say something else, but Rudy cut him off.

"Hey, *escucha*," Rudy said. Listen. He grabbed Enrique's collar, his fingers digging down into the soft skin about the kid's neck. He jerked him close so that Enrique could feel Rudy's breath in his ear. Then Rudy waited, let the words appear in his mind as he simultaneously spoke them. He said, "Tell your sister I know where she lives." He held the boy's head another instant, then gave it a shove, feeling the sudden release of tension. He hadn't committed himself to hurt this kid, might never have to. He breathed heavily, sighed. Sometimes the demands of being who he was tired him. He was relieved to get a break.

Enrique stumbled when Rudy released him. He took a second to regain his balance, then asked, "Which sister?"

Rudy laughed, a good, honest, mean laugh. The kid wasn't being a smartass, Rudy could see, just trying to get it right. "Tell them all," he said. Enrique's face was so open, he might have actually been a baby, Rudy thought, a baby miraculously given the power of speech.

"You want the water?" Enrique asked.

Rudy felt again the softening of the steel band, a sudden tension behind his eyes. It angered him, but it also connected him with this boy, this boy who was still unsullied by the world outside Apuro. Enrique Calzado didn't think himself any better or different. Rudy could see that, could hear it in the kid's speech.

"No," Rudy said, "no water."

Enrique did not know what to do next. He realized that his heart was pounding fast, and he was feeling something more than fear. It was part fear and part something else, part of it was like the feeling he had watching Ms. Anna Ordaz—he knew it wasn't sexual, but it had that excited sexual feel to it.

Rudy looked back at the house, then turned to go, but he hesitated, feeling an urge, something like the desire to hang out with a friend, and nothing inside stopped him from feeling that urge. He suddenly wanted to give this boy something.

"You ever been high?" he asked, and Enrique became a statue, as if he were trying to actually remember if he had ever been high, as if he were listening and considering it, as if words could go from one person to the other, and they would actually be *heard*.

Enrique, for his part, paused for a moment because he didn't want to assume the boy meant drugs. He could have been talking about the mountains.

Before Enrique could think to say anything, Rudy said, "Didn't think so. Ready to try it?"

"I've got to water the yard," Enrique said, immediately ashamed at the lameness of the excuse, his face flushing, turning as hot as his hair had been earlier. He threw his arms toward the impossibly green swatch on the ground that was, Rudy could tell, still barren beneath, just crappy sand down deep where it mattered. Rudy laughed and began walking home, realizing that he had almost lost something, that something had almost been taken from him. He realized, too, that the boy was special, that he was of a different category. Which meant that he was the key to getting to Cecilia Calzado. This boy would permit Rudy to get her. How, he wasn't quite sure, but Enrique was the kind of kid others responded to and did things for. That would be her undoing.

Enrique, to prove that his embarrassing lie was the truth, walked over—he stepped on the grass!—hopped off the grass, and turned on the hose, putting his finger over the opening, as his father did, to make it spray. The water that spurted out was so hot he flung down the hose, and stuck his burned fingers to his mouth, glancing up at the boy, ready to be completely humiliated.

Rudy was already two houses away, paying no attention to Enrique, looking instead at the house whose yard he had cut through. He heard the leaves of the tree he'd stood beneath rustle, and he understood that he had mistaken this slight sound for the slight sound of Cecilia's dress rustling, and hearing it again now, even understanding that the sound was a tree and not a girl, he nonetheless felt a weight slip down into his balls. He would fuck her, he decided. He'd make her do it. He'd let others watch.

He cut through the yard again, thinking this time to look into the corner, wanting to see what weird thing he had seen before out of the corner of his eye. At first he couldn't tell what it had been, and then he saw the birdbath, a reddish ceramic bowl and pedestal. Three birds lifted from the rim as he walked near, soaring skyward, water flying off the wings. There was nothing chrome about it. That part had come from inside him, he reasoned. That part was all his.

And the world better not try to fuck with it. He planted a foot on the rim of the bowl and pushed it over.

Enrique turned the water off and circled round the grass to the kitchen door. Inside, his sister Cecilia immediately grabbed his shirt. "What did he say to you? I saw him whisper. What did he say?"

"Said to tell you he knows your address." Enrique shrugged at the utter strangeness of this. "Why didn't he come in and tell you? Although if he came in, obviously he'd know your address, which he would also know if he was sitting in our yard, which he was, so I don't get it."

"I was hiding at the window," she said, touching her fingers to her mouth in a funny way, like she was typing her lips. "Every time he looked, I ducked." Then she added, "That's Rudy Salazar."

"Hey, we're not supposed to play with him!" Enrique said. "Dad's going to be mad." Rudy Salazar was the boy who had broken his brother's nose in a basketball game *on purpose*.

"He followed me home," she said. "Don't tell Dad."

"Should we call the police?"

"For what? For following me home?"

"He trampled the grass."

"What if Dad came home and found a policeman here?"

"Yeah," Enrique agreed, shaking his head. "Not a pretty sight."

"I'm calling Rita." She turned and hurried away out of the kitchen.

He offered me drugs, too, Enrique thought, but he didn't want to tell his sister that. Maybe then they'd have to call the police, and he didn't want to. His brother whose nose had been broken had said that Rudy was sick, which made Enrique think immediately of that guy in *The Silence of the Lambs*. No way he wanted that guy mad at him. He wondered what River Phoenix would do. *Follow him*, Enrique thought. That's what River Phoenix would do. He turned to the refrigerator to get a drink of cold water, and then realized he still had the Coke he had bought at Arzate's Grocery in his hand and he hadn't even opened it. He had to do something about his *mind*! It buzzed about like a fly in a hot room, and if he didn't do something as soon as he thought of it, he would forget it until he wound up somewhere else without his notebook, holding a Coke he hadn't even opened, his hair singed down to the skull.

He bolted out the front door. He would follow Rudy Salazar before he forgot. Salazar was already gone, but Enrique knew that Rudy lived across river. Enrique, too, had lived in Apuro, back when he was little, but he didn't remember it very well, and he hadn't returned there since they'd left. He had been, what, four when they moved? How could it be ten years since they moved and he had never been back when it was right across the river? Was there some kind of secret? An excitement began to grow in his chest as he thought of River Phoenix having flashes of his previous life, his mostly forgotten life in his own private Idaho. This was why the movie had grabbed him so powerfully, Enrique believed, because he had his own private Apuro just beyond the river, riddled with memory, no doubt. He felt he had to see it. And as he thought this, his mind seemed to settle on it, to focus all his thoughts until they seemed like a single beam of light shining brightly on the foreign and familiar soil of Apuro.

Within minutes, Enrique stood on the river shore, looking first at the distant bank, which was a few minutes' walk north of Apuro, and then at the shallow water at his feet. It occurred to him that he would be a *negra* now if they had not moved, and his life would be entirely different. Better or worse, he didn't know. Electricity certainly seemed handy, but there was something appealing about the idea of candles and what? Flashlights? How did they get by over there anyway?

He didn't want to get his pants wet, and while he couldn't see anyone in either direction, he felt a little uneasy about taking his pants off and crossing. What if Rudy Salazar saw him in his underwear? Downriver, at Apuro ledge, there was a secluded place to cross, but the water was deep there, and the only way he could keep his clothes dry was by stripping entirely naked, and there was no chance he'd do that. The water stayed fairly shallow up-river, but he would have to walk past Calle Blanca, the one street—a dead end—between the highway and the river. Just beyond the end of Calle Blanca were a bunch of trees crowding the water. He could cross there un-observed.

As he trudged upriver along the bank, he tried to remember more about Apuro. Logic told him that he would be a *negra* if they hadn't left there, but it seemed hard to believe. Then he realized that if his parents had not moved from Mexico, he would be a Mexican. He would live in Juárez, or wherever his parents might have wandered. He had relatives in Mexico City, an aunt who said it was one of the great cities of the world. It was possible that his parents' decision to come to the United States had ruined his life, had made it meager and common, while he could have been a resident of one of the great cities of the world.

Of course, he couldn't entirely believe it. He knew Mexico was poor. He believed that the United States was the greatest country in the world. He had enough imagination to know that other kinds of life existed, but it didn't seem possible that whether he was an American or a Mexican was simply a matter of his parents picking one piece of desert over another. Be-ing American seemed a lot deeper than that, but maybe it wasn't. Or maybe it was in some ways and wasn't in others.

Then he began thinking that maybe what his parents had really given him by leaving first Mexico and then Apuro was that sense of a place lost, that private place of . . . *longing* was the word he was looking for, but he could not name it, and because he couldn't, it lost none of its power, so that it rode with him not just in his mind but in his body, in his very nerve endings.

Lost in these thoughts, he forgot about the monsoon. A distant roll of thunder woke him and he dashed for the single tree nearby, a mesquite out by the river. The rain hadn't even begun yet. Once again he had scared him-self. The mesquite would provide lousy shelter against the rain, besides. He decided to make a dash for the more distant trees, but before he could take a step, he spotted a girl in the window of the nearest house. She was looking out the window, up at the sky, the dark roll of clouds, her neck long, pale, and beautiful.

In another second he recognized that it was Rita, his sister's best friend, which at first disappointed him. But immediately she became to him like the family he'd seen through a window in Tucson—an ordinary girl made extraordinary by his view of her through an ordinary window. She was sitting up close to the glass, and suddenly she swung her feet around—bare feminine feet. Lovely feet. He couldn't tell exactly what she was doing, but those bare feet swinging into view had caused some kind of movement inside him— like watching his teacher's bottom as she walked to the front of the class, but these were not a woman's bottom, these were feet! Seen at a distance! She had put them into the kitchen sink, he realized, but she wasn't washing them. She was staring out the window, at the sky, the dark sky. He had seen a million people stare at the sky, but seeing her through the window, after seeing her naked feet—he couldn't move for staring at her, while his heart, suspended on a rope, banged against his ribcage.

She was a year older than he—in high school—and he had no more chance with her than he had with Ms. Anna Ordaz, but even as the thought passed through his head, he knew he had to overcome it. He imagined Rita and himself together, and yes! If he needed proof, there it was: when he tried to imagine her breasts and his head in the same frame, he saw them, his head sort of bounding against her breasts—he had no idea they were so large!—and then he rubbed his face around them. He didn't know what to do with breasts exactly, although he thought about them a great deal.

Then she lowered her eyes and turned to gaze at the river. Before he could even think, he was on the ground, rolling over the grass, off the ledge, and into the river, suddenly submerged, his world black and liquid, weightless, airless—all this, and he did not even know if she had seen him, one little stare in his direction and the world was irretrievably altered.

He rose from the water, crouching to peer over the ledge. She remained in the glass, her face slightly turned, her lips moving, rainbows of light arcing through the window. He crawled up to the tree once again, standing near it now not for shelter but to be hidden from her so that he could watch her once again raise her head to the turbulent sky.

It rained on him for more than a minute before he realized it was raining. A sizzle of lightning suddenly illuminated her window, making her shine in the brilliant blue flash, a penetrating bolt of light like an X ray impressing the image of her very bones onto his soul.

The explosion of thunder that followed made him drop to his knees, and as he fell, she again directed her gaze at him. He continued falling, holding his eyes on hers as long as he could, even as his chest struck the wet ground, and he rolled again into the river.

By the time he started home, the rain had passed on and he'd forgotten all about Apuro and Rudy Salazar. He was sopping and muddy, his good shoes squeaking and spraying out water, his clothes soiled terribly, after hiking all that way to keep them clean and dry. While walking home, he saw at a distance a white van crossing the street on which he stood, while from the opposite direction a black sedan crossed. Sunlight, brilliant against the white sides of the van, was swallowed by the black sedan in an exchange so secret that it could take place openly on the street and nobody—almost nobody—would recognize it, an exchange of power and light, of forces dark and luminous, an exchange of realities, leaving in their wake a wash of asphalt unfiltered by the illusion of reality, a bare, black, cruel pavement, a horrible spot on the planet.

Then normal unreality swept back over it all, and it became once again just a piece of the road, the same road that Enrique was standing on, his clothes soiled from rolling in the river mud, and soaked from standing in the rain to look at his beloved's feet through her kitchen window. How long had he been standing there? He didn't know. Not long, he suspected. An eternity.

He crossed the street to the opposite sidewalk. He was just fourteen years old, yet he believed he had witnessed a moment that was in some essential way *true*.

Enrique breathed deeply in the rain-laden air and hiked homeward in his heavy, wet shoes.

Sex

9

Shoeless, in sweaty gym shorts, a Persimmon Tigers T-shirt, and white tube socks, his hair wet with perspiration and sticking up, Denny hunched boyishly beside Gay, embarrassed to be caught without his sneakers. He had left a note wedged between her front door and its jamb (*I'm at the gym*—Denny), but Gay had arrived at a funny time. The lone man in the gymnasium, a Hispanic man with pitted cheeks and a beautiful goatee, who'd been practicing free throws, had gone into the locker room to retrieve Denny. He now faced her, sheepish in his smelly gymwear, while the Hispanic man edged his toes up to the free-throw line once again. Gay did not feel awkward. She had changed after work into Levi's and a striped boatneck shirt, smart black flats and art deco earrings. She had even put on makeup. The contrast between them amused her.

"Why don't I get dressed and we go somewhere?" Denny said. The ends of his socks stuck out an inch beyond his toes and reminded Gay of the bunny slippers Rita had worn as a child.

"Somewhere?" she said.

"Somewhere," he said. "As in 'somewhere else.' "

"I like a decisive man," she said, pressing her advantage. The Hispanic man laughed, but he didn't turn his head and he didn't make his free throw. "I walked over," Gay said. "I don't own a car."

"How can you live without a car?"

"I depend upon the kindness of strangers," she said, and watched his face to see if he caught the reference.

"I'm not a stranger," he said, and turned to go. "Give me five minutes."

"You don't read, do you?" she said.

"I read," he said, continuing toward the locker room. "I just don't read Tennessee Williams." He disappeared through the locker room door.

"Help," the Hispanic man called.

Gay had a second to imagine that he actually was in trouble before the basketball bounced past her and into the folding bleachers. It rattled about, coming to rest at her feet. She wondered if he had simply thrown the ball there, various clichés popping into her head about the ball being in her court. She bent to pick it up and tossed it back to him.

"You want to shoot a few while you wait?" he asked her.

She immediately looked him over more carefully. Besides his perfect goatee, he was an ordinary-looking man in his middle thirties. His T-shirt advertised the dog track in Juárez. "I'll play a game of horse with you," she said. "I shoot first."

"Are you a ballplayer?" he asked, tossing the ball back to her. He wore an opal earring in one ear.

"No," she said, catching the ball. She stood at the free throw line and tossed up a shot. It fell short of the rim. "Okay, I give," she said. "My name's Gay. I like your earring."

His name was Salvador Rillos. "Are you Denny's girlfriend?" he asked her.

"Hmm," she said. "I'd prefer to be thought of in nonpossessive terms." When he stared blankly at her, she said, "We're not at the boyfriend/girlfriend stage. More like the I-hope-he's-not-a-Republican stage."

Sal Rillos blinked. "I guess I'm not sure what that means."

"Men have different concerns, I guess," Gay said. She was reminded of how few men actually understood her. "It's something like the I-hope-she-doesn't-believe-in-crystals stage."

"That one, I follow." He had a handsome, square smile, but each of his limbs twitched, one after another like the consecutive mechanical motions of a windup toy. "That Denny's a hard one to read."

This comment surprised her. "He seems pretty straightforward to me," she said. "In a lot of ways."

"Some yes, some no."

Gay said, "You ever read Tennessee Williams?"

"I don't think so," he said, then his face brightened. "But my uncle has a record by Tennessee Ernie Ford."

"Close," she said, "but no cigar. Now, if it were *your* record . . . "

Sal shook his head sadly. "Caught trying to appropriate my uncle's culture."

"There's a lot of that going around. Are you a coach, too?"

He wasn't. "I am an undiscovered folksinger temporarily masquerading as a high school counselor. Democrat, if that's a factor. It's only fair to add that most people prefer my company to Denny's." He shrugged. "Just so you'll know." He smiled then and took another shot, which thudded against the rim and bounced directly back to him. "I'm actually a terrible basketball player. I was the kid who was always picked last. Had to guard the fat boy or the girl. No offense. I'm just here to manipulate your boyfriend—or whatever he is."

"Denny."

"Him. You want another shot?"

She shook her head. She liked him. He reminded her of her husband—sweet, smart in his own way, and slightly silly.

"Me neither. It gets humiliating after a while." He rolled the ball in the direction of the locker room door, then raised a finger to his pitted cheek and gently rubbed one of the scars. "The last coach was a prick. Excuse my French. Treated the kids like cattle. He was the cowboy and they were the steers."

"You're in the anti-cowboy camp, I gather."

"There are a lot of us, but none of us can make a decent campfire." He paused to see if she would laugh. "I'm no good with jokes—or fires."

"You rub two sticks together," Gay said.

"But how do you make it funny?"

Denny emerged from the locker room, his hair still wet from the shower. "You wouldn't have a comb on you, would you?" he asked Gay, picking up the ball that had come to rest by the bleachers and tossing it to Sal Rillos. Damp splotches on his cotton shirt clung to his chest and shoulders, which reminded her of their swim in the Rio Grande. "I hurried," he said. If he held any residue of embarrassment from being caught in his socks, Gay couldn't detect it.

"Nice meeting you," Sal said to Gay. "Let me know whether he's a Republican." He dribbled head-down to the locker room.

"What was that about?" Denny combed his hair with his fingers.

"He entertained me in your absence. You know how to build a fire in the wilderness?"

Denny nodded. "Sure. I can do propane or even those little canister things."

The parking lot asphalt was still marked by puddles from the afternoon shower, and they reflected the sunlight brilliantly, like pools of glass. For a moment Gay was reminded of the time she had been sick, when she'd had the breakdowns, how such a landscape would have frightened her, the expanse of asphalt covered with large and random fragments of glass, how the ordinary had been infused with the treacherous.

"How long does this so-called monsoon go on?" Denny asked.

"Depends," Gay said, coming back to herself. "Never long enough. I haven't eaten, have you?"

They decided on the diner, officially known as Frieda's Cafe but almost exclusively referred to as "the diner." His hands on the steering wheel were slightly larger than she remembered and rough at the knuckles. She recalled the hand on her bottom. The car, however, was exactly as she recalled: dingy, old, and layered in gum wrappers. "So how was that guy trying to manipulate you?" she asked him. "He told me he was trying to manipulate you."

"Sal? He's the official bleeding heart at the school." This turn of phrase made him smile. He drove cavalierly, two fingers of one hand resting on the bottom of the steering wheel as he guided them out of the high school parking lot. "Wanted to make sure I wasn't going to exclude kids for being Mexican, basically, or 'having a history' with the last coach, who was a turd, from what I gather."

Gay nodded. He kept glancing over at her as he drove, as if he thought she might disappear. "What did you tell him?"

"The best players make the team. Period." Sunlight angled harshly across his face, and air from the slightly opened window lifted and rippled his hair.

"This thing have air conditioning?"

"Sure." He lowered his window all the way. "How's that?"

"Lovely. So are you a Republican?"

"I'm a nothing."

"An independent?"

"A nonvoter. A dropout."

She paused, appraising him. She felt the urge to give him the benefit of any doubt, but she distrusted the urge. "You think the democratic system in this country has devolved into a meaningless beauty pageant? Or you're just lazy?"

"Hmm. If I ever actually thought about it, I'd think the former, but I'm too lazy to even think about it."

"Don't like to be categorized, eh?"

"Given that I coach high school basketball, you can see why I want to avoid generalizations."

Air from his open window fluttered her hair into her eyes, obscuring her vision of him, and she let it happen. Sometimes the wind in your hair felt good, she thought.

The diner had a good soup of the day and decent pies, as well as the obligatory burgers, Mexican food, and steak. Denny followed her to a window booth, which provided a view of the traffic on River Road and the post office, a spotted dog asleep on the sidewalk in the shade of a pyracantha bush the postmaster kept watered. Once they were seated, Denny said, "So what's the deal with you and your husband?" The Formica table between them held a cheap vase filled with plastic flowers. He began to finger the blooms as if looking for bees.

"I can do what I want," Gay said, hesitating long enough for the sentence to have some weight. "He does what he wants. That's the *deal*."

"But why?"

"Why what?"

"Don't pretend not to understand. Your marriage is strange. Before I go barging into the middle of it, I'd like to know why you two have such a strange arrangement. Is that an unreasonable thing to ask?"

His directness she found oddly stimulating. "Let's order first," she said, as the waitress was already hovering, a young Mexican woman Gay did not know. She had only one hand, her left arm ending in a stump and a wrinkled scar. Her name tag read LUCINDA. "What can I do you for?" she asked, then smiled as she scribbled their order on a pad wedged against her stump. She winked at Gay before walking off, a wink that had to do with Denny's looks.

Gay ignored it. "Are your parents together?" she asked Denny.

"In the ground," he said.

Gay nodded. "I don't even know where my parents are. They disowned me when I was in high school."

"Sex?"

"Drugs. Nothing serious. Nothing even interesting. Bad pot that made your head ache. I got busted, and they wouldn't get me out of jail. 'We wash our hands of you.' That's what they said."

"So, naturally, you live two hundred fifty miles from your husband and each of you—"

"Have a little patience. Are you like this in bed? Everything a rush to the punchline?"

"Isn't everybody?" He laughed. "Okay, I'll shut up."

"Most marriages are lousy," Gay said, and the dog on the sidewalk rolled over as she spoke, turning its back to her. Everyone's a critic, she thought.

"The people are miserable, their children are neurotic, and ultimately two people who used to love each other come to wish the other dead."

"That's—can I speak?"

She worked not to smile at him. "Keep it short."

"That's a bit of an exaggeration, isn't it?"

"A little, but a lot of marriages aren't all that great. Can we agree on that?"

He nodded, shrugged, began to say something, but she was quicker. "So I love Sander, and Sander loves me, but we're—how old were you in 1968?"

"Ten."

"I was afraid you might be younger than you look. I'm glad you're not."

"Is this part of the story going to turn hippie?"

"Hush. Why does everyone bring up hippies with us? I'm talking about idealism." She had not even been ten in 1968, but Sander had been in high school, and it was one of the questions he asked people. *Have to get my bearings with folks*, he liked to say. "Sander and I wanted to make a different kind of world, and I still do. A lot of people do. So this is my part. I've invented a new kind of marriage."

Denny's expression could be read as a half smile or as a smirk. It seemed to be his dominant facial gesture. "I wouldn't say 'invented.' A lot of people do what you're doing. They just call it by a different name."

"What?"

"Dating your ex." He began playing with the plastic flowers again, rubbing the petals between his fingers.

"Once a month, he comes down and we spend two nights together. On special occasions, I take a day off work, too. While he's here, we play. We tease. We fuck like bunnies." She wanted to get a rise out of him, but saying it reminded her that she had thought of Denny while making love with Sander. She turned to the window to avoid his gaze, afraid she might be blushing. An old woman carefully stepped over the spotted dog, which immediately began to run in its sleep. "How many married couples that live together—we've been married fifteen years—how many have sex as often as we do?"

"How do I know?"

"*None* is the correct answer. We're happy. There are some limitations, but I get to have my own life. He has his own life. We see other people, have some adventures, but we're also married, in for a lifetime. It's a careful, considered, artful arrangement."

"And the sex is good."

"The sex is wonderful."

"These are plastic," he said, aiming a fake rose at her.

"You could be a detective."

"So is my part in this grand scheme that of 'random dalliance' or 'mean-ingless affair'?"

" 'Not-always-charming dinner companion,' at present."

"Just so I know where I stand."

The one-handed waitress returned with their dinners, and they were po-litely silent while she set the plates before them. Gay could not help won-dering why a woman with one hand would want to be a waitress, but she was impressed with the woman's ability to balance the serving tray on her arm while she removed the dishes. Every meal she didn't spill must feel like an accomplishment.

"So why do you keep Rita in the dark?" Denny asked her. He lifted his club sandwich. Gay hoped he wasn't one of those men who paused in mid-sentence to eat, only to finish the comment through a muffle of food. "If this is all sort of idealistic," he went on, staring at the sandwich, "then why not let her know?" He paused another second, and then bit into the club.

"So she can have a normal life."

He swallowed before continuing. "You call that normal?"

"She thinks we're divorced, and yes, that is perfectly normal. Her father spends two full days a month hanging out with her—plus close to a month in the summer. That's probably more than most kids spend with their fathers."

"If you told her the truth—"

"She'd think we were weird. She'd feel funny. Kids think they're at the heart of every problem." She glanced out the window again. The spotted dog was up and gone. "She'd want us to live together or change, somehow, just like you do."

"I didn't say that. I like the plan."

The conversation stalled while they ate. Her salad—iceberg lettuce, tomato quarters, and curls of carrot draped heavily in bleu cheese dress-ing—did not please her. Salads in diners were generally a bad idea. When-ever she was out with men, she tended to order salads. When she was with other women, she often ordered red meat. Sander was the exception. When they were together, she might order anything. "Sander says that our deal takes away the everydayness, but that's just my point. Although I can see what he means with Rita. He misses stuff. But she thinks seeing him is a treat, and she doesn't feel that way about me. It all evens out. *I* don't feel trapped. My life is my own. I like it."

Denny leaned back in the vinyl booth, a cynical but amused expression spreading across his face. "Now I'm supposed to say, 'I've never met anyone like you.'"

"No, you're supposed to change the topic and carry your end of the conversation for a change."

"Oh." He straightened up. "How 'bout this weather we're having? Monsoon, you call it?"

"It's almost over, and then it'll be hot and dry all day long, and we won't have a thing to talk about."

He responded with a vague head movement, then began to eat his sandwich. Gay poked at her salad. Denny said, "I guess I better read Tennessee Williams. I *was* in a play once. I played the butler. High school. I don't remember the name of the play. The teacher was a *hippie*, sorry to bring up that word again, and she painted my face brown and had me speak like somebody out of 'Amos 'n' Andy.'"

Gay felt a sudden and inexplicable rush of desire for him. Maybe she liked for men to be self-deprecating. Maybe she liked that he tried to be funny. She said, "I bet that made you popular."

"I don't know why she decided that would be funny—but she was right. Audience laughed at all my lines." His smile was crooked, like Heart's, but, unlike hers, it was beautiful. "I could never run for office, though. Somebody'd produce snapshots of me in blackface."

"I went to live with my cousin after I did my time—one weekend in jail," Gay said. "I was seventeen, and she was twenty-two. Now I've taken her in. She lives in my house."

"You haven't seen your parents since they cut you off?"

"I used to drive by their house sometimes." She could picture the house more clearly than she could her parents. "Once my father was searching for the morning paper, which was in the gutter—I could see it. I thought about stopping the car and getting his paper for him. But I didn't stop. Then they moved to Florida somewhere."

He pushed his plate aside and put his hands and elbows on the table. His eyes were blue. "You want to do something this weekend? A movie? A real meal? Something?"

"You want to wait till the weekend?" she said.

He thought about it. "My place isn't really put together yet. How do you respond to chaos?"

"I don't want to sleep with you yet," she said. "But I'd like to see your chaos."

He had moved into what was euphemistically referred to as a cottage, but more closely resembled a garage. Actually, it had been built in the 1920s as a chile-drying shed, an adobe rectangle, open at one end, which in the past decade had been plumbed and given an adequate roof. The bathroom took up one corner, leaving the remainder unobstructed, a short counter to indicate where the kitchen began. The clutter of boxes and dirty clothes did not put Gay off; in fact, she was surprised that there seemed to be so little. "I travel light," Denny explained. "My books—you were about to ask about them, weren't you?"

"No," Gay said, staring at the scrabble of sheets on a bare mat. "I was about to ask when you were going to get a bed."

Denny glanced at the mat. "My books are in those two boxes over there." He pointed to brown boxes stacked in a corner bearing the label "Libby's Lite Peaches."

"You don't have any furniture," Gay said.

Denny looked around the bare room. "A fair appraisal," he said. "You don't have any manners."

"Yes, I do," she said, picking her way past a pile of dirty clothes to the boxes of books, which were still taped shut. "Let me see," she said. "I want to pull out just one as a sample of your personality."

Denny took a kitchen knife from the counter by the sink and joined her. "One book is a kind of small sample, don't you think? What if you pull out the *Odyssey*? You going to think I'm an intellectual?"

"I don't know what I'm going to think," she said, and again she experienced that queer rush of sensation. Maybe it wasn't desire, she told herself. Maybe she was catching the flu.

"You like games, don't you?" he said, cutting the tape on the box.

"Not really," she said softly, feeling suddenly unsure of herself. "I don't think so."

"You like to think of yourself as unusual," he said. "Or maybe you'd just like me to think of you as unusual."

"Is that what I'd like?" she said, lifting the flap just an inch and sticking her hand inside. She withdrew a pair of boxer shorts.

"Wrong box," he said.

"Oh, I don't know," she said, breathing again. She hadn't been breathing. The shorts had cartoon pigs and hearts on them. "This reveals a lot."

"Reveals I have a daughter," Denny said. "She's six and a half." He slid the box to the floor and began slicing the tape on the bottom box. "I am in the very usual position of being an ex-husband whose ex-wife would like him to dry up and blow away. I know it pales in comparison to your colorful marital situation, but—"

"Do you have a picture of your daughter?" Gay asked.

Denny dropped the knife and pulled out his wallet. A little girl in a pink and white coat and matching hood stood in a yard full of snow. Gay took the wallet from him. The girl had his eyes. "How often do you get to see her?" Gay asked.

"She's going to move out here second semester," Denny said. "As soon as I can get my life in order. Her mom's busy. She's a pretty good mom, I guess, but it wears on her."

Gay flipped the plastic sheath holding the photograph over, but there was only one picture. "How long have you been divorced?"

"Year and a half." He took the wallet back from her. "It's getting late," he said. "Reach in and get a book, but don't show me, okay? Take it home and read it." He leaned close to her and kissed her on the lips, and Gay knew she was in trouble.

He pulled back from her. "You know what? I can't do anything this weekend. I got roped into dinners and whatnot with faculty."

She could feel her face color. She turned from him and moved to the other box. "Female faculty?"

"Potluck with a big crowd of people one night, and a family barbecue the next. Once I know these people better, I can be rude to them. How about a week from Friday? A real meal and a movie?"

She fiddled with the box. "What is it you teach, anyway?"

"Social studies, and one PE course. My degree is in biology, but they already have someone who has been teaching biology here for six years. Her degree is in math."

She took a breath and faced him. "What's your last name?"

"Redmon," he said. "You really don't know much about me, do you?"

She reached beneath the cardboard flap, and retrieved a book, which she slipped under her arm. "You should offer to drive me home."

"Let me drive you home."

"It's still light out. I'd rather walk."

"You might get rained on and ruin my book," he said.

"The monsoons come and go," she said. "They don't linger."

She kissed him again at the door, a nice kiss, but just a kiss. Possibly she had been imagining, magnifying some natural attraction. She quickly turned and began the walk home, resisting an urge to look back at him, choosing instead to picture him in the doorway watching her.

The streets were damp from the rain and shone brightly in the light of dusk. She felt a curious resistance to looking at the book's title. What if it were a joke book or one of those sappy pop-psych self-help books? It was a hardcover, which she found encouraging, but she had known that pulling it out, had picked the hardcover out of the surrounding paperbacks in order to give him a better chance at making a good impression.

A boy on a tricycle suddenly wheeled onto the sidewalk from a hedge-lined driveway and barreled toward her. "Honk, honk," he said. He looked to be three.

Gay stepped into the street, but the boy stopped anyway, just before he would have run into her, making a loud braking sound. "We don't crash," he said, then turned the wheel, making a sharp reverse turn, and pedaled back home.

She stepped back onto the sidewalk and looked at the book. *The House at Pooh Corner.* Oh, she thought, he's a good father, which was, at that moment, an attribute she found terribly sexy.

10

Just south of Apuro, by the irrigation ditch, in the shade of an acacia, behind the living stump of what must have once been a huge tree, Rudy could conceal himself and watch the dirt road. The old stump was covered by leafy suckers, a perfect refuge for spying. But upon arriving at the spot, Rudy realized he could not hide. Not in Apuro. He could not reconcile his dominance of the place with hiding. He merely stared at the shady spot, confirmed that it would have suited his purposes, then turned around and began hiking back through the soft sand.

He needed to know precisely when Humberto Douglas left for El Paso. Humberto would visit his "brother" as he did every Saturday. While he was gone, Rudy planned to break into Humberto's adobe house. He didn't think this would be difficult, but how could he know for sure? He didn't want anyone to see him enter. He might have to be patient. Once inside, it could take a while to search through everything.

He needed a task with which to occupy himself outside, near the road, an unobtrusive means of observing Humberto's departure. He found his answer in the rattling approach of Luís Magana's old Ford truck. Luís's Guatemalan wife sat beside him, and Fred Chavez beside her. The truck was loaded with water bottles, tall blue plastic bottles filled from a hose in Persimmon. A group of men took turns retrieving drinking water. Rudy's father had once been among them, and Fred Chavez had asked Rudy to help after Rudy's father left Apuro. Rudy had declined with a snorting laugh. Later that same week, when the water carriers had declined to leave a bottle on the Salazar doorstep, Rudy had simply walked next door, thrown open the Obregons' door, and taken their bottle.

Today he would help. He would lug the bottles into houses until he saw Humberto's Chevy leave Apuro.

When Luís Magana cut his engine, Rudy stepped up to the truck and lowered the tailgate. No need to talk, he thought, grabbing a bottle and heaving it up into his arms. The bottles had no caps and had to be carried upright, water soaking his shirt before Rudy reached his own doorstep.

Humberto had received a letter from the Anglo reporter. Antonio Nieves, who worked at the diner across from the post office, had seen Humberto reading it in one of the diner's booths. Rudy wanted to know what the woman had written. He had not seen her after grabbing her ass, but Antonio claimed that she had been back while Rudy was at school. Now, just over a week later, she was corresponding with Humberto. Rudy carried the bottle into his house, surprising his mother, who stared at him suspiciously, a large grapefruit in her hands—her breakfast. She ate more fruit than anyone Rudy knew. He swept past her and set the bottle on the counter by the back wall. His mother had slept late and was not yet dressed for the day, draped in a nylon robe that featured the insignias of gas stations—Esso, Texaco, Sinclair, Conoco, Exxon, DX, and others. Rudy had given her the robe. It had been in the window of the Conoco, part of some promotion, and he had taken it for her.

"*Gracias*, Rudy," she said. "*Mil gracias.*" She set the grapefruit on the counter, poured what remained in the old water bottle into the washbasin, then handed the empty to him, the suspicion giving way to hope, which was always the way with her. "You're a fierce boy. Fierce? *¿Fuerte?*"

"Strong," he said, holding the empty bottle by the neck with one hand, as if this proved his strength.

"Strong, *sí. Recuerdo* back when *tu papi*—"

"Don't give me any line about him," Rudy said. "You get stupid about him. You get boring, *sabes*? Boring?"

Her face flattened, and she turned to the basin, began washing herself.

"He use to smack you, too, *recuerdas*?" Remember? He waited, but she acted as if she could no longer hear. "I gave you that robe, you know. Not him." He stormed out of the house.

"Appreciate the help," Fred Chavez said in his Tex-Mex accent, both a flatness and a twang to every word. An old man in his forties, he wore a black cowboy hat ringed with sweat. Bald guys liked hats, Rudy thought. His wife was long dead, and his kids were grown and living in Chicago, Los Angeles, Chihuahua, and some tiny place in Chiapas. Rudy lifted another bottle without acknowledging Fred Chavez, thinking of all the things he knew about this man's life. His wife had died in their bed from pneumonia, Fred Chavez returning from the chile fields to find women on his doorstep weeping. One of his sons, the one now in Chicago, had lost an arm in a tractor accident, the limb shaved off above the elbow. His only daughter had miscarried her first pregnancy while at work across river. The Anglo doctor who had driven her back to Apuro had said, "She lost the baby," and Rudy, just a boy then, had overheard and wondered about that, about how a person might lose a baby just as you might misplace a wallet. Fred Chavez had thanked the doctor and walked him back to his expensive car, but Rudy had hated the man for saying that, hearing in it what Fred Chavez could not hear, that an Anglo woman would not have been so careless. Then, as if Rudy had needed more proof, the Anglo doctor had to unlock his car door, had to slip keys from his pocket and slide one into the metal hole. In Apuro for five minutes, he locks his car to frustrate the inevitable thieves and keep out the stench.

Rudy carried the second bottle to the Obregons' house, pushing their door open with his foot, walking in without knocking. The airless room smelled of glue. He set the bottle on the bed, which was made, a wet circle immediately forming on the light blue sheet, then glanced about for the source of the odor. A pyramid about a foot high sat on a spread of newspapers, a kid's school project, evidently. Their boy was too little for such an undertaking, which meant that a neighbor kid, probably one living in a shack without a real floor, had come there to work. Rudy went to one knee, pushed open the swinging doors at the base of the pyramid. Inside were white floating spheres. He could not believe it, and looked again, five tiny white globes floating in the gloom. His throat tightened uncomfortably. He leapt up, threw open curtains to let in more light, then he looked again. A domino stood upright in the center of the pyramid, its five white indentations no longer appearing to float. He grabbed the empty jug left by the door.

Rudy delivered two more bottles before returning to the truck to find Humberto Douglas in his car idling beside the cab, his passenger window down, his body stretched across the front seat of the Chevy, gabbing with Luís Ma-gana's wife, a woman Rudy knew only as Baby. Rudy watched from a short distance. Humberto could talk forever about nothing to anyone, little wonder he hit it off with the reporter.

Baby said something, her caustic voice cutting through the space as Humberto's musical voice did not. The Maganas were a mystery to Rudy. Luís was tall and not ugly, probably as old as Fred Chavez but he looked years younger, while his wife was squat and square-headed, with a gap in her teeth. Her Spanish sounded like it came from the back of her throat, like she was chewing on something while she spoke, or trying to hawk something up, an accent so irritating that Rudy would change direction to avoid her. He had never heard her speak English, couldn't imagine how she might garble that.

What did Luís see in her? Why her? They had met in El Centro, California, Rudy knew, where she was awaiting deportation. By marrying her, Luís, a legal U.S. citizen, had stopped the deportation. Rudy could see some satisfaction in that, in walking into a room crowded with foreigners and selecting one, letting her know that he could save her from her fucking miserable country if he wanted. But why her? Were all Guatemalans built like woodstoves? When he pictured Guatemala, all he saw was Ciudad Juárez and the scrub desert that surrounded it. Guatemala had to be worse, nothing but sand and cactus and ugly women like Baby Magana.

Humberto finally quit talking to her, waved, and shifted his car into gear. Rudy heaved the final bottle into his arms. He didn't like to leave a task unfinished. Fred Chavez appeared as he lifted it, his shirt wetter even than Rudy's. "*¿Adónde?*" Rudy asked. Where?

Fred indicated the trailer of Maria de la O. "Last one," he drawled, and stepped past Rudy to shut the tailgate. It occurred to Rudy that this load of bottles served only a fraction of Apuro. Fred and the Maganas would be heading back to Persimmon to make another trip.

Rudy banged on the cheap metal door. He didn't like stepping inside the trailer. The low ceiling and narrow passages made him feel tense. A child opened the door, a little girl in underpants. "Shit," Rudy said, and shoved the bottle just inside the door. In Spanish, he told her to take the empty to the truck, then he pivoted and headed to Humberto's house.

The door was not locked. Like most of the houses in Apuro, it could not be locked from the outside, only from the inside with a sliding bolt. Rudy glanced about before stepping inside and shutting the door. Nothing to it.

He had not been in this house or looked in its windows since he was a child. What a *maricón*'s house was supposed to look like, he hadn't really imagined, but still he had some sense of disappointment. Not at all sissy, not full of pillows and things—Rudy couldn't articulate what he had expected to find, but the room disappointed him. A Coleman lantern dangled from a viga in the middle of the ceiling. Rudy found matches and lit the Coleman, although the morning sunlight through the windows remained bright.

Like most of the adobe *casitas* in Apuro, the house had only one room. Humberto had draped Mexican blankets over a wire to separate the back third of the room from the front. A black wood-burning stove for heat was situated in the center of the room, and an easy chair covered with another blanket faced it. A low table sat beside it with magazines stacked neatly upon it. Dozens of magazines. A counter with a metal sink lined one wall, three round holes where the faucet and handles would go, the big blue jug of drinking water on the counter beside the sink, delivered, no doubt, just moments ago. A mirror stuck out from the wall over the sink, and in one corner of the mirror, a photograph.

Seeing the photo made Rudy's heart race. He realized that he was looking for clues. Clues to why the reporter would want Humberto's opinions, clues to who or what Humberto really was, clues to why he, Rudy, had been afraid to enter this house for so many years.

The photo showed a man standing beside a green car, his hands linked and hanging low about his crotch. The man's smile suggested he had something to hide, the kind of smile you gave a woman who asked too many questions. A coy pose. Rudy didn't recognize him at first, but then he noticed that the man wore cufflinks, observed the man's perfectly combed hair. The same man Humberto had met in El Paso all those years ago, his "brother." For a moment, Rudy thought maybe they *were* brothers. Why would they still be together otherwise? *Maricónes* didn't marry each other. They just got humped by whoever was willing. Rudy slipped the photo back in the corner of the mirror. He saw then that the mirror was also a door, which was why it stuck out from the wall. Little shelves were perched behind it, holding a brush, a comb, toothbrush, toothpaste, a razor—all the things anyone might have. A few of the bottles Rudy didn't recognize, a box labeled Clairol with a picture of a dark-haired Anglo woman on it. Did Humberto have women visit him? Rudy would have known. Except for neighbors, no one visited Humberto. Rudy shut the mirrored door. He hated looking at things that he didn't understand.

He walked back to the curtain of rugs and lifted it, but there was no way to hold it up, and the rugs were stitched together, heavy and expensive blankets with colorful designs. He located a gap in the makeshift wall of rugs and stepped through. Humberto's bedroom contained a single narrow mattress on a low wooden platform pushed up against the wall, more a berth than a bed, but neatly made, covered with another Mexican blanket that couldn't possibly be of any use this time of year. A simple dresser stood at the end of the bed, and on top of the dresser two belts were coiled like snakes, alongside a tin of shoe polish and a single book. The book made Rudy push open the blanket door and examine the main room again. There were no other books. He would have expected Humberto to have some. He crossed back into the main room to look at the magazines stacked on the low table. He thumbed through them, half expecting something hidden to fall out. But there was nothing inside, just ordinary magazines like those sold at Gil Pharmacy. Magazines about the movies, about climbing mountains, about bodybuilding, about public affairs. A couple in Spanish that looked political.

He went back to the bedroom, to the dresser and lifted the book. The Bible, in English. He started opening drawers—socks and underwear, folded shirts and pants, a sweater with a paisley design. Nothing. Yet Rudy felt there was a quality to the room, to the air, that spoke of Humberto. Rudy could sense it but couldn't determine what it was.

Framed pictures covered much of the walls: a painting of the tops of buildings, a black and white drawing of a rainy street with a huddle of black umbrellas, a color photo of a house surrounded by black kids in caps with a bareheaded child staring out one of the windows. Nothing.

Rudy decided he would go to Nita's house one day when she and her girlfriend were out, would search through their things. Lately they seemed to be Humberto's best friends. By now everyone in Apuro knew that Anna and Nita were lesbians, although no one would say as much. Some people avoided them, but Rudy, like most everyone else, liked them. His reason, though, was very specific. He liked them because their curtains did not entirely close. Sometimes he just watched them move around, talking and reading. They had to know he was watching. It probably thrilled them. Women needed a man, even if they were afraid of his cock. Simple logic told him that. Eventually he would fuck them both. They couldn't let him watch, then expect to be left alone. He told himself he would do this, but some part of him knew it was not true. He told himself he was content for now with watching. Biding his time was, after all, one of his great pleasures. Some part of him knew he was more afraid of those women than he was of any man in Apuro.

The search proved useless. He inspected the place carefully, wanting to leave no trace of his presence. Then, before leaving, he succumbed to an impulse. He wanted to lie on Humberto's narrow bed. He didn't know why, but he wanted to put his head on Humberto's pillow and his body on the blanket, which had red and black stripes and was beautiful.

Not a comfortable bed, too small for Rudy. On his back, he stared up at the vigas and boards overhead, his arm draped off one side, his knuckles brushing the floor. It was little more than a cot.

To get up, he had to roll off, putting a hand and knee on the floor. It was the knee that felt the little ridge of papers stashed just beneath the bed.

He lowered himself to the floor, lifted the beautiful blanket: a short stack of typed pages and a paperback novel. Rudy took them both, stared again, but there was nothing else, not even dust. The title of the book gave Humberto away: *White Noise*. Rudy did not need to read any of it to know what "white noise" meant. It was come, and the book was about *jotos* doing it to each other.

Rudy replaced the book beneath the bed. The sheets of paper were a letter to Humberto from the woman Rhonda Hassinger. Rudy laughed out loud at his luck. He carried the letter to the table, sat down, and began reading. "Dear Humberto," it began, as if she actually knew him. As if she actually cared. Humberto was a fool.

> I hope this letter finds you well. I've decided, finally, to leave the questionable material in, and I thought I ought to let you know that, but I've cut back on the purple prose, which should be some compensation. I've kept the approximated dialogue, as all the editors here thought it sounded authentic.

These few lines incensed Rudy. He knew almost all of the words, yet he could not understand what she was saying, and it felt personal, as if she were ridiculing him. She did not know that he would ever read it, but that it was done behind his back made it even worse. Or so he felt, his anger too sharp and bright to permit him to reason anything out. The paragraph simply reminded him that most of the world operated at a distance and in a language he did not know. It was all he could do not to rip the sheets of paper into pieces, and he had to let himself calm down before he read more.

She had interviewed Humberto. She claimed that it was "the heart of the story." Kissing Humberto's ass, Rudy thought. She wrote about deeds and records, how there were none for Apuro, as far as she could tell, as if that mattered, as if that explained something. Rudy skimmed down the page to a paragraph in different type, something she was adding to her report on Apuro.

> *Their neighbors on the other side of the Rio Grande ("across river" is how the locals phrase it) have not totally ignored Apuro. Roughly forty years ago, they planted a row of mulberry trees along their side of the river. The trees, now tall and stately, obscure their view of Apuro, a living wall to deny Apuro's existence. A decade ago, to assist the efforts of the mulberries, cane was planted between the trees and the water, so that now there is a second living wall—over eight feet high—of dense cane. One literally cannot see Apuro from Persimmon except from the riverbank on the north and south ends of town. Stand there, shading your eyes against the glare of the sun off the water, and you can peer into the distance at the huddle of life across river.*

This paragraph angered him, too, but for different reasons. He didn't like to see his home written about in this fashion. It seemed improper. It lacked respect. To think you could spend a few days in a place and then pretend to know it—again he had to stop reading, let himself cool off.

He turned to the next page, which was nothing but script from her article. He tensed his stomach, as if in preparation for a punch, and then he read.

> *Apuro is not the only colonia in the area. In fact, they are springing up all along the Rio Grande. Some are no more than camping spots for people who have fled the poverty of Mexico to seek work in the United States. Others are the result of real estate swindles, parcels of land sold to people seeking to escape some other hell. The landowners arrive to discover that there are no utilities to the property or even available to it, unless they can pay to have wires and pipes run over dozens of miles.*
>
> *Apuro, however, is the only colonia of such long standing, and the only one in immediate proximity to a city. There have been, over the years, people in Persimmon who wanted to offer a helping hand to Apuro. Most recently, there was a movement to build a footbridge over the Rio Grande, which would permit the residents of Apuro to shop, work, and go to school without having to*

wade through the river. At present, the nearest bridge is fifteen miles away.

The local newspaper led the opposition to the footbridge, printing editorials and letters, which argued that a bridge would encourage more to settle there. "Apuro means 'danger' in Spanish," one letter to the editor began, "and that's just what we'd be inviting into our homes." Apuro, in my dictionary, is defined as "want, need, grief, sorrow," although most people in town think it is Spanish for "deep water," and the river is indeed deep next to the settlement.

This stuff didn't interest Rudy. If it didn't enrage him, it bored him. He was tempted to put the letter back and leave Humberto's house, but scanning the next page, he spotted his own name.

You don't need to worry about the Salazar boy. I've dealt with lots tougher than he. The story needs him, but I'm not sure how I should use the prick just yet.

Rudy reread the paragraph, an uneasy quiver moving up his spine, but he could not decipher what it meant, how she thought she could use him. The fucking bitch.

Nowhere else in the letter could he find his name, but, near the end, after talking about the weather and other useless crap, she began telling a story about Tito.

Sometime after midnight, I was up typing notes into my laptop when suddenly somebody's knocking on my door. Tito Tafoya stood outside my door, barefoot, in soaking wet clothes, saying he had something to show me. He was so sincere that I was out the door before I thought about the possible danger. I imagined that his visit had something to do with the story, like he was going to give me some kind of scoop. I felt like a character in a movie.

He led me out to the highway and across it, down the shoulder and through some bushes—and suddenly it dawned on me that I hadn't told anyone where I was staying. I asked him how he'd found me. "Everybody stays at the Oasis," he explained. Then we reached the river, and he stepped right into it. "It's black," he said to me. "*Negro*," he added, as if I might not understand his English. It took me a second to figure out that he meant the water. The water was pitch black. It looked like he was wading in Darjeeling tea.

"I didn't know who to show this to," he said. "Then I thought of you." He sat down in the water, leaned back and submerged himself.

I tried to tell him that the water was probably poisonous. There must have been some kind of huge dumping of chemicals or pesticides or something into the river—done at night, no doubt, to avoid notice. What else would turn a river black? But the boy seemed to think it was a miracle. Despite his urging, I declined to go in.

Rudy found himself in tears. He could not believe that he was sitting in the chair of a *joto* and weeping like one. It shamed him. He didn't know what in the letter made him cry, except that Tito had betrayed him because of this woman. But was that even true? Tito had come to him first that night. He had tried to take Rudy to the river. In fact, it had been Rudy who had brought up the reporter, who gave the *estupido* the idea.

Rudy couldn't sort it out, but he knew that he would make the woman pay for his tears, and he would make Tito a part of it. He turned through the pages again. She wanted to meet with Humberto again. Rudy memorized the date when she would next be in town. He stacked the papers together neatly and wiped his eyes.

He returned the papers to their spot beneath the bed. He straightened the blanket. He wanted no evidence of his visit to show. If only that woman had asked him about the deed to Apuro. He could have told her who owned the place. Now he would have to show her.

11

The back corner of the building now occupied by Persimmon Books had been added on years after the original construction. The appendage had likely been the cheapest way to tack on a bathroom, with the long, narrow storage room a bonus of the construction. The room was still uninsulated and unfinished, each wall made of a different material. An original adobe wall connected it to the remainder of the store, spottily covered with ancient stucco, a now-useless window beside the door, its panes painted black. The exposed brick of the neighboring building dominated one side, while the back wall was made of concrete block, a transom window above the metal door the only connection to the light of the outside world. The final wall featured exposed studs connected by splintered beams. The floor, of bare concrete, and the ceiling, stark rafters and plywood, complemented the decor. A hot, ugly room that Rita liked.

If her mother hadn't commented on the room, Rita might never have thought about it. Gay had stood in the doorway and swept one arm out in the direction of the bookstore, the undulating adobe walls and ceiling made of pine vigas and aspen latillas, saying, "This is who we were." Then she flapped her other arm at the mean, patched-together storage room and added, "This is what we've become."

Rita and Cecilia had rolled their eyes at this decidedly typical adult cynicism, as if it mattered what a storage room looked like when the whole idea of storage was to get things out of sight anyway.

Heart had said, "I lived back there for a month when I first moved to town. This was an office supply store then. I paid fifty dollars for the pleasure." She shook her head at the memory. "Like living in a barn."

Rita liked something about the room that she couldn't quite name. If pressed to identify the feature, she might have said "variety," pointing to the different colors and textures of each wall, but that wouldn't have been the real answer, just one of those things you say when you can't find a way to express what you really mean. She knew she liked the way the sunlight came in through the high window, how even with overhead fluorescent tubes switched on, it created its own separate tunnel of light. But that wasn't the whole reason. She liked that it was patched together and ugly, that it was unfinished, that it was rough and raw, that her mother hated it. Some ugly things were attractive, like billboards and electric signs, like the stores at a mall, like Burger King, whose building was mostly plastic and done in burger colors but Rita always wanted to stop there. Ugly but alluring, trashy but unabashed, the storage room felt comfortable and real. Rita preferred it to the bookstore, which somehow seemed phony.

She and Cecilia had come to the room to finish the inventory, their third day of after-school work at the bookstore. They had, by design, dressed up that day, Rita wearing her green velvet Heart dress and Cecilia in her communion dress, with her best earrings, tiny red jewellike glass surrounded by silver—elegant because they were so small. Rita had sifted through her collection of earrings, ranging from monkeys that hung by their tails from her lobes to authentic zirconiums on gold studs, and had chosen silver hoops in an attempt to match Cecilia's elegance. Heart had asked why the fancy getups, but the girls had declined to answer. They had no answer.

All afternoon they had counted and recorded books. Now only the ones in storage remained. Pizza was on the way. In the back room, a single bookcase held extra copies of books that sold well—or at least sold well in other stores, as nothing seemed to sell especially well in Persimmon Books. Also, stacked against one wall were five cardboard boxes of books and magazines that had been part of the stock Heart had purchased but which she did not want to carry in her store.

Lately, when Rita and Cecilia were together, their conversation hinged on developments in the Rudy Salazar saga. The first exchange on the subject had been the best, Cecilia coming over to Rita's house on the pretext of doing homework assigned on the first day of school. "I told my mother we had a project to do, and she believed me," Cecilia had said after they rushed into Rita's room, "but it isn't really a lie because of what I have to tell you—"

"What? What?" Rita demanded.

Cecilia told her that Rudy Salazar had followed her home and sat in her father's grass.

"He followed you all the way home?" Rita narrowed her eyes and cocked her head, sensitive to exaggeration. She felt a queer mixture of fear and jealousy.

Cecilia nodded dramatically. They sat together on the floor, their legs folded and knees splayed. Rita pushed her doll house out of the way, as if the nature of the conversation demanded more space. "He followed you past where we split up downtown?"

"He came all the way to my *yard*," Cecilia insisted, flushed and eager to talk, indignation welling in her voice. "He sat on that little grass patch Papa waters every day and doesn't let any of us touch. Enrique told him not to sit on it, or our papa would get mad, and you know what that bully did?"

"He punched Enrique!" Rita said. "Enrique's only in middle school!"

"No, he didn't hit him. Although he almost did. I could tell by the way he acted. But what he did was he got up, just like Enrique asked him to."

"Oh."

"But then he went over to Enrique all friendly-like and whispered in his ear."

"What?" Rita asked, leaning close and whispering herself. "What did he whisper?"

"He said, 'Tell your sister I know how to get into her house.' "

Rita rocked back in astonishment. "No, he said that? What did Enrique do?"

"He said, 'Which sister? Cecilia?' And Rudy Salazar laughed in a very mean way and said, 'Yes, Cecilia,' and then he left, just like that."

Rita stared at her friend for a moment in silence. The enormity of Cecilia's problem caused in Rita a wash of envy. "What are you going to do? Did you tell your parents?"

"No way," she said. "And I made Enrique promise not to tell either. My father would think I had led Rudy to the house. Besides, he's been sick and he doesn't need the worry. He might tell Rudy to stay away from us, and that would just make Rudy mad, and who knows what would happen?"

Rita crossed her arms then. Her tone became dismissive. "You can't let yourself be afraid of guys like him."

"He didn't follow you home. If he'd been sitting on *your* grass, you'd feel different."

Rita straightened her arms and legs and leaned back on her elbows. "We don't have any grass in the front yard. Not enough to sit on. He'd have to go 'round back." Suddenly she thought of the man she'd seen from her window. She had assumed it was her father come to get a look at her mother, but what if it had been Rudy Salazar come to look at her? "I just thought of something," she said. "When did he come to your grass patch? Was it before the rain?"

"Of course it was. He followed me home."

Rita grabbed her arm, an afflicted look of excitement taking over her face. She began explaining about the man, his movement, the way he rolled into the river.

"That doesn't sound like Rudy," Cecilia said. "Hiding like that." She shook her head and made a face. "I don't think so."

"So you think he would go to your house but not to mine?"

"I didn't say that, although he did come to my house right out in the open daylight. But even if he would go to your house, and even if he did figure out to go around to the back, I don't think he'd hide if you saw him. He isn't going to hide just because he thinks you or your mother or *any*body spots him."

Rita thought about it for a moment. "I guess you're right." She felt thoroughly deflated. "But who was that, then?"

Cecilia considered the question, then her eyes grew wide with amusement. "Your secret lover."

Rita liked this, and the next thought occurred to her so forcefully that she almost spoke his name, *Mr. Gene*. He had seen her steal the notebook, and then he had come to the house to spy on her. This, however, she didn't mention to Cecilia. It became her own secret fantasy, a daily exercise in creating a life for a man who hid the facts of his own existence with such care that it had to be fascinating.

In the week that followed, at school and after school, they had discussed the menace of Rudy Salazar. They sneaked glimpses of him at school, compared his brute physique to the Arnold Schwarzenegger poster in the window of Gil Drugs, and walked home side by side to protect themselves from his constant threat. He, however, paid no attention to them whatsoever. Rita increasingly turned her imagination to the question of Mr. Gene.

It made sense to her that a man too shy to speak aloud to a girl would roll into the river if she caught him spying on her. It made her want to spy on him. But it was a pretend desire, she knew, one she would never act on. He was interesting to her only so long as her own life was essentially boring.

She had hoped to see him in the bookstore. He was becoming too theoretical. Shouldn't the boyfriend help with the inventory? But they were almost finished, and he hadn't shown. She and Cecilia worked slowly in their best clothes, discussing reasons why Rudy Salazar continued to pretend to ignore them. Despite their chatter, they finished the books on the storage shelves.

"Are we supposed to open up these boxes?" Cecilia asked. Her communion dress had a streak of black across the rear where she had swept her hand all afternoon before sitting. Their hands had grown grubby from handling so many dusty books.

"I don't think so," Rita said. "She's not going to sell that stuff anyway."

Cecilia's interest in the boxes persisted. "Why wouldn't she sell it?"

"Doesn't like it, I guess. I don't know."

Cecilia examined the stack of boxes. They were sealed with wide bands of packing tape. The beam of light from the transom window now provided only faint illumination, and the fluorescent tubes suddenly seemed brighter. Cecilia said, "This one is marked 'Gruesome.' "

"Heart doesn't like violence," Rita explained. She joined Cecilia in studying the box, looking it over carefully as if it might leak blood. "She won't watch television unless you promise her 'no guns.' "

"You don't have a television."

"We don't, but I still know that about her. She only goes to movies about England, or stuff like that. My mom won't get a TV because she says it causes blindness."

"Your mom's weird sometimes."

"Tell me about it."

Cecilia squatted to look at the box beneath "Gruesome." She found its label in Heart's minuscule scrawl. "This one says 'Reactionary.' "

"I don't know what that means," Rita said. "You'll have to ask Heart."

"Help me lift these," Cecilia said, taking hold of 'Gruesome.' "I want to see what the bottom ones say."

Together they moved the boxes, restacking them bottom to top. The next box bore the label "Cars, etc." and the one after that, "Spanish Serials."

"If the books in here are in Spanish, she ought to put them out there," Rita said. "She might actually sell one or two."

Cecilia had already begun her scrutiny of the final box. "This one's been opened." She pointed to the place where the tape had been cut and then pressed back together. "Look." The box bore the label "Crud."

"Huh," Rita said.

Cecilia had gone to her knees to read the box's label, her dress now sporting slashes of dirt across the front, too. She stood and tiptoed to the door. Rita whispered, "Look through the glass. There's a spot." The black paint on the redundant window had been scratched off in one spot about the size of a thumbprint. Cecilia had to put her knee on the adobe sill of the window to raise herself up to the spot. "Your mom and Heart are both at the front desk," she whispered. "They're looking at some book with pictures in it. Wait! There's a customer."

Rita knelt before the box, wiping her hands on her velvet dress before touching the dusty flaps. She lifted one, gritting her teeth theatrically at the sticky noise the tape made. There were not books in the box, but magazines. Cecilia quickly joined her. On the cover of the top magazine, a naked woman held on to a bedpost, a naked man planted squarely on top of her. Black censoring dots covered the points of intersection.

Rita felt an excited flutter in her chest.

"Open it," Cecilia whispered, patting Rita on the back.

Rita handled the cover delicately, only her thumb and pointer finger touching it, as if it might burn her. On the first page, in black and white, a naked couple lay side by side ready to begin sex. Although they did not look in the direction of the camera, they had lain so that their genitals were fully exposed. It looked uncomfortable. The man's penis appeared to be as long as Rita's arm from the elbow, the head of it roughly the size of her fist.

"Gross," Cecilia said. "But interesting."

"I don't see how that's going to fit," Rita whispered. She looked up at the window as if a glance at the glass constituted checking on her mother and Heart.

"Whole babies come out, so that has to be able to go in," Cecilia said.

"I know," Rita said. "I just don't see how."

"Turn the page," Cecilia suggested.

"*You* turn the page."

"She's pretty," Cecilia said, "but he's almost bald."

"I don't think he got the job for his hair," Rita said. She began giggling and Cecilia joined her. "They can't all be that big. Pants would have to be made different."

Cecilia, still giggling, ran to the window, and lifted herself on one knee to spy again on the adults. "We should listen for the front door," she whispered, hurrying back. "They'll come for us when the pizza guy gets here."

Rita began turning the pages. A series of closeups showed the penis entering the woman's vagina, pulling back, and entering again.

"This reminds me of something," Cecilia said.

"Oh, yeah?" Rita said, teasing.

"No, something like you do with cars. My brother Arturo used to have these car books with step-by-step pictures."

"He's changing spark plugs," Rita said, and let out a breath, which was like laughing, only quieter.

They paged quickly through the remainder of the magazine. None of it looked like fun, the people all appeared serious and distant, often in pain. Still, it was compelling. Toward the end of the magazine, the couple got gymnastic, which was entertaining, and then the penis came out of the vagina and spewed all over the woman's face.

"Ugh," Rita said.

"It's supposed to be good for your skin, I think," Cecilia said.

"I thought it was more . . . *regulated* than this," Rita admitted. "I didn't know you could move around so much, and get into such funny poses."

"Funny ha ha or funny weird?" Cecilia said.

"Both," Rita said. She tried to imagine her mother and father doing these things, and couldn't. She knew her mother had done it with a lot of men. It didn't seem gross, particularly, but unlikely. In some ways it definitely seemed appealing, though not with a bald guy, and certainly not with the men her mother dated. She studied the bald man. He looked a little like Heart, or like what Heart would have looked like if she were a man and bald and big. Then it occurred to her that the people in these pictures were paid to do this. Which seemed especially strange. Professionals at making love.

Cecilia began looking at the covers of the magazines that remained in the box. The top few looked similar to the one they had just studied, but near the bottom of the box were magazines whose covers showed men, without women, gripping themselves. Inside, men kissed other men. They had sex together.

"They're not supposed to do that," Cecilia said.

At the very bottom, a magazine featured women in bed together. It didn't seem to matter whether the people were men or women, or whether they were with somebody of the same sex or the opposite sex, they all had that look of consternation and suffering. No one was smiling or laughing. It appeared to be serious business. Which made Rita think her mother probably wasn't very good in bed. She liked to kid around too much. One camera angle revealed the ceiling over the woman's head, the same bare rafters and plywood as the storage room.

They heard footsteps, and hurried to fill the box and pile it with the others. The door opened and Heart stuck her head in. She didn't really look like the bald man, except for something about her eyes. "You at a point you can take a break, girls? The pizza's here."

"We're finished," Rita said.

Heart smiled at that and said something about coming up to the front to eat. As soon as she left, Rita began restacking the boxes. She wanted "Crud" back on the bottom. Cecilia helped her. Through the lacy top of Cecilia's communion dress, Rita could see black dots.

"For my little brother," Cecilia whispered. "He still doesn't get an urge. My parents are worried."

"Enrique? Doesn't like girls?"

"That's what they're afraid of. He never noses around after girls the way a boy should. Arturo was in a lot of trouble by the time he was this age. But poor Enrique. Nothing."

"Do you talk to him about it?"

Cecilia gasped and threw her hand over her heart, but the magazine came between hand and heart. "I would never *speak* to him about it." She made Rita promise to keep silent.

"Does he jerk off, at least?" Rita asked.

"I don't think he does," Cecilia said sadly. "Is there some way you can tell?"

"There is, but I don't know how."

Cecilia tapped the magazine beneath the fabric. "This should help, don't you think?"

"You should let me sneak it out," Rita said. "I can see it right through your top. Unzip me."

Cecilia shook her head. "I'll put it in my notebook." She shook her head seriously as she pulled the magazine out. "This is a sin," she said. "Stealing."

"Yeah," Rita said, and began laughing.

From the next room they heard Rita's mother calling them. Cecilia opened her notebook. They had not examined this magazine, a young man and a young woman on the cover, naked on an oriental rug, the curled feet of a couch just above them, a handsome man and a beautiful woman joined at the waist by a dark circle.

12

SEPTEMBER

Gay had to work late Friday and told Denny she would meet him at his house. During her hours at GEM Transport, she wore a wireless headset so that she could write travel coordinates in a log, or simply meander about the office while she talked with truckers. She kept track of their deliveries and mileage, their hours on the road and hours at rest; she relayed new orders and spoke with superiors; she filled in a grid with numbers and codes. A monkey could do it, she sometimes thought, but she knew that wasn't true. Not a normal monkey, anyway. Maybe one of those chimpanzees they'd trained to read and type—what was the name of that chimp? Bongo or something like that. She had always wondered whether they could be taught musical instruments. Could a chimp play Mozart? Chopin? Billy Joel?

Billy Joel almost looked like a chimp. It didn't surprise Gay that his wife the supermodel had dumped him. Margaret had told her this. She argued that Gay could have been a model. "I don't have the temperament for it," Gay had said, and believed it to be the truth, but she had liked it being said that she had the looks of a model. She stepped to the lone window in the room and studied her faint reflection in the glass. Headphones were becoming in a way. They made you look competent and otherwise engaged. The second-story office provided her with a view of Main Street, which she took in after tiring of her reflection. The angle of the sun made for long shadows, a Gothic effect inconsistent with the brick buildings from the fifties, the adobe ones from earlier times. Sitting on the sill, a child's aquarium, a remnant of her boss's first marriage. Tiny, shiny fish called neons darted about in the tank, their bodies shimmering red and blue as if electrically lit.

GEM Transport delivered cars nationwide, a fleet of semis and trailers pulling new cars to new destinations. None of them actually stopped in Persimmon. Gay merely plotted courses and directed shipments. "You get any inside information?" Denny had asked her. She had not seen him since their trip to the diner, but she had spoken to him a number of times over the phone. "You have any advice for someone who needs to buy a new car?"

"Sure," she had said. "When you get your new car, don't drive behind one of our trucks. The cars often slip off."

"How often?"

"All the time," she had said, an exaggeration, but it was the single thing she knew that could vaguely pass as inside information. The only real benefits of GEM Transport were the pay, the medical and dental insurance, and the opportunity to talk to some of the truckers. Most were boors in all the predictable ways—"You remind me of my first wife," came the voice through the headset, or, "I'd like to get you a present. What's your bra size?" Many had volunteered to detour through Persimmon in order to take her to dinner, to buy her a drink, to pick her up and take her on to Los Angeles. "A weekend with me will change your life forever, babe," one trucker insisted.

"Sounds like you have a disease," Gay had responded. Most of them had never seen her face to face, but she guessed they didn't get to talk to many women in this line of work. Some of her regulars she very much liked, and she'd had a fling with one of them, a boisterous man with large, knobby hands and a wife in Dallas.

Her work was not something she would ever have thought she would enjoy, but she did. Her supervisor spent just fifteen hours a week in this office, which meant she decided most things on her own. She knew that she was not making a difference in the world with this work, but she was comfortable with it. That she lived a private life of her own design helped her reconcile herself to it.

She had made a few decisions, looked for improvements in her daily life, purchased items, discarded items, pursued ideas and people who interested her—and these things had defined her life. She had made her bed, and it had turned out to be a fairly comfortable place to lie. Denny, she had come to understand, posed a threat to that life. Or so she had thought. Talking to him on the phone without seeing him had been smart. It diffused the strange power he seemed to hold. She did not want to disrupt her life. She loved Sander, and she liked occupying a design of her own making. There was room for Denny in it, as long as his part was restricted. For them to become simply another couple would, in the long run, destroy everything.

As soon as she finished the logs, she locked the office and walked to Denny's cottage, a short stroll that took her through a shabby but not dangerous neighborhood called Barrio Tampoco. Many of the houses here were among the oldest in town, small adobe boxes alongside cheap tract homes from the sixties. The new police station had encroached upon this neighborhood, causing many old houses to be torn down. A big bulldozer was still parked on the lawn of the police station. Gay had opposed the location, but she hadn't wanted it in her neighborhood either. The bulldozer looked identical to the one that had briefly occupied the end of her own street. The decal of an American flag showed in one window.

The middle-class neighborhood where Denny lived was separated from Barrio Tampoco by an irrigation canal. The houses across the canal became immediately larger, as did the yards. The canal was only a few feet wide, but not all streets traversed it, which permitted it, in this part of town, to take on the job historically belonging to railroad tracks, that of separating the have-nots from the haves. Of course, the river did the real work, Gay acknowledged, separating Persimmon from Apuro and, farther downriver, the United States from Mexico.

When Denny opened his door, she could not help noticing the bed—new, made, and queen-sized, covered with a quilt, the room's centerpiece. A strange charge darted about inside her chest, like the neons in the aquarium at work. "You've been shopping," she said, enjoying the little ignitions that caused her skin to tingle. She was going to have sex with this man tonight.

"First things first, I always say," he said. "Do you like it?"

"It's an improvement." She kicked off her clogs and lay her body across it. "Foam pillows?"

"I can't afford feather."

She rolled to the center of the bed. "It's firm enough for one, but I don't know what it will be like with a man on top of me. Men never think about all the weight women—and the box springs—have to bear. And then there's all that thrusting besides."

"There's only one way to really know for certain," he said.

"Purchase a brand-name mattress?"

"Even that could leave some room for doubt." He showed her his crooked smile as if it were a gift. He had ironed his shirt and slacks.

"Come lie beside me," she said.

As soon as he crawled onto the bed, she rolled over on top of him. "Well?" she said. "I don't weigh as much as you, of course, but we have the same cumulative pounds per square inch."

"Feels great," he said.

"Spread your legs," she said. When he did, she began thrusting against him. "And now?"

"It's a great bed."

She slipped her arm beneath one of his knees and then the other, raising them so that they buckled back against his chest, and she pushed harder against him. "How's this?" she said.

"Uncomfortable," he admitted. She stopped thrusting. "But it's not the bed's fault. I don't bend so well that way."

"I know the feeling," she said. "Where are we going to eat?"

"Would you mind if I get my knees out of my face?"

She climbed off him and stepped from the bed. "Chinese?" she asked, straightening her dress. "There's a decent place in El Paso."

"I may need to lie here for a while," he said.

"How did you come to be a teacher?" She wandered over next to the sink and stove. The stove was so clean, she guessed that he hadn't yet used it.

Denny sighed and sat up. "By default." He stood and began tucking in his shirt without loosening his belt, just shoving it down. "They started calling bums 'the homeless,' which made me feel sort of pretentiously unemployed. So I began substitute teaching, and I sort of liked it."

"You say 'sort of' a lot."

"Lucky for you, I'm drawn to difficult women."

"Oh, am I the lucky one? Isn't that *sort of*—"

He raised a hand, showing her his palm. "One of many faults. Let's go."

She wasn't ready to go. After the initial thrill of seeing the bed, she had relaxed, which was both a relief and a disappointment. "Where is your daughter going to sleep?"

"I'm getting a couch that folds into a bed. Let's go. I'm hungry. You want to drive?" He dug his hand into his pocket and removed a wad of keys, which he extended toward her. The pose reminded her of classical statuary, the model's arm stretching out into space, and reminded her, too, of a pose from a movie.

"Sure," she said, the keys in flight toward her before she had even spoken the word. She caught the keys.

"I thought you would," he said.

Fully clothed but beside him again in the queen-size bed, she reached for her purse and produced a condom. Her hand shook, she noted, her body, once again, advising her. Despite what she wanted to believe, this was not an ordinary flirtation. The Chinese place had gone out of business, and they had eaten mediocre Italian, but the wine had been good and plentiful, and he had continued talking with her all night in that immediate way he had.

She never had to resort to small talk, and she had not for a moment been bored. The restaurant was located on the bottom floor of a split-level strip mall, and from their table they had watched the legs of strangers, cut off at the hip, meander past, the tailored slacks of men and women in suits and the bare legs of teenagers in their ridiculous shoes.

A fragment of a dream had come to her while they were eating, little more than an image, one that she had forgotten upon waking. She and Denny were figures on a billboard and then had come alive. That was all of the dream she could recall, and she did not tell him about it.

After dinner, while they finished their bottle of wine, Gay had looked again out the window. Night had fallen while they had eaten, and she felt the wide expanse of the night sky. When the legs of strangers again appeared, she was startled by their proximity, and it occurred to her that, of course, the sky stretched to the very surface of the earth. She hadn't needed to say anything because Denny had been looking out the window, too. They drank the good wine—she had meant to jot down the year and vineyard—and studied the high window. The dark lent to those limbs, disembodied and scissoring above them, an odd beauty and a sense of human inevitability and mortality, which engendered a peaceful, melancholy feeling.

Upon their return, she slipped off her shoes and reclined on the bed, which had seemed safe, a way to lead them back into her territory. But she still did not feel safe or in command of her emotions because the sense of peace that had begun at the restaurant had settled into her now more profoundly, which made her uneasy with it. It reminded her of the rush of relaxation that immediately preceded sleep, but she was not sleepy and she could not imagine into what state of being she might be about to slide.

Sex, though, she knew and could handle. While she fingered the packaged condom, he told her a story about his misspent youth—a rambling tale of taking psilocybin with his buddies, stealing golf carts from the local country club, and playing bumper cars. "I suffered from what was back then known as stupidity," he said to her. "It's likely that I still suffer from it, but I've come to understand that I was from a dysfunctional family, so I was the victim all along, and not those people whose property I destroyed and whose livelihoods I endangered."

"How did this dysfunction rear its ugly head in your family?" Gay asked him.

"Hard to say. Mother was a lousy cook, and my dad once drank my science project—a long story, but it involved growing mold in a Pepsi bottle."

"Ugh." A sensation like laughter but that was not laughter flashed through her chest and sent ripples through her extremities.

"He liked a little carbonation with his rum."

"Ah, substance abuse, plus they clearly inhabited traditional roles."

"Throwback abuse," he said. "It's a wonder I survived at all." His eyes flitted down her body, stopping at the hand that held the condom. "If you want me to," he said, "but I haven't been with a woman since my divorce."

By saying this they skipped over some part of their mutual seduction, and Gay felt the rush of that acceleration. "What makes you think this isn't for birth control?"

"Oh, just a guess."

"How long were you married?" Her voice skidded into whisper with the final word.

"Ten years," he said. "Some of them long ones."

He was like a man who had stepped out of a movie, she thought. The idea had nothing to do with what they were saying, but with the ease of their talk and the attractiveness of his person. Wasn't everyone supposed to want a movie star? How had he learned to behave this way? Her attraction to him felt strangely generic, like the appeal of a packaged vacation. On the one hand it felt too easy. On the other hand, who could resist?

She had a moment to believe herself silly. She would tell Sander about all of this, including her willingness to delude herself, she thought. But then he began to kiss her neck.

In another moment, someone was pounding on the door. Denny immediately donned a pained look of disbelief. "No one visits me," he said, standing awkwardly, dipping a hand into a pocket to hold down the lump in his pants. Gay laughed out loud.

The pounding came again. "Hold your horses," Denny said, which made Gay laugh more. He swung open the door. A uniformed policeman stood before them, his official billy club in hand. He had evidently banged on the door with it.

"Hello there," Denny said.

The policeman stared past him at Gay, his eyes meeting hers. They were compassionate eyes, she could tell, embarrassed to glance down at her legs, which were exposed to him, she guessed, by the manner in which she lay on the bed. But she did not change her position, waiting instead the few seconds it took for him to meet her eyes again. He said, "Somebody here dial 911?"

Gay smiled at him and watched it register on his face. "Not yet," she said.

He asked to use the phone, then apologized as he checked out the bathroom and closet, even glanced beneath the bed, talking all the time about their regulations and obligations, about emergency calls being automatically traced. He telephoned headquarters from Denny's phone and explained the situation. "Not a chance," he said to someone on the line. He was inside the cottage less than five minutes. "Carry on," he said deadpan, and disappeared.

Denny bolted the door behind him, then turned to Gay, who had covered her legs but had not risen from the bed. His mouth spread open but he didn't have anything to say, and neither did she, the man had come and gone so quickly and with such mystery that there seemed nothing to say.

Time then gave up its hold on them, and they were in bed together, and they were naked, and they pressed their bodies one against the other, and they were creatures of those bodies, and the passing of an hour meant no more to them than it did to any other creature, just the unregulated flow of the dark that would end eventually in daylight, or in darkness without end.

It was only after, while they were lying in the dark, that he said while it was true he hadn't been with a woman since he left his wife, there had been others *before* he left his wife.

She immediately reached across him and switched on the light by the bed, making him squint. "You lied to me," she said calmly. "You shouldn't have done that."

"I don't have AIDS." He made a two-finger salute without sitting up, a childish thing, but he was able to pull it off with some charm. "Scout's honor. It's not that easy for a heterosexual man to get it, unless he's into the needle, which I'm not."

"It still should be my decision," she said.

"Okay, you're right. I apologize. I did 'fess up, at least."

While he had apologized, he did not appear to have any regret. Nonetheless, Gay couldn't muster anger. In fact, she felt more like herself than she had before, no longer made flighty with false emotion. Rather than anger or indignation, she felt something like curiosity. What was the makeup of this man's character? It seemed like an old-fashioned question, but it was precisely what she needed to know. "Why were you with other women while you were married?"

He didn't look at her but at the ceiling, the sheet covering him to the waist. "My marriage was everything you say marriage is. We hated each other after a while." He paused, slipping his hand beneath the sheet and placing it on her thigh. He continued to stare at the ceiling, fondling her leg, adding, "But at least we hated each other a lot."

"What is that supposed to mean?" She faced him but he continued to study the ceiling. It seemed to her that all men did this, and she wanted him to look at her.

"We didn't work out some halfway deal, some—"

"You two see each other now?" She gave him a little shove at the ribs, but he would not face her.

"Not if we can help it."

"I rest my case." She kicked the sheets off them, the hand on her thigh dislodging momentarily. When it returned to the very same spot on her thigh, it had become altered. Now it radiated heat, a deep, sensual warmth.

"There was actually only one woman while I was married."

"Besides your wife?" she asked, her voice faltering

"Besides my wife." He moved the hand, but she still felt it there, a phantom feeling. She wanted to tell herself that this whole nonsense with him involved phantom feelings. Something in her life was causing this. A midlife crisis, only she wasn't old enough for that. She closed her eyes to concentrate, but she could hear him breathing beside her. Suddenly she thought he might be falling asleep. "There were two women, then," she said. "You were in love with her, the other woman?"

" 'In love.' " He spoke the words to the ceiling, slowly and with comic emphasis as if they were foreign to his vocabulary. "Hell if I know," he said. "You 'in love' with your part-time husband?"

"Yes," she said without hesitation.

Finally he rolled onto his side and looked at her. "You 'in love' with me?"

"No," she said equally quickly, but she began to tremble, which made her feel ridiculous.

"Take your time. Consider it carefully. Wouldn't want you to jump to any conclusions."

This is preposterous, she thought. She made her voice calm and stared not at his eyes but the base of his throat. "Are you trying to tell me that you're in love with me?"

"I was actually saying that I'm not even sure I was in love with Laurie, so how—"

"Your lover."

"My ex-lover from my ex-marriage."

"You divorced them both, wife and lover?"

"It sort of worked out that way."

"Sort of?"

He nodded, pursing his lips. "I got this job out here." He tapped the bed, as if it were the source of his employment. "Laurie didn't want to leave her job—or her husband, really—and I don't know. I guess I wasn't sure I wanted her to come."

Gay sat up in the bed, taking in the ugly room, his handsome body, the little puddle of business on the sheets. She leaned over him, her breasts swaying above him, and looked down at his head on the foam pillow. His blue eyes moved from her face to her breasts and back. She said, "I thought you'd been divorced a year and a half."

"Officially," he said, his face contorting, as if in pain. "But we made up for a while. I only moved out a couple of weeks before I headed down here."

What she had thought was an emotional connection—love, why should she lie to herself—had been an instinctive distrust, she thought. She was not infatuated, she was furious. "What other half-truths have you pushed off on me?"

"Let me think."

"I'm not laughing," she said tersely.

"The truth is . . . " He raised his hand to her bare shoulder, pushing her gently aside, then sat up and faced her. "The truth is, I have more mixed feelings than I admitted to about difficult women. I am drawn to them, but they often turn out to be a pain in the ass."

She started to roll out of bed but he grabbed her, his arms around her waist. He held her tight. She felt unaccountably dizzy and wanted to dress.

"I'm not attracted to you because you're difficult," he said, speaking into her ear, the effect of his breath like a strain of distant music, "and if you could manage to be less interesting, I'd appreciate it. However, I am power-fully attracted to you." His grip on her tightened as he said this, taking her breath. "I am over my failed marriage, and while I probably was 'in love' with my lover, we never seriously considered having anything more than a controlled, sort of limited relationship—an idea you, I know, are acquainted with—and I never slept with anyone for the past ten years but those two women—both of whom are married and extremely low-risk partners—and I'm already about halfway in love with you, despite every damn thing about the relationship telling me that I'm acting the fool."

"And you say 'sort of' too much," she said.

"And I say 'sort of' too much."

"All right then." She quit resisting. His hold on her loosened. This man was going to destroy her marriage. She shook her head in response to her own thoughts. She rolled back toward him, throwing a leg over him, pushing him back against the mattress. It seemed that there was, inside her, something heavy tied to a string, and each time it swung about, she would have to respond. Now she wanted to push him into doing something. She wanted to regain control of the evening, which might even permit her to get a grip on her own feelings. She said, "I suppose we can make love again."

"Right now?" He tried the half-smile, but with her looming directly above him, it was less effective. "We just finished," he pointed out. "Give me a little recharge time, will you? You want a beer?" He slid out from beneath her.

"All right."

He stood so quickly he almost lost his balance and threw his arms out to steady himself.

"I do like your butt," Gay said. She searched about for the condom, finding it in the wad of sheets at the foot of the bed. She pulled the sheet over her, luxuriating in the idea that she was going to ruin her marriage, destroy the life she had carefully constructed. This, she said to herself and half believed, is the beginning of the end, the beginning of the undoing of her current existence. She felt drunk with the heady power of her own destruction, the reality of it still distant enough to permit her to enjoy the sensual rush of falling.

Denny threw open the refrigerator door and poked around for beer. "This fridge smells funny and I haven't even started spilling things yet," he said. "How can that be?"

She saw them together in her house, sleeping in her bed, eating with Rita and Heart at the kitchen table. She said, "This is going to be tight quarters once you add a six-year-old."

He bent at the knee and stuck his hand deep into the refrigerator. "That's starting to look iffy already. Her mother is squawking about my living out here. I may not have Jenny until the summer. Got it." He pulled out a can of Tecate. "I can pour half into a jar if you want, or we can take turns." He didn't wait for a reply but started back to the bed.

"Are you going to have a custody fight?"

He shook his head. "If I fight, she becomes bullheaded. If I'm patient, she more or less forgets the conflict. She's not cut out for raising kids. She and I were happily married until we had Jenny. Then it all went to hell."

"I had a breakdown after Rita was born," Gay said, and that delicious feeling wound through her body again. She would tell him her secrets. She could feel herself tumbling into herself and pulling him along, a slide into the dark.

"What kind of breakdown?" He crawled back into bed, offering her the first sip of beer.

"I'm a good mother," she said, not defensively but thinking of his ex-wife, feeling expansive and generous. "Did you give your wife a chance to adjust to being a mother?"

"A million of them. She's in AA now, and as long as she's sober, she gets Jenny. I could give you more details, but it isn't interesting."

"I shaved Rita's head. The day she was born." As she spoke, she could see the baby, could feel the madness—not all that different from being in love. "She had a surprisingly long shock of black hair, and I took my Lady Bic, and I shaved her hair off. Her scalp bled and scabbed, and she could have been taken from me, but she wasn't."

"Why the hell did you do that?"

"I could give you more details, and it *is* interesting, but I don't want to yet." She put her arms around him, her face against his chest. "Have you had sufficient recharge time yet?"

"I haven't even finished my beer."

"Our beer." She put the condom packet to her mouth and made a tear in the serrated package.

13

The magazine had simply materialized beneath his pillow. It was not *New Woman*. Enrique had no explanation for what it was.

When his family had lived in Apuro, everyone had slept in the same room because the house had only one room. His mother had told him this when he asked about Apuro. The two adults and one or more of the six children slept on the double bed, while another child or two slept on the sofa, with the remainder on blankets or mats on the floor. Upon moving to Persimmon, their father had built three bunk beds, assembling them in the two children's rooms because they were too big to pass through the doors. Enrique shared a room and a bunk bed with his brother Arturo, who now attended college in Las Cruces. Cecilia had her own room now, too, although there was still a pair of bunk beds in it like archaic pillars to a ruined palace, and his sisters still slept there when they visited.

The beds were made of four-by-four posts, with two-by-four rails and scrap lumber of various sizes serving as slats and stabilizing rails. Because their father was not a carpenter by trade, many stabilizing rails had been necessary, so that the mattresses were walled in on three sides by scrap lumber their mother had painted white, but that long ago had been covered by artwork, stickers, baseball cards, and photographs. The mattresses their mother had made from foam squares and old sofa cushions. The beds had long been the envy of all their friends.

Despite Arturo's prolonged absence, Enrique still slept on the top bunk. Climbing up involved slipping one's toes between the unevenly spaced rails at the foot end of the bed, then swinging around the rail onto the mattress—which meant that Enrique had to make his bed himself. His mother required that he make it every morning, and she checked. If he didn't make it, she would simply pull the sheets and pillow from the top and leave them in a pile on the floor. She never made the bed herself, which meant that Enrique's bed was private. Once, to test the privacy, he had written the word "damn" in pencil in one corner of the bed. He left it there and waited to see if he would get a talking-to from his mother, but it never came. He erased it, though, after a week because the tension had been too much.

Before turning a single page of the magazine, he slipped back down the rail ladder and got his flashlight. Then he climbed down again and pulled a comic book from the pile beneath the lower bunk. If his mother came in and asked what he was reading in bed instead of sleeping, he had to have something to show her. He slipped the magazine and flashlight beneath the sheet, then pulled his blanket over himself, too, to contain the light. It was a warm night, and he immediately began to sweat. He opened the comic to a likely page, the X-Men standing on a rocky precipice pointing to a distant shining city. Had he read this comic? He turned a couple of pages. Oh yeah, the one where they all get mad at each other and one of them almost gets killed by one of the others. He paged back to the precipice, then placed the comic within easy snatching reach.

Finally he opened the magazine. Immediately he banged his head against a rail. She had it in her mouth! He peeked out of the blanket, checked the location of the comic, then pulled the blanket up higher still. He knew this was called a blow job, but her cheeks weren't inflated. In fact, he could see dimples in them. He had never understood why people thought dimples were attractive. Did Rita have dimples? He didn't think so, but if she did, he probably would think they were attractive. That must be how it worked. Once you liked something you felt obligated to figure out why and then came up with rules, like saying dimples were good looking. He looked back to the woman and banged his head again. Why did this picture make him jump?

The penis itself interested him. Either it was much larger and thicker than Enrique's own, or the woman had a very small mouth. Which made him think of Monica Gutierrez, whose mouth, Enrique believed, was too small for her face, which was why she always wore a lot of lipstick. On the other hand, she talked a lot and about anything, so people said she had a big mouth, an irony that made Enrique smile, until he remembered she wouldn't dance with him because her brother's feet stank, and big little mouth that she was, now probably the whole school had Enrique confused with her stinky brother.

He protected the spot on the back of his skull with his hand and returned to his magazine. He hadn't noticed her tongue before, which was sticking out of her mouth and licking the underside of the man's penis. There were likely other things he had missed, but he had to turn the page or get a headache.

Now the woman and man were doing it in a bed. Several different angles showed him on top of her with clear pictures of the combination of their parts. Enrique had spent a lot of time imagining such an event, but here it was in black and white. She was biting her lip and had one eye closed, then in the next frame still biting her lip but with two eyes closed, then her mouth was open and her bottom teeth showed with a little spit on them.

There were close-ups, as well, of the penetration, which made Enrique realize that there had to be another person in the room with a camera. What a lousy job, he thought, nosing around some man's testicles with a camera, saying, "Excuse me. Could you slow down? Could the two of you hold still? The last picture was all blurry." And they would say how they didn't want to hold still because everyone, even an eighth-grade virgin who thinks about sex all the time, knows that you have to keep moving around or the whole deal doesn't work.

The man on top started explaining as much to the photographer, and then the woman started to put in her two cents. "Enrique." Not the woman. His mother! He jerked his head out of the covers, banging the identical and already sore spot against the rail, grabbing at the comic, which slid off the bed and fluttered to the floor.

"What do you think you're doing up there?" his mother said, and he tried to think of an answer, but she didn't wait for one, having already stepped into the room and lifted the comic book to her face. "X-Men aren't going to get you to college, no matter what any person tells you different. It's an hour past your bedtime, on a school night, and—"

"Sorry, Mom," he said, rolling onto his stomach so that he covered every inch of the magazine with his body, lying on top of the magazine just as the man in the magazine had lain on top of the woman. He had an erection? He hadn't realized it until he turned over.

"—to sleep right this second," his mother finished up, closing the door behind her as she stepped out of the room.

He waited awhile in the dark. If Rita saw him now, she wouldn't understand that a boy sometimes can't help getting an erection, even though the naked woman isn't the girl he loves, so he shouldn't be blamed at all. Not that Rita would actually care, since she didn't even know that he liked her, and she didn't have any feelings for him at all, unless she secretly didn't like him and told Cecilia every day what a wimp her brother was, who didn't even have a girlfriend and there was this rumor about the odor of his feet.

He sighed and rolled back onto his side, the magazine crackling beneath him. The flashlight was still on. Had his mother told him to shut it off? He didn't think so, but he missed some of what she said. Maybe *she* had put the magazine in his bed? She worried about his preoccupations, he knew, but this possibility was too humiliating to consider. He shone the light on the magazine. The vein at the bottom of the man's penis stood out like some kind of inverse river. His mother hadn't given him this, or his father either, which only left Cecilia. But where had she gotten it?

He turned the page. The previous man and woman were replaced by a woman driving a convertible and a policeman standing by her window writing her a ticket. She had forgotten to button all the buttons on her blouse, and Enrique considered for a moment that this was what she was getting the ticket for. Then she was on her knees in the driver's seat, unzipping the cop's pants. Did this kind of thing go on all the time?

First she put her face next to it, her tongue slipping just out of her mouth, a look of pleasure on her face like maybe her favorite song had come on the radio. "Born in the U.S.A." came to mind. He couldn't tell from looking whether she would like Springsteen or not. She kind of looked like Madonna, with the same kind of blondish whitish hair, but that didn't mean she would like her music. Enrique turned the page. Now he was pulling off her blouse. She didn't wear a bra, and her breasts were round with very dark nipples, like targets—which was probably helpful for babies who are trying to hit the nipple, seeing this big target. But did that mean that the notion of the target was something people were born with, or were all those bow-and-arrow targets stuffed with straw and left out behind the gym to get ruined in the rain based on nipples? The world was just too weird sometimes.

She crawled onto the hood of the sports car, a Corvette maybe or a Z car, and all her clothes were off, and the policeman stood over her. He was blond, too, and had stripped down to his underwear. But he was wearing bikini underwear. There was no way a cop would wear bikini underwear, which made it all seem fake. Not that Enrique had thought a lot about what underwear was on underneath a policeman's uniform, but bikinis couldn't be regulation. Besides, what about traffic? Some driver would see this naked woman on a Corvette or maybe a Z car with a policeman standing there in bikini underwear, and crash, there he would go right off a rocky precipice to a sure death, unless he was somehow saved, but Enrique wanted to keep the X-Men out of this.

He heard footsteps in the hall and quickly shut off the flashlight and closed his eyes. The door to his room opened. "Finally," his mother said, and then the door shut.

Enrique closed the magazine and slid it back beneath his pillow. He closed his eyes and saw the policeman and the woman driver smiling at him. Both were blondes, but in his mind he worked to change the woman into Rita Schaefer and the man into Enrique Calzado. His imagination only partially cooperated. Rita's head and his, too, appeared on the grown-up bodies, but they were still blondes. And still smiling, Enrique noted. He pushed his imagination forward, but it just seemed too rude to have Rita lie on the hood of the car, which would likely be hot and definitely be hard. Instead, he had her come home with him, and she did. By the time he pictured Rita and himself in their house, they were both clothed and in their own bodies, although Enrique still had the policeman's hair. His parents had made them a big meal, and Cecilia had set up a stool so they each could climb up onto the counter and stick their feet in the sink. "I like your family's custom," the blond and debonair Enrique said to her. Drifting toward sleep, he felt himself smiling, knowing that he and Rita were never going to make it into his bedroom in this fantasy, although he kept wanting to picture her climbing up the rails. His mother was saying, "You two look as happy as your father and me back when we were young."

"Million years ago," his father said. "Her pet sabertooth used to jump up in my lap." His mother pretended to be angry while the others laughed, melodic laughter, rising and falling, an intake and exhale, that led Enrique into sleep.

Rita found herself alone in the house and snooping around Heart's room. It was Saturday, and her mother and Heart were both working. Heart had a checkered quilt over her double bed, which was centered in the room, against no wall. The slope of the roof wouldn't permit it. Rita had to duck to get past the bed to her dresser, which was an antique.

She went through Heart's few socks, her underwear, her folded shirts. She found one letter, from Heart's mother in Carbondale, Illinois. A terribly boring letter about people Rita didn't know, weather that had already come and gone in a place she had never seen. One sentence stood out for her, and she memorized it. "Cordelia is retrenched in the old ways." Part of her fascination centered on "the old ways" and how poor Cordelia might be retrenched in them—Rita couldn't help wondering.

The closet held four shapeless dresses, but high on a shelf at the back of the closet she found a box of photographs. All of them were family pictures. Black and white. She could not find one with Heart holding Mr. Gene, which was what she wanted. She understood this while she went through the photos. She wanted to find some evidence of Heart's attachment to Mr. Gene—or better, evidence of his attachment to her. Instead, there was Heart with her parents, her brothers and sisters. All of the photos were family pictures. Black and white. In one a boy stood in the foreground, his hand raised against the sun, while Heart and another girl—a prettier one—stood in the background smiling on. Rita wondered if the other girl was Cordelia. Heart had hardly changed at all. None of her siblings resembled her. It must have been difficult being the ugly one. The only thing interesting about any of the photographs was the constant smile on Heart's face. She didn't seem like the sort of person who'd had a happy childhood, but the photos argued otherwise. For that matter, she seemed happy now, although Rita couldn't see why. The bookstore had to be boring, and it didn't make much profit, and then she'd come home to Gay and Rita. Maybe Rita's life was dull, too, but she knew it could be interesting later. And her mother was pretty, and interesting things happened to pretty people. But Heart's life didn't seem to have any possibilities. Except for Mr. Gene. He must keep her happy, Rita thought, and she shuffled through the pictures again for his image.

As she was returning the pictures to the closet shelf, she glanced through one of the dormer windows and spotted Cecilia below, crossing the buckling sidewalk.

Rita ran down the stairs and to the door, which she threw open. Enrique stood beside his sister, although somehow Rita hadn't seen him from above.

And his hair! His hair was blond. She stared through the screen door at it the way one might stare at a deformity.

"My brother wanted to come with me," Cecilia said to her on the porch.

Rita opened the screen door and held it for them. Enrique was very pretty, his features both soft and angular, his eyes a sweet shade of brown, but he didn't have that boyness about him that attracted girls, that insolence and cockiness—with or without blond hair. "Hi, Enrique," she said.

He immediately glanced at his sister.

"He wants to be called Henry," she said.

"It's my name, actually," he said to Rita, smiling.

"I thought your name was Enrique," Rita said.

"That's Spanish for Henry. You can call me that if you're speaking Spanish. But if you're speaking English, which we are, then I go by Henry." He threw open his hands as if he'd just solved a riddle.

Rita led them inside and got Cokes from the refrigerator. Rita, in Spanish, would still be Rita, they guessed, while Cecilia, if it was Spanish, might be Ceal or Cee-cee in English, which they all thought too girly. In her mother's house, a person was called whatever she wanted to be called. Rita didn't find it hard to call Cecilia's brother Henry, although Cecilia obviously didn't like to.

They didn't know quite what to do together, stumbling over conversation in the kitchen and then in the living room. Their usual topic of late—Rudy Salazar—did not feel like something they could bring up around Henry. Finally, while Henry went to get another Coke from the refrigerator, Cecilia pulled Rita into her room and shut the door. She confided that she had agreed to bring him along so they could work to "cure" him.

"Have you shown it to him yet?" Rita asked.

"I tucked it beneath his pillow, but I haven't noticed any change, except he dyed his hair, which I don't think the magazine made him do, and he decided he wanted to come with me to see you. I thought maybe you could cure him without the magazine, but I brought it just in case."

"We're not going to look at it *with* him, are we?" The idea horrified Rita.

Cecilia just raised and lowered her eyebrows mischievously. "We need to get him *interested*," she said, unbuttoning her blouse. "Just *interested*." She pulled the magazine out. "If we can get him interested, then we don't have to use the magic sex magazine."

"What are you guys laughing about?" Henry called. "Where are you?"

Rita went to her knees on the floor and lifted the dollhouse. "Put it under here," she said. Cecilia slid the magazine under the base of the house.

Henry knocked on the bedroom door. "You guys got your clothes on and stuff?"

They laughed again and told him to come in. He carried Cokes for all of them. "What are you laughing about?" he asked again.

"Our dirty minds," Rita said, which made their laughter rise.

Henry smiled at this and handed them their sodas. "Like what?" he said, but they didn't have an answer and just giggled. He looked over Rita's room. He couldn't believe he was actually standing in her room. She slept on that bed. Under those sheets.

Cecilia said, "It's awfully hot. Don't you think we should change?"

"Slip into something more comfortable?" Rita said. Almost anything either of them said made them laugh.

Henry laughed with them, although he had no idea why. "Slip into what?" he said.

Cecilia waved her arms to make him leave, a hand-flapping gesture their mother used when she wanted him to go outside and get out of her hair.

"I've got three Cokes here," he said.

"We'll be out in a minute," Cecilia said.

He stepped into the hall, stood next to the closed door a few seconds, then carried the Cokes back into the kitchen. He put two of them back in the refrigerator, which was packed with stuff. Had he eaten today? He didn't think he had, but he wasn't hungry. The excitement of being in Rita's kitchen overwhelmed his hunger. She ate at this table. She put her feet in that sink. She walked barefoot over this floor to this refrigerator to eat at night. The floor was blue! And here he was, kneeling before a refrigerator packed with food, but he wasn't hungry. This was love, he had no doubt.

Then he recalled that he had eaten chorizo burritos for breakfast, and he might have had a bowl of Kix after that, but still, normally, he would have become hungry looking at all of this stuff, and he wasn't. He closed the door to the fridge and sat at the table. He had eaten a Snickers bar on the way over, but that didn't mean he wasn't in love with Rita Schaefer.

Suddenly the girls stepped into the kitchen wearing bathing suits. Henry banged his knee against the top of the table, causing his Coke to rock in its plastic bottle. "Ow," he said, rubbing his knee, but he recovered quickly. "You look great. You two. You girls. You."

Rita's bikini was two years old and cut into her neck and hips. Her stomach was not flat, and if there had been a real boy and not Cecilia's little brother in the kitchen, she would not have worn it. Cecilia had put on Rita's new one-piece, which fit like a gunnysack.

"Let's go swimming in the river," Rita said.

"You can wear your boxers," Cecilia said to him.

"Okay," he said, then thought again. "Maybe I should run home and get my trunks."

Rita said, "I think you'd look . . ." She turned to Cecilia for help. Cecilia covered her mouth and whispered "Sexy" in Rita's ear. Rita laughed and said, "I think you'd look *nice* in boxers."

"We'll meet you down there," his sister said. They left through the back door.

Enrique took a big gulp of his Coke. He was going to be with Rita in his underwear. What she had on was the same as underwear only made of waterproof material. They were going to be in their underwear together. In the river. This was no coincidence, he knew, standing as the thought came to him, banging his knee again against the table, which caused him to limp into the living room. He looked into the mirror over the couch. His hair, so blond that it was almost white, looked pretty natural, he thought, except for his dark eyebrows, which he hadn't thought about, but probably lots of people had dark brows and blond hair.

Immediately he took his shirt off. Luckily he didn't have hair on his chest, but he did have some under his arms, and it was dark—not that Rita didn't know his hair was really dark, like hers, but dying his underarm hair could have helped the illusion. Were his boxers clean? His mother had always warned him that something like this might happen, some weird circumstance where people would be staring at your underpants. How did mothers know this stuff?

Then he remembered that he had changed all his clothing before coming over with Cecilia, although it might be a good idea to get a safety pin and make sure the flap stayed shut. Maybe that was why Rita suggested he swim in his boxers, so she could get a peek! He kicked off his shoes, sat on the couch to peel off his socks, lifting his feet one at a time to check their odor. Not perfect, but hardly a menace. If Monica Gutierrez could see him now, about to strip and go to the river with a high school girl, she'd quit harassing him. Not that she had actually said anything besides that one time, but inside his head she was still harassing him.

He pulled his jeans down and tugged them off, then stood before the mirror again, checking out the flap, posing with it open, partially open, bending over—

"Hey," his sister yelled and he jumped, his hands flying to the gap in his shorts. He turned but she was calling from the back door. "You coming?"

"Just a sec," he yelled. He straightened and examined himself a final time in the mirror. Tall and blond.

He looked great.

The three of them spent the next two hours at the river, lying around on a white blanket that Rita retrieved from the house, swimming, and splashing one another. Rita did a lot of bending and posing in front of Henry, per Cecilia's instructions. Late in the day, Cecilia and Rita wading in the water and making up gossip about people in their classes, Cecilia suddenly slapped Rita's leg and whispered in her ear, "He's got a boner!"

Rita stared at Henry, who was on his back in the shallow water, his eyes half shut but jittery, like he had been watching them. His wet boxers clung to his skin and bulged in the middle. "Are you sure?" Rita asked. The erections in the magazine had a quality to them that involved defying gravity.

"I think so," Cecilia said. "See how it bumps up there."

"It would make some bump anyway, wouldn't it?"

"No, that's definitely a boner," Cecilia said. "I think."

"Make him stand up," Rita said. "Then we can tell for sure."

"You already made him stand up," Cecilia said and laughed.

Suddenly Enrique slid himself deeper into the water, immersing himself to the waist.

Cecilia pointed. "It floats," she said. She began clapping her hands. Then she grabbed Rita's wrist and they ran from the river to the house, their work completed.

Henry heard the shower from the bedroom. He had pulled his pants up over his wet underwear, but there were damp splotches right where he didn't want there to be damp splotches. "Think," he advised himself. The first thing that came to mind was how he had hiked out to the same spot in the river and looked at Rita through the window. He stepped into the kitchen and stared out the window at the mesquite tree, which was quite near where they had been swimming. This thought reminded him of what little time it took to get from his house to hers. He slipped out the back door and began running to his house. He would change and be back before they got out of the shower.

If he happened to run past the junior high track coach, Henry thought, he would no doubt be recruited, as he seemed to be flying. He felt the heat on his back, but he didn't feel especially hot. His legs carried him forward effortlessly. He wondered if serious runners felt this way all the time.

He found himself waving to people, not that many had braved the heat on a Saturday, but the few he saw he waved to. They, too, like Rita, like himself, seemed extraordinary, perfect in a way he couldn't name. Rita must like him. He wished he had the afternoon on video. He wanted to review the tape. She kept sneaking looks at him. Suddenly he saw a woman standing before a window in her house, spraying the glass and wiping, the bottle of blue spray nestled in her right hand, her reflection in the glass also wiping, and through the glass, just visible, another person wiping, getting the spots on the other side. How incredible it was, this woman, her reflection, and it looked like her husband, yes! her husband, all wiping at the window at the same time. A thing of beauty. Rita liked him, wanted to be his girlfriend. Every step revealed new wonders.

The girls showered and dressed, but they could not find Henry. "Is he hiding?" Rita asked. "Did we embarrass him?"

"He embarrasses easy," Cecilia said, "but usually it doesn't bother him." They decided Cecilia should take the magazine back to the house just in case this day's work didn't stick. "The combination of live models," Cecilia said, "and illustrations of the actual deed," she tapped the magazine before folding it once and jamming it in her purse, "should fix him good, don't you think?"

A knock came from the front door before Rita could respond. She wanted to keep the magazine for a while, but she did not want to admit the desire, even to Cecilia. She stepped into the living room and looked through one of the tall windows. Henry had run home, put on fresh clothes, and come back. "Here he is," Rita said. When she opened the door, Henry scooped her up in his arms and spun her on the porch. He kissed her. A little, dry peck, but right on the lips.

"Cokes?" Rita said, turning away from him, the feel of his lips lingering on hers, a strange texture to it, like she had been kissed by a sweater. She took Cecilia's hand and led her directly to the bathroom.

"He's crazy about you," Cecilia said. She put her hands on her hips and ran in place. "He's completely changed. I even think his hair is starting to look good, don't you? Funny, but good, once you get used to it."

"I don't know," Rita said, unsure whether to feel happy or wary. It had not felt like a kiss. More like a swipe.

Then Cecilia said, "Oh, Rita, you've cured him."

Hearing that gave her such a heady feeling, the feeling she might have had if it had been some other boy who had grabbed her, whirled her, and kissed her lips. She felt things moving inside herself, and she suddenly could not stop smiling.

They went back to the kitchen, where Henry had opened three Coke bottles and poured them into glasses. His hair looked fine to her now. Just took some getting used to. He really was pretty.

"Pop?" he said, offering a sweating glass.

"Sure," Rita said, and took it from him. Their hands touched exchanging the glass of Coke.

Over the course of the afternoon, without a word on the subject spoken, Henry Calzado became Rita Schaefer's boyfriend.

14

Like everyone else in Apuro, Antonio Nieves normally walked across river, but this afternoon he had driven his Yugo to Persimmon in order to have the spare tire repaired. He invited Rudy to join him for a drive around town after work and a lift home.

Antonio set Rudy up in the rear of the diner, a ladder-back chair situated beside the greasy screen door that overlooked the alley. "You can catch a breeze here," Antonio said, then he hurried off to haul in a big tray of dirty dishes to the sink. Rudy had a textbook to read about the Civil War. He didn't like people to see him doing schoolwork, but he had to do some if he wanted to play basketball. He tried to focus on the Battle of Gettysburg until Antonio swung by again. This time he heaved a great gray rack of plastic cups through the swinging metal doors. It looked like hard work, but that was just what Antonio wanted him to think. Antonio was probably showing off. Still, he was more interesting than the Civil War.

Antonio wore the Whole Earth T-shirt that he claimed he had bought for a quarter at a lawn sale. White originally, the shirt had turned gray with sweat. The hairnet that he rarely took off had a silver safety pin through the netting on the side, just above his ear. The pin held a couple of little figures meant to go on a charm bracelet, a tiny silver car and an equally tiny Sacred Heart.

The cook, a big Mexican in a sleeveless T-shirt, with a tattoo of an eagle on his shoulder, had a hairnet identical to Antonio's. It had never occurred to Rudy that Antonio was required to wear the hairnet at work. "Pete's a genius with a spatula," Antonio said of the cook during one of his passes through. "Don't call him Pedro unless you want to lose your . . . Ah, you could probably take him, but he'd carve a piece outta you. Learned to cook at La Tuna. Did two years for smuggling *mota* and resisting arrest. Used to be a major *pachuco en* El Paso. Don't call him a low rider, either. He's picky about what you call him."

Antonio had another two hours of work, and evidently he had decided to entertain Rudy all that time, despite the textbook Rudy obviously needed to read. Twice Antonio gestured for Rudy to come to the swinging doors to check out girls, the first an Anglo woman in a short skirt that showed off her thighs, the second a young Chicana smoking a cigarette in a booth with two other women. A few minutes later, Antonio put a clean plate still steaming from the dishwasher in Rudy's hand. "Trust me," he said. "I got an eye for this. Only stuff nobody even touched." He scraped a half portion of french fries from a plate, carefully avoiding a smear of catsup and the ashes and butt of a cigarette. In another minute he added a slab of ham from another plate, then half a grilled cheese.

"I eat like a fucking king here," Antonio said. "Doesn't cost me *nada*. Honest to God. I eat here, take home stuff, get freebies on my days off."

Rudy took a bite of the grilled cheese and nodded to express his approval. He hadn't eaten since lunch, when he had commandeered the tray of a freshman and stuffed down a lousy cafeteria hamburger. The diner had good food.

"Told you, *ese*," Antonio said. "You keep eating. I'll keep shoveling it your way."

Antonio had two modes of behavior, his happy, hustling, "everything's cool" disposition, and then the dark anger that came when he drank. Maybe it came at other times as well, but Rudy had only witnessed it when Antonio was loaded, which was often enough. Now he was busy convincing Rudy what a great job he had; later he would drink and curse his stinking, sweaty work.

Rudy ate and watched. He read about Lee and Grant and Abraham Fucking Lincoln. At eleven he went out to the Yugo and sat while Antonio mopped the floor to finish his shift. Antonio exited the greasy door wearing a fresh shirt and carrying the Whole Earth T-shirt, which appeared to be soaked. He also had a six-pack of beer. He swung open the driver's-side door, took a clothes hanger that had hung over a rear window, and slid the wet T-shirt over the hanger.

"Washed it with dish detergent," he said. "Saves me washing my work clothes at home. I take a hanger with me even when I walk." He handed the six-pack to Rudy. "They let me keep stuff in the cooler. I got a cardboard box with my name on it. Got some *naranjas* and stuff in there if you're still hungry." He started the Yugo and pulled out of the lot. "Pop me one, *ese*."

Rudy opened a beer for each of them.

"Bought Lite because it was on sale. You don't mind, do you. Figured, free *cerveza*, hey, who's gonna complain it's Lite? Not Salazar."

Because Rudy didn't drive, each time he was in a car he studied the driver's actions, the signaling, the glances in mirrors, the shifting of gears, the flicking of lights, the braking and accelerating. People claimed it was simple, but he worried that you had to start young to master it. He said, "Where we going?"

"Cruising," Antonio replied, backing the Yugo out of its parking place near the alley. "See what's up." Then, as if intentionally to contradict himself, he turned off the lights and put the car in park. "*Esperamos un poco*," he said. We're going to wait a little.

Rudy thought maybe the car's engine needed to get warm or some other mystery of automobiles had come into play, but then he saw a late model Oldsmobile, a low rider, creeping down the road past the post office. Antonio evidently wished to avoid them.

"Those *cholos* just looking for somebody to blow away," he said. "*No quiero ser un* moving target. They make fun of my car, anyway."

Rudy turned in his seat to get a better look at the Oldsmobile, which hunkered low to the street, the windows dark, something shiny tied to the top of the radio antenna, the music loud but impossible to decipher, just a heavy bass line thundering across the parking lot. "You know them?"

"They're like you, *ese*, got a noodle in their heads about their *turf*. Whole planet's out there waiting for somebody to take it, and they're here shooting each other about who went to whose party in whose part of *este* shithole town. You follow me?"

"No," Rudy said. The car finally disappeared.

"I was stopped at the traffic light on Rio Road, and they pull up next to me—maybe not them in that car but some car like it—and they stare in at me real nasty-like, so I say, 'Yo, homes, what's going on?' And this fucking *cholo* guy in the passenger seat—the whole car's full of guys—so this fuckwater in the passenger seat says, 'That a car or a washing machine? You put wheels *en la lavadora de tu mama*?' They all laughing, and you know me, I hate this car, but hey, it's my car, so I say, 'Fuck you and good night, 'cause the light's changed anyway, and I'm heading home, but these dudes pull up even *con el* Yugo *otra vez*, and this same guy's pointing a big-ass pistol at my face." Antonio shook his head, turned the lights on, and twisted in the seat to look behind the car as he backed up.

"So I hit the brake," he said, braking as he said it, " 'cause I can't outrun a fart in this car, but they brake, too, and I know I'm *un muerto* motherfucker, but I hear somebody say my name. Some *cholo* in the backseat knows me and saves my butt." He spun the car around and headed out of the lot, drinking from his beer as he drove.

Rudy drank too, surreptitiously watching Antonio shifting gears, accelerating and braking. Something about the incident Antonio described nagged him. "That same car?" he asked.

Antonio shrugged. "You'd think I'da memorized that car, but I was concentrating on saving my *cojones* and trying not to piss on the upholstery. Seriously, I had to stop at the *campo santo* and piss on a grave. Couldn't make it home."

"We ought to fuck 'em up, then," Rudy said.

"I just told you I couldn't pick out the car—"

"You've got to make somebody pay for that kind of shit."

Antonio didn't respond. He made another turn, then slowed in front of a trailer court. "I used to have a girl lived in there. Met her at the diner. Lucinda." He shook his head. "Shoulda married that girl. I'd see her face and I'd—"

"What are they up to?" Rudy asked. "They just look for anybody to blow away? Where's the pleasure in that?"

Antonio turned from the trailer park. "They want to get even with somebody, but they don't know who, so they figure anybody'll do. Mostly they fuck up other Chicanos, *como tú y yo*. We ever done anything to them?"

"Not yet," Rudy said.

Antonio stared at him a moment, then pointed to a trailer. "Right there. Lucinda Olivares. Her old trailer. We broke up a while back, and last week she moved. One time we stayed up all night playing rummy. Stupid game, but what the heck, it was fun. She's gone to Washington State now." He shifted into gear again. "Know why I didn't marry her? I thought she wasn't really *bella*, you know? Didn't have the hot bod."

"Next time you've got a problem," Rudy said, "you let me know."

"Yeah, *bueno*, shit," Antonio said, and he directed the car toward the highway. "Might as well head home, no?"

Rudy knew any gangs in Persimmon would have to be minor league, anyway, but the idea of taking out anyone handy offended him. To cover your eyes and swing blindly, then peek to see what your victim looked like—he couldn't see the pleasure in that. What was the point? It might feed a certain curiosity, but it couldn't touch on that deeper satisfaction. They played with violence, and that pissed him off.

Rudy had designated two specific people for violence, and whatever he wound up doing to them, he would feel satisfaction from it. Rhonda Hassinger, who had put her nose up the wrong *culo*, and Cecilia Calzado, the carrier of a generational virus, one that would inflict Rudy no more. Waiting for the right moment, letting them stew, having patience—these were central aspects of the deeper pleasure of fucking someone over.

The thirty-mile drive to Apuro took most of an hour on the bad roads. They drank the beers. Antonio lost his edge of optimism. "My life got nothing in the middle of it, you know? Like this guy works days, Anglo but *suave*, got the same job as me, but this fucker drives a Cadillac, nineteen fifty-something white Caddy. Works on it every day. Got the tuck-'n'-roll job from Juárez with real leather. Even got a CD player in it." He hammered his fist against the plastic dash. "You and me, we need something *como la* Caddy."

Rudy shook his head. "I got plenty," he said.

"Like what, *ese*?"

Rudy didn't answer. He could not explain the dimensions of his life, the pressures of his dominion, the steel band that inhabited him, the rigorous, volatile demands of his soul.

"*No hay nada*," Antonio insisted. There's nothing.

Rudy arrived home tired and restless, annoyed with Antonio's incessant chatter. The house was dark. He paused in the doorway to let his eyes adjust, then tossed the textbook on the dining table. He had finished the chapter, but couldn't understand why he'd been asked to read it. What difference did the old wars make now? Cities had been razed, brother had taken up arms against brother. So what else was new?

He knew enough to pass the test, and that was all he wanted. He waited to give Antonio time to pour himself into bed, then he headed back out the door to make his rounds. It was after one in the morning, but he performed his duty. No one could say there was nothing at the center of his existence.

A half hour later, he settled down on the couch, which his mother had made for him. But he still felt uneasy. If the textbook hadn't been so boring, he would have gotten it out and read by flashlight. Something to pass the time, to encourage sleep. He felt his thoughts turning to the future, not to playing basketball or getting even with the reporter bitch, but to some more distant time, after school. He loathed school but it provided him many of the things he needed. School and Apuro, but what was the value of one without the other? He would have to get a job or find a way to make money without working.

He rolled over on the couch, as if he were turning his back on the future. He didn't want to consider it. Didn't want to see himself as some low rider with a gun, harassing complete strangers just to get off. It denigrated who he was.

He got up, found the flashlight. He kept a stack of magazines and catalogs that he had stolen from Persimmon mailboxes, a stunt undertaken out of boredom. The magazines interested him not at all, and most of the catalogs were equally worthless. He had studied one that showed Anglo women in fancy underwear, but ultimately it had enraged him. He hated the women's smug non-smiles, the skimpy, worthless panties that cost more than his shoes. He'd torn it up and put a match to it.

But there was one catalog he liked to look at. It shamed him, and he did not look at it when others could witness it, but he was drawn to it. From the bottom of the stack, he withdrew The Sharper Image. On the cover, a ball with a number, like a pool ball, but if you studied it, you discovered it was a gearshift knob for a car. Inside the catalog, a woman held a white telephone with a short antenna to her ear, a garden hose in her other hand. The phone didn't have a cord. She could walk around anywhere with it, could take a crap with it. Her shoulders were bare, and the phone nestled against her bare flesh, the curves of her jaw and neck matched by the perfect angles of the white plastic.

Rudy's favorite page had no people. It showed a black floor. Situated on the floor, a device shaped like a horseshoe, only elegant and elongated, too large for any hoof. At the top, rising above the horseshoe, a chrome circle shimmered in an invisible light. It was calibrated, white numbers appearing on its black face, forming a circle within the circle. Centered and written in red, the words "Health o Meter." A scale. Nothing more than a scale, despite its name. Nevertheless, the shapes hovering one above the other on the black floor, the orbit of numbers within the chrome circle, the curving top and tapering base, the thin red indicator that would sweep over the dark face, these excited in Rudy a nameless desire, which he reshaped into a craving he could endure.

He imagined a woman's naked feet on the scale, imagined water running down her pale thighs, dripping from the ends of her hair, from the tips of her nipples, but some part of him knew the woman was secondary. The scale itself had given him his erection, that perfect circle, those curves and elevated angles, the black and white beauty of it. It cost more than he could spend in a month—unless, of course, he were to purchase the scale itself, slide it beneath his own bare feet, watch the red needle rise to indicate the number that indicated his weight in the world. The Health o Meter, as if health were a thing that could be not only measured but won over, that could be identified and then seduced or stolen, that, for eighty-four dollars and ninety-five cents, could be owned.

15

Her mother's tap on her door found Rita writing in Mr. Gene's notebook. It was her day to see her father, which meant she'd had Mr. Gene's list a month now. During that time she had acquired a boyfriend, which had only made her more curious about Mr. Gene. Although she liked having a boyfriend, they didn't have all that much to do or talk about while they were together. She looked forward more to talking to Cecilia about Henry than actually to being with Henry.

But Mr. Gene, she knew, made Heart happy. Rita no longer had any intention of returning the notebook. She had erased "Make love to R" and substituted "Ravish R," which had a more literary ring to it. Then she had reinserted "Make love to R" so there could be no confusion. She then added "Kiss R," wondering whether she shouldn't erase the other two so that the kissing came before ravishing. But the paper was already thin from her earlier erasure. She wrote "Make out with R" and "Give R scarves." She wished she had taken the scarves from the truck along with the notebook. She would wear one and dare Heart or Mr. Gene or anyone to say a word.

Henry would not likely ever give her scarves. She couldn't entirely take Henry Calzado seriously. But he was good practice. After all, she didn't really have any idea what Mr. Gene was like, only that he was shy and that he liked Heart. The rest she had made up herself, which didn't necessarily make it less true.

"You ready?" Gay said, appearing in the doorway. "It's a hot one," she said. "Heart will take you."

Heart accompanied Rita to the Nissan, and Rita tried to speculate whether Mr. Gene would prefer Heart to herself. She was fifteen and Heart was over thirty. Heart was ugly but thin, while Rita was young but heavy, and if not exactly pretty, still better looking than Heart. Rita knew she had big thighs, but her ankles were average, and she wasn't really fat. Her mother and father thought she was beautiful, but then they evidently thought each other beautiful. Her father was too sloppy to be beautiful—sloppy wasn't the right word because he was actually very neat around the house. But there was something lazy about his looks, a softness in the eyes and he had unruly hair. He didn't take himself seriously enough to be beautiful.

Her mother did not have that problem, and she was pretty, Rita knew, but not beautiful. She was thin enough, and maybe she was even pretty enough, but she was too aware of it. She was the same way about being different from the whole main gaggle of people out in the world. Rita's father was different because he couldn't help it and didn't know how to be any other way, but her mother made a point of being different, refusing to have a car or television, unwilling to even come by the motel and shake hands with Rita's father. As Rita saw it, her mother was the same way about her looks, wearing clothes that exaggerated everything—like that dress she had worn into the river. No one truly beautiful would feel she had to wear such a thing. Anyone would look great in it, even Heart.

She glanced over at Heart, who was shifting from second into third, her bangs flying back in the wind of the open window, a drop of sweat perched on the tip of her nose. Maybe the dress wouldn't help Heart all that much. Why, then, did Mr. Gene love her? Why did he prefer Heart to someone like Rita—not a beauty, she conceded, but young, with some looks, and long legs, even if they were fat.

She tried to imagine Heart without hair, back when she'd had chemotherapy. She had seen the breast that had been cut up, a scar like a frown above the nipple, making the breast pucker. Heart put her elbows against the steering wheel and hunched forward. She would look awful in the dress, Rita decided. Her mother had looked wonderful, but Rita had known why she was wearing it. To be with some man, some man Rita would never meet. Maybe that was why Rita had a crush on Mr. Gene. He was the one man in town she knew for a fact her mother was not fucking. Thinking this startled her. Putting it into words, even without actually speaking them, made her chest wobble, but she could not question their validity. She knew, of course, that most men didn't have a chance with her mother, but she could never be certain who did and who didn't. Except for Mr. Gene. Gay would never fuck Heart's boyfriend. Rita knew that much about her mother.

Her father was sitting on the concrete stoop outside his motel room. From inside the room, she could hear the television tuned to a baseball game. He was reading a paperback book.

"I thought we'd drive up to the Gila Wilderness," he said to her as she got out of the car. He offered Heart an odd little half-salute, then to Rita he said, "Give me a hug."

She bent down and put her arms around him. "I don't want to go anywhere," she said. "I'm wearing my bathing suit."

Sander shrugged and climbed to his feet. "The pool's clean," he said. "I always check it."

"Why? You never swim."

"Habit." He had already started walking toward the chain-link fence that surrounded the pool. The motel was in the shape of an L, and the pool, bordered by a parking lot and driveway, was centered in the remaining space. "Besides, I swim now and again."

"Why don't you ever swim with me?" She'd already tugged off her shirt and was unbuttoning her cutoffs.

He opened the chain-link gate for her. "I'm always working when I'm with you."

"You're not working now."

He waved his book at her. "I'm reading. Trying to improve my mind." He said more, but she dove into the cool water and lost his voice.

She often tried to imagine what her life would be like if her parents had not divorced. It was difficult to see how the two would combine. Her father's place was nothing like the Persimmon house. It was called "ranch style," like Cecilia and Henry's house, which seemed to mean single-story with low ceilings, cheap carpet, and virtually identical to every other house on the street. While her mother's house was full of light, the Bloom house seemed always dim and slightly dingy. Not dirty. Sander had a thing about dirty dishes and the trash. He washed while he cooked, and he'd empty the garbage when all it had in it was a milk carton and a couple of candy wrappers. Clean, but dingy. The furniture was cheap, most of it homemade—wood frames and lots of foam pads, that kind of thing. Only his stereo, which was old but first-rate, and the furniture in Rita's room were even remotely suitable. He'd purchased her a canopy bed back when she was eight, as well as a matching dresser and vanity.

Her father's yards, both front and back, were as green and groomed as Gay's were sparse and abandoned. His work had started as a yard service, and he still liked working in dirt.

July—her month to visit him in Albuquerque—was a busy time for the pool service. Rita would ride in the bucket seat of his pickup, wearing just her bathing suit, her back stuck to the vinyl seat, one foot lolling out the window, the hot desert air whipping her hair and chafing her skin, the radio blasting Golden Oldies. Sander liked to sing along with the radio, especially old Motown songs. Even now, in equally hot Persimmon, those months with her father seemed sultry and decadent, as if they were desperadoes brazenly pool-hopping across the west, or lovers going from one secret place to the next, or wanderers in a desert land that, to their enduring bewilderment, held one oasis after another.

In reality, her father couldn't afford to take off work for her monthly visit, and tried to make the best of it by letting her swim while he worked. Every night, after Rita was in bed—or was supposed to be in bed—he'd lie on the living room floor in front of his stereo and listen to jazz, his beloved CDs, smoking a joint, one knee raised so he could tap his sock-covered foot. But he did not sing along, not even when Billie Holiday sang "Willow Weep for Me," or Sarah Vaughn sang "Cry Me a River"—songs even Rita knew the words to. One night she asked him why.

"Walking around, driving around, I sing because the music makes me happy," he explained. "At night, I listen because the music makes me sad. I don't sing while I'm sad."

"Why do you want to be sad?"

"I don't *want* to be sad, but I *need* to be sad. Otherwise I more or less forget my life."

Rita kept the coins from her allowance in an old five-gallon aquarium that had a crack on one end. "You know what they say," her father said to her once, sticking his face into the top of the aquarium. "Save all the change in your pockets—never spend a dime of it—and after ten years, you should have one big hunk of metal." He raised his head and looked at her. "Spend it now and again, you could have, you know, tunes, food, adventures—a life, basically."

"You blow all of your money on pot," she said self-righteously.

"Touché," he said. "Bingo. The girl has hit the bull's-eye. Why, if I quit smoking, I could save up enough money to . . ." He frowned and raised his eyebrows in mock consideration. "To redecorate! Down with the old paint, and up with wallpaper—pink flamingo wallpaper in Rita's room!"

"That sounds great," she said. "Do it."

"No, no, no. I've got a better idea." He sat on her bed, pulled a Baggie of pot from his shirt pocket, and started rolling a joint. "With my new-found savings—" he paused to wave the baggie. "This stuff is already paid for, you understand. No point in wasting it. But now that I've turned over a new leaf, so to speak, I can take all that money and—"

Rita cut him off. "Put your daughter through college."

He blushed. She hadn't meant it to be a mean thing to say, but it embarrassed him. He tucked the pot back into his pocket. "Save your metal, if that's what you want to do. Never hurts to have a little silver stashed away." He quickly left the room.

But she wasn't saving the money because she wanted to buy something, not even something as abstract and unimaginable as an education. She didn't know why she kept all the money she retrieved from the pools.

After a dozen laps, she put her elbows on the ledge of the motel pool near his lawn chair, and asked him about living with Gay and Heart on the commune.

He lowered his book and gave her a suspicious look. "What about it?" He shifted in his seat—a short aluminum chair with cucumber green webbing.

"Why you and mom broke up," she said.

His face flattened. "Aw hell, Rita, do we have to talk about this now? I haven't even had a joint yet. It isn't even noon. Don't you want to eat first?"

She shook her head to indicate no. "Mom told me some stuff," she said.

"She did?" He looked at his paperback a final time, then dog-eared the spot. She finally caught the title: *The Mismeasure of Man.* "You have to understand," he began, putting his hand to his face to shield the sun from his eyes. Then he dropped the hand and shook his head sadly, tapping the book against his thigh. He took a deep breath and edged out of the chair, squatting on the pool concrete. "People don't always know why they do things. They just act and then try to make sense of it."

Rita shifted her elbows on the concrete ledge of the pool to get comfortable, her chin resting on her folded hands. She could tell from the way he squatted and from the deliberate gestures that this was something he took seriously. His hands were especially large and dark from the sun, the hair silver below the knuckles from years of chlorination, glistening in the sunlight just above her head.

"Heart and I have always liked each other. We were good friends back then." He dragged the lawn chair over and resettled in it, but as soon as he began speaking again, he slid back out of it into a squat. "Your mother . . . oh, I don't know. Between them there was some small little bad wish. Not now, I don't imagine, but back then . . . neither one would admit it, but . . . and Gay being pregnant just made it worse. She felt fat, and . . . " He had begun staring at the sky, and when his eyes settled again on her in the sky blue water, he seemed startled. "Maybe I just imagined that," he said, and pushed himself back into the chair, squirming now, sliding the chair back away from the water.

He tried to rake his hand through his hair, but it was too tangled. Sliding from the chair to his knees, he dipped his head into the water—his whole head all the way into the water to his neck. He came up snorting and shaking his head like a dog, spraying her. "Your mother and Heart were pals even then," he said, then spewed away the water that dribbled down his lips. "Really. They were." He sat again in the green lawn chair. "Look, I hate to say this, but your mother will tell what she wants you to hear. What did she say about all this?"

Rita rolled her eyes. She was already tired of his worried response. "She said there was a bet in a card game—"

He blanched and grabbed both arms of the lawn chair. "That? She used that?" He raised himself up inches above the seat of the lawn chair, as if he were about to leap into the water.

"She said you took off Heart's wig."

"It was meant as a joke." He stared at her oddly, a disconnected look, and dropped back into the chair. "I'll tell you the whole story, all right?" His face regained its color, and he may have been blushing again—it was hard to tell in the bright sunlight. "I'll give you the whole lowdown." As he said this, he seemed to come back to himself. "Not just your mother's idea of the truth." He shook his wet head and rose from the chair in one motion, as if the force of his thoughts had lifted him. "Climb on out, Rita. Let me chlorinate here. But I *will* tell you. You can bet I'll tell you."

"Dad," she said. "This is the Desert Oasis. We're not working."

He stared at her a second before laughing. There was something in that stare, but she couldn't put her finger on it immediately. Before she knew it, he'd dipped his hand into his pocket. "Here goes," he said and tossed a handful of sparkling coins into the air.

While she was under, snatching the quarters and dimes as they floated down, she realized what she'd seen in his face. He had been afraid. Because he'd forgotten where they were? She wondered, but she couldn't answer. She retrieved the silver coins first, surfacing several times for air. Before she dove for the pennies, she spotted a bill floating near the drain. A five-dollar bill. She tried to show it to him, but he'd gone to his room. His paperback lay on the concrete in a puddle of water.

.   .   .

In the truck, he became cross with her. She'd left her shirt and cutoffs by the pool, and they'd had to return to get them. Then when she had gone to his room to dress, she'd merely slipped them on over her wet suit. "Christ, Rita," he said. "I don't see how we can go to a decent restaurant with you dressed like that."

She glanced down at her shirt, the wet bathing top showing through. "I don't want to go to a decent restaurant. I want to go to the Pizza Palace," she said. The Palace was her favorite restaurant, but it was in El Paso, thirty miles away.

"Even if the restaurant doesn't care, you should care," he said.

He stopped at the Conoco next to the river to get gas, and went inside while a boy filled the tank. Rita refused to get out, sitting in the truck with the windows up, sweating and listening to rock and roll on the radio, hoping to run the battery down, thinking that if she died of heat prostration he'd really be sorry.

When they were on the road again, she finally had a rejoinder ready. "I, at least, plan to comb my hair," she said.

This seemed to get to him. He grew quiet, and she caught him surreptitiously trying to run his fingers through his wet locks.

However, she realized she'd left her brush in her bag at the motel. She threw open the glove box to look for a brush. A Baggie of pot rolled forward, and she had to catch it before it fell to the floor.

"Close that," her father said.

There were rolling papers in the glove box, maps of New Mexico and Colorado, the truck's registration sheet, matchbooks from Sugar's Tavern, Boogie's Head Shop, and The Inn on the Square in Santa Fe.

"Close that, *please*," he said.

"What were you doing in Santa Fe?" she asked. Beneath the maps were two more paperbacks: *On the Road* and *What We Talk About When We Talk About Love*.

"I like Santa Fe," he said. "I go there all the time. Now close the glove box."

A Victoria's Secret catalog lay beneath the novels, and beneath the catalog, condoms in their little packages with pointy edges, like the little packets of crackers you got in a restaurant.

She shoved everything back in and shut the glove box door. They rode silently with the windows down to the Pizza Palace, then sat opposite each other in a garish green and orange booth. After they ordered, Sander began his version of the story Gay had told Rita the month before. "Heart came to the farm—that's what we called the commune. Heart came a month or so after I did, then she brought your mother out there a while after that. So I knew Heart before I met your mom. Heart and I were buddies. She had a thing for this guy who lived there, too, a friend of mine—"

"Miguel Delgado?" Rita said.

"She told you his name?" he said, disgusted. "Miguel is blameless in this. No matter what anybody says." He shook his head and covered one eye with the palm of his hand.

Rita slid her plate toward the pizza that had just been set in front of them.

"That was fast," her father said to the waitress, who only smiled in response, revealing a gold tooth. What a strange thing to have in your mouth, Rita thought. The waitress sliced the pizza with a roller cutter. Sander remained silent until she left, as if she might be a spy.

He trimmed the cheese away from two slices, then commenced talking again. "That night . . . was I up to the night of the card game? Heart, that night, was three sheets to the wind, which is how in polite conversation you say that someone was stinking drunk. You're not going running to Heart with this, are you?"

"No," Rita said. "Were you drunk, too?"

He merely gave her a look. "We were all playing cards. Heart and your mother had taught Miguel and me to play bridge, and then made us be partners. We rarely won, which suited all of us. Neither Heart nor your mother cared for losing. Have they taught you bridge?"

"Nuh-uh," Rita said.

"I'll teach you. I play by a whole different set of conventions now." He shook his head, and took a tiny bite of pizza. "Heart wanted to make a funny bet, and we let her. Your mother didn't want me to agree to the bet, but I didn't know that. *She* agreed to it, but I wasn't supposed to. If Heart hadn't been . . . damaged, you know, the cancer . . . Sometimes a person has a problem and finds a way to make it work to her advantage."

"What was the bet?"

He nodded and sighed. "It was about all of us staying together. Getting a place together. If they won, we were going to leave the commune but share a house. The four of us. Your mother thought I should just *understand* that she didn't like this idea." He took another chomp of pizza, looking off into the crowd of tables while he chewed. Noise from the video game began to sound like background music.

"So?" Rita said.

He pursed his lips, holding his breath, then suddenly exhaled. "The question we still had was, What if the boys won? Heart already knew she had an amazing hand, so she didn't care what it was. I came up with Heart taking off her wig. It just occurred to me, so I blurted it out. Everybody thought it was funny. But your mom made some mistakes. She was real pregnant, and maybe couldn't concentrate so well. They lost when it had seemed like there was no way they could lose. Maybe I shouldn't have insisted they pay off, but I thought it would be weird not to collect. Condescending. Miguel and I almost never won, and if we didn't collect when we finally did win, then it wasn't really betting, it was something else."

"And Mom got mad?"

"Heart never put the wig back on. Wore that stupid hat to chastise us. That's the way it felt, anyway." He took another bite of pizza. "Your mother felt responsible. Heart's head wasn't like Sinead O'Connor's or that woman on the new 'Star Trek.' She was not completely bald—"

"Like a coconut," Rita said.

"Yeah, honey," he said sadly. "Like that. It turns out your mom loved Heart more than me. I don't blame her for that. Heart was dying and all. Well, not dying, obviously, but sick. Love between people is never perfect. You can't just decide to love one somebody more and another somebody less. It's messier than that. Anyway, that's the story."

He ate then, though not all that much. "I pleaded with Heart to quit wearing that stupid hat," he added.

Rita didn't say anything, comparing the two versions of the story in her head. She couldn't see any reason for the differences. She wished she could ask Heart, but she didn't really think it mattered. It all happened so long ago, why should anyone care? Another mystery of the lives of adults. Like her mother running into the river. Like Mr. Gene preferring Heart.

16

OCTOBER

It was supposed to be a middle school party. Henry never would have taken Rita to a high school party—it was just asking for trouble, wasn't it? The girl, Melody Mendez, who had been in the choir with Henry when he was in choir, had a big brother who was a junior or senior, and her brother had invited his friends.

Henry had worn a tie, which his mother had suggested, although Cecilia had told him it was a bad idea. Rita, though, when she met him at her door, had said, "Nice tie." She had on one of those dresses she called a Heart dress, which Henry liked, although no one at his school ever wore anything like them. Rita had her own style.

He had imagined the party taking place in Melody's basement, although Henry had never been to Melody's house, and almost no one in Persimmon had a basement. He pictured the party going on in her basement while her parents were upstairs reading newspapers and being tidy—maybe making cookies, which they would bring to the party, as they would always be looking for excuses to come down to the basement and make sure everyone was behaving. There would be music and not very much light. A few couples would dance, while the others would play some kind of game, like Parcheesi or poker or something involving blindfolds. He had actually hoped that there would be lemonade rather than punch. He didn't like punch, and if you spilled lemonade it didn't stain your shirt. He had worn a white shirt.

He and Rita walked from her house to Melody's—about six blocks—holding hands. This was their fifth date, but the first time they had been out together alone. Usually, Heart chaperoned and drove them about, and Cecilia often came. Twice they had gone with Rita's mother and her boyfriend Mr. Redmon, the high school basketball coach. The first time, he had encouraged Henry to come out for the team. "Your brother was a starter last year, wasn't he?" Mr. Redmon asked.

"I'm still in middle school," Henry had said. He neglected to add that he wasn't going out for the middle school team either. While he was tall enough, he didn't have much sense about physical games. Guarding people seemed rude to him in some way he knew better than to describe—all that lurking and trying to steal the ball. Baseball was even worse. He always played right field, and there was so much time between plays, he inevitably forgot about the game. Once he'd been wondering about the size of telescopes and how much of the sky they could see—he started out by wondering whether you could see more stars if you had a whole baseball park or only an infield from which to look—when a line drive hit him right in the shins and knocked his feet out, so that he fell on his face. The second baseman had run to him and dug the ball out from under his body before he could get up. "Nice stop," he said after hurling the ball back to the infield. Henry had limped for a week.

It hadn't been an easy meal, but the second time had been worse. They had gone to Rondo's, which was the best Mexican place in town, and he'd spilled salsa on his pants, right exactly in an embarrassing place to have a stain. Rita's mother kept talking about things he didn't know anything about, but he didn't want to let on that he didn't know everything. This was one of the dangers of dating an older girl, he knew. To make things worse, every time Mr. Redmon spoke, Henry felt this pain in his shins. Then Rita's mother started talking about some music only astronauts and crystal heads liked, and when she said "crystal heads," Henry said, "Geologists?" and when they'd laughed—including Rita—he'd said, "Geographers? I always get those mixed up," but they never would tell him anything, and Rita said forget it and squeezed his hand underneath the table. She was great, and he had decided to practice basketball some to please her.

But this party was the first time the two of them had been alone together in what turned out to be a big crowd of high school kids. Right as they walked in the door—which was wide open and Pearl Jam was pouring out of it—some big kid in a *Viva la Raza* T-shirt and dark glasses, even though it was inside and night time, crooked his arm around Henry's neck in a stranglehold, and dragged him away from Rita—Henry managed to wave at her, trying to act like he wasn't worried—through the crowded living room and into the crowded kitchen. "Hey!" the guy dragging him yelled, "look at this *pendejo*'s hair." Which he then grabbed up in a fist.

"Put him down," Melody Mendez said from the kitchen table, which she was sitting on top of, crammed back into a corner and surrounded by chips and dips. "This is still my party, and he's my guest."

"Hi, Melody," Henry said from the big guy's choke hold, noting her shiny patent leather shoes, and thinking that she probably had the same idea for the party as he'd had, although now there was some ranch dressing on her shoes, and the front of her dress was covered with chip crumbs. His neck was starting to hurt.

"You like this chicken taco? Brown on the outside, but inside all white meat. Ain't that right, taco? *¿Qué piensas?*" He yanked Henry's blond hair while the room filled with boys' laughter. From his limited vantage point, Henry could see six or seven other boys huddled around the refrigerator, holding beer cans and smoking cigarettes. There were a couple of girls in shorts leaning together by a screen door counting money, and another girl, whose head was practically shaved and who had an earring in her nose and was wearing army clothes, drinking from a liquor bottle that she was sharing with a boy. It looked like a good party, he guessed, if you weren't getting strangled.

"You're choking him," Melody pleaded.

"You can't choke a taco," the boy said. "Anybody here ever hear of a choked taco?"

Henry raised his hand.

"You don't count, bubba head." The boy let go of Henry's hair, but maintained the stranglehold and lifted Henry slightly off the ground, which made Henry think of the old westerns he'd seen on television, all the hangings where outlaws kicked and shuddered in the noose just the way he was kicking now. The boy bent down and stared into Henry's face, saying, "Why'd you do this to your hair?" He seemed sincerely upset. "You wanna be an Anglo boy, that it? Or you wanna be chicken meat?"

Henry tried to answer, but he couldn't force any words through his throat. *River Phoenix*, he tried to say.

"He's turning green!" Melody yelled, bumping the Doritos bowl with her knee so that it tipped over.

"Hey, watch it," the boy with the girl with the shaved head said to Melody. He shoved the chips away from the edge of the table, then presented his hand to the girl, who laughed and licked away the orange powder. Even in his present predicament, Henry thought that was cool.

"Let him go, Benny," one of the boys said. "He's so little he ain't even got a dick yet."

While it wasn't a complimentary thing to say, Henry was still happy to hear someone else asking for his release.

Another boy piped in. "You better let him go, or his girlfriend is going to beat you up."

Benny turned then, knocking Henry's backside into various drawer handles and partially opened drawers. He caught a glimpse of Rita, who had pushed her way through the doorway past two boys gesturing with their hands and one couple feeling each other's butts. Henry tried to note the precise placement of the boy's hand on the girl's bottom for future reference. His mother had taught him to make the best of a bad situation, and he was trying. He was afraid, though, that he might pass out.

Rita grabbed Benny's arm, her fingers brushing Henry's lips, and he instinctively kissed her fingertips. "Let him go," she said angrily.

"Does your lover boy think he's white?" Benny asked Rita. "Look at this—"

Rita slapped Benny across the face. He dropped Henry, who fell to a heap on Benny's boots, his head bounding against Rita's bare legs. He took a quick, desperate gulp of air. A lot of whooping had started up in the room, which turned to laughter and whistles.

By the time Henry could pull his feet in under his body and start to rise, Benny was jabbing a menacing finger in Rita's direction. Henry jumped up beneath the boy's hand, knocking it out of the way. "Thanks for the party," he called to Melody, who had an almost full Fresca can in her hand and was threatening to throw it at Benny, screaming something Henry couldn't understand, tears running down her cheeks and falling into the spilled Doritos.

Before Henry could maneuver Rita through the doorway, Benny's hand landed square on his head and forced him down to his knees, while a tidal wave of people lunged at Benny from behind. They were tugging him back, away from Rita—which was good, except that Benny managed to grab Henry's tie, and Henry was dragged back into the kitchen, too. He sprawled across the tile floor, which smelled of beer and mud, the tail of his tie still in Benny's fist, even while people held tight to the guy's arms.

Benny struggled with the boys trying to contain him, jerking Henry about in the process. Henry caught a chair leg in the face, and his nose began to bleed. His sister had been right about the tie. "I'm bleeding," he yelled, thinking that might cause everyone to stand back in concern, but no one even responded, except Melody, who began chanting, "He's bleeding! He's bleeding!"

Rita had fought her way back into the room and was slapping at Benny's hand, trying to make him drop Henry's tie. Then the girl with the shaved head and an earring in her nose pulled a Swiss Army knife out of her pants and starting sawing at Henry's tie—which was actually his dad's—cutting through one strand before the other slipped through Benny's hand, so that Henry's chin hit the tile, right in a puddle of beer. He tried to get to his feet, but his feet were being dragged by Rita and some boy through the kitchen doorway away from Benny, while Benny, who was being held now by the shoulders by a whole crowd of people, was raising and lowering his feet in a stomping fashion—weird, Henry thought, until he realized that the boy was trying to kick him in the head.

Outside, in the front yard of Melody Mendez's house, the boy who had helped Rita drag Henry out of the kitchen now lifted the back of Henry's collar and cut through the tie, which was knotted so tightly Henry had been unable to loosen it. His name was Tito, and evidently he knew Rita from school—at least he talked to her as if they knew each other. To Henry, he said, "Ties are bad luck, like the chicken with the extra toe."

"What chicken?" Henry asked. He tilted his head back to stop his bloody nose.

"Don't ever chew on a chicken feet that's got a extra toe," he said to Henry, but smiling the whole while at Rita.

"You eat chicken feet?" Rita said.

Tito's face clouded over. "Just a saying, you know. 'Bout *pollo*. You all right?" he asked Henry.

"It was my dad's tie," Henry said.

"That guy doesn't scare me," Rita said. "Bullies are really cowards."

"He was faking it pretty good, though," Henry said.

The music from inside the house stopped. Tito said, "Maybe we ought to get away down the street *un poco*."

Henry kept his head tilted back, holding Rita's hand and walking on the sidewalk, Rita guiding him, saying things like, "Curb," "Big crack," "Sprinkler," so he wouldn't stumble or get sprayed. The cloudless sky had filled with stars, Henry noted. He heard Tito walking in the street beside them. "Where do you live?" Henry asked him.

He didn't answer immediately, making some throat noise first. "Across river," he said finally.

"Apuro?" Henry forgot himself and looked at Tito, the telltale darkness below the knee. "I grew up there," Henry said. "Well, not really grew—oops." He tilted his head back again. Blood trickled across his lips. "I was just a baby, I guess, like about three or four, when we moved to here."

"*Vivimos aquí dos años*," Tito said. His voice sounded cheerier, but Henry wasn't sure what he had said. "Me *y mis padres* and my sister. She's got bad *pulmones*, you know, you breathe with."

"Lungs," Rita said.

"Yeah, so we moved to U.S.," Tito said.

"Where are we going, anyway?" Henry asked.

"I'm taking you home," Rita said. "Or we could go to my house, and Heart could make you stop bleeding."

"Nah," Henry said. "I don't want to bleed on your mom's rug. Where are we? You're supposed to be able to tell where you are from the stars, but I can't even tell which direction we're going."

"I've got you," Rita said.

A few seconds later Tito said, "So I'll see you at the school or some other place, no?"

Henry waved to him, but kept his head tilted back. He and Rita walked alone in the still night air. Wasn't there some kind of circus performer who walked like this? He wondered but he couldn't name one. He hadn't said anything for a while. "You know," he said, "that's got to be the worst party I've ever been to."

"Are your parents going to be mad?" Rita asked.

"Because I got beat up?"

"Because your dad's tie got cut, and your shirt is covered with blood."

Henry looked down at his shirt. It looked like he had been shot, which, while a mess, had an appealing look of danger to it. His nose seemed to have quit bleeding. Rita had blood on her Heart dress, a streak that wandered riverlike to the hem. Blood matted her hair. *His* blood, he thought. He took her hand again, and tilted his head back, although his nose no longer bled. He closed his eyes, so that the number of stars in the heavens multiplied. "Let's pretend I'm blind," he said to her.

"Okay," she said. "You're blind. Now what?"

"The whole world is completely black," he said to her, sidling up closer to her, linked now at the elbows. "Guide me home."

"What if I don't take you home?" she said. "You're at my mercy."

Henry liked that idea. She began telling him about the street they were on, making it fantastic and funny. Then she described the man and woman who founded Persimmon, the Chinese immigrant and his Anglo wife, their groves of persimmons. How the man fed his wife ripe persimmons, splitting them open with a knife he carried in his pocket. How she would close her eyes while he raised the fruit to her lips, pausing to inhale the fruit's odor before biting into the meat of it. Henry had never seen a persimmon, which permitted him to imagine it as the perfect fruit. He asked Rita to describe it, but she was more interested in the couple. She had imagined them thoroughly. The woman was taller than the man and wore a visor. The man rolled the cuffs of his pants unevenly. He spoke perfect English, except when excited or tired. The fragrance of persimmon blossoms made them intoxicated and languid. She liked him to kiss her neck, to bite her white shoulders. He liked to bathe her in warm milk. She would cut his hair on the back porch by the light of a bare bulb. He would read to her in bed. Neither wore socks. They were, Rita explained, the ideal couple, and she imagined that they had lived in her house, slept in her room.

Moved by this imaginary world but still blind, his head tilted back, Enrique reached to hug Rita and grabbed her breast. Thinking he had her shoulder, he squeezed gently. When she put her hand over his, he understood his mistake. "Oh, my love," he said, withdrawing his hand, his eyes still shut, imagining the startled face of his beloved.

Rudy led Tito to a tree stump across the highway from the Desert Oasis Inn. Their pantlegs, still damp from the crossing, dripped onto the dry leaves at their feet. Because Tito had been fooling around at some party, they were late getting themselves in place. Rudy worried that they had missed their opportunity. He stood on the narrow stump, leaned forward against a neighboring tree to look over the rise of the riverbank and the highway. The Desert Oasis shown brilliantly across the road, green neon palms with red coconuts waving seductively in an electronic wind. He couldn't see the parking lot, though, only the motel's sign.

In Spanish, Tito asked why Rudy was angry.

"Shut up," Rudy said. "Come on." They climbed the slanting bank, weaving among the trees in the dark. "Watch for headlights," he said. "Don't let anyone see you."

"Qué hacemos aquí?" Tito asked. What are we doing here?

"Get up here," Rudy said. He squatted to study the lit room beneath the glowing red MANAGER sign. Through the glass door, a bald head appeared behind a high counter. He would not be able to see them cross the road. The motel was situated north of town, surrounded by farmland and the river.

"Maybe she's already gone to El Paso, to the airport," Tito said, still speaking Spanish. "What makes you think she's in town, anyway? Maybe she's not ever going to come back here, so we might as well go home."

"We're staying," Rudy said. Only three vehicles in the parking lot—the K car that belonged to the bald manager and was always out front, a beat-up old American car that this reporter woman wouldn't drive, and a pickup with stuff in the back to clean the motel pool. She hadn't come in yet. They were not too late. He sighed and tapped the trunk of a tree with rough bark. How was it that he could speak two languages but did not know the name for a tree he had seen all his life?

"Yo no—" Tito began, but Rudy cut him off.

"Why do you think you can speak Spanish to me? You think that makes us friends? You think I *like* that?"

"I just know Spanish better," Tito said. "We talk in Spanish a lot."

"Not tonight, *entiendes*? No fucking Spanish."

"Okay, *inglés.*"

Headlights appeared on the highway. Rudy ducked, slapping at Tito to make him do the same, but the car didn't slow for the motel and disappeared up the highway. "When she shows up. We wait until she goes to her room. Then you knock on her door. You tell her you need to talk to her. Tell her something has happened, and you've got to let her know about it."

"What? What's happened?"

"Nothing. But you say it has anyway. When she opens the door, you step in and hold it. I'll be hiding behind her car or something, and we'll both go in."

"Then what?" Tito said. "Why you want in her place?"

Rudy didn't know how to answer this, wouldn't know what he was going to do until he was in the act of doing it. He might just scare her. "She got in our place, didn't she? Got her nose in Apuro, no? I'll put my nose where I want it."

Headlights again swept by. They were quiet while the car passed. "I read the thing she wrote about us. Found a copy at Humberto's." He waited to see how Tito would respond to this lie. He had only read the letter that described the article.

"She a good writer?" Tito asked. "Humberto show it to you?"

"I go wherever the fuck I want," Rudy said. "Humberto can kiss my . . . He can get . . . Forget Humberto."

"She talk about me?" Tito asked. It should have been a question that made him afraid, Rudy thought, but it didn't. He sounded even hopeful.

"It's shit. She thinks we're shit. Some poor beggar people."

"Well," said Tito, shifting to his butt, "Tata Rosales *does* beg. She got that 'Will Work for Food' sign. See her at the Conoco sometimes."

"You are so fucking stupid."

"I don't think she ever works for food, 'cause mostly it's people there getting gas, so they're all going somewhere where they don't need Tata Rosales and they probably don't got food there to feed her anyway. *Creo que* they just give her some change or buy her an extra Twinkie at the Conoco."

"You know what she said about you?" Rudy said.

"Tata Rosales?"

"No, *estupido*. The fucking gringa in her report. Says you're a *joto*."

Tito's mouth hung open, and his eyes darted around like he was studying the dark, but Rudy could tell that he wasn't really seeing anything. He said, "I don't do that."

"Says Humberto fucks you in the ass, and you like it."

"Humberto? Me?"

"I know you don't," Rudy said. "So I'm gonna fuck her up." He had said it, and now he would have to do it. It had just slipped out, but now he was committed. "She can't say that shit about you, see what I mean?"

Tito said nothing. He got up on his knees and stared at the Desert Oasis. His breathing sounded funny. "I don't care what she writes," he said. "*Vamos a casa.*" Let's go home.

"No," said Rudy. "You fucking crying? You better not be fucking crying."

"It's me she says this—"

"Shut up. You're doing this." After a few seconds of quiet he added, "Don't touch anything in there. Don't put your hands on anything."

"I won't," Tito said. "I'm not crying." After a moment he said, "What are you going to do, Rudy?"

"I'm going to . . ." He waited, hoping Tito would say something, hoping he wouldn't have to answer yet, but also letting it come to him, letting it appear. But it would not come to him yet. He would have to remain vague until he stepped into the room. "I'm gonna fuck her up," he said again, relieved to find a way to dodge the specifics. He might only have to push her around.

"*Ay, Dios,*" Tito said. He began praying.

"Shut up," Rudy said. "Shut the fuck up."

The car slowed well before the motel, the headlights so bright that Rudy's eyes threatened to tear. "Get ready," he said. The headlights slowly grew near, turned, aimed into the motel driveway, but then the car wheeled around, the lights pointing out to the street. Rudy ducked, which caused him to slide down the bank. He flattened himself against the ground. Tito, just above him, slipped his skinny body behind a tree trunk and kept watching. The headlights stayed steady for a few seconds, and Rudy feared they had been spotted. As he waited, the fear turned into a furtive hope, but the headlights began moving again. They had not been seen. He would have to follow through.

"Just turning around?" he said.

"Wait," Tito whispered.

"What?"

"Somebody dropped her off. *Mira.*"

Rudy raised himself to his knees. He saw the woman disappear into a lighted room, the door closing behind her. "Come on," he said.

They came out of the trees, hesitating, checking for cars before crossing. He couldn't let them be seen. The understanding hit him as he was crossing the street, struck him in the chest like a blow from a club. He was going to kill her. He could not fuck her up and then leave her to speak to the police. He was going to kill her, and then he and Tito would go to school in the morning as if nothing had happened.

The marquee below the neon palms had been impossible to read from the trees.

AMERICAN OWNED

CHRIST GIVES

ETERNAL LIFE

COUPLES $20

Tito began praying again, muttering under his breath. They paused at the chain-link fence that surrounded the pool, which was lit by lights under the water. They stared for a moment at water, the below-water lighting. Rudy could see that Tito was about to speak. "Don't say anything," he whispered.

The bald head remained motionless behind the high counter. Watching television, Rudy guessed. He crouched and trotted across the parking lot to the pickup truck, where he squatted. Tito bumped against him when he squatted, but Rudy did not lose his balance. "Go on," he said, pointing to the room where the woman had disappeared. "Knock on her door. Don't touch anything."

Tito nodded. He didn't look as nervous as Rudy had expected. Tito stood, then ran his hands through his hair, as if he were going to ask her out. He walked up to the door and knocked. A few seconds passed. Tito tapped his hand against his leg. The door opened. An apron of yellow light cut across Tito's face and body. Rudy leaned away from the light. A voice said, "Yes?" A man's voice. Rudy raised himself to look over the hood of the truck. An Anglo with long hair stood in the doorway. She was here with her fucking boyfriend.

"Hi," Tito said, fidgeting now, rolling his shoulders. "Hello. Is the lady Rhonda, who a . . . Is she here?"

A woman appeared in the doorway, too. An Anglo, but she looked nothing like the reporter. Tito had fucked up.

"Rhonda?" the man said. He looked to the woman. "You know any Rhonda?" The woman shook her head.

"Okay, then, well." Tito flapped his arms about in an exaggerated shrug. "If you see her, just say Tito says hi and so on and like that."

The woman disappeared but the man remained, staring, nodding. "Tito says hi," the man repeated. "If I ever meet a Rhonda, I'll tell her."

"Hey, that's great," Tito said. " 'Bye now." He turned from the door smiling, but stopped smiling as soon as the door closed. "Wrong door," he said.

"How the fuck you think that woman is her?" Rudy asked, getting up. "That woman's ten feet tall."

"Yeah," said Tito, "but I couldn't see her face. She just had that kind of clothes on that I thought was her."

Rudy pivoted and began marching back across the lot. They could do nothing now. "Hey," Tito called. He leaned against the chain-link fence, staring at the pool. "I like how it's lit up," he said. "I wonder can you see it from an airplane, like some kind of like some, I don't know, *island* down here."

Rudy had stopped walking to listen. An island of water in the sea of the desert, all lit from below.

"So I guess," Tito said, "I guess we might as well go home, no? I shouldn't have said her name, I guess. Or mine."

It came to Rudy then. He heard what the words meant to conceal. He understood that Tito had made the mistake intentionally, that he had only pretended to think the tall woman was the reporter. Rudy expected anger, but felt instead something else, something he didn't know how to name. The moment was rare. Someone had been looking out for him.

"You got the *cojones* of a two-year-old," Rudy said, his voice soft at the edges, shaky in the middle.

"Hey, you know, a pool like this to swim in, just to swim in, not even for drinking or washing or nothing, you get one of these, you got to feel like, like, you know, *good*." Tito smiled his too-wide, too-open smile.

They crossed the street together, waded the river together. The reporter would be crossed off his list, Rudy thought. Nothing he could do about her. He felt the pain of that relief, but it reminded him of his other responsibilities, the other obligations he could not let slide.

Tito said, "We ought to put some lights under here." He waved at the river before them. "Light it up and everybody will want to walk in it."

"*Callate*," Rudy said. Shut up. But he liked the image of the river water lit up like a sky, the whole murky wash of water illuminated from here to Mexico, the sotted garbage and the befuddled fish made visible, the silt and human shit, a stream of savage light like a steel ribbon through the heart of the valley. "Come on," he said, not stepping onto the bank, remaining in the water, wading home with his friend.

Love

17

"Hubby would have come," Margaret said to Gay and secondarily to Heart, "but he said there were a few other things he'd rather do, including being beaten half to death." She smiled at the other women. "Not a sports fan, Hubby. It's one of his redeeming characteristics."

Because the team was undefeated, the Persimmon High School gym was crowded, and Gay was squeezed between the other two, high up in the bleachers. Heart had spent the day draining and covering the cooler in the bookstore, and Gay wished she had bathed. Her body odor had been hardly noticeable in Margaret's car, but in this crowded room it wafted up whenever Heart moved her arms. As luck would have it, arm-moving was an integral part of several cheers, including one that required raising your hands above your head and waving them back and forth to a high school jazz band version of "It's a Thin Line Between Love and Hate," with the new lyrics, "Go Tigers, We Think You're Great." Gay thought the original line was more appropriate. Gay declined to participate, but Heart cheered eagerly. When the noise stopped, she pulled one of her cigarette-sized drinking straws from the front pocket of her ugly dress and began puffing on it.

"Denny looks nice, doesn't he?" Margaret said. "It's a shame he doesn't have to wear a uniform like they do in baseball. Wouldn't you like to see him in his little shorts? Of course, you get to, anyway, but Heart and I could use the stimulation."

"I wouldn't mind it," Heart said. While she sat leering, her hands in her lap to aid her concentration, the familiar smells of popcorn, perfume, and hot dogs wafted up to Gay's nose. She never thought the combination would be so welcome. Heart and Denny had become friends. Gay had even suggested a double date with Heart and her boyfriend, but she had declined. "Mr. Gene is just too shy for that sort of thing," she had explained. "He doesn't like to be in a car with more than one other person."

"That sounds . . ." Gay had stopped herself from saying *certifiable*, and instead said, "a little neurotic."

"More than a little," Heart had said enthusiastically. "He's a nut about that sort of thing."

While Margaret analyzed Denny's anatomy with Heart, Gay scanned the student bleachers for her daughter. Current teenage fashion seemed to be based on the circus aesthetic, she decided. Boys with waterwheel Mohawks sat next to girls with brilliant green beehives. Tattoos flourished on both sexes, although many had to be of the washable variety, Gay speculated, unwilling to believe so many children had marked themselves up permanently. Leopard-skin dresses were popular, as were nose studs, lip rings, eyebrow piercings, and purple eyeshadow. Rita sat in her homely Heart dress, her dark hair pulled straight back, nothing but her earlobes pierced. She sat between Cecilia and Henry Calzado, Cecilia dressed for a church wedding and Henry in hand-me-downs from a heavier, shorter brother. Henry didn't please Gay as a boyfriend for her daughter. He was a sweet boy, but goofy and distracted, with no sense of how to dress himself or romance his girl. His features were nicely arranged, but he was more a child than a boy, a pretty child, but his looks were forever linked to the cuteness of a kid rather than . . . than what? The sexiness of a tattooed hoodlum? Did she really want her daughter to have a sexy boyfriend? She did and she didn't. She wanted her daughter to have the thrill of being with a boy who could make her legs wobble, but she didn't want the worry—or the danger. Henry was safe, and there was something to be said for that—a lot to be said for that. On the other hand, it saddened her that her daughter wasn't popular, that her boyfriend was in middle school and likely a putz even there.

"Let me have a puff on that," Margaret said to Heart.

"You can have one of your own." Heart produced another short drinking straw.

Margaret accepted it and inhaled. "Hmm," she said. "I'd need a lobotomy to go with it. Oh, look." Margaret used the straw to point. "There's Claire. I told her we'd be here." She stood and called to her, waving, then spoke under her breath to Gay. "She looks like a soggy sandwich, doesn't she? That outfit says 'nineteen seventy-six.' "

Claire spotted Margaret but did not wave or smile, merely began climbing the bleachers, pushing through the seated crowd. Her long hair looked wet, which shifted her appearance from Farrah Fawcett of the seventies to Joni Mitchell of the sixties. She wore an ugly, clingy pantsuit. Had such a thing ever been fashionable?

Gay took a moment to wonder why she had become suddenly obsessed with appraising the dress of the crowd. Probably because she had no interest whatsoever in basketball. If Denny weren't coaching, she would feel like Randall, willing to take a beating rather than watch pimply kids display their aggression in a condoned fashion. She had worn tight jeans, a sleeveless blouse, and black flats, a casual but attractive combination. She could generally pick the women who were going to interest her by the way they dressed. They needed to have some sense of style and some sense of themselves, an edge of daring, plus a combination of what was new with what fitted their own age. Margaret managed this well enough. Heart was so hopeless that she transcended all categories, while men, in general, or at least in towns like this one, only dressed well if their wives or girlfriends directed them step by step. In this way, all men were projects. Denny, tonight, wore the pants, shirt, and tie she had selected for him on a shopping excursion at the mall in El Paso. He'd balked at buying new shoes, standing flamingo-like on one leg to reveal the amount of tread left, and now his ugly brown loafers were the only failing in his appearance. She could no longer pretend not to be in love with him, especially not while sitting in a crowded gym smelling Heart's body odor, waiting for the beginning of a high school basketball game, worrying about his shoes.

Claire suddenly blocked Gay's view of Denny, still working her way up the bleachers, her pace determined but laconic. "Where's she going to sit?" Gay asked.

"Oh, we can make room," Margaret said. "Slide over some, Heart." They all three stood as if on command.

"I may just walk home," Heart said. "I only came along to see why a grown man would want to spend all his free time coaching boys in a meaningless exercise of virility, anyway."

"You practiced that line," Gay said without actually discouraging her from leaving. Her body odor had swelled anew when she stood.

"I intended to say it in front of Denny," Heart explained, "but the time seemed ripe."

Ripe, Gay thought, was a word Heart should avoid until she bathed. Heart had stank back when they lived together on the commune, Gay recalled, but everyone at the place stank, and Gay had gotten used to it. That people on the outside wore deodorant had caused much smug head-shaking and even occasional laughter.

"Claire," Margaret said, "we saved you a place."

Claire stepped past Margaret and faced Gay. "You never got back to me," she said.

"Oh," Gay said. "You're right. I'd forgotten. It's been months and . . . well, I had to leave that party. This is Heart. We share a house."

Claire sat without acknowledging Heart. The other women wedged themselves in around her. Her pantsuit was wet, which was why it looked so odd. Very wet, Gay noted, trying to scoot away from her, but there was no room, and all she accomplished was making Heart shift her arms.

"You're soaked," Margaret said, touching Claire's damp leg, but Claire didn't seem to hear. She was glaring at Gay.

"I know you're seeing the new one," Claire said. "Denny Redmon. I know you and he left Margaret's house together. It doesn't surprise me to see you here."

"Is something wrong?" Gay asked, while Heart at the same moment whispered, "Is she all right?"

"It was three months ago—one, two, three," Claire flicked three fingers angrily, "which doesn't make any difference, does it? You said you would talk to me. I lied to Mr. Dick. I emptied Margaret's ashtrays. You never got back to me."

"Claire," Margaret said, taking the woman's arm, but Claire would not shift her gaze from Gay. Margaret grasped Claire's chin and forcibly turned her head. "Claire, honey, you don't seem to be yourself."

"Who else would I be? Is there somebody else I could possibly be?"

The national anthem began. They all stood. Heart whispered to Gay, "She's having a breakdown." Halfway through the anthem, Claire joined the singing—a little loudly, but she had the words right, and her voice was steady and in key.

After they resettled, Margaret affected a cheery tone and asked Claire about her husband. "How's Dick? How's everything at the police department?"

"He just works there," Claire said. "It doesn't have anything to do with how he is."

"And how is your semester going? Do you have a good class this year?" Margaret asked her. The game began, the ball tossed high into the air while the two tallest boys leaped to slap it.

"My class? My kids?" Claire turned her head to the gym's rafters, while below the Farts wound up with the ball and sent it rocketing downcourt. An easy shot was missed, but the tallest Fart, trailing on the play, stepped into the colored zone just as the ball bounced off the backboard. He grabbed the rebound and neatly tossed the ball in. A roar went up, and during the roar, Claire spoke. Gay, who had been concentrating on her while pretending to watch the game, leaned close to hear. "They're the only relief." She turned to Gay and whispered in her ear. "I bought them all Tootsie Pops, and we just sucked them. 'No biting,' I said. I wanted them to last as long as they could. I gave a prize to the slowest one."

Gay leaned back to look at her face, which now wore an expression of earnest pride. "What was the prize?"

"Five dollars," Claire said. "I went to the SoLo in El Paso right after class and bought a whole case of Tootsie Pops. My little reserve against chaos. Anytime I have to have it, I can make them sit quietly for half an hour." She made a slight hissing sound. "For five dollars, the little grubs would slit their throats."

Margaret put her arm along Claire's shoulders. "Has Dick . . ." She paused while another blare from the crowd rose and died. "Has Dick been acting strange?"

"How would I know?" she said. "Strange. What a ridiculous word that is. How can you tell what's strange if everything's always been strange?"

Heart whispered to Gay, "Maybe we should take her out of here."

"Isn't that the truth," Margaret said. "The world is so strange."

Gay said, "You've changed your hair since the last time I saw you."

Claire glared at her again, but only momentarily. The anger suddenly left her eyes, and she touched her hair. "Just wet. It's not raining, you know. My hair is wet but it's not raining."

"It hardly rains here at all," Gay said, imitating the light timbre Margaret had adopted, "once the monsoon is over. My daughter loves monsoon season. I don't think you've met her. You can see her, though. She's right over there, across the court."

"Where?"

"Count up five rows," Gay began. Meanwhile, Margaret reached beyond Claire's shoulders to tap Gay's arm. She held a slip of paper between her fingers. Gay took the note without pausing. "Look for the boy in the brilliant orange shirt," she said.

"Orange," Claire said.

The note read:

Heart
Go get Hubby. Meet us in lobby at halftime.

Gay surreptitiously passed the note to Heart. "Just to the right of that boy is a skinny boy—that's Henry, her boyfriend. Rita is holding his hand, and that's her best friend on the other side of her, Cecilia."

"She's Mexican," Claire said.

"Her friend is," Margaret put in. "So is her boyfriend."

"I'm going to use the bathroom," Heart said, pocketing the note. "You guys can spread out a little bit."

Claire tapped Heart on the shoulder before she got away. "You smell," she said, then turned to Gay. "Your daughter's not pretty like you. She's pudgy. A little pudgeball."

"She's beautiful," Heart stated flatly, glaring at Claire a moment before continuing down the bleachers.

Margaret said, "Rita's just finding herself. She's going to be really lovely. You wait and see."

"But not like her mother," Claire said, staring again at the teenagers. "He's Mexican? The boyfriend? He has a blond head."

"Oh, look," Margaret said in her artificial voice, "they've tied the game."

"Do you really," Claire began, then turned to study Gay's face. "Deep down, do you really trust Mexicans?"

Gay felt a litany of responses bubbling up, some knee-jerk and politically correct, some an attempt at a complicated kind of honesty, some concerned only with Claire's well-being. Finally she said, "I almost married one."

Claire nodded. She said, "I don't either."

Rita sat in the bleachers, pressed between Henry and Cecilia. It was strange to date her best friend's little brother, especially when most of the time she preferred Cecilia's company to Henry's. The game was close and evidently exciting as Henry kept jumping to his feet, stepping on Rita's toes. She and Henry had started kissing this past week. Not the dry pecking that had passed for kissing, but truly experimental mouthwork. He was game for anything, but he didn't press. Her mother sometimes dated younger men, and Rita had begun to understand why. She could set the rules and control the doings. Nevertheless, older men still interested Rita more.

She imagined herself sitting at the game next to Mr. Gene. The image sent a pleasant vibration through her chest, but, of course, he wouldn't come to the game. She looked across the floor to find Heart, as she had earlier, sitting next to her mother and Margaret Lamb, and now some other woman was sitting there with them.

Mr. Gene would have his own ideas about what they should do. Rita liked this notion and didn't like it at the same time. If she wanted to go to the game, then why wouldn't Mr. Gene come along? But why did she want to go to the game, really? Was it the event itself? She glanced at the scoreboard. Persimmon led by four. There were moments when the game involved her. A boy would leap gracefully, or he'd grimace and stomp around, or Mr. Redmon would run out to talk to the referees and stick his fists on his hips. A lot of the girls had a crush on Coach Redmon. Rita might have too if her mother weren't already screwing him. It seemed like the kind of thing her mother was always doing, although she couldn't think of another example.

Besides, there was something about Mr. Redmon she didn't trust. If he was as great as he looked, why wasn't he a doctor or a senator or something? She could see why her dad was happy with his pool service. He didn't want or need very much from life. But Mr. Redmon wasn't like that. Her mistrust of him could simply be jealousy, she understood. Besides, if she didn't trust him and didn't even pay attention to the game, what was she doing in the gym?

A crash of bodies underneath the basket temporarily distracted her, but she wanted to reason this out. Had she come to the game to be seen? To see if something provocative was going to happen? To avoid being called a hermit? Because Henry and Cecilia wanted to come? Was she really here just to please her boyfriend, even if he was younger and she wasn't really all that attracted to him?

She didn't think so. The desire to go to the basketball game had to do with possibility. Something could come up that could lead to something new. Things could happen. Opportunities could present themselves.

Why, then, had her mother come to the game? She certainly had no interest in the game as contest or as spectacle. They had lived in Persimmon twelve years, and the only game she had seen before this season had been when Rita forced her to go. Obviously her mother attended the game because she was dating the coach. But why did that determine how she spent the evening? It wasn't like he was playing, and they certainly couldn't talk during the contest. It was true that he did sometimes stand and gesture, but mostly he sat with a towel in his hands and yelled at his players. He didn't go to GEM Transport to watch her work, did he? But the gym was packed with people, which proved that his work was more public than hers. What of all of this did her mother enjoy? It wasn't possibility. She wasn't looking for a party to go to, or trying to avoid the label of hermit so that she might be popular with others. She certainly wasn't here to fend off other women attracted to Denny. Rita snorted at the idea. Her mother wouldn't think any woman in Persimmon more attractive than herself. It was probably why they lived there. It was probably why she surrounded herself with mean-looking women, like Margaret Lamb, and unattractive ones, like Heart. Was her mother enjoying the attention that belonged to Denny? Was she attracted to men who were in some small way famous? Maybe *famous* wasn't the right word.

"You want a Coke?" Henry asked her.

She studied him for a moment before answering. He was as good looking as any boy here, she thought, and he liked her so much and so exclusively it might frighten her if he were a different kind of boy. But why did he like her? "Yeah," she said, and she smiled at him just to watch him respond. His face widened, all his features expanding. "Do you have enough money?"

"Of course," he said. He touched her hand, then he leaned past her and asked his sister if she wanted a Coke. The boy loved Cokes. In another moment he was picking his way through the people seated below. The game had stopped, a time-out. Persimmon led now by five. Rita decided to bring Cecilia in on her ruminations. "Why do we like this?" she asked her.

"You're not having fun?" Cecilia said.

"I am, but I don't know why."

" 'Cause everyone's here and we're winning," she said. "Even your mom's here."

Rita leaned closer to Cecilia and spoke into her ear. "Why do you think Henry likes me so much?"

Cecilia immediately turned to answer. "He thinks you're the most amazing person who ever lived."

"But why does he think that?"

Cecilia shrugged. "Once he gets something in his head, he turns into a train. He's all choo-choo after a certain point."

"But there have to be reasons."

"You've driven him mad with your sexual aura."

Rita laughed. "I'm serious. I'm trying to figure things out." A horn sounded and the players slowly edged away from the benches. "I can see why the players would like playing the game. It's exercise and competition, and they want to win."

"And they want all the girls hot for them," Cecilia said.

"Is that what we're supposed to be doing?" Rita asked, genuinely perplexed. "Getting hot for the players?"

"Arturo had like a million girls in love with him after he made varsity."

"I haven't even been paying attention to the players."

"That's because your passion for Henry has made you blind to other men."

Rita turned to be certain that she was joking, then they both burst into laughter. One of the Persimmon players stole a pass and raced downcourt for a lay-up. While everyone else stood and cheered, Rita put her mouth to Cecilia's ear. "The thing is," she had to shout, then modulate the volume as the crowd quieted, "I like having a boyfriend, and I like Henry." She paused, while Cecilia nodded and smiled. Rita had almost said, "But I have more fun with you," but some instinct told her not to reveal that. They both knew that boys were supposed to come first. Was that why she felt more attracted to older men, even if they didn't like the same things she did, even if they weren't as good looking as Henry or probably anywhere near as nice? Simply because as a kid you were always wanting to be like the adults so that you could have more freedom, so that you could at least pretend to be more fully like them? Was she thinking about older men because she wanted to be more like her mother? That couldn't be it, although her mother would certainly be the adult woman she had imitated as a child. Did her mother go out with men she really only liked as friends? What was Rita doing here with Henry?

Cecilia suddenly put her mouth to Rita's ear. "There he is again," she said, her voice urgent and breathy. Rudy Salazar had returned to the game, walking slowly, insolently, while the referee held the ball and watched. Rudy had forgotten about Rita and Cecilia, as far as they could tell, but they had not forgotten about him.

And then there was Enrique, climbing the bleachers, carrying three Cokes, stepping on some guy's hand and apologizing, kicking some woman in the thigh and apologizing again, the Coke rising up to the lip of the cups and running down over his knuckles as he tried to stop the dripping by licking his hands. She found herself smiling. He made her smile.

"Hey, whoa," he said. "There was a line from here to kingdom come. What's the score?"

Cecilia told him the score while taking her Coke. Rita said, "What's that mean, 'kingdom come'?"

Henry squinted and sat beside her. She could tell he was really thinking by the various expressions that crossed his face. There seemed to be a direct link between his intellectual processes and his facial muscles. "It's like when you die and go to heaven," he said, "that's the kingdom, which by that time has come, so I guess there'd be a big line to get in." Suddenly he smiled. "That's the one line where no one would be taking cuts. Just when you think you have it made, you step in front of Gandhi or somebody, and some angel taps you on the shoulder and gives you a ticket to the hot place."

Rita laughed. "The hot place?"

"My mom never let us say H-E-L-L. This guy at church says 'H-E-hockey sticks,' but I didn't get it for a long time because who knew what hockey sticks looked like? So we always said 'the hot place.' "

Rita leaned next to him and took his hand.

No one could shoot worth a shit. The crush of bodies inside became acute. Rudy had one boy on his hip, another he hooked behind his elbow, while a third stepped in front of him. The ball cut an arc high above them. He kneed the boy in front of him, making the boy's leg buckle just as the ball struck the rim. Rudy leaped then, giving the boy at his elbow a little shove as he went up, and grabbed the rebound, turning as he came down, ready to make the two-handed outlet pass Coach Redmon had taught him, but bodies and limbs blocked the passing lanes. He landed firmly, holding the ball close to his chest, elbows out, then managed a short bounce pass to Cone, the Anglo center—pale as an ice cream cone—who made a quick baseball-style pass downcourt. Rudy fell then into the boy whose knee he had pushed, forcing the kid to the floor, letting him have an elbow in the neck, but making it look clean—just their legs tangled up—and jumping quickly to his feet, in time to see the lay-up at the other end.

The new coach had not only let Rudy come out for the team, he had made him a starter. The first week of practice, when Rudy had knocked Cone to the floor going for a rebound, Coach Redmon had blown his whistle. Rudy had readied himself for a confrontation, but the coach said, "All right, Salazar, you're our enforcer. Every team's got to have one. You're our Karl Malone. Nobody who plays us gets away with anything, the Enforcer sees to that. How's that sound?"

Rudy hadn't smiled, although he had felt the urge. "I can handle that," he said.

"The only thing you have to work on is taking it out on the *other* guys. Your job is to protect *these* guys."

Coach had taught him to bend the knee of a taller player if the guy had position. "The refs look up here," he said, waving his hands. "Don't try to get away with any pushing, checking—nothing using your hands or elbows. And the feet they watch. No kicking, stepping on toes. But they can't watch everything. The old knee trick, even the good refs don't spot it, and we won't have a good ref all season. You'll be amazed what you can get away with."

It wasn't the only trick he'd learned from Redmon. Push off the side of a guy's foot, and it looks like honest foot confusion but is just as effective as standing on his toes. Shove a guy around with your butt, not your hands or arms. If the opponent is a lot taller, then you get smaller, shift your center of gravity down lower by squatting a little, and keep him off balance, make him fall back into you.

"You ever heard of the verb 'to glower'?" Coach asked him one day.

"No," Rudy had said. "So what?"

"Well, you're doing it right now. That's a glower on your face, and I want you to do it during the game. You're only six what, two, three? And you're our power forward, so you're going to be guarding bigger guys most of the time. We can't make you any taller, but you glower at them—and play smart like I've taught you—and you can make them *smaller*."

Rudy liked thinking of it that way. His job was to make people smaller. He had been practicing all his life.

The team was 4 and 0, but they were struggling this night against mediocre opposition. No one could put the ball in the hoop. It wasn't his job to shoot unless he had a shot right by the basket. He rebounded, he played D, he threw screens, he enforced. In the very first game, against the Mayfield Bulldawgs, he had knocked the opposing center down twice without a foul, using his butt, tangling their legs. When the Bulldawg coach ran onto the court to complain, Coach Redmon had come out and defended Rudy. Dirty play, the Bulldawg coach complained; aggressiveness, Redmon had said back. The Bulldawg coach pointed at Rudy: "This *thug*," he'd said, "This *hood*," which made Redmon yell, "Don't you slander my boys." After the yelling had stopped, Coach had called a time-out. In the huddle, he leaned in close to Rudy and said, "They're scared shitless. Back off now so you don't get a technical." He'd given Rudy a wink and then started clapping his hands and addressing the whole team.

Rudy had felt a strange sensation, an unfamiliar revolution in his body. He wasn't accustomed to being defended, congratulated, promoted. He didn't want to like it, or to like Coach for doing it, but he did. After that first game, in the locker room, Coach had said, "You just routed a pretty good team. You've got a rare opportunity. The opportunity to be champions."

The old corny bit. Rudy knew this routine, but he could see it working on the others. He also saw Coach looking at him differently, ironically, almost winking again, as if acknowledging that he had to do this crap with *boys*, and only the two of them, Rudy and Coach, would be aware of the manipulation.

At the other end of the court, one of the players was bleeding, a Tiger guard. Play was stopped while they slapped on a Band-Aid. Rudy folded his arms and looked over the crowd in the gym. There were no Fart yells this year. Rudy had told the boys who instigated the business to cut it the fuck out, and they had. Instead, there were the normal cheers, including one that they did for each player, using his name. The cheerleaders would shout it, and the crowd would yell it back. Hundreds of people yelling for him, calling his name. He looked over their faces, as he almost never did during play; in fact, when he was playing well, he would forget that people were watching. It had happened to him once or twice in years past, but this year it happened all the time. The crowd disappeared, even the building vanished, and he didn't really hear, either, although he could respond to Coach's instructions. He couldn't explain it, but he went through spells in a game when he existed outside of time, beyond the senses, when he was free of thoughts, feelings, free even of the steel band. He became light. That was the only feeling, a lightness, like he might, at any moment, float up to the top of the gym.

Whenever the game stopped, even like this, just a delay, he returned to himself, felt the full weight of his existence, of his heavy obligations—one of which was to keep from taking any of this crap to heart. When the season ended, the people who cheered him now would once again piss on him—or try to. Let them try. He looked forward to their trying.

Even now, he could see what they thought of him.

He's a starter on the team, but he's still a negra.

The coach had to buy him sneakers and tell him not to wade the river in them.

He shits in an outhouse.

He could hear them just by looking at their faces. That ability to hear was his gift. Fuck them all.

Except there stood Tito, waving maniacally at him. Rudy gave him a nod, a slight jerk of his head, acknowledgment enough. Tito was a child, but

Rudy was determined to teach him. Tito thought he could be one of *them* without giving up who he really was. Rudy would show him otherwise.

One semester, years ago back in middle school, Rudy himself had decided to buy into their way of life, even though it had meant selling out his. He had started getting up early in the morning to do his homework, had started saying "yes, sir," and "no, ma'am," willing to try to believe that *words* could make a difference. He'd quit speaking Spanish as they had seemed to want. The teachers hadn't wished to give him a chance, but he had forced them, forced them by doing his work, by being prepared—he'd even begun raising his hand to give an answer or, rarely, to ask a question.

It had worn on him, turned his stomach, and he hadn't been able to sleep well. Every night this strange anxiety came over him, this nervous invasion of his body that made him tremble in bed. But in the morning he would re- solve again to do it, to make it through another day not as Rudy Salazar, but as this other boy, this kid who had something to gain in the world from be- having as they wanted him to.

One day, in his English class, they had been updating a play, a Shake- spearean play about a guy who makes another guy think his girlfriend is a whore, and so the guy kills his girlfriend. Rudy had liked the play, had even said as much to the teacher. He'd had trouble understanding the writing at first, but once he got the hang of the language, he'd understood it. It touched him. He had never read or seen anything better, the way the bad guy could manipulate the good one, could make him believe ridiculous lies.

In the class, they were rewriting it, setting it not in the past and not in the present, but in the future, on something called the *Enterprise*. The main guy in the play became the Captain, and Arturo Delgado got that part. All the parts were recast to fit in this futuristic world that everybody seemed to know about but Rudy. When it came his turn, they made him the bad guy, the one who tells lies about the girlfriend. "You'd have to be a Klingon," somebody said. Rudy had laughed because everyone else had, but he had discovered the truth later. He'd asked somebody in the cafeteria what a Klingon was, and they told him: an alien. An evil alien.

It hurt him. He had put himself in a situation where they could hurt him, and of course they did. But he told himself he was stronger than they were, that he could ride out their taunts. A lot of them had once been illegal aliens themselves.

A week or so later, in his math class, he had finally asked why all semester he had been turning in pages of homework, while everybody else just handed in one sheet of answers, as if they'd done the problems in their heads. The teacher had gone to one of the students and asked him for his "pocket calculator." Rudy remembered the term because it had sounded so weird, like what did pockets have to do with anything? The boy had not reached into his pocket but into his backpack, which Rudy saw had a patch sewn onto it that said MEGADETH, as if that patch were a clue, as if it were trying to speak to Rudy. The pocket calculator looked like a toy. "They don't cost that much," the teacher had assured him. "You do remember my saying that calculators were okay for homework?"

Rudy remembered, but he had pictured the squat machine that sat on the counter of Arzate's grocery, the tube of paper rolled like toilet tissue perched on top. "I'll get one," Rudy had promised.

It wasn't that day or the next or the day after that. Rudy couldn't remember the day that he'd given up, but he hadn't done another math equation by hand, and he had not eaten any more shit.

Play resumed. Rudy let his man work his way to the three-second zone, let him think he had position, while Rudy kept his hand on the fleshy part of the boy's middle, a little hand-check on the soft place between the hips and the ribs. Then, just when the guard self-consciously looked the other way while bouncing the pass inside, Rudy pounced, the hand on the boy now an iron gate that would not permit movement. He intercepted the pass, his arms rising above his head to make the two-handed pass to a guard already breaking downcourt. The muscles in his back announced themselves beneath his jersey as he cocked his arms, then thrust them forward, hands and ball whisking over his head, the ball flying through space, as the gym disappeared, as sound itself vanished, the steel band within him obliterated by the torque of his body and the pristine silence of the floating, spinning basketball.

With thirty seconds to go in the half, the clock stopped for free throws, the Farts ahead 32 to 25, Margaret suddenly cursed, "That idiot." Gay jerked her head around. Randall stood in the lobby doorway beside Claire's husband, Dick Brownlee.

"What on God's green earth do people see in this?" Claire said, watching a boy on the free-throw line loft the basketball toward the basket. "Why bother?"

Margaret leaned past Claire and whispered to Gay, "I'm going to distract those men, tell them we'll meet them all in the car. You get your boyfriend to take you and Claire out through the lockers."

"Why?" Gay said, and Claire said, "That's what I say, 'Why bother?'"

"Something's up with her husband," Margaret whispered. "I don't want to let Dick at her."

"How do you know that?"

"I can just tell." To Claire, Margaret added, "You two carry on without me." She began hurrying down the bleachers. "Look out," she called to the people on the bleachers below her. "I'm wearing heels," she threatened.

Gay took Claire's elbow. "Come with me."

Claire permitted herself to be led. They trailed Margaret down the bleachers, taking advantage of her wake. They reached the locker room entrance just as the half ended. Players rushed by, sweat gleaming on their shoulders and dripping from their hair. Denny shoved his hands in his pockets as he approached them.

"Something wrong?" he said, glancing from Gay to Claire. He didn't seem to recognize her.

"We need an unblocked exit," Gay said, motioning with her head toward the lockers.

He nodded, as if this were not at all unusual. "Intrigue," he said, then extended his hand toward the locker room door.

"I know you," Claire said to him, but his assistant coach had begun talking to him, and he didn't hear her.

Claire's hair frizzed in the arid night air and slight breeze. Her clothes no longer looked wet. "Where are we going?" she asked suddenly. They had cleared the school grounds and strolled past a deserted convenience store, an orange poster in the window advertising milk at a price out of the distant past.

"My house," Gay said. "I live near Margaret."

"I know that," Claire said. She walked slowly, a flatfooted amble that made her seem old and feeble. Gay let her set the pace, but directed them down a narrow residential alley. She didn't want Claire's husband to realize he'd been tricked and then find them strolling along the street. Normally, Gay would not walk down such an alley at night, but it was lit at either end by tall vapor lights, and Claire's ineptitude made her feel competent by comparison, almost invincible. Besides, every male in town was crowded into that gym.

"I'm sorry we never got to talk," Gay said. "I didn't realize it was important to you."

Claire said nothing, watching her feet as she walked. The alleyway was bordered on either side by high fences that hid the yards and houses from inquiring eyes, while also hiding the grim alley from the families' view. Wood fences abutted walls made of concrete blocks, which connected with fences made of linked wire and woven metal strips. Dented metal garbage cans leaned convivially against one another on the pitted asphalt, their openings overfilled with dead leaves and clippings, yellowing newspapers, rotting vegetables and coffee grinds, the plastic remains of toys. If Gay were with a friend, she might say they were wandering down Rejection Lane and try to turn it into a rock-and-roll song. Of course, she would never find herself in such an alley with a friend. In any case, she understood the burden of conversation lay entirely on her. "I suppose I was embarrassed after going off with Denny like that."

"You're bragging. You weren't embarrassed," Claire said, clucking her tongue after she spoke.

Gay sighed, eyeing an empty plastic barrel that looked large enough to stuff Claire in. "No, I wasn't. But I do apologize."

Claire nodded dismissively. She pointed at graffiti on a concrete block fence, a crude, spray-painted woman's body, circles and dots and wavy lines, the single black triangle. "My father tried to cut my mother's tongue out. He held her down on the kitchen floor to work a Swiss Army knife into her mouth."

"Jesus," Gay said. The asphalt gave way to soft sand and the sky suddenly grew darker and pressed down heavily upon them. A tattered pair of panty hose, snagged on the rail of a fence, drooped artfully to the ground, one toe daintily touching the sand, a prancing, flesh-tone ghost. Gay regretted taking the alley.

"His name is Earl. He's all dead now. My mother moved to Fresno to live with her sister." She walked purposefully, practically wading through sand. Gay didn't know what to say to her. She could smell something dead in one of the trash cans. The tall fences now made Gay think of the cheesy Old West façades popular along freeways, phony walls disguising and denying the business they fronted. Claire said, "She killed him. At least I think she did. Poison, probably. Maybe she poured something in his ear. Isn't there something you can pour into a man's ear—something hot? Or is it a bug? You let a bug crawl into his ear and eat his brains."

Fear began to dominate Gay's emotional state. She had started the walk as a caretaker, but now she found herself in a narrow corridor with a crazy person. Ahead, beyond one of the walls, a huge mechanical shape loomed, a dark metallic figure with angles and corners and incredible weight. Merely a piece of machinery, Gay told herself. She tried to make her voice sound neutral. "What did the doctor say was the cause of death?"

"Heart attack," Claire said. "Can you imagine? Ridiculous." She shook her head violently.

"It happens," Gay said.

"You're naïve." Claire narrowed her eyes, staring at Gay with an intensity that unnerved her. "You look like you're the sort of person who knows things, but you're not. You don't know anything. Do you know what Dick did to me tonight?"

"No." They stopped walking, the end of the alley just a dozen paces ahead, their skin ghastly in the vapor glow. A television from nearby projected canned laughter. Gay took a few trial steps, but Claire did not follow. Gay turned to her, waiting.

"You don't know one fucking thing," she said.

"I guess I don't," Gay said. "Let's get out of this alley."

Claire suddenly looked around her. She began an exaggerated trot, swinging her arms in long arcs, and kept it up until the alley ended. Gay stayed a few steps behind her, feeling both ridiculous and gratified to be running. She emerged from the alley with such a profound sense of relief she almost felt she had accomplished something. Taking the alley had been only a small lapse in judgment and brought on logically by the circumstances, but she felt extraordinarily lucky to have survived it undamaged.

She led Claire to the highway and across, recalling how, years ago, she and Sander had participated in a nocturnal march in Albuquerque to decry violence against women. "Take Back the Night" had been the event's title, and marches had taken place in cities around the West, maybe all over the country, she couldn't remember. What she did remember was that a little girl had disappeared in one of the cities during the march, a girl eleven or twelve years old. A response to the march from the other side, from the forces of darkness.

"What does that mean 'peckerwood'?" Claire asked suddenly. "Why would anybody call anybody else a peckerwood?" She smiled dimly and looked at Gay, expecting some kind of response.

"People say ridiculous things," Gay said.

Without streetlights, Calle Blanca was darker than the alley had been. They left the street and walked on the sidewalk. "For some reason, they won't put lights on this side of River Road," Gay said.

"Peckerwood," Claire responded.

Gay folded her arms and picked up the pace. She hated Claire. The woman was damaged and deserved sympathy, but she was also a hateful, tedious jerk. Gay believed she could have sympathy for her and still hate her. She pointed. "That's my house."

Claire slowed, then stepped off the curb and into the street. "You live in the spook house." She said something to herself and began shaking her head. "Why don't you do something about this yard? Cut down some of these trees?"

"I like it like this," Gay said, and turned to walk up her buckling sidewalk, but Claire remained in the street. "Aren't you coming?"

"I'm not sure. I'm a little worried about this."

"Dick doesn't know where I live."

"Not that. He could find you. He's a policeman. He's a detective. He knows where everybody lives and how to get there."

"Then my house is as good as the next."

"It's this sidewalk. This spook house. I'm not sure I should."

"Take my hand," Gay said. "I'll take you across."

Claire stared for a moment at the extended hand. She lifted her arm hesitantly, not taking Gay's hand but placing her forearm in Gay's grasp. They walked slowly. "Watch it here," Gay said. "It's uneven." Then she herself stumbled, which made her laugh. "I'm not cut out to be a guide."

Claire had not laughed at the stumble, but she laughed hard at this statement. Too hard, Gay thought. They stood on the walk in the dim moonlight while Claire doubled over with laughter. When she finally straightened, Claire said, "I know Margaret's little secret, too. I bet you don't. You think you're her friend, but I bet you don't know."

Gay shrugged, a weariness settling upon her, as if she had borne Claire's body the whole way. "Beats me," she said, trying to keep her voice light. "Let's go in."

Claire pushed away Gay's hand. "They had a baby in Phoenix. She and Randall Hubby Randall. They adopted a baby through some kind of payment and underground business. They got a baby out of Tennessee or Mississippi, one of those Confederate states."

"You're right," Gay said. "I didn't know that."

"You don't live with a detective."

"You want to go inside?"

"I'm not finished, peckerwood. So Margaret and Randall Hubby got the baby like they had wanted forever. She's sterile, we think, or he is, or they both are, but the point is, they got the baby through this deal, by paying this woman some thousand dollars, and then you know what?" She smiled savagely. "They sent the little bastard back." She began laughing once more, bending at her waist, her hands on her knees, roaring. A nasty laughter, like a person with wax caught in her throat and trying to cough it out. The laughter hurt Gay, not quite like blows to her body, but the ugly cackle caused her pain.

As abruptly as the laughter had started, it stopped. "Crack baby, we think," she said. "Or maybe, who knows, just a retard. That's why they moved here. You think they'd choose to move here? They had shown off with the neighbors, paraded their *son*, and then they shipped him back to the Confederate state he came from. So they moved here. Isn't that a hoot?"

Gay felt weak through the shoulders. A pressure began behind her eyes. She felt short of breath.

"You don't have a sense of humor," Claire said. "Why'd I want to talk to someone like you, anyway?"

"I wouldn't know," Gay said softly.

"Mr. Dick didn't want me to come see anybody tonight. That's why he held me in the shower. He thought that would stop me." She stomped her feet on the concrete.

Gay nodded, sniffed, and took a breath. "It didn't stop you."

"No," said Claire, stepping high over a crack in the sidewalk. "Nothing has stopped me. Except when you didn't get back to me."

"I understand that," Gay said.

"Do you know what my father did to me?"

"I think I might," Gay said.

"You should cut down these trees. All these trees. I hate trees," she said. She raised an arm as if against the threat of the branches. "My father loved me. Now Dick loves me. There's a whole country of men who love me. Am I spending the night?"

"If you want," Gay said. "I have a comfortable couch."

"How many men have you fucked on it?"

Gay took her elbow. "A few," she said. Claire jerked her arm free, stumbling from the force of it, falling off the walk. She screamed, "Get your hands off me."

Gay was not touching her but her arms were outstretched. She dropped them and stepped back. Claire crawled in the bare yard away from the sidewalk. "You pushed me," she said, her voice childlike with indignation. She climbed to her feet and ran, disappearing first in the dark yard and then into the darkness beyond.

18

Henry's brother Arturo and two of their sisters—one who lived in El Paso and one who lived in Phoenix—had come home for the weekend, even though it wasn't a holiday and the Thanksgiving break was coming up soon. Henry expected his brother to give him some grief about his hair, but he didn't. He merely put his hand on Henry's shoulder when he'd stepped from his car, and led Henry to the house. "I understand you're not Enrique anymore," his brother said.

"Only if you're speaking Spanish," Henry said.

"Fat chance in this family," Arturo said.

His sisters didn't say anything either, although they eyed his hair and made faces at each other that he wasn't supposed to see. He suspected that their mother had told them not to tease him about it. Maybe they told him how he'd already been beaten up by strangers over it, so he didn't need any family misery. One kid, a seventh-grader but *big*, now spat in Henry's hair every day just before second period.

Only Henry's oldest siblings were missing from the gathering—one sister who was pregnant and lived in Chicago, and one who was in the army and stationed in North Carolina. Their father had been on a vacation from his job at the elementary school for the past week, and it seemed to Henry that he had wasted most of it just lying around the house. "This is what I want do," his father had explained. "You're going tell your papa how he can use his time off?"

"It doesn't look like much fun," Henry had said.

"Fun is for kids. Grownups want relaxation. Besides, your brother and sisters are coming this weekend. That will be fun, no? Quit your thinking 'bout me. Tend to your own doing. Have your own fun while it's good."

Eating was always the main activity for any family reunion. Their mother had made a big spread—green chile, pozole (their father's favorite), flautas, fried chicken, refried beans, rice, cole slaw. She had stocked the refrigerator with beer, as well, and he and Cecilia were given the privilege of sharing a Miller Lite. "Just one," their father said. "We don't want you two running through the streets making silly." Cecilia had taken a drink and then, while trying to swallow, had snorted it out her nose. Henry sipped judiciously, and finished the remainder of the bottle. Arturo then slipped him another.

Before the meal was over, their father said, "This vacationing wears me out. I think I'm going to lay down. I see you all in the morning."

"You didn't eat your pozole," Henry said. Cecilia slugged him beneath the table on his thigh. "Ow," he said.

Their father, who was rising from his chair, said, "That boy's got eyes like a fox. Give Henry my pozole. Growing boy needs pozole with his beers."

The family laughed at that, and their father's pozole was poured into the bowl by Henry's plate. What Henry noticed was that their father had said Henry instead of Enrique, without stuttering or stumbling or correcting himself, and right in front of everybody, which made him think that it had been their father who told the others to say nothing about his hair and his name. This realization, along with the beer, made him feel warm and cheery inside.

Henry and Arturo cleared the table and swept beneath it with the short broom their mother kept in a corner behind the kitchen door. These were their traditional chores. Their mother and sisters washed the dishes, huddled around the sink, the radio playing softly from its corner—the same radio they'd had practically all of Henry's life. According to the family story, their father had come home with it the first week that they'd moved into the house, while Henry was still a toddler. "A new radio," their father had said, and their mother had said, "The old one still works." Their father had smiled and said, "But this one has a plug!" Then he had swung the cord around in a big circle so that their mother and all the kids had to duck down, laughing and whooping at their father's behavior. "He loves his electricity," their mother used to say.

"Wait here," Arturo told Henry, grabbing his arm and holding him still in the center of the living room. Arturo then disappeared into the kitchen. Henry heard his mother say, "Don't you get that boy drunk," before Arturo emerged with two fresh bottles of beer. Henry hadn't finished his second one yet, which was warm now.

"Chug it," Arturo said, gesturing toward the bottle in Henry's hand.

"Like all at once?" Henry said.

"Just like that," Arturo said.

Henry raised the bottle to his lips and drank, not really chugging as he'd often done with sodas, racing against friends, afraid that he might start snorting bubbles as Cecilia had. He eyed his brother while he drank, who gave him encouragement, nodding and shaking his fist. The warm beer started dribbling out around his lips, and he had to open up wider to avoid a major spill. He finished the bottle and sat it down too hard on top of the television, making a whack against the console.

"Good drinking there," Arturo said, handing him the cold bottle, then picking up the empty. "Let's go outside."

"Sure," Henry said, a big burp building uncomfortably inside him.

"Go on," Arturo said. "I'll meet you out there." He returned to the kitchen to throw away the empty.

Henry stepped out into the evening air, which was warm but not hot. In another few minutes, he knew it would be perfect out. The fall was the best time of year in southern New Mexico—mild days, beautiful nights. He lowered himself to the sidewalk, misjudging the ground slightly so that his butt hit the concrete heavily. "Whoa," he said to nobody, looking up and down the empty street. The yards that were kept up were still green, though none as green as his father's—none as small, either, he noted, but really it was plenty large, especially since you couldn't walk on it anyway. What would be the point of making it larger? He smiled at this logic, the intelligence of his father illuminated by pure reason. He twisted off the beer cap.

Arturo came through the front door with two lawn chairs. "Here," he said, handing one to Henry. "Don't ever sit on a sidewalk while you're drinking beer. It makes a bad impression."

"Oh," Henry said, glancing up and down the street. He wished he had his notebook with him. "Sorry."

They positioned their chairs to face the green square of grass and sat together, but Arturo stood almost immediately. "We need a little entertainment." He walked over to the faucet and hooked up the hose. He tossed the sprinkler into the center of their little yard and turned it on. The yellow arms of the sprinkler spun slowly. Arturo adjusted the faucet until the spray reached all but the corners. He took his chair next to Henry again. "That's better," he said. In companionable silence they watched the water fly from the spinning arms. Henry felt incredibly happy.

"So you've got a girlfriend, I hear," Arturo said.

"Yeah," Henry said.

"Cecilia's friend."

"Yeah," Henry said.

"She pretty nice?"

"Yeah," Henry said, "she's *real* nice."

"You and her, you using, you know, protection?"

"Oh," Henry said, thinking he was referring to the high school party, "she protected me some that one night, but mainly I protect her."

Arturo didn't say anything for a moment. Then he said, "That sounds fair."

"Yeah," Henry said. Then he added, "I love her."

Arturo looked him over, raising his eyebrows. He took a drink of beer. "That's good, too, I guess."

"Yeah," Henry said. He drank from the bottle, and immediately after the swallow was down, the big burp came up.

"Bless you," Arturo said, which made Henry laugh, and Arturo chuckled with him. He gestured toward the house, which made Henry look. "Mom's got Cousin Don on the phone. You remember him?"

"The nurse," Henry said, which made him think of his trip to the hospital in Tucson. "Hey, I know," he said, "what I've been thinking lately is about Apuro. I've been trying to remember it and stuff. You remember it?"

"Sure," Arturo said. "What about it?"

"Well . . ." Henry found that his thoughts had tumbled around without focusing, so he couldn't think, really, and he'd have to just start and hope it all came out right. "See, there's this kind of memory I get that isn't really a membering—remembering, I mean—so much as it's like a *picture* that means something I can't understand, you know what I mean?"

"Maybe," Arturo said uncertainly.

"Like I'm walking down the street and there's nothing out there but what's, you know, out there, and I'm thinking about stuff, nothing important, maybe I'm thinking how some girls have that little shadow right up between their eyes—you ever noticed that—bitty little shadow shows up there if you talk to them. So I'm just thinking about this and suddenly I get this picture in my head of someplace—someplace I'm not, and I can see it, and there it is, but it isn't there, and I was thinking this had to do with Apuro, 'cause I can't remember it."

Arturo paused for a moment, then took a long drink of his beer. He held his bottle up. It was almost empty. He drank again, finishing it off. "Let me see yours," he said.

Henry raised his bottle. More than half remained.

"Maybe I should finish that one for you before it gets hot," Arturo said.

"Oh, yeah," Henry said. "Good idea." He handed the bottle over. "I don't need another one just yet. Maybe later."

"Maybe later," Arturo said. Then he said, "You want to walk over to Apuro? Look around?"

"Hey, sure. I tried to do that myself once, but I wound up rolling into the river—long story. Yeah, that's a great idea."

"Pack up the chairs," Arturo said. "I'll turn off the entertainment."

.   .   .

While they walked to the crossing spot on the river, Arturo talked to Henry about moving from Apuro. "I didn't like living over here," he said. "Not at first. I was in second grade or something, and I would be going home and halfway cross the river before I realized I didn't live there anymore. Was like I had to get wet to remember."

"What did you miss?" Henry asked.

"My friends. The neighbors. It seemed more like a real place over there, while our neighborhood here was just a street with a bunch of houses on it." He stopped talking while they crossed the highway. "I missed the river, too," he said as they walked up to the river ledge. "One day I came home with black knees, and Pop took me out to the backyard and said if I went over to Apuro again, he was going to hit me with a paddle."

"You're kidding," Henry said. They stood on the sandy bank. Arturo balanced himself on one leg and slipped a shoe off without unlacing it and then his black sock. He balanced himself on the bare foot and removed the other shoe and sock. He didn't speak until he had folded the socks and stuffed them into the shoes.

"Pop was tougher on us older kids than he was on you and Cecilia. Come on." He stepped down into the riverbed, and began walking through the water. Henry had his shoes off and was hopping around trying to remove his socks without falling down. He finally sat to avoid falling, tucked his socks into his shoes, and followed his brother into the river, feeling slightly amazed, as if he were suddenly living out his own imagination.

Arturo picked up his story again. "Pop said I had to quit going to Apuro. Said, 'We live here, now.' That's how he put it. I didn't tell him I wasn't really going over there. I was just forgetting. I used to be kind of spacey as a kid, you know what I mean?"

"I guess," Henry said.

"But that cured me," Arturo said. "I grew up after that. Made me hate the old man for a while, but I got over that, too."

The water covered Henry's ankles and on up to mid-calf, the river shallow and warm from the day's heat, although now the air had turned cool. It was almost dark.

"Only one other time I ever hated Pop," Arturo said. They had come to the opposite bank, but Arturo hesitated, standing in the water, holding his shoes. He turned and looked up the river and down. "We should have brought some more beer," he said.

Henry pointed up river. "Rita lives thataway. You can't see her house."

"Rita," Arturo said. "I remember her being about ten and playing tea party with Cecilia. She used to be a little on the fat side."

"She's perfect now," Henry said.

Arturo stepped up out of the riverbed. He sat on a big rock. "Same rock we used when I was a kid," he said, running a foot over his pantleg to free it of pebbles. He pulled on a sock over his damp foot. "Same river, same rock." He patted a spot beside him. "Room enough for two," he said.

Henry copied his brother as precisely as he could, running his foot over the leg of his jeans to clean his sole, balling up the sock so that it would go over the wet foot more easily. Like the rituals of a ceremony that had been denied him, his brother's movements seemed to speak of a culture Henry did not know.

"Wonder if old Humberto is still around," Arturo said, rising. "You want to meet people or just look the place over?"

"I don't know," Henry said. "I haven't thought that far ahead."

"Want to know a secret?" Arturo asked, then answered before Henry could say. "I was born in Mexico."

"No way."

"We already lived up here, but we were back there visiting family, and I came out early. To hear Mom talk about it, Pop freaked. Mom was fine, I was fine, but he was all worried because to be a citizen I needed to be born in the U.S. They didn't have any papers or anything themselves back then. We left the night I was born, and when we got back here, he and Mom drove all the way to Las Cruces. Went to the hospital and said I'd been born in the car on the way over. So I got a U.S. birth certificate, but I'm Mexican."

"Cool," Henry said. "I never knew that."

"It's a story they quit telling."

They walked among the houses, waved at people who nodded back. A whole family of Anglos lived there, Henry noted, which surprised him. Arturo commented on it, too. "Used to be strictly Mex," he said. He didn't seem that interested, Henry thought, probably because he could remember the place with regular memories, while for Henry, Apuro lived not as recalled landscape or events, but as the coloring that made one thing stand out from the other, the way a bloom stands out from the leaves of a plant. He couldn't entirely articulate this in words, which disappointed him, because he felt his brother was giving him something, and he'd like to give something back, even if it was only an explanation of his desire.

"Hey, I know somebody who lives here," Henry said. "This guy named Tito. He helped Rita drag me out of that fight. Had some kind of advice about chickens, but I didn't get it all 'cause my nose was bleeding. Nice guy."

"You know which house he lives in?"

"Nuh-uh," Henry said. "No idea."

They continued walking. A small place, but there was a lot to notice—the potted plants and the geraniums, the old cars and the new ones, the Porta Potties all lined up in a row, and then the lights in the houses, as they came on, the strange whiteness of the lights. The houses were jumbled together, as if they had been tossed like dice and left wherever they landed. What did it mean to have lived in such a place? What did it mean to have left it? In an old white car, he saw two small boys playing, one turning the wheel wildly back and forth, the other pointing and talking. It occurred to Henry that his family had been poor when they lived here. That was obvious, he guessed, but he had never considered the possibility.

They were leaving, heading back to the crossing point, when Henry spotted Rudy Salazar standing beside one of the houses, his back to them, leaning on the wall—no, looking in a window. Which made Henry think of the family he had seen through the window that night in Tucson. Had Arturo seen *My Own Private Idaho*? Then he thought of seeing Rita and her bare feet through her kitchen window. For a second he felt connected to Rudy Salazar, who bent now at the knees to get a better look through the glass. Then he remembered that Rudy Salazar had broken Arturo's nose. He tugged on his brother's shirtsleeve and pointed.

"Let's avoid that clown," Arturo said. "Unless *you* want to talk to him."

"He broke your nose," Henry said.

"No shit," Arturo said. "Maybe I should say hi."

"He came to the house one day and sat on the grass. I told him not to, but he was already sitting there."

"What did he want?"

"I don't know," Henry said.

"Stay away from him," Arturo said, and as he said it, Rudy Salazar pulled his head away from the window and walked off, never noticing them.

"What do you think he was looking at?" Henry asked.

Arturo shrugged. "Take a look."

"Really?"

"You wanted to see Apuro. Look behind closed curtains."

Henry took a couple of steps, then looked back. Arturo said, "Hurry up. I'm ready for another beer."

Henry nodded. He tiptoed up to the window, which was lit, but the curtain was pulled shut. He stood where Rudy had stood, to one side, and peeked through a gap at the very edge of the window. A bedroom, mattress on the floor, sheets rumpled and haphazard, bright red plastic bins stacked on top of each other and filled with clothes—women's clothes. Then a woman walked through the room, passing so quickly through Henry's slice of vision that he could barely see her, but he could tell that she was in her underwear. It embarrassed him, excited him, and before he could turn away, she appeared again with a skirt, which she stepped into and pulled up her legs. Her bra was white and lacy and the woman's nipples showed through. And then he saw her face. Ms. Anna Ordaz. His heart tumbled about in his chest, and she disappeared, and the sheets moved—someone was still under a sheet. He could see the outline of a leg, and then a foot. The toenails were painted pink.

He ran back to his brother. "Anything?" Arturo asked.

Henry shook his head. The pink toenails rather than the glimpse of nipples through the bra, stayed with him as they walked over the path to the rock, where they removed their shoes and still wet socks, and where they stepped again into the river. Had Ms. Ordaz been in bed with the other woman? Were they sisters? Lovers? He used to think about her a lot, he recalled.

"That other time," Arturo said, jerking Henry back to the night, the water, the moon as it appeared in the water, his brother wading beside him and speaking, "was when he didn't let me play Sancho Panza in the school play."

"Who didn't?"

"Pop. Wouldn't let me because, he said, it was a demeaning role, that I should have been the star. But the truth was, I had some lines in Spanish. The director—Mrs. McMichael, she's still at the high school—had this idea about making the play a border story, so it was in *Spanglish*. Dumb, probably, but I wanted to do it, and he wouldn't let me. I hated him for that. For . . . oh, two months." He put his arm around Henry and pointed up at the moon. "Moon," he said, and Henry looked. The water barely covered their ankles.

"He's never done anything mean to me," Henry said, staring up at his brother's finger silhouetted against the moon. "He barks at me sometimes, but nothing mean like that."

"Yeah. He's been a good father," Arturo said, his voice, like the moon's reflection in the water, breaking up.

19

Rudy preferred sex with the Anglo girl, Marcia Ivygale, to sex with the Mexican girl, Crystal Rodriguez. Both were from across river, and neither was choosy about who she slept with. Crystal was better looking. Rudy wasn't fooling himself. He wasn't one of those guys who thought any Anglo girl was better looking than the best-looking Chicana. He knew Marcia wasn't particularly attractive to anyone. Her hair was good, long and light brown, but she had a peculiar nose, the nostrils slightly different in shape from each other, and her eyes had a sad, hangdog look about them. "*Ojos de perro*," Antonio had said of her once. Eyes of a dog.

Crystal had a better body, too, and she certainly had a better sense of humor. But Rudy got off more fucking Marcia Ivygale. She had rules. He had to talk to her for an hour before she would fuck him. No quickies. She wouldn't do two boys at once. And, as she put it, "No circus business." Just the basics.

Rudy liked these rules, appreciated them, but they weren't why he preferred her. He didn't know why.

He met Marcia at the Conoco station, around the side, by the bathrooms. He checked his watch as she walked up, 9:15. He wouldn't be able to fuck her until 10:00 at the earliest.

"Let's walk," she said. She was carrying a paperback book.

"You going to read?" Rudy asked her. "Think you going be bored?"

"I thought you might be late," she said, shaking her long hair as she spoke. "Come on."

"I don't want to walk to anywhere," he said.

"No one will see you with me," she said patiently. "I thought we could go down by the river where there's that cane."

"Fuck that," Rudy said. "I like it here." The Conoco abutted an empty lot, the sand greasy from illicit oil changes. Broken glass glinted in the moon's faint light.

"There's no place to sit," she said, her imbalanced nostrils slightly flared.

"Already thought of that." He displayed the key to the Men's room. "Way ahead of you."

Marcia shrugged and folded her arms. "All right, I guess."

Attached by a thick wire to the key was a wide piece of flat metal almost a foot long that bore the word M-E-N in magic marker. Rudy opened the door and held it for her. She flicked on the light as she walked in, pausing just inside to give the little room an appraising look. The toilet sat at the far end of the narrow room, with a floor urinal and sink against a side wall. A cracked mirror was positioned above the sink, a condom dispenser next to it. She walked over to the toilet, flushed it, then lowered the black lid and sat on it. "Where are you gonna sit?"

He leaned against the door. "Don't need to sit," he said. "So . . ." He knew what she expected. They had to talk for a while, and he had to initiate some of the conversation. "How are you, anyway?"

She lifted one side of her mouth. "I've got Fowler for chemistry. He's supposed to be a prick. But Dombrowski is teaching calculus this semester, and I like her. I had her for geometry."

"She's the one carries her tits like—"

"She doesn't have any tits," Marcia said definitively. "You're thinking of what's-her-name, teaches government. She wears some kind of shoebox bra. Mrs. Shoebox." Marcia made a gurgling noise, which was as close as she ever came to laughing. "This guy I know swears he saw her in a bar in El Paso wearing a red miniskirt and shaking her butt across the floor. Can you imagine?"

"That's not Dombrowski?"

Marcia shook her head. She liked gestures that made her hair move. "Dombrowski's nice."

"But no *chichis*."

"She's *little*, like this tall." Sitting on the toilet lid, she raised one hand even to her head. Marcia, standing, came within an inch or so of Rudy's height. A tall girl with long hair, maybe that was why he preferred her to Crystal, the crown of her head only barely reaching his chin.

"I've seen her," Rudy said.

"She didn't major in math in college. Biology. Taught for a while at some college in California, but she got married and her husband moved them here."

"Who's she married to?"

"How do I know?" Marcia cocked her head and widened her eyes. "Some dipshit named Dombrowski. What an ugly name."

"You write a report on her or something?"

"We talk. She tells me stuff." She paused, her mouth shaping a word, her eyes flitting back and forth. "Like she had an abortion when she was going to college. Don't tell anybody that."

"No sweat," Rudy said.

Marcia shifted on the toilet, crossing her arms and legs simultaneously. "You're not really talking to me, you know."

"I can't help it you run at the mouth about this *puta* math teacher."

She shook her hair again, angrily this time, and shifted again on the toilet seat, tugging fiercely on the skirt of her dress. "She's my friend."

"*Pues, depende.*" He felt a specific pleasure begin in his chest, a warmth, a sweetness. "She *acts* like your friend. That doesn't mean she's your friend *de veras.*" He made a mocking face at her as he spoke, savoring the moment.

"Like *you* are."

He shrugged, trying not to smile. "Not her either. She feels sorry for you, you *pobrecita.*"

"Fuck you, Rudy. She's my friend."

"Yeah? You hang out with her? Outside school?"

"I've been to her house."

"You hang out with her?" He waited but she couldn't say anything, staring down at her lap, letting her hair cover her face. The pleasure he had taken in tormenting her hardened in him, turning to contempt. "Don't be stupid. You take these classes and you think you're smart, but you act stupid."

She spoke without looking up, running her finger along the pages of her book. "You can have friends you don't rob liquor stores with, or whatever you and your friends do."

"I don't rob stores, and I don't have friends," he said. Tito Tafoya's preposterous smile flashed before him. Tito was the exception. No need to muddy the waters with exceptions. "Friends are for children."

"You're pathetic," she said, turning to face the graffiti on the wall.

"Looking for your phone number?" Rudy asked. "This friend of yours, you tell her how you like to fuck? Huh? Why don't you tell her that if she's your friend?"

"Fine, we're not friends. Okay? How did we get started on this, anyway?" She ran a hand over her arm. "I just wanted to tell you I like one of my teachers, and you turn it into something awful."

"Hey, I like all my teachers."

"Give me a break."

"Why shouldn't I? They're teachers and we're students, so, *bueno*, maybe I don't *like* them, but I respect them. Until they try to fuck me over, then—"

"Then you blow out the windows in their car."

"Didn't have no choice, girl." He had told her about the previous coach. For a while she had liked for him to talk tough while they fucked. "Some things I've got to do. Just like you."

"It's not the same," she said, her voice tightening, her eyes not red or teary but thick and wooden, "and you know it."

"What's with the book?"

"What's *with* it? I'm reading it."

"Why?"

"Because I want to. I *like* to read."

"Don't have to get pissed, *chica*. Just asking you a question. What's it about?"

"Nothing. Forget it."

"I'm just asking what your book's about."

She puffed her cheeks and sighed. "It's a book about a family."

"Yeah?"

"They're a fucked-up family, and the girl who the story's about . . ." She stopped and looked up at the ceiling, which appeared yellow in the poor light and traversed with cracks, the paint curling along the cracks. Like veins, Rudy thought. Like the ceiling was a part of a living thing.

"Go on," he said.

"She's beautiful and they're rich, but she doesn't like it at home, so she gets money out of her father's private account—her father's having an affair with this girl's friend—and she pretends to run away, but really she goes to another friend's house. That's as far as I've got so far."

"Sounds like a good story."

"Yeah, only parts of it are fake. Like they never watch TV, and she has this real nice guy who is crazy about her, and he's *perfect*, but she won't look twice at him, so you know they're going to wind up together at the end."

"How do you know that?"

"It's how these stories work. They're stupid really, but I like reading them. I don't actually enjoy them, but, okay, I do enjoy them but I don't respect them."

"That's what I was saying about teachers. I don't like the cocksuckers, but I respect them."

Marcia closed her eyes. "We're not the same," she said quietly. She grew pale, her skin almost luminous. With her eyes shut, she looked to be made of marble. "I *need* boys to fuck me. All right? Does it make you happy to hear me say that?" Beneath their lids, her eyes darted to one side and then another, like something trapped. "I don't know why, and I don't care. It's just this thing I have to do." She took a breath and opened her eyes. "You're not like that. You're . . . you're not going to like this word, but what you are is a psychopath."

Rudy smiled at the sharp pain this caused him, like a sting from a wasp. "So you think I'm a crazy Mexican, that what you're saying? *Un loco* motherfucker?"

"That's not what I said." She turned again to the graffiti.

"Oh? Just *un poco loco*? Huh?" He squatted to put his face level with hers. He scooted closer to her, remaining in the squat, leaving parallel trails across the dirty linoleum. She wouldn't look at him, didn't say anything. "Okay, then why—"

A pounding came from the other side of the door. "Pardon me. You're holding up the restroom," a voice yelled. "There are people here."

"Get the fuck away from here!" Rudy yelled. He leaped up and hammered on the door. "You hear me? Go fuck yourself." He waited until he heard steps leaving the door, a man talking to a boy. When he turned his head, Marcia was smiling at him. "What?"

"He must think you have the worst case of the shits in history."

Rudy grinned and exhaled sharply. "Some dumb asshole with a kid." He looked at his watch, 9:40. "Show me some more leg. Come on, Marcia. Little bit of white."

Marcia looked to the floor, but she took the hem of her dress in her hand and pulled it up a few inches, her thigh white and clean, like a band of snow. "Mrs. Dombrowski says I can get a scholarship to almost any school I want."

"Higher," Rudy said. "What color your panties?"

She tugged the dress higher, her thighs touching, her underwear the gray of winter skies. "She says I should go to Michigan. The University of Michigan. That's where she went."

"They take psychos there? 'Cause if I'm a psycho, I know you gotta be one. Maybe they give me a scholarship, too."

"In what?"

"Spread 'em out some. Pull the panties—not down. Did I say down? Pull them aside some. Yeah. You think that book fit in there? I bet it would. I bet you could fit a whole library in there."

"You don't have to be mean to me, Rudy."

He had to think about that. It seemed to him that he did have to be mean to her. Not just for his sake, but for her sake, too. Without it, what would they have to pass between them but flat and idle words?

"You played well against the Eagles," Marcia said, her dress bunched at her waist, the fingers of one hand tracing a figure scrawled on the wall. "I was at the game."

"Okay, pull 'em down now," Rudy said.

Marcia put her book on the back of the toilet and took her panties off. Then she stood and grabbed the hem of her dress, but she paused. "What time is it?"

Rudy looked at his watch: 9:45. "Ten," he said.

She pulled the dress over her head. "Where can I put this?"

Rudy took it from her and tossed it onto the sink. "Turn around," he said.

She swung around and leaned over the toilet, putting her hands, then her elbows, against the wall. Rudy unzipped himself and ran his hands over her butt, using his foot to spread her legs. He lifted the toilet seat.

"Why are you doing that?" she asked him. The filthy bowl was dappled gray like certain horses.

"Shut up now," Rudy said, his fingers inside her body, spreading her open. "The talking part's over."

He laced his arms under hers and gripped her shoulders, pushed himself way inside. He pumped against her hard and fast. He wanted to feel that he was hurting her and that she liked it, but she didn't seem to feel anything. Why did she want to fuck if she didn't feel anything? He could understand if it made her feel bad. A lot of people wanted to feel bad. But he couldn't understand it if she felt nothing. It pissed him off. He pushed against her harder, but she just leaned against the wall, then put her hands on the back of the toilet to balance herself. He felt himself losing it, going soft. The bitch.

He took her nipples in his finger and pinched.

"Ow," she said, but it didn't sound like real pain, just an announcement to make him stop. He grabbed her shoulders again, pulled himself up on her back, so that she leaned over more, riding her back as he fucked her. He raised his knees and pressed against her thighs, making her bear not only his weight but the pressure of his thrusts at the fulcrum. She bent lower still, her head against her arms on the toilet tank. Rudy freed one of his hands and flicked her book from the top of the tank. It fell into the toilet.

"Goddamn it, Rudy," she said, and reached down for it, but he yanked her shoulder up at the same time, his feet slipping back to the floor, the feeling growing in his cock again. She was crying now, crying over the fucking book while he felt the buildup, the moments before the surge. She was supposed to be so smart, but here she was crying over this book when he'd tossed in the toilet to keep from having to hit her. She had no comprehension of his compassion. "Stupid bitch," he said as he came, shoving himself as far up inside her as he could.

He pulled his pants up and zipped. He rinsed his hands. She was no longer crying, but trying to step past him to get her dress. He stepped from side to side to block her. "Don't bring no fucking book next time," he said. "You think I like that?"

"Let me get dressed," she said.

Rudy grabbed the dress. "Maybe I ought to take this home with me. I could use this, I bet." He held the dress high when she tried to reach it.

"Give it to me," she said.

"I already gave it to you," he said smiling. He thought she might cry again, but suddenly she quit reaching and put her arms around his chest. She pulled her naked body close to him, her head pressed against his shoulder. "Here," he said and tossed the dress back on the sink. He waited. When she didn't let go, he pried one of her shoulders away, then grabbed the doorknob. "I'm turning this key in. You better get dressed quick."

She nodded, and he felt the urge to do something else, a different kind of urge, not sexual, the urge to touch her hair, a caress. He gave in to the urge, running his hand gently down the back of her head. But it caused a turn in his stomach, a feeling that he could describe only as weakness. He threw the door open and stepped out into the dark.

20

Rita had the best horse and she made it run. "Last one in has to brush them all down," she yelled, the others already too far behind her to catch up. Neither Henry nor Cecilia were familiar enough with riding even to try, and Heart, she knew, would linger with them in any case. For two weeks, Rita had asked to go riding, but once she mounted the horse she knew she had only wanted a gander at Mr. Gene's ranch and, ideally, at the man himself. He had not presented himself, despite the presence of his truck. How could he be elsewhere if his truck was in the driveway? Shyness was one thing, but this was rude.

The ranch was more rundown than she remembered, the driveway lined by barbed wire all the way to the main road, with bits of trash caught in the barbs, including several Styrofoam cups from 7-Eleven, all dangling like ugly Christmas ornaments. The driveway opened to a wide yard of gray dirt, a single big tree off to one side, its branches stark and desolate, a rope hanging from one branch that ended in a sour fray, as if the original swing had been dissolved in acid. The barn, too, disappointed her, just a row of stalls, the ceiling so low that the horses almost banged their heads if they whinnied with any enthusiasm. A ladder led up to an attic—or whatever you called a garret when it was in a grubby barn—where he evidently kept hay, based on the mess on the floor beneath the opening. The house produced more frustration, a shabby little bungalow with rotting siding and patches on the roof, a dingy front porch whose uneven planks reminded Rita of the rolling floor of the fun house at the county fair. A measurable layer of dust covered everything.

Even the weather seemed sleazy, a cold front arriving this morning, the sky the gray of dirty linen, a chill that led them all to wear ugly caps and old sweaters ragged at the elbows.

Rita had prettied up her memory of the place and had arrived half expecting a stone mansion perched beside a mountain stream. The reality of it annoyed her. This was a place where a person did hard work for little reward, where the prize of solitude and self-sufficiency came at the expense of menial labor, squalid living, and daily exhaustion. It turned her stomach. She guessed then that she had done the same to Mr. Gene, that he was really just some guy who wouldn't talk.

Riding in cold weather didn't help her temperament; it made her feel petulant and selfish, and so she took off on the horse, announcing the race as an afterthought, knowing they wouldn't have a chance of catching her even in a fair contest. She galloped down a dirt road, through a pecan orchard, the limbs bare now, the cold air making her nose run and eyes water. She would be sore, she realized, feeling it already in her butt and thighs. The horse began snorting, little clouds showing and disappearing in the cold air. She worried that she had harmed him by making him run so hard and that's why he was snorting, a healthy black gelding she had named Blackie when she had known him a few years ago, but Heart had called him Ace.

Rita realized the ranch lay just ahead. The horse was simply eager to get back to his barn, his cozy stall. No sooner had she thought this than she sighted Mr. Gene standing beside his ugly truck, opening the tailgate. He had his eyes on something in the truck bed, turning his head from side to side. He put one knee on the tailgate, beginning to climb into the bed, but then he heard Ace beating the dirt with his hooves. He halted movement for less than a second, partially into the bed, one knee up, one boot still on the ground. His head turned. He saw Rita approaching.

His next move was toward the house, but Rita waved wildly and called, "Wait! Wait!" The heavy gallop of the horse, the waving, the yelling. He would think there was trouble. Where were the others, after all? Rita had not consciously misled him, but she didn't mind the misunderstanding. She pulled on the reins, watching Mr. Gene, while Ace huffed and slowed. He was not as handsome as she had recalled, but not ugly like his farm, just a man, a face and body that went together well enough.

He shut the tailgate to the truck, then turned, raising his hand to his eyes, as if to block the sun, but the sky was drab and sunless. As she pulled even with him, he put the flat of his hand on the mammoth jaw of the animal, his face tense, deep declivities in the flesh between his eyebrows.

"How are you?" Rita said.

One kind of tension left his face, but it was quickly replaced by another. The lines in his forehead and around his eyes relaxed for less than a second, but she witnessed it and it left a charge.

"Where are they?" he asked softly, then ducked slightly, patting the horse, hiding from her.

"They're coming," she said. "We were racing."

He looked down at his boots, which were a brown that was almost red. He muttered something about the barn, the brushes.

"I can't hear you," Rita said. She began to dismount, but Ace stepped forward abruptly, and she waited.

Mr. Gene said, "Careful." He glanced at her, offering a quick smile as he turned and began heading for the house.

"You're being rude," she called.

He stopped, slowly turned, tipping his hat down to shade his face, not turning all the way, facing the tree with the rope but speaking to her. He spoke so softly the words seemed to drift before reaching her. ". . . can't help . . ." was all she could make out. He stepped up onto the rotting porch and let himself inside his little house. He might have said, "I can't help it," or "I can't help myself." Possibly he said, "I can't help you."

In the bed of the truck, a big cat eyed Rita suspiciously, her head poking out from a filthy nest of burlap. He liked cats, she thought. She had discovered that much about him. The truck smelled of manure.

"That's no way to act." Heart had said nothing until the Nissan had cleared the Calzado driveway. Rita waved again to Henry, who stood in the doorway watching her depart. "You don't invite people out and then abandon them," Heart went on. She hunched forward as she always did when she drove, her hands and elbows touching the steering wheel. "It's ugly."

You're what's ugly, Rita thought, anger rising up in her to match Heart's. "They didn't mind," she said. She folded her arms and lifted her feet to the dashboard, wishing now she had remained in the backseat. She didn't need a lecture from Heart.

"They think too much of you to guess you were being rude," Heart said, her voice changing, a strange quality swimming up in it—disappointment or grief or an emotion Rita didn't know the name for.

"You don't have to get all mad." Rita turned her head away from Heart so sharply her nose touched the cold glass of the passenger window. The squat houses lining Cecilia's street, built to handle the intense summer, looked shabby in the cold. The sudden chill had caused the remaining leaves on the deciduous trees to turn gray and fall. They ringed the trunks like grime left in a tub. "I said I was sorry."

"No, you did not."

"*They* understood I was sorry. I didn't have to spell it out for them. *They're* my friends."

Heart braked too hard, the car stopping several feet before the stop sign. Rita rocked forward, her chin brushing against her raised knees before her body snapped back against the seat. The coffee thermos tumbled from its spot on the handbrake to the floorboard, and the soiled washcloth Heart used to wipe condensation from the windshield flew from the dash and landed on the seat below Rita's legs, unfolding as if it had spilled out of her.

"Buckle your seatbelt," Heart said, "and get your feet off the glove box."

Rita sighed noisily but obeyed. The car made a drumming sound. Heart had shifted into park and was gunning the engine. There was another sound, beneath the engine's beating: Heart's ragged breath. She was about to cry and racing the engine to hide it. "Don't ask me to take you riding again," she said, the same something rising in her voice, navigating through the rending gasps. She could have been drowning. "I won't do it. I will not do it."

"Fine," Rita said, her mood now completely black. "I won't ask. I didn't like it, anyway."

Heart tapped her fingers angrily against the steering wheel, the tips striking dully because she chewed her nails. She let the engine recede to an idle, shifted into drive, and lifted her foot from the brake. The car rolled forward to the stop sign, and she braked again. A man appeared at the corner, bent over, eyeing the Nissan before chasing a brown paper bag into the intersection, finally stamping the bag with his foot. He carried a hammer in one hand. When he stood, the heads of nails shone in his mouth, erupting from a face otherwise as serene as those on dollar bills. He hopped slightly to show he was hurrying from the street, a little jig for their benefit. A way of being polite.

"I had a friend who went on a field trip in high school," Heart began, the engine humming now beneath her voice, an accompaniment. "And the parent who was supposed to be watching the kids decided she had to have a drink and just left them on the battlegrounds. Didn't say a word."

"What battlegrounds?" Rita asked. The trees, shorn of leaves, looked like steel sculptures, like imitations of trees. She felt peculiar, a strange urgency filling her chest. "Are we just going to sit here?"

Heart glanced in either direction, then turned up the blower on the heater, as if such an act required secrecy. She pulled out into the intersection. The street was utterly dead, even the man with nails in his mouth had vanished. "A battlefield from the Civil War," she said. "The area I grew up in was full of them. When this parent left, my friend got worried." Her voice had become steady, the forced calm adults developed to keep children from panicking. Rita felt a prickle along her spine. She was afraid, although she knew this story was about the past. Heart continued, "It was hard enough on my friend just to be out there with those other kids. You don't just abandon people. Decent folks don't behave like that." She braked again and in the same motion began a U-turn. "I ought to check on the store while we're out this way," she said.

In the surrounding gloom, the downtown buildings seemed to shrink, as if hunching in the cold, while the angled white lines on the street, entirely free of vehicles, suggested a purpose besides parking, something grander, something of larger consequence. Heart veered over them, driving on the wrong side of the road, the parking lines passing beneath the car like ties beneath a train. She stopped the car before the large window and glass door of the bookstore. Steam rose from the sewer grate, a smelly steam Rita imagined so thoroughly she ran her finger beneath her nostrils.

Heart left the engine running, the heater on high. She made no move to leave the car. About the corner of her mouth, a slight yellow stain showed, a birthmark, Rita guessed, although she had never noticed it before. It seemed unfair that Heart should have this discoloration on her face, which was ugly anyway. Why did her body offer nothing but indignities, while

Rita's mother had not only an attractive shape and a pretty face, but also a symmetrical smile and flawless skin?

"A little cold weather," Heart said softly, "and people think it's the end of the world." She pursed her lips, then drew her hand across her mouth. The yellow spot streaked, nothing but a trace of coffee on her skin. Rita's indignation faded away.

They sat silently in the idling car, which was becoming overwarm. Rita knew she had been rude, but she was not used to Heart's anger, and she didn't know what to do now to regain their customary balance. She didn't want to say the wrong thing and set Heart off again. Had she ever seen Heart cry? She had—at the movies, while reading a book, once when Rita had tearfully reported the unkindness of a fellow sixth-grader. On the door of the bookstore, a handwritten note taped to the glass read, *Closed until one p.m. Saturday*. Even her penmanship was ugly.

Rita said, "Why was your friend so nervous?"

Heart turned from the store, her crooked mouth open slightly. "I don't think I'm going to open up today," she said solemnly, as if passing judgment on a serious matter. "Nobody's out, and I don't feel like it."

"Do you want me to take your note down?" Rita asked. "I don't mind doing it."

"Some people are just born nervous," Heart said. "They can't take the pressure of being out in the world. You can't abandon them. Ever. So you find some way to stick it out. Even if it's a ridiculous way." She gripped the gearshift and located reverse. "Nobody's going to read that note anyway. Let's just leave it." She backed the car into the vacant street, although Rita couldn't see a reason for backing. It occurred to her that Heart might be talking about Rita's mother. She tried to recall details of the story about the bet and the green felt hat. "Why did you decide to leave the commune?" she asked, her voice steady but soft, little more than a whisper.

Heart touched her eyes, her glasses rocking up as she rubbed them. The car remained in the middle of Main Street, straddling the yellow center line, unmoving except for its exhaust making clouds that rose up over them and then vanished in the cold air. "You're always making decisions," Heart said, "whether you know it or not. It's handy if you know it, but most of the time you don't. You understand what I mean?"

The tone of her reply made Rita regret the question. She was going to get more than she had asked for. Which meant that merely asking had been a decision, which now had the consequence of having to listen. "Yeah," she said, "I know what you mean."

"You have to pick between your responsibility to one thing and your commitment to something else. You can't please everybody." Her eyes flitted to the rearview mirror. She waved at a car behind them. The passengers, a whole family of people in coats, gazed in the Nissan curiously as they passed.

"We're sitting in the middle of the road," Rita said. "Isn't this illegal?"

Heart didn't seem to hear. "It got too easy on the farm. Same thing all the time. And I missed people. Your mother didn't live with me there for long, but . . . we had a falling out. You know about it?"

"Maybe. A little bit."

Heart lifted her foot from the brake. The car began rolling down the street and into the proper lane. "Nobody was to blame," she said, arms and elbows against the wheel once more. The car picked up speed and her answer seemed to be over, which relieved Rita. But she began to wonder about a person's history, how you do things and those things accumulate, and then the accumulation starts affecting you. Heart surprised her by speaking again. "I wanted to be a part of your life," she said.

"*My* life?"

"I own that ranch," Heart said. "I've always loved horses. We had horses on the commune. I couldn't think about leaving until I had enough money to take my horses with me."

"You own it? The ranch?" Rita said, this information erasing what had come before it. When Heart nodded, Rita said, "Is that how you met Mr. Gene?"

"Not exactly, no." She almost smiled. "I never wanted to live out there, but I like horses and he likes . . . that kind of life."

"Well," Rita said, thinking maybe she had discovered something, but not at all sure that she had. What did this new information reveal? She was not sure, but she knew what to say. "I'm sorry I was rude," she said. "Sometimes I just get an urge and I do it."

"Oh, yes," Heart said. "We adventurous types have to act on our urges." Her smile was so large and so crooked that it misshaped her entire face. She pressed the accelerator, and the Nissan vibrated slightly, a mild tremor that shook them both, then went away.

21

DECEMBER

Gay flattened herself against Denny's bed while he massaged her back and shoulders, a knee on either side of her waist, the balls of his thumbs pressing into her skin. Naked, having already made love, their sex too urgent to satisfy the magnitude of their desire, they traded now in the pleasurable agony of deep massage and talk, "catching up," Gay wanted to call it, as if being apart and falling behind were the same thing.

Circumstances and the basketball schedule had temporarily separated them. They had not seen each other since the brief exchange at the locker room door the night Gay had guided Claire from the gym, and this was why Gay thought of Claire, because when she and Denny were last together, Claire had been present. "Her husband had held her in the shower to keep her from going out," Gay said, her speech punctuated by Denny's thrusts to her sore spots. "He's—"

"What's that clown's name?"

"Dick," she said. "Detective Dick." Dick Brownlee's bald head and arrogant eyes flitted before her when she closed her lids. The prick. The son of a bitch. All of her epithets were sexual, she realized. The bastard.

Denny worked her neck, pushing her head against the mattress, the white sheet that still smelled of laundering. He had become meticulous about the bed, which she appreciated, especially now. A "rubdown," he had called it, warning that he was well practiced, and that his rubdowns hurt. Now a burning that began at the tips of his fingers ran down her body in separate trails, causing her to lift her feet from the mattress, her back arching in anguish. "He beats her," she said, groaning at the pain, "or something that has the same effect. It may be something sexual he does." Denny's hands moved from her neck to her shoulders, rubbing them gently at first, loosening the muscles but causing her to anticipate the coming torture. This was no ordinary massage.

"She ought to be in a hospital," Gay went on, taking advantage of the relaxed spell, "but she went home. Randall Lamb has given her medical leave." Her talk seemed to extend the gentle part of the rub. "She thinks he's holding her position, but Margaret says there's no way you can teach third grade after having a major breakdown." Gay paused, a sudden tingling in her chest, a warmth separate from the exhortation of his hands: the excitement of temptation, the thrill of revealing more of herself than the naked body splayed at present across his bed. "I had a breakdown myself after I got out of jail," she said. "I told you about jail."

"A little." His hands slowed but pushed slightly harder, rings of pressure growing from his fingers. "Smoking dope—lousy dope, I believe you said— and your folks wouldn't come pick you up." The pressure turned to pain, his fingertips insinuating into the muscle and tissue.

"Not . . . jail . . . that caused . . . breakdown," she said, her speech made telegraphic by the kneading. Her parents had never spoken another word to her, leaving her in the city jail, the police befuddled and amused.

"They're the ones who sound crazy," Denny said, lifting his hands, his body lifting too, as he bent forward, his weight on her shifting. The knob of his elbow lodged in her back just below a shoulder blade and began rolling on her skin in small circles, digging in deeper with each revolution.

"Am I going to hear your ugly family stories," she asked quickly, partly to divert him, "or is this strictly a one-way confessional?"

He let out a grunt that sounded almost like laughter, the motion of the elbow slowing as he spoke. "One of my old man's tidbits, one of his not-so-enigmatic sayings, occurred to me while you were talking. He said if you kept putting your dick somewhere, your heart would eventually follow."

"Ugh."

"You asked for ugly." Then the point of his elbow turned into a knife, and she let out a scream. He sat up. "You want me to let up?"

"No," she said immediately, before she had even caught her breath. "It just hurts."

"Your back is all balled up." He leaned forward again, the elbow resting beneath her other shoulder blade. "So what happened to you in the slammer?"

"Nothing. Heart got me out." If she talked, she delayed the pointed bone from screwing into her back; however, she knew all she had to do was tell him and he would stop. She didn't want him to stop, but she talked quickly nonetheless, to make him pause. "I didn't know Heart at the time. She heard about my predicament through the family grapevine and drove down from her commune. The charges were dropped, and I went home with her. We were strangers, although her parents and mine had grown up in the same town." She took a quick breath. "Then, my first morning on the commune, I couldn't get out of bed. I had a breakdown." The knife again sank into her back, and she screamed again, but he did not stop this time, and her back burst into flame.

"That feel better?" he asked, rocking back, the surface of her back calming like water after a storm. He flattened his hands and rubbed gently. He encouraged her to continue her story.

She told him about being crazy. Heart had arranged a phone call with several friends from home. A boy who had been arrested with her told her about his parents' reactions, while another boy picked up on an extension and began pleading with her to come back, but she had thought it was the first boy altering his voice, trying to mess with her head. While she described it, the memory of that phone call returned to her with such clarity and completeness that it frightened her. She felt the same strange distance from herself, the suspicion and dread, the anxiety and certainty all in one radiating pulse, which shifted, abruptly, to pain, her lover's knuckles now burrowing into her spine. Pain cut through the distance effortlessly.

"How long did this breakdown last?" Denny asked. Already he had let up. She could tell by the speedy way he covered her middle back that he would not use his elbows again. She felt both relieved and disappointed by this revelation.

"I got better after a couple of weeks," she said, "but I wasn't entirely myself for months. Once I recovered, I managed to get pregnant in no time flat." She'd had sex at the commune on Heart's old sofa, and her sensitized back could almost feel the ribs of corduroy on that overstuffed couch against her bare skin. She recalled how her butt would slide uncomfortably into the crack between the cushions, and the dark thrill of being a teenager and fucking a grown man in her cousin's living room. She even remembered the smell of the place. Everything in Heart's cabin had carried the faintly sweet odor of unwashed bodies combined with marijuana smoke. "I stayed with Heart until Rita was born, then Sander and I got a house. What?"

He crab-walked his fingers and thumbs across her waist. She turned to look at him, and he was studying her so intently, she felt suddenly nervous. He said, "I get the feeling you're leaving something out."

She smiled and closed her eyes. "It's complicated." In the time it took to speak these words, she understood that she would tell him everything. He would like hearing about her bad behavior. He would love her for it. "There was this man that Heart liked, a guy named Miguel Delgado—"

"Delgado? Isn't that Rita's boyfriend's name?"

"That's Calzado."

"Oh, yeah. I'm bad with Mexican names. So Heart liked this Miguel guy."

She had his complete attention, she could tell, even with her eyes closed. He slid farther down her body, straddling her butt while his fingers started in on the meat of her hips. "Miguel and Sander had a floundering landscaping business. They lived on the commune to save rent money—not ideological types, those two. They were Heart's friends, and that's how I met them."

"She was seeing Miguel?"

"They were friends, but edging toward more." His knuckles seemed flush against the bones of her hips, a duller hurt, a purple pain after the searing red. She wondered how she would explain these bruises all over her backside to Sander. She was no longer as frank with him as she had been, not when it came to Denny. "Heart liked him. Miguel. A lot. She'd had a weird home life, from what she told me. Her dad spent a year in prison for bad checks, and one of her brothers was a shut-in or a recluse or something. Then she got cancer. Lost part of one breast." The crease in the breast, like a pleat in the flesh, curved like a crescent, a scar that would have its own beauty if it were not deforming the breast, turning the nipple up, making Heart forever askew. "She lost her hair, too, because of the chemo, but she wore a blond wig that looked better than her real hair looks now. Everyone at the commune liked her. Then I moved in, and . . ." Her heart kicked in, a rush of blood to her face, her battered back. "I wound up *dating* both Sander and Miguel behind Heart's back."

The prodding of her back stopped. "Interesting," Denny said, his hands slow to return to their business. She eyed him suspiciously. The smile he gave her indicated genuine pleasure. Everyone loved to hear of another's weakness.

"I was a teenager," she said, sounding defensive but not feeling it. "Heart saved me from jail and homelessness, so, of course, I slept with the man she wanted but couldn't get. Does my parents' decision to dump me make better sense now?"

"I'll reserve judgment," he said, backing himself farther down her body by shuffling backward on his knees. His hands settled now on her ass, the same rhythmic force, the same penetrating spurs, his fingers digging into the soft mounds up and down the cleft, creating now another suspense.

She liked his hands on her. She wanted no intimacy unshared. "I wish I could say I slept with Miguel because I'd had a breakdown and wasn't myself." She would leave no room for him to make excuses for her, and still he would love her. "But I didn't sleep with him until I was better. I had a crush on Sander, but Miguel wasn't even my type. He was sweet and kind, but I wasn't attracted to him until after we were lovers. Heart seems to be over all this now, but we never talk about it. Of course, she won't tell me a thing about her current boyfriend. I've met him, but she won't even consider having him over or anything like that. Not that I blame her."

He spread her legs to insinuate his fingers into the delicate flesh at the summit of her thighs and the narrow bridge between them. "When did fun and games end?" he asked.

"After Rita was born," she said, her voice sliding down a register, feeling herself glide out of the conversation for a moment, the birth of her daughter and this man's fingers melding together into a sensation that was neither memory nor experience but another category, lacking a name, almost a dream, a wholly sensual awareness, like the consciousness of the lower animals. Then a thought knocked her out of it. She wondered if he could feel the scar of the episiotomy.

He shifted his hands to her thighs and the heavier labor there, the shallow but immediate pain pulling her back the remainder of the way. She tried to pick up the thread she had left dangling. "Sander and I got married. Miguel left town. Heart stayed put. We lost touch with each other until a few years ago when she called me out of the blue."

"She ever get wise to you and Miguel?"

Gay nodded, keeping her cheek against the sheet. "One night we were high and playing cards. Heart and I were partners. I could tell she was up to something. She waited until she had a great hand, then made a bet: If we girls won, then the four of us would get a house in town, live together, and raise the baby. I was about seven months along, and she was stoned enough to think Miguel might want to live with her. Maybe unconsciously she knew she needed to make me part of the picture. Or it was just her way of broaching the subject. Bets like that aren't *binding*. She just wanted the idea in the air."

He clamped his hands over the top of one leg, making her jump, then the hands began an undulating movement down the tapering cylinder of her thigh. He said, "How did Miguel respond to this idea?"

"It was fine with him," she said, her back arching again at the pain, "but Heart didn't know that he and I were lovers. He shouldn't have agreed to it." She tried to explain her resentment. Neither man laughed off the wager or changed the subject. They forced Gay to be the one. "Heart didn't even consider that I might object. I wasn't into some kind of communal *thing*. I might have liked it, I guess, but it felt too weird. Besides, I knew the men both wanted me."

His hands stopped at the knee, then started in on the other leg. "You did or didn't know which one was the father?"

"I didn't have a clue," she admitted. Then she explained how bad had turned to worse. They had to determine the other side of the bet—what the consequences were if the boys won. At first, no one could think of anything, and Gay had hoped that the bet might be dropped. But then Sander had said, "If we win, I get to wear Heart's wig the rest of the night."

"Everybody thought that was a riot," Gay said, "except me. I'd already decided we were going to lose."

Denny began working on her calves. He linked hands and ran his forearm forcefully up and down the leg. She explained to him that, at that time, she felt she had to marry the father. To be fair to the baby. "I'd had that awful break with my parents, and I wanted to be good to this child I was bringing into the world."

Denny gripped an ankle, but he did not squeeze, just held it loosely. "But you didn't know who the father was," he said. "How could you . . ."

"My plan was to look at the baby and decide who the dad was. I thought it would be easy." Sander was slight, fair-skinned, and easy with people, while Miguel was big, dark, and shy around others. Telling him these details made her feel foolish, but she was determined to hold back nothing. "I've never told another person this story," she said and only then did he begin to rub her feet. "Sander has argued with me over parts of it, but I haven't even told him everything. I told Rita about the bet, leaving out significant elements, of course."

"Why are you telling me, of all people?" In the timbre of his voice, she thought she could hear a hopeful note. He did not stop jamming his thumbs into her soles, as if suggesting it was a trivial inquiry—which, Gay thought, proved the opposite.

"I was wondering the same thing," she said.

"Because you're passionately in love with me, and you've lost your head in my presence?" He burnished her feet intensely, quietly. She felt herself teetering, at the brink of saying something, wishing to separate truth and illusion. When she didn't respond, he said, "I hit it on the first guess?"

"I do like you," she said, then screamed as his thumb seemed to strike bone. He told her to finish the story. "That hurt," she said.

"I guessed that," he said. "Go on."

"I misplayed the hand," she said. "I had thought I could make it look like an accident, but Heart had too many points. We pretended I was in a phase of pregnancy that brought on stupidity, but everyone knew I'd thrown the game, and everyone understood why." After they lost the last trick, Sander had stood and walked over to Heart, laughing, trying to make light of the situation. He had lifted the wig from her head while she shuffled the cards. He had merely blanched, but Miguel had let out a gasp. "She never wore the wig again," Gay said sadly. "She bought a green felt hat and wouldn't take it off except to bathe. It took years for her hair to grow back fully."

Denny now handled her toes, rolling them like cigars between his fingers. "I didn't know there was this stuff between you two."

"She took me in when my parents abandoned me. She nursed me through my breakdowns. She loved me and thought the baby was going to unite us forever. She offered me her hand in a kind of matrimony, and I rejected her. That hat became a punishment. A reminder of what I had done. And then, what is amazing, ten years later, she forgave me. She heard from Sander about my moving here, how he and I had reinvented our marriage." It seemed to Gay that Heart had instinctively understood she was trying to change not just her marriage but herself. Heart had moved to Persimmon to join her. "I haven't always treated people well, maybe especially other women. I'd learned some patterns pretty well. It's taken work to give them up."

Denny finished massaging her and threw himself onto the mattress beside her, bouncing against her, his face landing just inches from hers. He kissed her. They settled in together, arms around bodies, legs linked. It had the feel of permanence, Gay thought, as if they might hold this position not just through the night, but for the remainder of their lives.

Denny interrupted her reverie. "Didn't you tell me you shaved Rita's head?"

She did not want to talk any longer, and especially not about this, but once a fall had begun, there was no way to stop it. "Heart came with me to the hospital, but I didn't want her there. I asked the nurse to make up a lie and send her home. She told Heart I was barely dilated, and the baby wouldn't arrive until the morning or later. I gave birth a couple of hours after Heart left."

"Why didn't you want her there?" He held her so snugly she felt the movement of his Adam's apple against her cheek.

"I wanted to look at the baby and make my own decision. I didn't want to think the child was Sander's because Heart loved Miguel. I especially didn't want to claim Miguel to spite Heart. I wanted to decide who I was going to marry without that hat there chastising me."

"I get it," he said.

"We had voted on names, but I decided not to use them. Rita was the nurse's name. I copied it off her name tag. And then later, when she brought the baby to me, that's when—Rita wasn't fair-skinned or dark, just raw and red the way babies are. But she had a big shock of black hair. When the nurse left us alone, I got out my travel kit and shaved her head."

"What did you think you were doing?"

"Her crown bled." She remembered the resistance of the razor, snagging on her daughter's new skin, blood in the fine, dark follicles, a crooked line of it running down the baby's face, pooling in her slight brow, a dark river of blood, so dark it was almost black, so dark Gay had worried something was wrong with the child. The memory made her shiver. "Rita could have been taken from me. I could have been judged unfit. But Heart lied for me, convinced everyone it was a postpartum, sleep-deprivation thing."

"Which it probably was, wasn't it?"

"I don't know what it was."

He let go of her, and his voice changed. He separated from her and sat up on one elbow in order to tell her what had happened. "You wanted to marry Sander, but the baby had—Rita *has*—dark hair. Your judgment was impaired by the whole giving-birth deal, you were in sort of love with Sander, and—"

"Sometimes I think if the baby'd had blond hair, I would have married Miguel." She put her hand on his chest. She was ready to be through with her past. She wanted to explore his body with her hands. She didn't want sex, just to touch him as he had touched her, to study his body with the tips of her fingers.

"It sort of makes sense to me now," he said, taking her hand in his, "this arrangement you have with your husband. You made up a way to live that puts you in charge of your life without turning your back on him. Does Miguel know he's Rita's father?"

The question made her suddenly alert. She retrieved her hand. "I never said he was."

"The circumstantial evidence—"

"Genetics don't interest me. Sander is her father." She tempered her annoyance to see if he could just let this pass.

"If Rita had his last name, she could get a college scholarship anywhere she wanted."

"You're disappointing me," she said flatly, but she did not let herself feel disappointment yet, holding it off, giving him time to make it right.

"Just being a pragmatist. If this Delgado is the real—the genetic—father, then she's half Mexican. She's legally eligible."

"Even if I were willing to tell her about all this, which I'm not, I wouldn't feel right claiming benefits meant for minorities. If she is Hispanic, it's only in the technical sense."

He produced the smirk that had become his dominant facial characteristic. At this moment she hated it. He said, "What other kind of sense is there?"

"Cultural—"

"*I* know more Spanish than her boyfriend. What's his name, blondie?"

"Enrique."

"*Henry*. He's eligible, isn't he? He's Hispanic, isn't he?"

"I don't want to talk to you about this." She turned away from him, rolling onto her back, which immediately began to burn, from the top of her neck to the ends of her legs, and this, she understood, was what she wanted right now, to live entirely in her body. She said, "You're sounding like a jerk."

She felt him lean over her, but she kept her head turned. "I'm just saying that blood is thicker than—or at least as thick as—culture. Hell, for that matter, all her friends are Mexican."

"Oh, please. Half the people who live here are Chicano. Are you implying there's an ethnic connection between Rita and her friends? As if she were *drawn* to—"

"No. I'm saying it's all arbitrary. Which side of the border you're born on, which side of the river your parents or grandparents were born on. Rita's on the other side of some imaginary and wholly arbitrary line. Why deny that? These labels are—it's hard to know what they mean, exactly, what they signify. Blood is every bit as thick as river water."

She spun herself around to face him, the burning in her body subsiding. She looked him steadily and sternly in the eyes. "What you're really saying is that if the system presents an opening, take it. It doesn't care whether you're only technically eligible, so why should you? But I hate thinking that way. It's small and mean-spirited, and your life becomes reduced to looking for ways to chisel and connive."

"If Rita's genetically a Delgado, she's more than technically Mexican."

"She doesn't even *know* it. How can you say she's suffered discrimination when no one, including herself, has any idea that she's Hispanic?"

He didn't say anything for several moments, returning her even stare. Then, as if he could read her mind, he did the right thing. He placed his large hands over her face, the thumbs on her forehead above her eyes, the fingers making a discontinuous line along her jaw. He pressed tenderly against the sloping contours of the skin, rubbing gently, as if his hands held clay and he were shaping it into something human. He said, "I've got a feeling there are more details about this whole business that you could tell me, that you *will* tell me whenever they crop up in that head of yours. This whole strange life you've made, it's something we could talk about in bed for years to come."

"You think we'll be talking in bed for years to come?"

"I sort of like the idea," he said.

"As an idea," she said, "it's appealing."

Later, when their bodies again locked together, she confessed the one true thing about herself that she had withheld. That she loved him.

22

Cecilia had brought the magazine to school to give to Rita. She didn't want it in her house. "My father's sick," she said, as if that explained why she had to get rid of it. Then she added, "He's home a lot of the time now." Finally she whispered, "He has cancer. He's dying. I'd suspected something bad, then my mother told me last night."

"Henry never told me," Rita said.

"We don't like to talk about things like that in my family," Cecilia said. "I don't even know if Henry completely understands. But my mother told me last night, and I had to get that magazine out of there. I couldn't leave it in the house."

Rita assured her that she would sneak it back into the bookstore, although she had no intention of doing this, and she guessed that Cecilia understood as much. Rita wasn't sure what she wanted to do with the magazine, but she wasn't ready to throw it away. The pictures in it were the opposite of mysterious, whatever that might be—obvious? explicit? Maybe that was the definition of pornography: the opposite of mysterious. Nevertheless, they had an appeal. She liked seeing precisely how a penis went inside a vagina. She liked seeing exactly how people planted themselves upon one another, the kinds of expressions they made. There was also a silly aspect to it. She could tell the people were acting, pretending. Not the sex part, that was clearly going on for real, but there was some other part to it that they were pretending about. Which made them look silly. She liked seeing adults looking ridiculous, especially if they were naked. And they were having sex, which made it, in a certain way, hysterical. In another way, it made it not funny at all, but still interesting. And exciting. She would eventually throw the magazine away, but not until she'd looked at the pictures again.

They had met in a breezeway, but they headed back to the far corner of the campus to make the exchange. Cecilia had covered the magazine with a book jacket made from a paper bag. She had drawn stars on the jacket with a red magic marker. "I would have drawn people, but I'm no artist," she said, smiling but upset, her eyes red from recent tears.

Rita made herself smile. She wanted to make Cecilia feel better. "If you'd written 'History' on it, I could pretend to be studying."

Cecilia nodded, about to cry. She handed the magazine to Rita. "He's pretending not to be sick, but he's too weak to work. All he does is watch TV and sleep on the couch until we get home." She wiped her eyes but kept them focused on the asphalt at her feet. "What would you do if you knew you only had a little time to live?"

Rita didn't get the chance to answer. A noise stopped her, a grunt, an animal sound. They looked up to see Rudy Salazar standing before them, just inches away, his big arms crossed. He stared at them humorlessly. Rita and Cecilia each instinctively took a step backwards, into the wall of lockers, the combination locks clattering against the metal, pressing into their backs. Cecilia raised her notebook like a shield in front of her. Rita did the same with the magazine.

Rudy eyed Rita maliciously, then looked at Cecilia. "I'm going to pants your brother," he said. "I'm going to ruin his manhood."

Cecilia immediately began weeping, without even a second of delay.

Rita said, "Leave her alone," but it came out softer than she expected and he didn't seem to hear her.

"Unless you do something for me," he said. "Nothing bad, you know. *No mucho*. Just a little kiss. You kiss my belly button, and I let your brother go." He smiled, then added, "With tongue."

Cecilia said, "I'm Catholic." She was trying to quit crying and couldn't say more, but Rita believed she understood. This was a spiritual matter. Her father was dying. She could not kiss anybody's belly button.

Rudy began describing the pain her brother would soon know, and how he'd never marry because "his seeds would be jammed up into his liver." It was only then that Rita realized that he was talking about Henry, *her* boyfriend.

She said, "I'll kiss your stupid belly button if you'll leave Cecilia and Henry alone forever."

A teacher appeared just then to investigate the crying, a tall man with curly hair, dark glasses, and a pencil behind his ear. Rudy glared at the teacher a moment, then pointed at Rita, jabbing his finger within a hair's breadth of her bra. "That's a promise," he said. "You better keep it." He sauntered off, almost brushing against the teacher as he passed, laughing victoriously.

Rita turned immediately to Cecilia. "Don't tell Henry," she said.

Cecilia nodded furiously but couldn't speak.

The teacher still stood there, his hands on his hips. He seemed to be staring at the magazine. "Is everything all right here?"

"Yes," Rita said. She worked her finger into the magazine, as if to mark a place. "We've got it under control," she said. Then she added, "Her father is very sick."

The teacher nodded then. His posture softened. He patted Cecilia on the back before leaving.

"You're not afraid of him?" Cecilia asked.

"No," Rita said, although fear coursed through her limbs, a charge of energy almost indistinguishable from desire, from hunger, from excitement. The finger she had inserted into the magazine, she ran up and down over the pages, as if her fingertip could feel the images, the graphic displays of that which was once a mystery.

Tito's face, shrouded by his hands, appeared in the window of Henry's classroom. Sweat dripped from his nose, his mouth crooked with fear. Henry knew immediately that Tito had come for him and that something was terribly wrong. He stood, waved. Tito spotted him then and waved frantically back.

"What is going on, Mr. Calzado?" asked his teacher, who had been at the blackboard diagramming sentences.

"I don't know," Henry said, already heading for the door. "Excuse me."

Tito gestured for Henry to hurry. He began speaking in Spanish rapidly as soon as Henry stepped outside, sweat flying from hair and the slick slide of his jaw.

"I don't understand," Henry said. "I don't speak Spanish."

"Your sister," Tito said. "Rudy's going to . . . I don't know the word for it. Something bad to her at the *peligro* john."

"Cecilia?" Henry said.

"I can't do nothing," Tito said. "We need someone can stop Rudy. You got a dad or *hermano* or something can stop him?"

The bell sounded before Henry could answer. "My dad's not home," he said. "He's sick."

"We have to get running," Tito said, grabbing him by the arm. "The *peligro* john is where he's doing it to her."

It was hard to run and think at the same time. Tito ran faster than he did, and it was all he could do to keep within yelling distance. Rudy Salazar planned to do something to his sister. Henry should get hold of someone, but who? His father and mother were in El Paso at the hospital, checking on some kind of test. They crossed one street and then another, Henry trying to concentrate, Tito encouraging him to catch up. As they reached downtown, Henry finally thought what to do.

"This way," he yelled to Tito, who was well ahead of him. Henry ran to the bookstore, bursting in on Heart as she spoke on the phone to someone. "You got to call Mr. Redmon," Henry yelled. "Rudy Salazar is after my sister."

Heart stared at him a second, then said, "It's Henry. He says someone is after Cecilia."

Henry ripped the phone from her hand. "Mr. Redmon—"

"No, Henry." It was Rita's mother.

"Call Mr. Redmon," Henry said. "Tell him to get to the *peligro* john. Any kid can show him where it is. Tell him to hurry. Rudy Salazar is after my sister there."

"All right, but what—"

"Call him!" He put the phone down on the receiver and ran back to Tito, who stood at the door, holding it open. They took off again. Tito was talking.

"What?"

"Don't tell Rudy I said nothing. I can't be the one said anything, because he's my friend and he would kill me," Tito said.

"Yeah," Henry said, huffing, his heart bounding ahead, his legs working to keep up.

Rita told her fifth-period teacher she had cramps. Male teachers would let you get away with anything if you said you had cramps. She walked home. She wanted to change clothes before meeting Rudy Salazar.

One of the *negras* had delivered the note.

Meet me in the *peligro* john after school.

The *peligro* john was a portable outhouse in a fenced lot where the city parked the garbage trucks and the street sweeper. Rita selected her favorite pair of earrings, the silver image of the African woman with jade hair. She had not worn them for a long time, and poked her neck with the sharp wires while inserting them. They were a little showy. Which led her to put on her green velvet Heart dress and a matching ribbon in her hair—so the earrings wouldn't stand out. She went into her mother's room, powdered her face, and put lipstick on her mouth.

She decided to hide the magazine beneath her dollhouse, but first she looked at it again. There was an image she recalled and wanted to examine. Not a woman, but a man kissing the soft skin of a woman's stomach. His lips seemed to brush against her belly button. In the next picture, his head was between her legs, and close-ups showed him licking her genitals. She paged back to the image of his head on her stomach. One of her hands gripped his hair, while the other hand was at her own mouth, a finger between her teeth. The top of her head was out of the frame. Rita could not see her eyes.

She closed the magazine and hid it. Rudy had said he would pants Henry. Rita wasn't exactly sure what that meant, but she guessed it involved pulling down Henry's pants and then inflicting some kind of pain. It seemed at least as sexual as kissing somebody's belly button.

In the mirror, she examined her hair, her powdered face, the slight additional redness of her lips. She touched the silver African woman attached to her earlobes, pressing against them until the wires again poked into her neck—painful, but a pain in which she could take pleasure.

A small group had gathered at the lot, all boys. She hadn't told Cecilia where she was meeting Rudy. Whistles met her approach, their stares lurid. They saw her in a new way, she understood, and she liked that.

Rudy had already ducked under the chain-link, just below the sign that warned *¡PELIGRO!* DANGER! He stood with his hands on his hips, a mean look in his eyes. Then he raised his hands above his head and inserted them in the metal links of the fence. He leaned forward, still peering at Rita, as if he could read her. She felt she could read him, the pose out of a prison movie, trying to look tough, trying to scare her. She was scared, but knowing that he was posturing lessened her fear.

Three garbage trucks faced the fence, as if they, too, were curious to see the outcome, their white bodies smeared with refuse. Parked beside them, a yellow bulldozer aimed its blade indifferently at the afternoon sky. Rudy held the fence up for her, his mouth awry, as if he had just gotten a taste of some strange dish, an expression that was neither a grimace nor a smile. The shape his mouth took frightened her. She crawled on her knees, then stood and dusted off her dress. She could smell Rudy Salazar's skin, which was not a bad smell, that human odor a body makes when it has begun to sweat but not yet begun to stink. He was breathing through his mouth, no longer looking at her. The crowd of boys watching them grew quiet.

He turned from her and stepped up to the plastic outhouse. "Let me check it out," he said as if there could be anything to check out in an outhouse. He turned his head but didn't really look back at her. "Wait here." He disappeared inside.

Rita stared out at the boys' faces. Not one of them could meet her eyes, glancing down at the ground or off into space, their feet tapping nervously in the dirt or moving them in small, uneasy circles. She felt the urge to strike a pose, to take advantage of the attention of all those boys, but she resisted the impulse. The stoic machinery within the fenced yard returned her gaze impassively. The door to the *peligro* john rattled. Rudy called out for her to enter.

He faced the other way, as if peeing. He had taken off his shirt. She could see both strength and softness in his shoulders and back. She imagined them walking together, arm in arm, but she knew that was a dishonest image. He would not want her, and she would not want him.

She let the plastic door flap shut. He turned, briefly pressing himself against her as he latched the door. His pants were open. His penis was hard, pointing to the ceiling, curling with the undulation of his belly. He grabbed himself and pushed his penis flat against his stomach. "Okay," he said. "Kiss my belly button. With tongue." His smile was big and yellow, and stank, it seemed to her, although, of course, it was the outhouse that smelled. The head of his penis covered his belly button.

His hand grabbed her hair at the back of her head. He pushed her down, forced her to bend, wedging her against the plastic wall. He thrust his penis into her face—against her cheek, her clenched lips, against her teeth, pushing her lip up. It slid into the cup of one eye. It prodded her nostrils.

She reached for the African woman, slipping the earring from her lobe. The head of his penis slid over her clenched teeth and into her cheek, making it bulge. She gripped the earring in her fist and shoved the pointed end of the wire into the soft, engorged skin of his penis. He made a little noise, and gave a jerk, which caused the punctured skin to tear.

Blood spurted from the wound, a fine spray that painted her face. She jerked back and gasped. Blood spewed against her tongue and over her face.

Rudy yelled something in Spanish—not in anger, she could tell, but in surprise. It almost sounded like an apology: he didn't know why he was bleeding on her. When he released the back of her head, she fell against the latched door. Rudy put his hands on his bleeding penis, and they instantly covered with blood. He lifted a bloody hand, a red stream trailing over his wrist and down his arm. He tried to reach past her to the latch, but his eyes rolled upward, turning perfectly white, and his knees buckled. He fell to the side, the plastic wall thundering as he collapsed, his head pitching forward, just missing the metal latch. Rita scooted to the side to avoid the falling body, as Rudy Salazar fainted.

PART II

1994

Body

23

Henry stood to pedal up the small incline. The bicycle had twenty-five gears, but Henry hadn't yet figured out how to use them all. It was actually Rita's, a mountain bike she called it, her Christmas gift from her dad. "I knew he was going to give me something big," she told Henry, "because of Rudy Salazar. Because he thinks I'm *traumatized*. You always get bigger presents if they think you're sick or something."

Henry had laughed with her at that, but later he thought the same logic applied when she gave the bike to him. "I liked getting it," she claimed, "but I don't really like riding it." The real reason, he decided, was that his father had died just after Christmas, and she wanted to give *him* a big present.

He had parked the bike just outside his algebra class and locked it to one of the saplings that the Daughters of the American Revolution had planted the previous spring. Round holes had been cut in the asphalt and now served as tree wells. Algebra was Henry's last class before lunch, and as soon as the bell had sounded he had run directly to the bike and begun pedaling across town to the high school. Rita's lunch started twenty minutes later than his, which made him think the whole thing was meant to be, a matter of fate. He would sit with Rita and his sister and Rita's new friends and eat Rita's lunch—she had given up cafeteria food in order to lose weight. Then he would pedal back leisurely after lunch since his next class had already started, and there was no reason to hurry.

For three days he had skipped his PE class, and no one had said anything. Mr. Cabrera didn't know that Henry had been absent only from his class.

Once he was caught, he would say he had been going home for lunch to be with his mother. A lie, but they would understand his desire to be with his grieving mother, while it was impossible to explain why he needed to see Rita. The bike-riding was more exercise than he ever got in PE anyway.

He didn't honestly know why he had to go to the high school for lunch. Three days ago, during algebra, it had occurred to him that he could get there in time to eat with Rita if he pumped really hard. Then he realized that he had parked the bike right outside the door, as if some deeper part of him already had known he was going to do it before his regular mind realized it was possible.

He wouldn't have considered it while his father was alive. His father would have disapproved, and because he had been a school custodian, in Henry's mind he was connected with all school personnel everywhere. Which meant Henry could never have gotten away with it.

Now, though, Henry made his own decisions. His brother Arturo had dropped out of the university during the winter break. He had come home to support them. Their sisters sent some cash each month, and their mom, who took in ironing and sewing, and who cleaned people's houses, made a little money, but not enough, apparently. Arturo had been given their father's job. He did not attempt to tell Henry how to behave.

Still, Henry could not explain why it was necessary to bike all the way across town just to eat with Rita. He saw her every day, after all, right after school. But he'd had this strange pull in his stomach, this anxious trembling feeling that demanded he check on her.

Despite the cool winter air, he broke a sweat. He had to make Persimmon High by the time lunch period started, or there would be no place to sit at Rita's table. Maybe his anxiety had to do with Rita's new popularity. He tried to evaluate this possibility as he rode past the downtown string of buildings. He might merely be worried that some high school guy was going to steal her away. Stabbing Rudy Salazar had made her a celebrity at school, and suddenly, over the last several weeks, she had lost weight, which had made outright strangers come up to her and say how good she looked. Henry couldn't see that she looked any better. Her legs were thinner and her belly was flat and her cheekbones stood out in a nice way, but she still looked the same beyond those things, with the same legs and belly and cheeks she'd had before, only there was less of them.

He tried to let himself worry about high school guys flirting with Rita, preferring that worry to whatever was really eating at him. But he couldn't work up much misery. He and Rita were too close, too *connected*. It was a phony worry, and he knew it. Nothing could possibly come between them.

He remembered this movie called *The Breakfast Club* that he and his sister had watched on TV, and this one girl, the strangest and most interesting one, was made over by one of the other girls so that she looked more like everyone else, and she suddenly started acting more like everyone else, and then everyone else liked her. Henry had seen this happen in a dozen movies. Now Rita had done the same thing by getting skinny, and sure enough, she had been rewarded with popularity, just like the movies promised. Some piece of the logic that drove this equation escaped Henry. The girls, for example, shouldn't care whether she weighed less, should they? An aspect of her transformation to popularity eluded him. It reminded him of needing to pee during a movie and returning to find that something crucial had occurred during his absence. What had he missed?

Being popular for getting rid of Rudy Salazar, he could understand. Henry had accompanied Rita to the school hearing. They had held hands so tightly his fingers had turned white, until Rita's father had tapped him on the shoulder and said that he had to sit elsewhere. He sat with his mother and father and Cecilia. His father had been in a wheelchair by that time, but he had insisted on attending, riding in the chair in the back of the Perez pickup. A few weeks later, almost all of the same people would be at the funeral, his father's emaciated body in a dark suit like he never wore, lying in the bottom of a wooden box, a smile on his face. Henry had known it was a fake smile, one orchestrated by the mortician, but it had looked just like his father's real smile, wry and modest, suggesting the secret happiness of a man whose life had exceeded his expectations.

Rita's mother and father had sat together at the hearing. Heart had been there, too, and Mr. Redmon and people Henry recognized but didn't know. Superintendent Lamb and some other men had sat behind a desk and listened while Rita told them everything, including Cecilia's tears, how Catholic she was, the size of the crowd at the *peligro* john, even the funny look on Rudy's face when he held the fence for her. She told them about seeing Rudy break Arturo's nose a year ago during a basketball game. "Rudy promised to do something awful to Cecilia's brother if she didn't kiss his belly button." Cecilia had already told Henry about this, how Rudy had still been after Arturo, and how Rita had stepped in to protect them all. Henry's father had tried to rise from his wheelchair when Rita spoke about this. He had wanted to make a comment, maybe about Rudy breaking Arturo's nose, but he could not stand, and evidently it had been a comment he needed to make on his feet. He wound up saying nothing.

Rita's parents sat on either side of her, behind a table in the center of the room. Heart pulled up a chair and sat directly behind Rita, resting her hand on Rita's shoulder, grunting at all the right moments, just like family. Rita told them that she had pulled Rudy's head—by the hair—out of the mouth of the toilet before opening the door. It hadn't seemed dignified, she explained to Henry later, to have him lying like that.

Rudy Salazar's father had been there, too. He had traveled from Las Cruces, where he had been living since leaving Apuro. At one point he stood and said, "I will take care of this," his manner so threatening as to make even Henry fear for Rudy, who was not present but confined to a hospital bed in far off El Paso. "My job to take care of this," he said angrily, pointing to his own chest. A hollowed-out man with graying hair and red, pitted cheeks, he looked nothing like Rudy. "My job," he said a final time, pointing now at the school board. Then he sat and remained silent while the officials huddled.

Rita interrupted them. "I don't want to press charges," she said.

While Mr. Lamb explained that it wasn't a criminal proceeding, Henry wondered why she wouldn't want to put Rudy Salazar in jail. He thought he might understand part of it, the desire to forgive, but shouldn't Rudy Salazar be put away? He asked her about it later. "I think he'll be a better person now," she said, smiling in a funny way. "I think he's cured."

Rudy was expelled. He disappeared from the hospital and did not return to Apuro. There were rumors around school: that he had gotten gangrene and had to have his cock removed; that the knife Rita had stabbed him with (no one believed Rita had used an earring) had been so deeply embedded it could not be removed, and so Rudy had a permanent boner; that he had a jagged, three-inch scar, which, coincidentally, spelled out RITA; that she had cut off his balls and tossed them into the toilet, and now Rudy Salazar was studying to be a priest.

At the funeral, Arturo had slipped away while the priest was speaking, pushing aside the hands of each of his sisters as he passed them. Their mother, through her tears, had whispered, "He's so upset." But Henry had seen his brother's countenance and understood immediately that Arturo had heard something outside. He suspected that Rudy Salazar had sneaked out of the hospital to disrupt the funeral. Anger had flared in Henry's chest like a struck match, but then he had viewed the body and seen that smile, so much his father's, and the feeling turned to something else. He had run out to Arturo and held him. "Go see Papa," Henry had said. "I'll stand guard." Arturo had nodded, touched Henry's shoulder, and they changed places.

Henry heard the lunch bell sound just as he brought the bike to a skidding stop at the high school gate. He locked the bike to a pole in the chain-link fence and walked to the cafeteria door, already scanning the rush of kids for Rita. He didn't know why he had to come eat with her, but he had to. The flutter in his stomach would not end until he saw her face.

Henry slid along the gray bench before the gray table, scooting all the way down to the end. Rita slid in beside him, followed by Cecilia. A whole group of kids joined them at the table. Anglo kids and a couple of Chicanos, a group of freshmen and sophomores that hung out together. Rita called them a "click," which Henry kept meaning to look up. They had adopted Rita since she had become both a hero and thin. Cecilia had tagged along and become a part of them, too. Henry got to sit with them whenever he pedaled over. He nodded a lot during their conversations, trying to be polite, feigning understanding. Rita shoved her macaroni pie in front of him. While he ate and listened to the others, he thought of his father in the hospital bed, how he had wanted Henry there to read the forms. His father had been more afraid of the forms than of the cancer. Now Henry wished for someone to explain what these guys were talking about, a translator to decipher lunch. Neither Rita nor Cecilia were any help. Some kid would start it up, and then another four or five would leap in, one mouth barely shut before another opened, the discussion becoming impossible to follow, full of references as strange as the sentence of Latin the priest had uttered at his father's funeral.

An Anglo girl with braces started them today. She wore normal jeans and a regular shirt but mismatched (one green, one purple) high-top Converses. "So I got into an argument with her about whether Kermit was really a member of 'Sesame Street.'"

"That's like Al Franken and 'Saturday Night Live.'" The boy who said this wore a T-shirt showing an eyeball dripping fluid and the words *For Love Not Lisa*. "Is he part of the cast or isn't he?"

Another boy, a Chicano with a just-scrubbed look and purple eyeglasses, spoke up, "He used to have a partner, some skinny guy with bad hair. You can see him on the old shows on VH1."

"You know what VH1 stands for really?" said For Love Not Lisa. "Vag Hole."

"What does the one stand for?" Henry asked, trying to join in, resisting asking what "Vag Hole" meant.

"It's just a number," the boy said, "like MST 3000."

"That's the coolest show," a new voice chimed in. "Is that on the Sci-Fi channel?"

"What is MST 3000?" asked a pretty girl with a nose ring. "Is that those guys who talk about cars on the radio? I hate those guys."

"Mystery Science Theater 3000, which is like the date when it's set, you know, the future. Right?"

"It's on Comedy Central, not Sci-Fi," said another boy. "This guy's been banished to the deepest recesses of way outer space, and he has to watch these corrosive old movies, and he's got these robots to help him trash the movies."

"They're funny as hell."

"They show these truly dumb—like that one with the giant ants. They find this humongous ant in like a space cocoon or something in this basement in, I don't know, England or somewhere—I didn't have the volume on for part of it."

"Al Franken had a partner?"

"Who is Al Franken?"

"That guy on 'SNL' who isn't funny."

"That could be any of them."

"So why isn't Miss Piggy on 'Sesame Street' anymore?"

"You still watch it?"

"I have a little brother, Butthead."

"She wasn't ever on it, Beavis. The Muppets are a whole different group, except for Kermit, and he never puts his feet down on 'Sesame Street.' He just does those bits. *I* still watch it sometimes."

"You see that guy over there? What is that guy—Hey, how's it hanging?— He eats that every day. I shit you not."

"Which guy? That guy?"

"Point, why don't you? Get a spotlight. The guy with the salad and four glasses of water."

"I know him. He's trying to eat healthy is all. As soon as he's done with that, he'll eat like a doughnut or something, but first he has to eat his salad and drink his waters."

One of the girls started coughing. "Panic attack," she whispered to another girl, loud enough for everyone to hear.

"We can go somewhere," the other girl said. "Should I hit your back or something?"

"Lift your arms over your head." The boy raised his arms as if he were in a holdup. "Like this."

"Panic attack," the girl mouthed to another girl down the table, then resumed coughing.

"Like this." The boy bounced his raised hands in the air.

"Are you okay?" Rita asked.

The girl gave a giant cough and placed her hand over her heart. "It's not a bad one. They're not so bad these days."

"We can walk around or something if you need to get away from this food," her friend said.

"If you lift your arms next time, it stops the coughing. Like this."

"The doctor said I'd pass out before I'd die, so they're not so bad now because I know I'm not going to die."

"Did we do something to make you freak?"

"I never know, usually. Sometimes, if there's a test, or when I got my learner's permit, but most of the time it's no telling."

"Was that the bell?" Cecilia asked.

"I haven't even started eating. How can they expect us to pay attention if we don't get to eat?"

"Not eating this stuff is a treat."

"That *was* the bell, guys."

"Did you read the chapter?"

"I started it, but it's really confusing."

"I read it," Rita said.

"All right. I'm sitting next to you in case there's a quiz." A boy said this, and Henry eyed him suspiciously, but he wasn't Rita's type.

"Hey," the same boy said to another, "don't stuff it down all at once, you'll pull a River Phoenix."

"River Phoenix?" Henry said. He had just begun to stand, Rita's tray in his hands. He stopped midway, bent at the waist and knees, his hair falling into his eyes, blond strands appearing at the crest of his vision.

"He'll pull a River Phoenix and OD on chow."

"River Phoenix OD'd on coke, not cafeteria food."

"River Phoenix is dead?" Henry said. He swallowed, a lump of air traveling painfully down his throat. The tray began to dip and Rita grabbed an end of it.

"He bought it way back on Halloween. Old news, but his pic was just on the cover of *People* with some other dead actor. Dead but still news. There're worm condos in his cranium by now."

"River Phoenix is dead?" Henry said again.

Rita took the tray from him and set it on the table.

"Cocaine," the boy with the purple glasses said. "You like know him or something?"

Henry shook his head, waved as the others dispersed. He might have been smiling.

"Are you all right?" Rita asked him.

"I'm just surprised," he said. He took a deep breath. "I'm all right. Surprised is all."

"Are you sure?" Cecilia said.

Rita gave him a kiss on the cheek. "I've got to get to class."

"Me, too," he said.

He followed them out of the cafeteria, nodded and waved and stood around until Rita and Cecilia had disappeared down the breezeway. He handled it fine until he unlocked the bike, the tears welling in his eyelids with the clack of the lock as it separated. He had to get out of the parking lot. Ducking his head down, he pedaled slowly but with a regular rhythm, leaning low as if to improve the aerodynamics. He headed for his home, staring at his knees rising and falling like levers, but picturing River Phoenix, larger than life on the screen, wind lifting his hair, standing with his legs spread apart on a stretch of asphalt and then, suddenly, dislocated, back in his private world. Now dead.

It occurred to Henry that four events had shaped his life. Seeing *My Own Private Idaho*, loving Rita, his father dying, and now hearing of the death of River Phoenix. It did not seem possible that River Phoenix was dead. Dead since Halloween, three months in the ground. Food for worms, that boy had said. Dead without knowing that he had changed another boy's life.

Henry then considered adding to his list Rita's cutting Rudy Salazar. Now that he dated a popular Anglo high school girl, other kids responded to him differently, took him seriously. Monica Gutierrez would dance with him now if he asked. Boys granted him respect. Older boys even acknowledged him—a nod usually, a tilt of the head. Even the guy who had dragged him around at Melody Mendez's party. Henry had seen him yesterday at the high school cafeteria, and the boy had lifted a shoulder to Henry, a begrudging salute.

But the Rudy Salazar thing had happened to Rita, not to him. He was a tag-along, like his sister in that click of kids. Rita was the famous one. She had gotten skinny and everyone loved it, while he had dyed his hair and gotten beat up for it. She had fought with Rudy Salazar and left him bloody, while he'd had to cut his father's tie to keep from being strangled.

Yesterday while he was waiting at the cafeteria door he had heard two boys talking. One started telling a joke. "What did Jeffrey Dahmer say to Rita Schaefer?" the boy began. Henry had lashed out at him before he could continue.

"You think that's laughing business?" he had shouted. "Shut up with that."

Only later, after the boys had slipped apologetically off, was he amazed with himself for having said anything, embarrassed about "laughing business," and distressed that people were making jokes about the girl he loved.

He pedaled home. At his house, he locked the bike to the gas meter beneath the kitchen window, squatting to fit the half-moon lock over the gas pipe. He heard his mother inside. He lifted his head above the windowsill. She sat at the table, her dark hair lifted up on the back of her head, knotted into a loop. Her head bobbed up and down. She was crying.

Henry's first thought, which would later shame him, was that she too had heard that River Phoenix was dead. Quickly he understood the truth, that she was crying for his father, for his father's death, a *real* death, the death of the man she had made a lifelong commitment to. Even the word "lifelong" spoke of death, Henry realized. The death of his father. Now more than a month gone. Worms would be working their way into his body.

He sat on the ground beneath the window and wiped away his tears. His mind slowed, emptied, until it became as blank as a cloudless sky, a startling vacantness that held him to the cold soil several moments, his thighs growing icy while his mind simply quit.

Then he got up and dusted off his pants. He unlocked his bike and coasted quietly away, no longer crying, embarrassed that the death of an Anglo actor had meant a thing to him. His humiliation and anger led him to start pumping again, each thrust a self-rebuke. River Phoenix had been offered the world and had chosen instead to squander his life, while Henry's father had been given nothing, had to struggle for everything, and then, in the end, had even his breath taken from him.

Henry would not let his priorities fail him again. He would care for his family. He would care for his people. He would care for the girl he loved.

Fuck River Phoenix. He could rot in hell.

· · ·

The girl stopped Rita by grabbing her bare arm. "Just waiting for my friend," Rita said, as if addressing a police officer. The girl was a junior or senior, a cheerleader and member of the student council, but Rita couldn't remember her name, and the girl assumed she knew.

"We need to chat in private," the girl said. She had long, silky, bleached hair and wore expensive jeans and one of those push-up bras beneath her white blouse. She headed toward the library, expecting Rita to follow, her hair waving behind her like the shiny flag of an exotic and desirable country. Rita followed, glancing back to see Cecilia appear at her locker. Cecilia gave her a questioning look, then pointed to the front gate. She would wait for Rita there.

"Oh, I need to grab this guy," the girl said. They had just reached the library steps. She set her books on a stair. "Hold on a sec." She called to the boy and went running to him.

Rita sat on the library's concrete steps, the cold immediately seeping through her Heart dress, although the weather was mild. She exhaled but could not see her breath. This morning she had called her father and left a message on his answering machine telling him not to come see her this weekend. He had been to Persimmon every week since her episode with Rudy Salazar—"the incident," her father called it, never even implying the sexual aspects of it.

Rita didn't want him to come this weekend. She was fine and tired of his worried questions. The last time he'd visited she had tried to tell him as much, but he couldn't be convinced. Her mother said that on the one hand he was scared, and on the other he was disappointed that his presence wasn't required.

"Do you want me to talk to this boy's parents?" he had asked Rita, pacing around in the tiny Desert Oasis room. The motel had just added cable, and Rita had been lying on the bed watching "The Tick" because some people told her it was funny. She hadn't expected it to be cartoons.

Her father said, "I could talk to the principal again. Make sure he's on top of the situation. Make sure there's not going to be any retaliation against you."

"Everybody hated Rudy," Rita said. A commercial came on for Fruit Loops. "I'm practically a god at school. It's funny."

"Yeah," he said, cocking his head slightly, walking heavily on the carpeting, each step reverberating in the room. "You were a little braver than I care for. You ought to report that kind of stuff to your mother. You two can still talk and all, can't you?"

"Of course we can." Rita hopped up from the bed, stretching. She clicked off the television. "I would have told her if I'd needed her."

Her father sighed and turned his head up toward the ceiling. "How about the superintendent? Your mom knows him. I could talk to him or one of your teachers. Is there anybody I ought to talk to?"

Rita thought for a second or two. "Yeah, there's one person."

"Who? What's his name?"

She sat again on the bed. "Mom," she said. "I'd like you to talk to Mom." Her parents had been together at the hearing, but they hadn't really spoken. This was an opportunity to make them talk, and she didn't want to let it pass.

Her father stepped in front of her, dropped to his knees, and took her by the shoulders. He looked her square in the eyes. "Is there something going on with your mother? Is there some reason you shouldn't be with her?"

His questions scared her. "No," she said, her voice choked and tight. "I just wish you guys would talk."

He let go of her shoulders. "I talk to your mother all the time. How do you think I heard about this business, anyway?"

Rita hadn't considered the question until now. Of course Gay had called him. "What do you talk about?"

"*You*, a lot of the time. And, well, other stuff, like when I'm going to be at the motel, and so on. That kind of thing. We're civil. We're friendly."

She understood that she could press him on this, that she could get him to reveal something about his private life with her mother. The "incident" had given her an advantage. She could ask him anything she wanted and he was going to answer honestly. Understanding this pleased her, but all she came up with was, "Does she tell you what presents to buy me?"

Her father smiled, which made her realize how nervous he had looked just a moment before. "She used to give me tips, but she was never any good at it. Your daddy-o does his own shopping."

The opportunity slipped away. What remained was the reminder that Rudy Salazar's attempt to hurt her had given her power. She had just used it by asking her father an easy question, and she became proud of that question. By calling him this morning and leaving a message on the phone, she would put his mind at rest. Rita had started to believe that she was not an ordinary person. She had been given a talent. The baptism in the black river had ignited in her a strange power. The power to cure Henry. The power to cure Rudy Salazar. He was out of the hospital now, she knew, and he had not returned home. He was making a new life for himself because of her.

Soon she would mend Mr. Gene, that poor man. Her parents, too, were suffering, and she would try to help them. She had already begun.

The girl reappeared and sat beside her books. "That boy put something moronic in the school paper about our group. He thinks he's smarter than everyone else. I hate human beings like him." She showed her tongue to display her disgust. "So my friends and I decided to attend to you. We think the chill you gave that felon is remarkable and all, but why go out with a seventh-grader? It makes you seem, I don't know, *moronic* is the word, I guess, and I know you're not. You could date a guy with a *car*, if you wanted to, and besides, it's bad for school pride, don't you think?"

"He's in the eighth grade," Rita said.

"It's hard to break up with a guy if his sister is your friend. That happened to me when I lived in Dallas. His sister said I was a bitch because . . ." She leaned close and whispered in Rita's ear. ". . . I wouldn't blow him." She laughed. "No way. I was basically twelve, and she wasn't doing that either with the guy she went out with, but since it was her big brother, she thought I ought to go all-out. Forget it."

Rita nodded uncertainly. She wondered whether she could explain how she had cured Henry and why she still felt some obligation to him. How could she talk about Mr. Gene without giving away his identity? A damaged man whose voice never rose above a whisper. She could not turn her back on him, either. Some things were decided for you. People were handed missions.

The girl continued talking. "I told my friend, 'The first guy I . . .'" She leaned in close to Rita's ear again. "blow . . . " she said, puffing in Rita's ear, ". . . is going to have to be special.' God, she abhorred me then, like her brother was the most remarkable boy on the planet Earth, like he was Mr. Red-White-'n'-Blue. I mean, if I'd been going with him a long time, I would have. After a while you don't have a choice, unless you want to break up. It's this *thing* they all have to have."

It was what Rudy Salazar wanted from her, Rita realized. She had found a way to give him instead what he needed. The feel of his penis sliding across her teeth returned to her. The pain in her mouth, a kind of tearing, and the taste of blood. Now and again the sensations came back to her, twisting up some inside part of her. Then she understood that this girl had brought up this subject on purpose. She wanted Rita to open up to her. She wanted the gossip about what had happened in the *peligro* john.

The girl had continued talking. "—and if you look at it that way, a seventh grader doesn't even count."

Rita said, "No one else has asked me out, but—"

The girl cut her off. "So you're available?"

"I don't know if—"

"That means *yes*," she said. " 'Don't know' is always a definite yes." Then she said, "Seniors—especially if you're a freshman—if you go out with them, you ought to, if they want it. *But . . .*" She leaned up close to her ear once more. "You don't have to swallow." She laughed again. "You can say, 'I'm on a diet. Don't you know it's fattening?' " She laughed again, then pointed at Cecilia, who was watching them from a distance. "There's Mama." She shook her sparkly hair. "I'll put out the word you're open season."

"No," Rita said. "You'd better not do that."

The girl jerked her head around, gave her a look meant to convey shock. Then she let it drop. She curled her lower lip and puffed hair out of her face. "It's your life. Let me know when you're reachable, and I'll see what I can do." She stood and touched the waist of her jeans, the tip of one finger accidentally tweaking Rita's nose. "This is what I get for trying to help someone," she said.

"See you," Rita offered to her back, but the girl did not turn. Her hair rippled from side to side as she walked. She had great hair.

"What was that about?" Cecilia asked.

"She wants me to join their clique," Rita said. "But I don't want to."

Cecilia nodded, spoke into the ground. "I wouldn't join a group that wouldn't take you, either."

Rita didn't say anything. Is that what the girl had been suggesting? That she had to drop Henry and Cecilia both? Rita had done the right thing without thinking about it. She felt large and generous, at the center of every good thing in the world. She had known how to act without understanding what had been asked of her. As if guided by an invisible hand.

Cecilia's real hand grabbed Rita's arm. She whispered urgently, "Is that the boy?"

"Where?" Rita said. "There? I don't see him." Henry had only recently revealed that a boy had run across town and back trying to protect Cecilia from Rudy Salazar. Rita and Henry knew him, but Cecilia had not met Tito. Every time they saw one of the *negras*, Cecilia asked if he was the one. "He's taller than that guy," Rita said. "And better looking."

Cecilia still gripped her elbow and now gave it a little shake. "Why would he run all over to save me, and now not even say hello?" Then she said, "Oh, my God."

Henry stood in the parking lot beside the bicycle, which he had leaned against a light pole. He had shaved his head. He lifted a hand from the handlebars and ran it over the smooth crown of his skull. "Notice anything different?"

Cecilia said, "What did you do to yourself? You look like a pumpkin on a stick."

"Really?" Henry said. "I was hoping more like Michael Jordan." He looked to Rita. "He shaved his *cabessa*, too." He crossed his arms and leaned back against the bike, which shifted. He had to jump to keep from falling, then jump again to catch the bike.

"I like it," Rita said, although she couldn't tell whether that was true or not. This new haircut was simply another circumstance to guide him through. She put her hand on his head, felt the smooth skin and the two round Band-Aids where he had nicked himself.

Henry said, "I was thinking maybe I could go by Enrique again. You know, my *nombre*, like I was born with."

Cecilia groaned. "*Cabizza*, or whatever you said, is not a word in any language. *Cabeza* is Spanish for 'head.' I don't know the word for 'beach ball,' but you ought to learn it."

Henry dropped his mouth open in a smile. "Hey, *bueno*, okay, I'm *trabajo*-ing on it."

"He say *trabajo* or Tabasco?" Cecilia asked Rita.

She only laughed and linked her arm with him. "Enrique," she said to him, then pulled his bald head to her lips. "You have owwies," she said, kissing the round bandages, the little padded targets signifying injury.

24

MARCH

The bones filled two huge glass jars. One of the metal lids still held a label: Hellman's Mayonnaise. The lid of the other jar was covered by the skull. A small skull, Rudy thought. The jars had come from the restaurant that Billy Valdez used to manage. Rudy now lived in the basement of Billy Valdez's house. Billy lived upstairs, along with his *abuela* Doña María, whom Billy just called Granny.

The jars, stacked one on top of another, were almost as tall as a child. The skull belonged to a boy. That was the story, anyway. An eleven-year-old who had shot two of *La Verdad*, one in the back, one in the thigh. He had done other things, as well, things none of *La Verdad* would talk about. They had killed him. "He just disafuckingpeared," Billy explained to Rudy. "We disafuckingpeared him."

Newspaper articles about the boy vanishing lay beneath the jars, but Rudy didn't know whether to believe that these bones kept in mayonnaise jars were really the boy's bones. Moreover, he didn't care. What interested him were the bones themselves. All his life he had been able to read things, to hear what was really meant, to see what others missed. Now these bones had something to tell him. He sat in the cellar on the air mattress where he slept and studied the bones, attentive to their narrowing and knobbing, their fragile lines.

He had spent almost a week in an El Paso hospital. He was suffering from shock, they told him. He believed it. Shock accounted for the way he had acted that long week of humiliation. They had made him piss in a bedpan. It had hurt to piss, as the nurse had warned. When he lifted himself for her to remove the plastic pan, he saw that it was colored with blood. He had screamed, a pathetic, high-pitched screech. Then something happened to his heart. It beat violently, a wild and furious thrashing in his chest.

He blacked out, just as he had in the *peligro* john. A disease, they told him. Shock was a disease like the flu or hepatitis or any other disease. It made you weak, but it would go away.

Lying in bed, he had gone over what had happened, seeing himself in the *peligro* john, seeing the Shopper there, latching the door. He had forced her head down to his cock, and then she had torn him, ripped him up. It had felt like something besides blood was escaping, a substance even more essential to his life. He could not determine exactly what it had been that had fled from him, but he began thinking that he could make his life anew. What he had been given was humiliation, and maybe he could use it. If he went back to Apuro, back to Persimmon, and he did not seek revenge against the Shopper, then he would be saying that he accepted the disgrace. That he would bend to its will. That he would be the boy who fainted at the sight of his own blood. He would be the boy who was undone by the Anglo Shopper girl. It was shit, but he had already eaten the worst of it.

His mother did not come to see him. Cops from New Mexico came. The Shopper would not file charges, but they were considering arresting him for some complaint he couldn't make sense of. He didn't need to make sense of it. Even as they spoke it, he could hear the truth in the gaps between their words: they could do nothing to him. They merely wanted him scared.

He had been polite. He had nodded and said only "Yes, I understand," or "No, sir." He had made himself say "sir," and there was nothing to it. Nothing inside fought him.

The only other person to visit was Tito, who brought Rudy burritos. "I didn't think you'd want *flores* or nothing," he had said, then he had begun rambling, talking nervously, standing and sitting. "Marcia wants to come see you. Said she got to get somebody to take her." He went into a long explanation of how he got a ride. Humberto had brought him. "Antonio said he can't come, and he said some other stuff. Doesn't matter. *Estás durmiendo?*" Are you asleep?

"I'm awake," Rudy said, although he had been slipping in and out of Tito's words like someone asleep, but it had more to do with space than sleep, like he was sliding in between one word and another and seeing that the distances were not equal, seeing that these inequalities meant something.

Then he saw that Tito was crying and confessing something, speaking entirely in Spanish, which in itself was saying something. Tito thought he had betrayed their friendship somehow, and although he could not apologize for it, it still made him feel bad.

"*No te preocupes,*" Rudy said, interrupting him. Don't think about it. He believed Tito was talking about the reporter, how Tito had intentionally gone to the wrong motel room. Rudy's life stood before him, his anger and his revenge, his steel band, his blind trust in cruelty—and it all appeared ridiculous.

"It's over," he said to Tito. They split the burritos, Rudy falling asleep with the warm tortilla still in his hand.

Later, the shock wore off.

One of the nurses, a black woman with a sneer for a mouth, held his penis up to clean his wound and said, "This right here what gets all you boys in trouble. Not even a quarter pound of sausage that the whole world got to endlessly pay for in grief."

He had felt a surge of anger, which served to remind him who he really was, anger that was a kind of clarity. He felt the steel band once again. The nurse dabbed at the wound, making it sting, a burn that both soothed his anger and justified it. His battles were ridiculous, but they were his. This woman was no less absurd, her job to handle the private wounds of others, the blood and pus of people she didn't even know.

That night he took his clothes from the closet and dressed. He stepped into the hallway, then ducked into another room when he spotted the black nurse. He had thought she would be off duty by now. He found himself in a room with two sleeping men, separated from each other by a curtain. He found their clothes in drawers, just as his had been. One had forty dollars in his wallet, the other twenty-five. He waited another few minutes and then strolled out of the hospital, the pain from the wound less severe than he had anticipated.

He strode down the wide and brightly lit street, stopping at a 7-Eleven. He bought a hot dog and a bag of chips, although he wasn't hungry. He just felt conspicuous walking the streets with nothing in his hands.

He veered into a residential neighborhood, deciding to sleep in a yard, beneath a tree or behind a bush. He would lie in the dark and make plans. Nothing could be as it was. He knew there would be people making jokes about Rudy Salazar. Little people. But he could not return and crush them. Instead he would have to plan something that would prove them wrong. At the same time, without making the thoughts into words, he came to understand that he could not survive in this city by himself. He knew nothing of cities. The police might or might not look for him. Did he owe the hospital something? Would they have any idea that he had taken the money from the men in the adjoining room?

For two nights he slept wedged between an oleander bush and a board fence in a bare, ugly yard. His clothes became filthy, and he knew he could not stay on the streets. He waited until the man who lived in the house drove off in his rattletrap car, then he broke into the house. One of the bedroom windows was unlatched. It was easy.

There was nothing in the refrigerator to eat but pork and beans in a bowl covered with aluminum foil, and nothing to drink but a single can of beer. Rudy took a shower. Until he played basketball, he had never taken a shower. All his life he had washed from a basin. He washed himself thoroughly, examining his wound, soaping it carefully.

When he was through, he left the water running, steam filling the bathroom, billowing in the harsh light of an exposed bulb. He stepped up on the man's bed and pissed on the dirty sheets. No blood in his urine. Each day it hurt less to piss, to walk, to carry himself like a man. The clothes in the dresser were too small, except for the socks. He took the three clean pairs the man had. Then he left the house, the shower still running.

If *La Verdad* had not found him that night, he would have broken into another house. Anything could have happened. The car pulled up slowly behind him as he walked down another residential street in a poor neighborhood. He had immediately been on his guard, thinking it was the cops.

The car pulled even with him, and he saw that it was a low rider. He thought immediately of what Antonio had told him, how they had pointed a gun at him.

"Hey, *vato*," a man's voice, the window partly down revealing only the man's eyes and his slicked-back hair. "You a dumbshit, *vato*?"

Rudy grabbed the door handle, jerked the door open. With the other hand, he grabbed the man's arm and forced it down. But he had no gun. "Move over," he said. "I'm with you."

He lived now in this cellar with a cot, a sheet, a blanket, a toothbrush, a cracked mirror, a change of clothes, and two large jars of bones capped by the skull of a child. Maybe they murdered this boy, or maybe they had taken the bones from a museum or some such place, and just used them to brag. Rudy didn't really care about their source. They spoke to him. They demanded his attention. The bones were the past, and they were the future. Here was what each human would amount to ultimately, no matter how he lived. Whether he showered in a tub or bathed from a basin, he would become bones. Whether he owned a television or listened to a battery-operated radio, he would become bones. Whether he understood what lay ahead or he understood nothing, he would become bones. They were the pure essence of every living body, and they would remain pure beyond death.

He had a score to settle back home. Then it would be his home no more. He would stay in this basement, live with these people, help them if they needed help, until he was ready to even the score. Then they would help him, and he would himself disafuckingpear. Nothing left but a shock to the minds of those people in Persimmon who laughed at Rudy Salazar's wounds.

Or maybe nothing left but Rudy Salazar's bones. If it had to turn out that way, he could face it. Sooner or later, it would turn out that way in any case.

La Verdad had given him a bed, acted as a family, but he was not fooled. He had no family. He had no friends, except Tito Tafoya, who had found a way to come to him when Rudy was suffering. If Tito were here, he would attempt to explain his agenda. He owed the Shopper and he owed Cecilia Calzado, but he would have the opportunity for just one act. They both were connected to the boy. Enrique.

Enrique Calzado would suffer for them. They would live for ages with the rattle of his bones haunting them.

· · ·

Upon leaving the restaurant, following a mediocre salad and half a bottle of mediocre wine, Gay wrapped her arms about herself against the cold, hunching so that she stared at her feet, and walked into Denny from behind. He had stopped at the edge of the concrete skirt that fronted the restaurant to point across the street. Rita stood between Cecilia and Enrique Calzado, staring into the window of a clothing store. If her friends had not been with her, Gay might not have recognized her daughter, so much had her body changed. Embarrassed, Gay ran ahead of Denny to his Buick, saying, "I didn't dress warmly enough," which was true. She had not wanted to wear a coat over the sweater dress, making a special effort to look good, as if doing so were somehow a conciliatory gesture.

"I can't believe the difference in Rita," Denny said softly as he climbed in beside her. His voice sounded light and false. He had become careful around her. He started the engine and let it idle in the cold evening air.

The long fight they'd had did not have anything to do with logic. Before it happened, Gay had been ready to divorce Sander. She discovered this when Rita was almost raped by one of Denny's basketball players. The rage she directed toward Denny educated her. That he'd had that monster on the team made her question his judgment. She had almost given up not only her husband but the life she had made for herself, all for Denny, and suddenly he seemed unworthy and deceitful. Not exactly a logical appraisal, but she could *feel* the truth residing in it.

She had hardly seen him over the holidays, and Sander still came down almost every weekend, tying up much of her time. But she wanted to forgive Denny, and he wanted to be forgiven. Across the street, Rita pointed at something in the window, then made a wriggling gesture with her body, as if sliding on the garment. The other kids laughed. None of them wore coats.

"She looks great," Denny went on, and Gay understood that this was also an attempt at reconciliation. He would praise her daughter, suggesting, without saying as much, that she had not been damaged by Rudy Salazar, which seemed, incredible as it sounded, to be true. "She takes off a few pounds of beef and suddenly she's her mother's daughter."

"Beef?" Gay shifted in the car, unwrapping her arms. He was offering to resume their old dialogue, the teasing and joking. She kicked off a shoe in order to thrust her foot against his hip. She had on stockings and let her skirt slide up her legs. They had not made love in weeks.

"Just trying to be colorful," he said, smiling, clearly happy she let him tease her. He handled her foot as he shifted the car into gear.

"It was more than a few pounds," Gay said, watching now as her daughter and friends wandered down the street. "Try close to thirty. I think maybe having a boyfriend—"

"Nah, carving up my power forward made her a favorite on our fine campus, and that popularity went from her head to her body. She's become a social butterfly."

Gay felt herself freeze up inside. He had gone too far, suggesting that the attempted rape had actually enhanced her life, but she knew he did not speak with malice. She consciously worked to deny the anger that gripped her. They were going to have a drink with Margaret and Randall, and Gay looked forward to having other people around. She was determined to be patient.

The kids drifted down the street and Denny pulled out of parking lot. "They don't seem to have anything to do," he said.

"Rita has to be home in twenty minutes," Gay said, glancing at her watch. "They don't need to do anything but stroll and chat. It's a school night."

Denny pulled her foot into his lap as he directed the car into the street. "You going to come to the game tomorrow?" He began fiddling with the heater to keep from looking at her.

"I won't abandon you," she said, although she had not been to a game since the incident and the season was almost over. Losing Rudy Salazar had damaged the team. The formerly undefeated Tigers—now once again called the Farts—had lost half their games and most of their crowd. "He wasn't one of our best players," Denny had explained, "but he was the only guy with muscle. On a given night somebody may get hot and make some baskets, but nobody's going to suddenly get strong. We get shoved all over the place."

When he had said this, during an earlier attempt to get back together, Gay had lashed out at him, saying she didn't give a damn about how his team might be damaged by the loss of that animal. It had been impossible then to contain herself, but now she thought she could manage it. She loved him, and her daughter was fine. She moved her foot about his lap, rubbing his crotch, her stocking sliding over the material of his pants with a scritching sound that reminded her of something, although she couldn't say what, taking laundry from a dryer, perhaps.

Denny drove them to the Alouette, a piano bar in the lobby of an old downtown hotel long ago converted to business offices, where they had agreed to meet Margaret and Randall. "You ever been to this place?" Denny asked.

"With Margaret," Gay said, recovering her shoes while he looked for a place to park. "It's got that art-deco-gone-to-seed look that passes for atmosphere in Persimmon."

Denny shrugged. "As long as the beer's cold."

When they stepped from the car, she took his arm, pulling him close, for warmth and to nurture their delicate truce.

The Alouette took up one end of the building, a long and narrow room with a handsome wood bar and hardwood floor. The windows had been blackened, and neon beer signs appeared to be the primary source of light in the place. The heat was on high, almost taking away their breath.

"I don't see any piano," Denny said. Garth Brooks sang an earnest ballad on the CD jukebox, while an elevated television showed a soundless ESPN Sports Center.

"This isn't the place I was thinking about," Gay said. "I thought I'd been here, but I guess I haven't."

Margaret waved to them from the far corner booth. She scooted around the table to sit beside Randall, sliding a drink along with her. Gay and Denny sat opposite them. "I thought this was a piano bar," Gay said. "How can you have a piano bar without a piano?"

"It's no longer a piano bar, if it ever was," Margaret said, shaking her head as she spoke, her mouth exaggerating each syllable slightly, which Gay understood as evidence Margaret had been drinking for a while. "It's now a whistle bar. A few minutes ago those two men at the bar started yelling at each other, and the bartender blew a whistle to stop them."

Gay turned her head. Two men in dark shirts with identical posture slouched over the bar, a single padded stool between them. "They look peaceful now."

Denny nodded at Randall. "How are you doing tonight?"

Randall gave his head a little shake. His face seemed inordinately red, and Gay guessed that he, too, had already had several drinks. His liver spot stood out strangely against his ruddy cheek, almost as if he had been branded. She looked at her watch. They weren't late.

"We skipped dinner," Margaret said as Gay looked up. "We've been here a couple of hours. Drinking our din-din."

"Is something wrong?" Gay asked.

"Claire Brownlee wants to be reinstated," Margaret said, screwing up her face.

Beneath his breath but audible, Randall said, "Crazy bitch."

"He's quoting me," Margaret said. "The school board cannot put her in charge of eight-year-olds again. Her husband has suggested a compromise."

"The bastard," Randall said, no longer whispering. He sat up straighter and pulled at his tie, a wide red thing with diagonal black stripes.

"He wants her on medical leave with full pay for this year and to be reinstated next year. Hubby may have to demand a psychiatric examination in order to keep her away from the kids."

"Jesus," Denny said. "How crazy is she?"

"The problem," Randall began, then he lifted his drink and took a gulp. "Get me another of these, will you?" He didn't seem to direct the question to anybody, speaking to the table. He covered his mouth and silently burped. Denny got up and walked to the bar to order. "The goddamn problem," Randall said, loudly enough for Denny to hear at the bar, and he waited until Denny glanced over to show he was listening, "is that we could get some flake evaluating her, and she could pass. Trust me, she should *not* pass, but it could happen, and then we'd have to reinstate her. I don't give a damn about the back pay, but I am not going to permit her in a classroom ever again." He put one of his meaty hands to his head. "If I can help it."

"Hubby's a little angry," Margaret said. She looked expectantly to the bar, where Denny waited for the drinks.

Gay felt a split in her emotions. She did not like Claire Brownlee, but she felt compassion for her. She also believed that people deserved a second chance. Denny set a round of drinks on the table and then scooted in beside her. Randall lifted his scotch to Denny as a thanks. Gay felt an obligation to say something on Claire's behalf. "But she could get better, don't you think?"

"Moot," Randall said.

"You don't know what-all's gone on in that classroom," Margaret said. "And we're not supposed to reveal any details." She sighed and patted her husband's shoulder. Then she returned her attention to Gay. "I hate to tell you—and I'm not supposed to—but you've been dragged into this." The Garth Brooks CD ended. After a few seconds of silence, the bar filled with grunge rock. The atmosphere of the place shifted with the music, becoming, Gay felt, slightly threatening.

"Me?" Gay said.

"That crazy bitch," Randall said again.

Margaret nodded. "Claire claims you slipped her something. She says— I'm certain Dick told her to say this—that you gave her some kind of drug without her knowing it."

Gay's first response was to laugh, but her reaction shifted. The sound she made sounded like a croak.

"She *is* crazy," Denny said.

Life was infinitely strange, Gay thought. The accusation shocked her, but it was so ludicrous she could not take it seriously. Instead, she felt the pleasurable pull of a mystery. Gay felt certain that Claire Brownlee was a mystery as incomprehensible as serial killers or that group of teenagers in Texas who had made a fad of suicide. "When was it I supposedly did this?" Gay asked.

"She's vague about the time and place," Margaret said.

Randall took a gulp of his drink. "Dick Brownlee may be a son of a bitch, but he's not stupid enough to pursue this in any legal way. They just want to use LSD—"

"They didn't name the drug," Margaret said.

"What the hell else could it be?" Scotch slid from the lip of the tumbler and painted his hand. "They want to pretend she was drugged instead of insane, and they picked on you because you're single, and you have a different kind of setup and so on." He drank.

"Claire hates me," Gay said. "I promised to talk to her one time—at that dinner party at your place—and I forgot about it. Now she hates me. God only knows what she wanted to talk about."

"Her husband, I'd guess," Denny said.

"Crazy fucking bitch," Randall said. He took the napkin from beneath his drink and wiped his lips.

They again drank silently for a few moments. The music slid back into country and western. Gay found it a relief to think about Claire and not about Denny or Rudy Salazar. This problem would bring her and Denny back together, she thought. In a circuitous way, this ridiculous allegation would reunite them. The singer on the jukebox claimed that all his exes lived in Texas. He seemed to sing off key intentionally.

"You could sue her," Denny said. "She can't just lie about you."

"You're not supposed to know," Randall said. "It was a closed meeting. Don't repeat any of this."

Margaret stirred the ice in her drink. "As soon as we left the meeting, I said to Hubby, 'We have to tell Gay she's being used,' and Hubby said, 'Goddamn right.'"

"He beats her," Randall said. He still held the napkin and touched his lips again. "Dick beats her."

Margaret shook her head. "I'm not sure it's that simple."

"Goddamn cops," Randall said. "Makes me feel like a college student again, all righteous and full of piss. Remember how it was, Mags? We were all righteous and full of piss. Now we're sitting here wondering—How the hell did we get to the point where now we're, *us*, we're . . . Now we're—"

"Old," Margaret said.

"Goddamn cops put on their goddamn uniforms and turn into fucking Nazis." He tapped Margaret on the shoulder, then slid himself out of the booth after she stood. "Excuse me," he said.

"Dick is plain-clothesed," Margaret said, after Randall was gone. She sat again, straightening her skirt. "But it doesn't seem the time to quibble."

"This is so upsetting," Gay said, although what she was thinking was how people often used small problems to permit them to ignore larger ones. She supposed this was a large problem for Randall, and she could see that he and Margaret were distressed to have Gay slandered. But Gay decided it was lucky. Crazy Claire and Abusive Dick were making up stories about her. Sander will get a kick out of this story, she thought, and then she felt a moment of guilt thinking of him while she was with Denny.

"Did they say any other stuff about Gay or anyone else?" Denny asked.

"They left you out of it," Margaret said.

"I was thinking of Rita."

Margaret sighed again and looked for Randall.

"What?" Gay said. The perverse pleasure she had taken turned on her, and she became tense. She would not permit her daughter to be smeared by the Brownlees.

Margaret looked at her lap and sighed through her nose. "I'm not supposed to tell you this, but they said awful things about her going into that outhouse with the Salazar boy. Implied you were, I don't know, just bad news. They know about your marriage arrangement. God knows how, but they think they can use it against you. They made claims about, well, that you have some history of mental illness."

"How do they . . ." Gay remembered what Claire had said about Margaret and Randall, about the baby they had sent back. *You're not married to a detective*, Claire had said. Gay shook her head, cleared her throat. "I want to know what *exactly* they said."

"Don't worry. Hubby talked to every board member privately afterward. Told them you were our neighbor and a good person and so on. Pointed out that Claire's behavior had gone on for weeks—we can document that. No drug caused her to pay kids five dollars to be quiet. You know what else she did? Took off her shirt and cleaned a window with it. Right in the classroom. In front of the kids. She had her bra on, unfortunately, or we could get the fundamentalists to nail her up. And that's not the half of it. Don't fret about this. Not one sane person there took her seriously."

The anger Gay felt was the same anger she had felt before for Denny, a deep maternal anger that words seemed inadequate to express. She did not care what Claire—or anyone else—knew or said about her, but she wanted her daughter left out of it. Finally she said, "I could kill her."

"You won't have to. Her husband will probably take care of that, but not in the next several months," Margaret said, and then sardonically added, "Alas." She pointed to her own husband as he stepped from the bathroom. "Shh," she said.

"I called a taxi," he said. "I can't afford to be picked up for DUI."

"I could drive us all," Denny offered.

Randall shook his head. "Shouldn't be seen with you two, either. Might look like I was passing confidential information."

"Which is just what we've been doing," Margaret said.

Denny downed the remainder of his beer. "We might as well take off, too, I guess."

Gay's drink sat before her on the table, untouched. She put it to her lips but could taste nothing.

"There's one other thing," Randall said. "Unrelated. More or less. You need to tell your daughter to quit wearing those damn dresses she's got. They're too short. She was warned about them day one, but we let it go. Obviously we shouldn't have."

"What do you mean by that?" Gay asked.

"We just shouldn't have. She could be putting herself at risk again by wearing them."

Margaret took in a sudden gasp of air and covered her mouth.

Randall kept his gaze steadily on Gay. "I can handle this other crap, but the school could be liable for not enforcing its dress code."

Margaret slapped him across his forehead. He turned to her and she slapped him again, her nail cutting his nose. She reached across the table and touched Gay's hand as it slid off the table. Denny was leading her outside. "He didn't mean that," she said. "He's under stress. He's been drinking."

"My daughter was not asking to be molested," Gay said.

"I didn't mean that, Christ." Randall touched the blood on his nose. "I'm on your side."

"Come on," Denny said, pulling Gay close, throwing an arm around her, as she knew he would. Randall called to them again. Margaret spat words at him furiously. The Lambs *were* on her side, she knew. Randall was just careless, and she was being unforgiving, uncaring, maybe even unreasonable, tucked under Denny's arm, sliding through the door and into the bracing night. She understood that they were going to his cottage. They were going to make love. She felt bruised, terrible, giddy, dirty, Denny leading her by the arm through the cold.

Rita watched from the loft of the barn, the afternoon quiet except for the heavy respiration of the horses in their stalls. His truck was parked in front of the house, and the front door was open. Only the screen door separated him from the outside world. From her. He was in there, moving around or napping—although he didn't seem the type to nap—or watching television, but she didn't imagine he could get cable out here, and there was no antenna on the house. He had to be moving around in there, she reasoned, which meant that sooner or later she would catch a glimpse of him. Unless he was reading. He did seem the type to read. She wished she had brought a book to fill the time while she waited and also place her in a type of communal action with him, both of them reading within twenty yards of each other. She made a mental note to bring a book with her next time.

She heard a door swing open and bang shut, but not a solid bang, another screen door, she guessed, the back door. He had gone out the back, which was not in her view, but it thrilled her to hear it, to picture him walking out the door. She waited, perched on a bale of hay, staring at the house through the barn's open window. Was it a window if there was no glass? Maybe it was a doorway without a door. She had seen a hay loader carry bales up to such a door in a different barn, the loader like a little escalator, carrying square bales. Where had that barn been? On television, she thought. She'd watched it with Enrique and Cecilia and their mother. Did she like Enrique for his television? Her feelings for him suddenly seemed so clear to her, how they were ultimately superficial, as flat as the characters on the flat screen. She had mended him and now kept him around for appearances, so she wouldn't have to date another boy, and to help him along after the death of his father.

Enrique loved her, but she was going to give herself to Mr. Gene, as soon as she reached double figures. Ninety-nine pounds. She would simply walk into the house, and she would be so beautiful—in a bathing suit so that he could see her body. Or naked. Just her perfect body and her. And he would understand immediately, would know why she was there, why she had come to him, and he would love her, would find some way to let Heart down. Rita would cure him, make him whole.

Not that he'd meant her weight when he'd written "Hope for double figures" in his notebook—she wasn't deluding herself. He'd meant the weather, the temperature, getting below one hundred degrees. But this was the way the world operated. A secret set of rules worked beneath the surfaces, and if you could decipher the hidden meanings, then you could get what you needed, what you wanted, what you had to have. Was she supposed to believe that she had found the notebook simply by coincidence? She almost laughed out loud.

Movement in the nearest window. A dark form walking quickly, with purpose. Something was the matter. Or he was involved in some work. There was meaning in his stride, intention, reason. She could garner more from his partly hidden gait than from an hour of Enrique's gab. Not that she didn't like Enrique. He was soothing. But predictable, and his kindness had no mystery, just Enrique being Enrique. While Mr. Gene adjusting the light in the room—maybe that was what he'd been doing—sent her tumbling into a world of possibility. She had thought he was outside, but he was moving about the inside. The back door slamming had been something else. He had let out the cat. Or he had set out some garbage. Or he had let some part of the larger world in.

The front door opened, the screen swinging wide, her heart swinging open, and there he stood, bareheaded, the fingers of one hand in his short locks, the other hand holding a portable phone to his ear, his shirt untucked. He wore no shoes, the white socks streaked brown. Who would have thought that he would have a cordless phone? Mystery without end. She would never know all his secrets, no matter how long they stayed together. He shook his head, said something. His malaise, his private suffering, evident to her in even the tiniest of gestures.

Rita exhaled. She had been holding her breath. He wore no belt, the bare loops visible only on one side, the tails of his plaid shirt hiding the other side. "This afternoon?" he said, the only words he spoke with sufficient volume to reach her ears.

She touched her breast, imagining that it was his hand. The softest of touches. He was a gentle man. He would need encouragement.

He disappeared back inside. She turned from the open window, leaned against the plank floor, breathing heavily in the dusty, hay-laden air. This was love, she understood. The tingling, the sweat on her chest and thighs, her breasts suddenly hurting—a specific pleasurable pain, like fear, like hunger. A love that was partly for him and partly for what she could do for him.

She heard the screen door bang again, and suddenly she was certain that he had seen her and was coming to drag her out of the loft and send her home like a child. Or to make love to her here in the hay. She dug her fingers into the bale she rested on, to await her destiny.

But no, the truck door opened, closed. She peeked out the window as the truck started, could see his form through the back window as he shifted into gear. The truck pulled away.

She began climbing down. There was no point in waiting there while he was gone. Already she was calculating when she would be able to come back and what she would bring with her to read. The horses made nervous sounds as she descended the ladder, and she made another note to herself—bring carrots for the horses.

The air still held dust from the truck's departure, a little cloud floating out beyond the house. The screen door had not shut tight. It must have bounced because she heard it slam.

She could go into his house, she understood. She could just walk right in. The thought had barely entered her head before she found herself on his porch. The dusty tracks she left blended in with his. It would take a detective to notice anything, and she already knew him well enough to know that he paid no attention to such things. She pulled the door open wide and stepped in.

The front room was small, the ceiling low. A couch and matching chair lined a wall, white puffs sticking out of the material. An end table separated the couch from the chair, holding nothing but a fine layer of dust. Homemade bookshelves had been built into a nook. The shelves must have been new because there were no books, only a model house on the top shelf. She went to examine it. Made of Lego and painted gray, the house had a pitched roof fashioned from aluminum foil. It was almost large enough to be a dollhouse. She pushed the plastic door open, but the inside was hollow.

She turned back to the real house, exploring the kitchen first, another tiny room, a metal table in the center, two chairs with the same looping metal legs as the table. The legs of one chair were dented and rusty. Not a single dish on the counter, and the sink was empty, too. He liked his house neat, she thought. She went back to the living room, glanced through the door at the empty drive, then hurried down the short hall.

His bed was made, covered with a patchwork quilt, a diamond design in the patches, with concentric diamonds of different colors, a white patch in the center, as if one piece had been torn off. On the faded yellow wallpaper above the bed, there was a drawing of a mountain with a cap of snow. Bold black lines from a magic marker drawn right onto the wall. It was the only decoration on any of the walls. It might not have been a mountain.

Rita wanted to look in his drawers, but she heard a noise. It was only the horses, she understood as she came into the living room, but it seemed to her that she might have been there a long time. She decided to leave. She stopped at the Lego house and opened again the miniature door. Enrique had given her a plastic ring that had come from a gumball machine. A joke ring in real life, but in this plastic house it would not be a joke.

She would begin the cure of Mr. Gene with this ring, symbolic of marriage, of completeness, fulfillment. She tugged the ring from her little finger and slipped it through the miniature door. A rush of words flooded her mind, sounds with meanings she could not perceive, except in their grander sense. They spoke of love, the power of love to heal, the body as the vessel of love, the beauty of the unpolluted body, tainted not by hate or greed, not by jealousy or fear, not by artificial markings or perfumes, not by the residues of bodily excrement or bodily functions, a virginal body unsoiled by sex, liquor, or food.

Spirit

25

Once the moon set, darkness hunkered down to the earth, the sky so dense it brushed his hair. But his feet knew what his eyes were denied. They led him up the old corridor to the invisible town, took him weaving among the houses made of mud, the tumbledown shacks, the familiar cars and trucks, these monuments of his cerebral landscape, shapes so elemental to his personal vision that it startled him to hear voices, to be reminded that these forms actually existed in the larger world, that people dwelled in them, that they went so far as to think of them as theirs.

Rudy paused to breathe in the air infused by rushing water, the river high and rising, snowmelt from distant mountains carrying the fresh smell of spring. He had not set foot in Apuro for more than five months, living instead in the Valdez cellar, doing what was necessary to keep his cot, his meals, his place in *La Verdad*.

He had gone with Billy Valdez and three other boys on a buy in Juárez, a few pounds of *mota* and a small Baggie of cocaine purchased from a nervous *chango* in a crushed white hat. Rudy had stuffed the coke in his pants pocket and carried the bricks of marijuana in a black garbage bag across the Rio Grande, which was no deeper between countries than it had been between communities.

Billy had waded the river with him, while the others crossed the downtown bridge—a safety measure, they claimed. Dealers in Mexico sometimes informed on the buyers in exchange for cash, making money coming and going. If the others were searched crossing the bridge, they would know the dealer was a snitch. "And if Billy and me get our asses caught," Rudy had said, "you'll come bust us out, no?" He had laughed at their rationalizations, their cowardice.

Billy had accompanied him across the river because he didn't yet entirely trust Rudy. Rudy did not begrudge him his suspicion, his healthy reluctance to embrace the newcomer too readily. It was part of the life. Rudy, after all, planned on screwing them all when he left, not out of spite but necessity.

To prove his allegiance to *La Verdad*, he had participated in two fights, neither planned. One had broken out at a dull, stinking party in a rundown house filled with housecats. The electricity had failed early in the evening, and the gathering degenerated into sitting on a carpet the cats had frequently sprayed and otherwise soiled, and passing around joints of weak dope that smelled and tasted like rubber. Other recreation was offered Rudy. Billy and his girlfriend smoked crack in the bathroom, but Rudy declined, his eye on the big picture. None of these others were even aware that there was such a thing, taking what pleasure they could find in the moment without anticipating consequences.

The fight amounted to nothing more than punching out one tough guy with a mealy beard and a hoop in his ear that Rudy took pleasure in ripping out, and shoving another *payaso* through a window. Shots were fired near the end, but no one had been hit, a fight having to do with race and region, territorial declarations no different from the cats' spraying. Rudy had no interest in the impersonal, manufactured reasons for such violence.

The second fight erupted at an intersection when the rear window of Billy's car exploded. Rudy had been sitting in the backseat and ducked out the door, his head so low he could smell the tires hot from the pavement. He spotted a kid running across the parking lot of an abandoned gas station, lugging a sledgehammer. Holding on to the sledge was his mistake. Rudy caught up with him at the antiquated gas pumps, grabbing him by the collar and jerking him to the asphalt, the long handle of the hammer ricocheting off the pumps. Rudy wrapped up the boy in his arms and heaved him into traffic. The boy bounded off a slow-moving pickup, denting the passenger door. He landed in the street on his knees, his jeans flaring red as if the friction had turned his legs to flame.

A car darted from behind the gas station, accelerating past the pumps, gravel pinging against the metal building. Rudy hurled the sledge, missing the darkened windows, the head of the hammer skipping over the hood and bouncing into the street. A trail of dents shone on the polished hood, catching the yellow of the traffic light, as if the damaged car bled butter.

When gunfire began, Rudy picked up the boy from the street to use as a shield, edging toward the truck that had dutifully stopped after the boy had bounced off it. Rudy shoved the boy into the pickup bed and climbed in after him, rolling over the kid and the ribbed bed as the driver pulled a U-turn, causing the truck to career off a city dumpster in his haste to flee the site.

The boy was crying, gasping for breath, his face contorted in pain, an expression that reminded Rudy of someone, sometime. The driver of the truck screamed that he was heading for the police station. Rudy ignored him, placed his finger in the finger-sized depression at the base of the boy's throat, and pressed. The boy's eyes enlarged, his breath halted, the crying ceased. The kid reached inside his jean jacket for his weapon, but Rudy grabbed it first. A cheap switchblade from Juárez, which he tossed over his shoulder and into the street. He leaned close to the boy, waiting for words to come to him, to alight on his tongue, to let him know what he believed. *"Estás muerto,"* he said to the boy. You're dead. He paused to consider his motive. Was he threatening the boy or giving him advice? He lost the links in his thoughts. "Get a life, *feo*," he said, and thunked his finger against the boy's forehead. Then he hopped from the truck as it slowed for an intersection. As soon as Rudy jumped out, the truck ran a red light and disappeared.

Two of *La Verdad* had been wounded. Neither seriously, scrapes that could have been from bullets or from their own clumsy fleeing. They claimed to have killed the driver of the car, but Rudy looked through the paper the next day, and the event, described simply as gang violence, did not involve any deaths. The boy in the truck had ended up in the hospital with busted ribs and a broken kneecap. He was eleven years old.

It all had felt like playacting. People could have been killed, but death did not discriminate against the frivolous. People died skiing or motorboating or climbing rocks for their own entertainment—that didn't make them serious. The fight had the contrived and self-important feel of masturbation. Courage had not been required, only bravado, reaction, and a certain degree of reckless stupidity. It was impersonal violence, having nothing to do with . . . Rudy searched for the word: *manners.*

The only thing Rudy had done with *La Verdad* that had required courage had been fucking Liz Trujillo. She belonged to Billy and was strictly off limits. But Rudy knew he had just a few days remaining with *La Verdad*, and he did not want to leave empty-handed. It had happened only that morning. He had strolled over to her house under the pretense of looking for Billy, knowing that he was at school. Liz had been suspended for returning from a lunch break so high she could not operate the combination lock on her locker. He was certain that she would be home and alone.

She stood behind the screen door giving Rudy the eye, listening to him, her black hair pulled away from her face, one hip jutting out, her limbs loose and defiant. Then she swung the door open saying, "You know he ain't here, *caca* breath." She smiled, a wide, unattractive, toothy spread, curling her lips and revealing her fillings, but a sexual act in itself, the wild stretch of her mouth, the graphic display of her pink, wet orifice.

As soon as Rudy stepped inside her house, he pushed his face close to hers. "You coming with us tonight?" he asked her. He had said he could secure a gun in Apuro, and Billy was taking him there. He had made it sound dangerous.

"You know I am," she said.

"You a brave girl, huh?" He leaned against her, his chest pressing against hers.

"Pretty brave," she said. She pushed him away, saying, "I've been expecting you." She led him to her bedroom, the foam mattress covered with a dirty pink sheet, which she swept with her hand and arm before lying down. "I like to eat in bed," she said, laughing at herself and making room for him beside her.

He hesitated in undressing her when he saw the scar between her breasts. "He cut me once," she said. "I'm going to get a tattoo to cover it, but I can't figure the right shape." She unhooked her bra to reveal the dimensions of her scar, from nipple to nipple with a loop in the middle. "We were fucked up," she said. "I cut him, too." She ran a finger over the scar. "Billy says a dragon would cover it, but who wants a dragon on her *chichis*?"

Rudy took a breast in his hand, rolled the nipple's hard button between his thumb and finger. "I got a scar, too," he said. "On my cock."

"Big scar?"

"Big enough." He leaned forward and licked the damaged skin between her breasts, his tongue tracing the corrugated flesh, the looping groove.

Their sex was quick, unceremonious, and electrifying. They fucked face to face, taking only a while to find a rhythm, a give-and-take, the sexual syntax that spoke what they had no words for, that powerful human linkage that fucking merely made literal. Rudy had not felt this way with any other girl. This sex was not the product of rage but of something else, a spiral of feeling that dwelled beneath the rage, sheltered by the steel band. Call it love. A brand of weakness he wished to embrace, a liquid burn in his chest, a reservoir of hot oil where his heart had been.

"Don't come in my pussy," she said to him, her lips and teeth at his ear, and it seemed to him it was her voice that made him come. He pulled out just in time, shuddering against her soft belly.

He spent the day with her, discussing what he had to do in Persimmon and how he could get away with it, eating tamales thawed in the microwave, drinking her father's beer, making love again in her hot room. She napped, her pale breasts rising and falling with her respiration, the looping scar expanding and contracting, her body a dark brown against the pink sheets, and for a moment Rudy saw her body for what it was, a vessel for the spirit, a fragile shell containing impossible riches. The sun shone in patches on the bed, hot on his limbs, sweat running down his chest. He was a little drunk, and the heat, the exertion of love and lovemaking, the image of this actual person naked before him, created in him a deep sense of sensual peace.

At the same time, the intuition of her spirit—how the beauty of her body both contained and disguised it—stirred a different sensation in him, a troubling thought. This thought did not occur to him in the form of language— he did not trust language, anyway. It came to him in the subtler form of physical recognition, the body remembering itself, announcing itself as his sole source of satisfaction. Any other pleasure was a lie, a pretension. He understood that the only justification for his existence was in the visceral pleasure his body could find.

He climbed out of bed, dressed, and hiked back to his cellar, the feeling staying with him, a haunting that made his mood dark, and that left him only when he set foot in Apuro. He stood now at the opposite end of the *colonia* from where he had begun. Billy and Liz waited for him across river, but he could not leave yet, the desire in him unrelenting. He started the trek again. This was his home and this walk his ritual of ownership, and if it was his home, and if it was also his vision, then the walking was nothing less than contemplation, his study of the dark buildings something like self-scrutiny, his walk not so much like a train of thought as like the impulse of thought, like the current of electrical charge circulating through gray matter, making its circle through familiar territory, a kind of meditation. It calmed him, his legs assuming their habitual stride, himself coming back to himself, here in this place, the only place he had really known, this no place, this trash heap, this miracle of sand bordered by moving water.

This would be his last journey over the sacred ground, he understood, and the knowledge lent to his walk a tenderness, a beauty. It was as if he were making love a final time, the woman a childhood sweetheart, his wife, the only woman he had ever loved, and now she was leaving him, and he knew that she was leaving him, but not until morning, and so they lay in each other's arms and kissed each other's lips and touched each other's flesh, and in the touch was sadness, not the sadness of loss, but the sadness of love. Rudy walked silently, his fingers brushing against the adobe walls, not thinking as he walked, but walking as a kind of thought.

It took him to the Dodge Dart, to the front seat, the glove box, whose cardboard backing he pulled away. The pistol weighted his hand, pulled it down, yet another kind of sadness.

He considered putting the barrel in his mouth, but he could not really think this evening in the conventional manner. Only his feet could think, and they took him through it all a third and final time, the house of Humberto Douglas, the house of Nita and the teacher, the house of his mother, the shack of *la familia* Obregon, this final pass among the touchstones of his elusive inner and outer life ended at the house that once was his sanctuary, the house that once was home to the Calzados, and it was not coincidence that his thoughts, his feet, had taken him here. He had been right all along, the whole of his pain was connected to the boy Enrique, son of those who abandoned him, brother to Arturo and Cecilia, boyfriend of the girl who stabbed him. A nice kid, Rudy thought, still moving, circling the house, *a nice kid*, words as strange as music and as beautiful as the river, which was where Rudy headed now. *He's a nice kid*, Rudy repeated the phrase over and over in his head, the liquid dark below his feet moving imprecisely among the jetty nooks. *He's a nice kid*. The weight of the gun in his hand matched precisely the weight of the future.

"Jackie O bit it," the boy said.

Enrique leaned across the cafeteria table to stare at the Chicano boy with purple-rimmed glasses. The semester was almost over and Enrique had come to like these kids, but he still didn't understand them, and he could never remember their names. This guy's name had something to do with butter. Buddy? Bread? Brad?

"First her old man," the boy in the purple glasses went on, "and now her."

Enrique touched Rita's thigh with his knuckles. "Eat something," he said. She angled her head to show him her eyes, a loving, teasing glance. He ignored it and handed her a spoon as encouragement. He tried to catch Cecilia's eye so she would help, but his sister was scanning the room, looking for Tito Tafoya, no doubt. Rita had introduced them and told Enrique that Cecilia liked him. "I like him, too," Enrique had said, although he hadn't seen him in months.

"Who are we talking about?" a girl asked.

"JFK."

"The guy or the movie?"

"The President. He was married to Jackie O, before she was married to . . . Mr. O. She just died."

Another kid joined the conversation, an Anglo boy with Clearasil smeared over his nose, grooves from his fingerprints showing in the flesh-colored smudges. "I get JFK confused with Dick Van Dyke. Like I try to picture JFK and Jackie O, in that car in Dallas, but I keep seeing Dick Van Dyke and Laura Petrie."

"Mary Tyler Moore," yet another boy said. "She did have that same haircut." Everyone at the table was becoming animated, except for Enrique, his sister, and Rita. He became wary, while Cecilia ate and listened, and Rita merely listened. These conversations were like lessons, distant and peculiar, full of foreign names and arcane references. Everyone in the group chirped in.

"Dick Van Dyke, JFK—they're both dead guys in black and white."

"With three-syllable names."

"Dick Van Dyke's not dead. He's just a stooge. Got that 'diculous gray mustache. I saw him on something."

"He was the one in *Mary Poppins*. My mom bought that video. Can you believe it?"

"If JFK hadn't gotten wasted in Dallas, we'd still be in the sixties. We'd all be saying *groovy* and shit like that."

"Who was that other guy got shot at the same time?"

"Martin Luther King?"

"The guy in the car that the bullet went though his wrist or something?"

"It was Jerry. You know, the neighbor with the stupid hair on 'Dick Van Dyke.' "

"That'd be a good 'SNL' skit. Doing JFK and Jackie O as Dick Van Dyke and Laura Petrie. Like when it starts and he comes in and stumbles over that foot thing."

"Doo-o-o-do-do, doo-do-do—" Others joined in singing. "—doo-do-do-do-do-doo-doo-do-dat-DAT-dat."

"And when he falls there could be this announcer like Dan Rather saying, 'He's down! The President has been shot!' "

Almost everyone laughed. Enrique wanted to laugh with them, but didn't think he should laugh about a dead President. Especially a Catholic one. He rubbed his eyes to cover not laughing. His eyes stung. For the third time in a week, he had awakened this morning to find himself in the front seat of the Fairlane, his mother staring through the driver's window and calling his name. "It's a good thing we don't live on a cliff," his mother had said to him as he crawled out the door. "You'd be some sleepy splatter down there on a bunch of rocks. Get going, Mr. Baldy. Time for school. I'm going to have to hire a search party every morning, am I?"

"If Jackie O loved him so much, why wasn't she Jackie K?" the girl with braces on her teeth wanted to know. "You'd think if your husband was President, you'd take his name."

"She did. He was Jack and she was Jackie."

"They should have made Laura 'Dickie' Petrie. Dick and Dickie."

"He was Rob Petrie on the show. You're confusing TV and real life."

"Dick Van Dyke has that lame brother who's on that other show, 'Coach.'"

"Ouch. 'Coach,' that's sinking low."

"But it's perfect. His brother could play Ted Kennedy in the sitcom."

"You mean the skit."

"No way they'd have lame-o's like the Dyke brothers on 'SNL.'"

"They'd have Dana Carvey or somebody playing Dick Van Dyke playing Rob Petrie playing JFK, and the guest host could be, I don't know—"

"Winona Ryder," Enrique said. They all turned to him. Some of them smiled. Rita squeezed his hand triumphantly.

"Yeah, Winona Ryder playing Laura Pe—"

"Mary Tyler Moore."

"—playing Mary Tyler Moore playing Laura Petrie playing Jackie O."

"Jackie K."

"The Dyke brother on 'Coach' is playing Jerry playing Ted Kennedy?"

"Jerry's got to be the guy who got shot with JFK in the car—not Ted Kennedy. The bullet went through his wrist and shit. He's got to be in the opening when Dick Van Dyke falls over the foot thing."

"I swear we could write for 'SNL'. They are so pathetic."

"So like *we're* pathetic?"

"You'd have to have somebody filming it, you know, the Zapruder character."

"How do you know all this JFK stuff?"

"Got the video," the boy in the purple glasses said. His name was Olin, Enrique realized: Olin/Oleo. "Seen it ten times," Olin said.

"Since we got 'Nick at Nite,' I've practically studied 'The Dick Van Dyke Show,'" another boy said. "I could major in it. I could write a dissemination on it."

"We don't have cable!" Enrique said. It excited him that he could name the reason for not understanding these people.

"Ouch," Olin said. "What do you *do*? How do you function?"

"We don't even have a television," Rita said, squeezing Enrique's hand again. He squeezed her back. She had stirred the chocolate pudding, but she hadn't eaten anything. He couldn't get her to eat. Her mother had taken her to a special counselor and then a psychologist. Her father had moved to Persimmon, lived now with them in the pink and green house, giving up his business in Albuquerque. All because she would not eat. Why would a person quit eating? Enrique realized that no one was speaking. It was as if Rita had admitted having some kind of disease, the No-TV virus.

Finally, Olin adjusted his glasses and said, "Hey, I envy your future. You've got a million shows to watch, and for you *none* of them are reruns."

"Zapruder sounds to me like a made-up name."

"Zapruder's the guy who shot the video of JFK buying it."

"The camera guy shooting the skit could be Zapruder. Maybe he could be Lee Harvey O, too. You know, JFK aka Dick Van Dyke is shot *by* video and *on* video by Lee Harvey O aka Zapruder, which makes him stumble and go down."

"And Laura—"

"Jackie O."

"Mary Tyler Moore."

"Winona Ryder."

"She was in *Heathers*, right? I've hated her since *Heathers*. She thinks she's so great now."

"In our version, Jackie O and Lee Harvey O could be sister and brother."

"Yeah, yeah, and she wants her *own* sitcom, and Lou Grant shows up and—"

"She wants to be President on her show, like Hillary—she could even *become* Hillary, and Clinton could play Lou Grant."

"My mom says that when JFK was shot, *her* mom came to school and took her home."

"Cool. Why?"

"I don't know."

"Maybe she was worried 'cause people were getting shot. That mom kind of worry. Your mom a worrier?"

"It wasn't my mom. It was *her* mom. My grandmother."

"Maybe they were a dysfunctional family."

"Her dad came home from work, too. She says they sat in the living room and watched the news on TV, and her mom held her, and they all cried—even my granddad."

"Yow."

"Maybe when Dick Van Dyke is shot and he stumbles and falls, maybe we should show some people watching it all on TV."

"Yeah, and how it all seems fake to them."

"Like they could be *watching* JFK in the convertible and he's getting blown away, but what they're *seeing* is Dick Van Dyke stumbling over the footstool."

"Who's the hero? You know, the star. It can't be the guy who plays JFK, 'cause he gets wasted, and the star never gets wasted."

"That's easy. The hero is the guy playing Lee Harvey O."

"No way."

"Way. If he doesn't shoot the guy, we've got no show."

"Yeah, if it weren't for him we'd all be saying *groovy* and wearing bell bottoms, and we'd have granola in our beards."

"Gross."

"But I thought Lee Harvey O was the cameraman, so can he be shooting the show while he's shooting the President?"

"Sure, he's Lee Harvey O and Zapruder. They're the same guy, and he's the hero—the guy with the camera, the guy with the gun."

The bell sounded.

"Shit. Once again, I've not had time to eat, and I've got Squarehead McKinley now."

"For what?"

"History. But I think he's showing a movie today."

"Thank God."

Outside, in the heat of midday, Enrique paused with the girls before heading for his bike. The Heart dress Rita wore hung loosely, and the hem fell lower on her thigh. It looked as if it had been lengthened, but it was she who had grown smaller, sticklike. "You feel okay?" Enrique asked her.

"Wonderful," Rita said. The smile she gave him seemed to generate light. He had trouble believing anything was wrong with her when she smiled.

Ahead, straightening after leaning against the stucco wall of the cafeteria, stood Tito Tafoya. "You cut your hair," he said.

Enrique immediately put his hand to his head, thinking something had happened. Then he realized he had not seen Tito since he'd begun shaving his head months ago. He ran his hand over the stubble of a few days' growth. "*Por favor*," he said. Please.

Tito gave him a funny look.

Cecilia said, "He means *por supuesto*." Of course.

"I still get those two confused," Enrique said.

"Oh, yeah, sure, *seguro*, that's what you say talking," Tito said, smiling in Cecilia's direction now. "You going to class? Of course you are, *claro*, but if you are, I could walk with you, you think?"

Cecilia nodded.

"I gotta go," Enrique said, but Rita held his elbow.

"Romance," she whispered into his ear, watching Cecilia walk off with Tito. "I willed it to happen," she added.

"Whoa, yeah, I guess," Enrique said, but she didn't let go of his arm. She wanted to borrow the mountain bike. While she explained her reasons, he watched her speak, the skin about her lips moving with the traffic of her mouth, words slipping into space, bearing meaning he guessed, but it was her mouth itself he studied. Why wouldn't she eat? Why would the person he loved suddenly quit eating? His father had wasted away before dying, but there was no cancer in Rita.

Or was there? Something that was like a cancer inside her that wouldn't let her eat. He tried to consider this, nodding to her about the bike as they separated. What was like a cancer but wasn't one? A riddle, like the riddle of that big statue in Egypt, the Sphincter or whatever. What walks on four legs when it gets out of bed, two legs at lunch, and three legs at bedtime? His history teacher had asked the class, and Enrique had been the only one to get it right. "Man," he had said, because he had heard one of his brother's friends call his penis his third leg, so that's what he had guessed.

What makes a person not eat in the morning or at lunchtime or at dinner? What makes a girl suddenly dislike the taste of all the things that keep her alive? He had plenty of time to figure it out. Without the bike, it would take him half an hour to get back to school.

26

Early that morning, before five because Gay again had not been able to sleep through the night, she found a mouse drowned in the kitchen sink, floating in gray water beside an egg-stained dish. It had almost been enough to send her over the edge, the sight of it and the smell of death. Her mind had begun racing. It could not be denied that such a thing seemed an omen. She imagined the mouse's tiny feet paddling desperately through the long night, the scrabbling of nails against the porcelain.

She left the kitchen and ran to her bedroom, falling on the bed beside Sander, holding him. He turned to her without waking. Three weeks earlier, down for his regular visit, he had driven to the house and walked in the door with Rita. As soon as their daughter left them alone, he said, "I'm not leaving town. Rita's in trouble, and I'm not leaving. I'll stay at the motel if I have to."

"I want you here," Gay had said, although until she spoke the words she had not known they were true. A few months earlier she had thought she would divorce him, had thought that the terms of their marriage would be changed by her love for Denny, not by this . . . this disease, this *thing* that was happening to their daughter. Now her time with Denny seemed like a lark, an amusement, the whole of the life she had created seemed like a luxury. "What about your business?" she had asked Sander.

"I'll call some people," he said. "Either they can keep it going, or they can't. At this point, I don't care."

After more than twelve years apart from her, he moved back into her bed, and they lived once again as husband and wife. Gay needed him there, she discovered, needed someone with her who had as much to lose as she did. Only Sander fit that description.

Rita, for reasons that baffled Gay, had not been surprised. "Let me put my hands on you," she had said to them. They had been at the kitchen table, and Gay expected a hug, despite the peculiar wording. But Rita had put a palm on each of their heads and smiled at them beatifically, as if she were the Pope.

Gay had become furious at that, but she had hidden it. She did not want to make Rita feel bad. The counselor had said they needed to improve her self-esteem. Even the term *self-esteem* infuriated Gay. It felt so made up, so *constructed*, a simp of a word. She knew it was crazy to be angry with words. She feared having another breakdown. Now, when her daughter needed her.

As she lay in bed, her dream of the past night came back to her. In the dream the river ran red, a vivid red like the juice of cherries, an obscene red, blood from an anus. She had awakened from the dream in a panic, relieved to find Sander beside her. Her dreams had become torments, and she could not escape them. In one dream she looked through the windows of her own house to see a strange woman carrying a dead baby. Then Gay saw that it wasn't a baby the woman bore, rather a girl who had been denied food, whose skin had shriveled over her bones, and whose bones the woman shoved into a high cupboard and nailed shut.

Denny was angry with her, although he tried to hide it. He pleaded with her to see him. "I understand why he's here," he had said after Sander moved in. "He's her father and he ought to be here, but that doesn't mean we can't—"

"Yes, it does," she had said, jumping away from him when he tried to embrace her. "For now, it does." He had said some angry things then, and she had returned them in kind. It had taken place in his little cottage, the two of them standing before the bed he had bought for her right after they met. "For now," she had said, when their anger had finally abated, "I can only think of what's best for Rita."

"All right," Denny had said. "I guess I understand." And she could tell that he had no conception. *Imagine this happening to your daughter*, she had wanted to say, but despite her anger, she could not suggest anything so cruel.

"You say it as if I were bad for her." Denny, for once, could not look at her when he spoke, could not produce the smirk. He had averted his eyes, as if studying a corner of the floor.

"What you feel doesn't matter," Gay had said. "That's not the issue."

"You're wrong about this," he had said then, but she had already opened the door and begun her departure.

Gay turned in the bed and pulled Sander close, running her hands beneath the sheet and over his chest to wake him.

"What is it?" he asked, instantly up on one elbow, blinking to make his eyes focus.

"Just a bad dream," she said, as if she hadn't already been up, as if she didn't know about the rodent floating in their sink.

"Rita?"

"Yes," she said, "although Rita wasn't in the dream. Nothing but the river, a red river. I wasn't even in the dream."

"I know what you mean," Sander said. "Everything I look at turns my thoughts back to her. *Everything*."

The counselor had said it was good that Rita wanted to finish out the school year, that goals and ambitions should be encouraged. An Eating Disorders Counselor. What a ridiculous title, Gay thought. Few boys got this sickness, almost exclusively girls, she had said, usually around Rita's age. "Low self-esteem," the counselor kept saying, a stick figure herself, with jet black hair, who, in Gay's memory, looked identical to the cartoon character Olive Oyl, that moronic damsel, thin as a rail, torn between the brute Bluto and the brute Popeye, as if there were no other options but fat bullies or pig-headed sailors, starving herself to please them, while they pounded away at each other, more interested in slugging than loving. Gay could imagine a Popeye sequel, Olive Oyl finally his wife, trying to care for a herd of children, bruises on her cheeks, her eyes black, the children battered, while Popeye meets Bluto in a bar to drink and complain about her.

Gay had been ready to hate the Eating Disorders Counselor, but then the woman had stopped Rita outside the session room, had singled out Rita for attention. "You have such intelligent eyes," she told Rita, and the two of them talked for a few short minutes, the woman saying that if Rita did not start eating a little more, her kidneys and liver would be permanently damaged. "You don't want that to happen," the woman said, suggesting that Rita eat another two ounces over the course of a day. "That's not much," she said, her hand on the small of Rita's back.

Something in these simple exchanges suggested that the woman really cared what happened to Rita, and all of Gay's reservations about her slipped away. For that moment, even her anger vanished, leaving her choked with the more painful emotions, reeling in the paneled hallway, afraid she would not be able to lead Rita to the exit, or to drive them home. But, of course, Rita knew where the exit was. She was not helpless, merely starving herself.

Gay had driven to the university in Las Cruces, found books in the university library on girls who starved themselves. The Barbie Cult, one book had labeled it, the Twiggy Response. The flip labels had made her so mad she had ripped out the pages. Karen Carpenter, the gooey singer who had performed with her brother—Gay could picture his bad haircut—had died from not eating. The woman's syrupy songs began playing in Gay's head. "We've only just begun," she sang, a dishonest lightness in her tone. "Just like me, they want to be, close to you."

Even her forms of personal torment humiliated her. Instead of demons ready to wrestle, the ghost of a bubble-gum singer tortured her, an emaciated body and a sticky sweet voice, and the cartoon antics of a spinach-eating thug. She pressed her head against Sander's shoulder, but he had fallen back to sleep. The books had said that girls who would not eat typically had domineering mothers. She did not feel she had been a bad mother. She did not believe she was domineering. Rudy Salazar had done this to Rita. He was to blame.

She shook Sander. He sat up, alert and ready again, that owl-eyed struggle to make the swimming colors stationary. "What is it?" he asked her, winded as if he had been running in his dreams.

"There's a mouse in the sink," she said.

"Trapped?" he asked, rubbing his eyes.

"Drowned."

"Oh." He started to lie back down.

"Get up. Get rid of it."

"Oh," he said again, climbing obediently out of bed. "Man's work."

She rolled over onto the warm spot in the bed he had left behind. The morning would quickly heat up, but this early it was still cool, and the warm spot comforted her. She willed herself to calm down. Several times during the past week she had felt herself slipping into the agitated state that preceded her breakdowns, but she had been able to calm herself, to pull herself back. It would be selfish to lose control now.

A few days ago she had mistaken Heart for Rita. They both wore those awful dresses, and she had seen the figure from behind, just a glance. Under normal circumstances, the mistake wouldn't have bothered her. But she had *seen* Rita there, and Rita had not been there. The anxiety that followed the mistake lasted for hours. She began thinking Rita was consciously trying to look like Heart, withering her body away until it became like Heart's. Other crazy things came to her and skittered off, little samples of paranoia, like airplane bottles of liquor, not enough to wholly intoxicate but sufficient to remind her of what it was to lose control. The episodes left her breathless and almost in tears.

Another time, talking with Margaret, only half listening to gossip, she had thought Margaret said, "Rita is the bone woman who drives the bone truck, the little cunt." Margaret, of course, had said nothing of the kind. The first time Gay had seen Enrique's shaven head, she had thought that he'd done it to ridicule her. That Rita had told him how Gay had shaved Rita's infant head when she was first born, and Enrique had decided to taunt Gay by shaving his. Then she remembered that Rita did not know the story, and that Enrique wasn't the kind of boy who would try to hurt her.

"I put it in a Pop Tart box," Sander said, standing now in the doorway, "and tossed it in the outside trash." He leaned against the doorjamb in his T-shirt and boxer shorts. "Can I come back to bed now?"

"What about the sink?" she asked him.

He slithered under the covers, pulled her close to him. "Drained it. Covered it with Comet." He pressed his lips to the back of her neck. "Washed the dish that was in there in scalding water." His breathing became heavy almost immediately.

"That's never happened before," Gay said. "I've hardly ever seen a mouse in here. Why does it have to happen now?"

"Hmm," he said. "Because you've got me here to handle it? That mouse's number has been up for years, but Mr. Fate held off until you had me here to stick it in a Pop Tart box."

She didn't laugh but she felt herself relax, the tension easing out of her. "If you weren't here, I wouldn't even have a Pop Tart box," she said. He made a happy, muffled noise into her hair. "That means . . ." She stopped herself. This was good, peaceful. They were both tranquil and still. But she said it anyway. "This means you believe things can still work out."

His trilling ceased. He took in a gulp of air and held it. "We have to believe that," he said.

"She's starving herself," Gay said, as if he didn't know that, as if that fact were not the new center to their lives.

They came bearing a philodendron, the newspaper editor Ron Morrison and his wife Ana Morrison, standing on the doorstep side by side in dark dress, too dark for the heat, a funereal dark, an unconscionable choice in clothing. Gay considered flinging the door shut, letting it slam in their faces. She guessed that they knew about Rita, that they were bringing the plant as some sick offering of condolence. But she would not permit herself to act crazy. If no one else thought of her as crazy, then she must be sane. She invited them in.

They followed her into the kitchen, commenting politely on the house, the furnishings. Gay could still smell death, although the mouse was gone, the sink scrubbed, the room scented. They seated themselves at the round oak table, while Gay watered the plant in its white plastic pot and set it on the windowsill. The school had just called. Rita, claiming to feel ill, had left early, the school secretary had phoned to say. "Is she home yet?" the woman had asked. Gay had not lied to her, although she had felt the temptation. "Not yet," she'd said.

The line went quiet for several moments, then the secretary said, "I thought you'd want to know. School policy—"

"Someone is at the door now," Gay had said and hung up, the phone banging against the receiver, but it had been the Morrisons on her doorstep, not Rita.

Gay took a paper towel, dampened it, and began cleaning the heart-shaped leaves of the stark, ugly plant. Small talk ensued, the stalling chatter of generalities. Civility made her anxious, but it became clear to her they knew nothing of Rita's condition, which granted her some relief. She hoped Sander returned before Rita. She did not want to hear the Morrisons gasp, listen to their polite inquiries. Sander was out interviewing for a job. Their money would run out if he didn't find work. Meanwhile she had taken a sick day—a mistake, she thought now, listening to the Morrisons' mock-friendly prattle. Get to the point! Inside her head, she screamed at them, slapped their smug faces.

Ron Morrison, as if he could hear her mental goading, said, "Have you read the article everybody's buzzing about?"

The question sent a chill through her. Terrible thoughts rocketed about inside her head. She worried—hoped—that she was once again hearing things. "No," she said softly, paying undue attention to the garbage can as she threw away the damp paper towel, not wanting to face them, imagining that her family's grief had somehow been made public.

"It's about Apuro," Ana said.

Gay took a deep breath, filling her lungs with the odor of garbage. She finally felt assured that this visit was not personal, at least not in the threatening way she had first imagined. She turned and faced the Morrisons, but she did not join them at the table.

Mother Jones magazine had published an article on Apuro. "It makes those of us living on this side of the river look . . ." Ron stared at the exposed beams overhead, hesitating. Ana offered an answer at the same time he finally spoke his. "Ungenerous," Ron said. "Bad," Ana said.

"I used to get *Mother Jones*," Gay said, shaking her head nervously, shrugging, avoiding their eyes. "But that was years ago."

"We're the cover story." Ron twitched his head back and forth and smirked, which was meant to convey resignation, Gay thought, but which she read as pretension. "I intend to do something about it," he stated, a definite quality to his voice, like a politician taking a stand.

"We don't want to sit on our hands," Ana said. "I always wished I had marched with Martin Luther King, or done something like that. But I was only a kid back then, and I didn't know better. The same with other causes. I don't seem to care about them until the marching is over. But we can be right in the middle of this one."

Ron said, "I'm going to launch a campaign this week, starting with tomorrow's editorial. We're going to do away with that blight across the river."

They talked about the quality of life over there, the poor living conditions, about the fact that there were no deeds and so they paid no property taxes. Gay nodded, following the conversation, growing less rattled with their presence in her house, but also wondering how it had anything to do with her—a woman whose daughter was starving herself. Eventually they came to that part.

"Rudy Salazar was named in the article, although the writer didn't know of his attack on your daughter," Ron said. "I gather that came after her visit here."

"You're in a special position to help your community," Ana said, her tone overly formal and practiced.

They wanted her to denounce Apuro. They wanted a family that had specifically suffered from "that element across the river" to plead for the destruction of the place.

"The other *colonias* won't be so easy," Ron said. "People have legal deeds, and the state will have to condemn the property and buy it from them. But if we can destroy Apuro—and I literally mean bulldoze the place—the movement may steamroll."

Gay did not know what to say to this. It offended her. Not just the stupidity of the argument, placing blame on the whole community for the actions of Rudy Salazar, but also because she now saw their place in this melodrama: the family with the damaged child, the family victimized. She saw, too, how the attribution of that role to her family took away all their other properties, made them pathetic and ruined. Although the paper would not paint them that way, but as courageous people standing up for their beliefs despite their sick daughter. Gay understood that losing her daughter might elevate her position in the community, and it sickened her.

Rage colored her face and made her limbs tremble, but she dared not speak for fear that what had taken hold of her was not indignation but madness. She no longer trusted her anger. It lived too near the surface.

At the same time, she recognized within herself the opposite reaction, an ugly desire to seek revenge against her daughter's ravaged body by destroying the lives of others. The plan offered her direction, a means of taking action. Stupid action, vengeful and arrogant action, but *something*.

Ana spoke about negative publicity and how to counter it. She said something about television, talk shows. Gay felt herself slipping on the words, but she would not permit herself to fall. No matter the terrific, terrible appeal of it, the leveling of Apuro would not make her daughter well. She knew this. It was wrong, simply wrong to take away people's homes. She would not give in to glorifying her grief.

She heard the front door open. She could not say how long she had been standing at the sink without speaking. Sander stepped into the kitchen carrying a rolled-up newspaper. He could see that something was amiss, but she could not explain to him.

He introduced himself and listened while Ron and Ana defined their plan again. He sat impassively at the table while they spoke. He pulled a chair over next to his, and Gay joined him there. She took his hand. She couldn't regain her calm, but she did feel a steadiness at the center, a stillness around which her chaos flamed, and she gripped his hand harder.

"Developers get away with anything they please," Ron said. "You know that, and so do I. The legislature should have plugged the loopholes that let them subdivide willy-nilly, but money talks. I admit that I haven't always been on the right side of that issue myself. I may have supported the wrong policies, even the wrong candidates. But now we have people living in *ghastly* conditions." He hesitated, measuring his hold on them. "We could try to nab the developers, but what are the chances of that? And while that would affect the other *colonias*, it would do nothing to Apuro. Instead, I say we do away with the problem at its root. We start with Apuro precisely because there are no moneybags developers blocking the way. The legislature will leap to prove they're capable of action if we can just press the right buttons."

"The right buttons," Sander said softly, almost a question.

"They're freeloaders," Ana pointed out. "And drug users."

"And not a one of them is a U.S. citizen," Ron added.

Sander turned to Gay. "The right buttons," he said to her.

Ron Morrison continued to look expectantly at Sander, avoiding Gay's eyes, clearly happy to have a man to reason with. But Sander would not return his gaze. He didn't speak but looked instead at Gay, his eyes soft and patient. They didn't need to confer. He trusted her to speak for them both.

Gay began, but her voice was too frail. She cleared her throat and said, "I'd appreciate it if you'd get the fuck out of our house."

Sander turned to them and nodded. "Ditto," he said.

Ron Morrison said something cruel, something guttural and mean, but Gay could not understand him. He seemed to be snarling at her, and it looked as though steam were about to rise from his collar like in the comics.

She could not tell what was really happening and had to look away. Sander's voice cut through the film. "Take a hike," he said, and when she turned, the Morrisons were gone. She took a breath and sat at the table beside Sander. He put his arms around her.

"You've got a way with words," he said.

She did not wish to be comforted, but she let him hold her, felt herself calm. Still she had to say it. "There has to be some way we can save her," she said and then wished she hadn't, not wanting to hear *we're doing all that we can*, not wanting to hear him patiently list the therapist, the Eating Disorders specialist, all the useless things they were trying. But he surprised her by saying nothing, reminding her again how well he knew her, which made her wonder how long she would want him to stay once the crisis was over, but this thought grabbed her heart, as she could no longer believe that it could have an end unless it was her daughter's death, and that was a possibility she could not face. She was weeping. The river rushed outside her window—not the river, she knew, that lay beyond the range of her hearing, but the wind, the spring wind blowing through branches. No matter, the wind turned to water, a torrent of red river, syrupy thick but not syrupy slow, river running red, river running bloody and cruel, river running mad, all about her, surrounding her house.

Suddenly she jerked free from his embrace and stood on the kitchen's deep blue planks, which seemed to pitch and throb. "Where's Rita?" she demanded. "She left school. She should be here." She felt it begin to crack all over again, that fragile shell of sanity.

Enrique began running without knowing his destination, but it came to him as he ran. He had started out in the right direction without knowing where he was going. Rita had disappeared. She had left school early and had not come home.

Her mother stood in the river calling her name, wading upstream. Her father, in the white pickup, drove downstream searching the water for her. They believed she was somewhere in the Rio Grande. Heart had told Enrique this. She was stationed in the house by the phone. Mr. Redmon was scouring the school grounds. Margaret Lamb was hiking from the school to Calle Blanca. Randall Lamb was inquiring in all the stores of downtown Persimmon. She had disappeared, which, Enrique thought as he ran, was precisely what she had been trying to do for some time. To disappear. To weigh, finally, nothing at all.

He ran toward the ranch of the man she called Mr. Gene. She had spoken about his barn, had said she liked to be there among the horses. A strange thing to say, but not that much out of the ordinary lately. Enrique believed he would find her at that ranch. She had taken the bike. She wouldn't be in the river with the bike.

He could not picture Mr. Gene, but he imagined now that she was with him, that he would not let her go. Rita had pointed him out to Enrique once before, but all Enrique could recall was the man's crushed cowboy hat and his hands, which were red, as if his arms ended in shreds of meat.

Enrique knew how to get to the ranch. He had gone there once to ride horses. It was at least three miles, but Enrique had run two and a quarter miles last year for his PE certificate. He could make it, although this year he would not get a certificate. He was failing PE because he did not attend in order to have lunch with Rita. He would have to take a summer class to graduate from middle school.

When she asked for the bike he should have realized something was wrong. But he often felt something was wrong. She no longer looked like herself. It was as if he were looking at a photograph that was identifiably Rita, yet had failed to capture some essential quality. She had said that she felt weak and didn't want to walk home. He should have volunteered to pedal her there. She had ridden on his handlebars before, but now she said they hurt her, and he had to believe her. She was nothing but a slip of skin over bone.

Rita's parents acted like she had a fatal disease, and Enrique understood the attraction of thinking that way, but Rita wasn't sick. She just wouldn't eat. They needed to find something she would eat. All people wanted to eat, didn't they? His feet started to flap hard against the asphalt but he made himself run harder, go back up on his toes. He had begun believing, without knowing it, that he was running for her life.

The wind was at his back, blowing the dust from his heavy feet ahead of him. At the edge of town, he passed a group of construction workers taking a break, huddling in the shade of a tall tree, two of them perched like birds on a fence railing, their shirts off, their jeans covered with dust. They stared at Enrique but did not wave or nod.

"Can one of you give me a ride?" he called, his voice breaking. He could not catch his breath. "Just down the road a mile or two. It's an emergency."

All of the men stared at him. One of the shirtless guys cocked his arm and looked at his watch. "I've got five minutes," he said, dropping from the fence rail. He pointed to a pitted white Camaro, two shirts resting on the hood, their arms intertwined. "Get in," he said. He left the shirts on the hood, calling out something to his friend, something Enrique didn't catch. This guy was only a boy, really, just a little older than Enrique himself.

The windows were down, and the interior of the car was covered in dust. Wires protruded from the dash, running to a cassette deck wedged between the bucket seats. The boy started the engine and shifted into first gear simultaneously, the car fishtailing in the dirt from the acceleration, the shirts sliding up the hood to the windshield, hesitating there, blocking their vision, then flying up over the roof and vanishing behind them.

"What kind of emergency?" the boy asked.

"Somebody's disappeared," Enrique said, trying not to cough in the dust. "I think she's at a ranch just down the road."

"The one by the oil well?"

"Yeah," Enrique said, nodding, "that one."

"That's more than two miles," he said, shifting again, accelerating even more. "My boss is a prick." He took the curve in the two-lane highway without slowing. There were no seatbelts. Enrique clutched at the door handle to keep from pitching into the driver's lap. The boy said, "Why's this person disappeared?"

"It's my girlfriend," Enrique said. The boy nodded as if that explained something, but Enrique didn't think it did. "She's been . . . something's going on with her. She's—"

"Probably just showing off," the boy said. "Never can tell, though. My mother tried to hang herself once." He made a disgusted face and shook his head. "I'd do without women if I could, but I can't do it. Most of us would be halfway normal if we weren't out chasing pussy every night, thinking about it the rest of the time." He looked at his watch. "Fuck." He pressed the accelerator to the floor. "Without pussy to chase, what's the point?" He glanced at Enrique and smiled, a slash of white across his ruddy face.

"She won't eat," Enrique said. "She passes out. Her clothes don't fit. She's starving herself."

The boy stuck his head out his window, the wind whipping his hair, and spat. "That's weird," he said. He was careful not to look at Enrique but steadied his gaze out the windshield. "I'm sorry," he added, almost a whisper, and Enrique could tell that he meant it.

The oil pump appeared and the boy braked, the Camaro skidding sideways down the asphalt, stopping crosswise in the road. "See you," he said as Enrique jumped out, and he took off again before Enrique could thank him. The parallel lines of rubber made a curl on the road. One of the shirts had caught on the rear bumper and flailed wildly. Enrique waved to the fluttering sleeve before he could catch himself. He crossed the road, running again down the rutted driveway.

The small barn had been painted some years ago and had faded in the intense sunlight to a shade of white that suggested the original color without revealing it. The afternoon sun on it now made it radiant and mysterious. Enrique's heart raced from exertion and fear. Perspiration streaked his dirty face.

There were no horses in the barn. Along one wall hung some kind of horse apparatus—Enrique could not name any of the pieces, leather straps and fragments of bent metal hanging from nails, cruel-looking things. Horse accessories, he thought, thinking for a moment of the boy and his car, the deliberate tough manner of the guy who, nonetheless, had done him a favor.

Enrique checked each stall, taking in the smell, which made him think not of horses but of the river, a certain kind of outside smell that he associated with the river. Why did Rita's parents think she was in the water? Some part of him understood the impulse to start searching in the river, but he could not convert that intuition into logic, into words.

The bicycle leaned against the wooden ladder that led to the loft, and Enrique's heart leapt. He began climbing the rungs. By the square opening that viewed the house, he saw not her but an impression of her left in the hay, the straw's memory of her body. Beside the depression lay her clothes, flat and disheveled. Unlike the hay, they retained nothing of her.

The view of the house revealed the open front door. Enrique thought to take the clothes with him, but changed his mind, not wanting to bother things he did not understand. Besides, she might return for them while he was gone. He didn't want her left without clothing. There was no time to reason it out.

He quickly descended the ladder, missing the bottom rungs, falling into the scraps of hay around the ladder. He ran through the barn and across the dirt yard. He pounded on the door, which was not latched, and called out "Rita!" his voice a shock to himself, the desperate pitch and commanding volume. He pushed the door open wide and entered, taking in the room, bookshelves built awkwardly into a wall, an old-fashioned chair and matching couch pushed against another wall—no room for a body behind it. Each wall was bare, utterly bare. He rushed into the kitchen, glanced beneath the table, opened a closet door, and then hurried through the hall into a bedroom.

He found her there. On the floor. Naked. Her back on a Mexican rug.

Goosebumps had risen on her arms and across her chest, which made Enrique think of the dead white skin of plucked chickens. Her ribs corrugated her flesh, and the bones of her pelvis turned her waist into a bowl. He feared for her life.

He knelt and put a finger beneath her nostrils. She was breathing, the intake sticky with mucus and blood. A trace of blood from her nose trailed over the milk of her shoulder. He put his face next to hers to smell her sweet breath. He did not know when she had last eaten. He did not know whether she would wake.

He ran back to the front room and called 911. He asked for an ambulance. He explained their location. He called Heart. "I found her," he said through a sudden rush of tears. "She's passed out," he said and explained, wiping the tears and sweat from his face with the back of his hand.

"What is she doing *there*?" Heart asked.

"I don't know," he said. "Something about the horses." He knew this wasn't entirely true, but he didn't want to bother with the truth, which, anyway, he could not claim to know. "Get her mom," he said and hung up. He ran back to her.

He did not want to leave her to fetch her clothing. In the top drawer of Mr. Gene's dresser he found handkerchiefs, white and folded into piles, as well as long red ones folded into triangles. Bandannas, Enrique thought, and pictured one over Mr. Gene's face as he held up a bank. On the wall, above the bed, a strange kind of graffiti. A jagged black peak on the yellow wallpaper, another line to show the crown. A breast, he realized. Had Rita defaced this wall before passing out? Nothing else on the wall, on any wall in the house. The house was strange, ugly. It gave him the creeps.

In the next drawer he found T-shirts, his hands soiling them as he pulled them out. He hurried into the kitchen and washed his hands in the sink, then ran back and dried them on one of the shirts.

He pulled a clean T-shirt over Rita's head and down her body, which he lifted to the bed. She weighed nothing, but her slack body was awkward to carry. He decided she should not be in the bed, and then that she should not be in this house. He slipped his arms beneath her again and carried her through the bedroom door, careful not to let any part of her brush against the narrow jamb. Her skin had become translucent, like the skin of an onion, and he feared tearing it.

He carried her through the living room and out onto the porch. He sat in a kitchen chair on the covered porch and held her in his arms. An ambulance was on its way. He had to wait.

Nothing in the yard moved. The old boards that made up the floor of the porch were warped and uneven, rising in the middle like a sneer. The silence of this place, the stillness, induced in Enrique a state of terror.

He tried to make her comfortable, lifting her head so that her neck was not unduly bent. Her hair still carried the odor of hay. He could see his own tears as they appeared in the dark strands. He held her, bewildered by this turbulent love he possessed and by the dust stirring in the yard as if nothing had happened, lifted by an uncaring wind, made visible by the indifferent sun.

He did not see the brown truck until it rounded the barn and came to an abrupt stop in the dirt. Dust whirled about the vehicle like flame. Enrique tightened his grip on Rita. He tried to think what to say.

Mr. Gene stared out at them from the driver's seat. He stared for a long while, then opened the door and climbed from the truck, his head down, the top of his leather cowboy hat creased and wrinkled like the hide of a rhinoceros.

He approached the house slowly, glancing about, as if anticipating an ambush. He stopped at the steps to the porch, sneaking a quick look at Enrique and Rita, then staring at the porch floor as he spoke. "Are you someone I know?" he asked Enrique.

"No, sir," Enrique said. "But you know Rita."

He turned his back to them, taking another furtive peek at her as he turned. "Is Heart here?" he asked as he bent at the knees and waist, a half-squat that looked uncomfortable. The hair that emerged from his hat appeared matted, and Enrique could smell him, the rancid odor of an unbathed adult.

"No, sir," Enrique said. "Rita came out here on a bike. She passed out or something. She doesn't eat."

He nodded without facing Enrique, then sat on the porch steps. He faced the barren yard and stared at his truck or the trees or something else out there that Enrique couldn't name. After a long while, Mr. Gene said, "Should we do something?"

"I called an ambulance," Enrique said.

Mr. Gene stood. He put his hand to his hat, which effectively covered his face. "I'll be inside, then," he said as he stepped past them and through the screen door, which shut with a slap.

Enrique held Rita, and he waited.

27

JUNE

Gay saw the flowers and her heart sank. She looked furtively about the GEM Transport office, as if for a place to hide. *Beware of men bearing flowers*. Who had said that? A head appeared from behind the roses. Denny did not smile, but beneath his sober exterior he was smiling. It was not his daughter who had been hospitalized, and he could not help but gloat, even though he tried to keep it hidden. She could see it—or she was losing her mind. Yellow roses. She was grateful they were not red roses, but she could not tell him that because it sounded, even to herself, like the words of a woman gone mad. This morning a bumper sticker had made her cry. She'd had to pull Sander's truck off the road to compose herself. The sticker was meant to be funny. I WANT TO BE JUST LIKE BARBIE, the top line read, beside a caricature of the doll's face. The bottom line said, THAT BITCH HAS EVERYTHING! Why would a grown woman—why would a sane person—weep over that?

Denny opened the glass door without knocking, hesitating in the doorway, wearing a thin black tie and a wrinkled beige jacket, cowboy boots that looked new, shiny even in the dulling fluorescent light. He stepped to one side after closing the door, leaned against the wall, the flowers held low now, as if they had sprouted from his crotch. She realized he was waiting for her, as if there were a line of people here to speak to her, instead of just him. He watched her patiently. She had said nothing about his flowers, but she was wearing the headset. He assumed she was listening to someone on the set. "Okay, then," she said into the microphone. "We'll talk tomorrow," she said, as if signing off, as if she had been listening to a long-winded trucker.

"Thank you," she said to Denny. "They're lovely." Her voice sounded fine. She touched the huge heads of the roses, but withdrew her hand, the curling petals all turning inward, circling on themselves, convoluted and untrustworthy. They were grotesque. She had once tended plants for a living. She had once loved roses. When had that ended? What was he doing here?

Finally he offered that smile of his, crooked and toothy, but an affectation, she decided, as all smiles were, little lies the lips told. "I know they won't actually cheer you up," he said, "but I thought I'd bring them anyway." He seemed to be admitting that the flowers were for his benefit, a way to assuage his guilt for being there, something to give him a pretense for a visit. She thought this but she didn't trust the logic.

"I hear Rita's out of the woods," he said. "I'm happy."

Out of the woods? What could that possibly mean? She was out of the hospital and home, but she was barely eating. She did not eat enough to sustain a sparrow.

He spoke again. "My little girl's not coming at all." The roses, wrapped in their green paper, he lay on her desk. The huge blooms on the long stems made her think of the bulbous joints on the emaciated limbs of starving children. The flowers were thoughtless and obscene. Long-stemmed yellow obscenities. "First my ex backs out of the spring semester—I half expected that—but now she won't let her come for the summer. I'm going to have to get a lawyer."

Gay nodded. She felt no compassion for him. She knew that she had loved this man, that she still loved this man, and yet she felt nothing. She loved him, but so what? What did it matter? His daughter now would spend the summer with her mother. He would have to travel if he wanted to see her. His perfectly healthy daughter. This demanded her sympathy?

"I miss you," he said.

"Oh," she said, a shallow breath, a respiratory syllable.

He stepped toward her, his arms lifting as if suddenly weightless, his expression set now, decided, determined. "I want to make love to you," he said softly, so softly, a voice like mist. "I think it would be good for both of us. Don't you?"

"Why?" she said bluntly. "Why would that be good?"

"Help you relax," he said, the soft edge in his tone quaking, his determination faltering even as he took her in his arms, wrapping her up, pulling her close, her heart beating faster but not in desire, in fear, his arms suffocating.

"No," she said. "I can't."

"You can," he said. "I'm going to insist. I'm right about this. We mean something to each other. You know that. You're just frazzled. You need to—"

"My daughter is starving herself," she said, the clarity of the words startling to hear, weapons that traveled into her head and hurt her. "Having sex with you isn't going to change that."

"Not making love to me isn't going to change that either," he said, glancing for a second at the floor—the body's instinct for honesty betraying him. "And it could help you. And me. Make us both feel . . . *human* again."

"I feel human," she said. "I feel all too human."

"It'll let you quit thinking for a while." He released her arms, stepped past her to the receiver. "There some way to turn this off?" he said, staring at the buttons and lights.

She saw that it was off, that she had been wearing the headphones but the receiver had been off. She had pretended to be on a call with the receiver off. "Okay," she said, to make him look away. She removed the headset, the microphone sliding coldly against her cheek. "Okay, then," she said, believing he would think her crazy if he knew that the receiver was off. He would think she was breaking down. How long had she been pacing this floor, wearing the headset with a dead receiver? The room suddenly seemed darker. How late was it?

He had his arms on her again, and there was his tongue inside her mouth, slick and busy, not painful but not welcome, a living thing in her mouth, like eating her food without killing it first. And this, she understood, was how the sex would be—no damage to her, no suffering, but just this piece of him entering this part of her, just the sliding about of bodies and body components. She let him back her up against the wall, his tongue still in her mouth, wriggling and alive. She thought to lock the door, stepping away from him to click the bolt, a sane thing to do, she thought, pulling down the blinds, pulling up her skirt, hooking her panties with her fingers and tugging them to her knees. He high-stepped his boot between her legs, above the panties, and pushed them down, stepped on the panties, pink panties from Wal-Mart, harmless, asexual panties bearing the shape of his booted foot.

He unbuttoned her top, his hands all over her breasts, but it wasn't sexual. She thought of a doctor's examination, of butterflies beating against her chest, only larger—bats, harmless bats flapping their wings against her. Then it was inside her, the cock, the tongue, both inside her, and his movement, her back up against the wall. Sex. The familiar thrusting, the eagerness of the man embodied in the repetitive thrust, the penetrating push—this was all about him, about his need, about his famished desire, no matter the concern after, wondering how she had liked it, whether she had come. This was for him.

It brought her back to herself. Not as he thought, not in release. There was no release for her. But she saw clearly what was happening, what she was doing. It was not making love, and it was not rape. It was a kind of housekeeping, a taking care of business, a sexual appeasement, the kind men often needed—good men and lousy men—a serving up of herself that she had done many times in the past, as a way to get around them, to get them out of the way. Not rape; often, in fact, her idea, as much her doing as his, this turning it into a business transaction. Just a reality of loving men. Maybe a reality of loving anyone. Had Sander made love to her in this manner at times? She was certain he had. Not a gift so much as the fulfillment of an obligation, that human obligation to recognize need in another and to do something about it.

Sander's moving into her house had meant that she had given up the manner of life that she had invented for herself, given up the parameters of her marriage, but it hadn't been enough. It had made no difference. Nothing had made a difference, and she had found herself wishing that creatures would come and pull the hair from her head in bloody clumps. If it would matter. Now this, this servicing of a man she had loved, seemed to make a difference. It would not make her daughter eat, but by being thoughtless and weak, Denny had inadvertently permitted her to stay sane, and that might help her daughter. She had saved herself by helping him, by seeing the truth.

He came inside her, which made it less messy. "Oh," he said to her under his breath. "I've missed you. I love you."

"Yes," she said, gently moving him to the side, using her panties to wipe the few drops that ran down her thigh, then tossing the panties in her purse. "It was good for me, too," she said, knowing that he had no idea what she meant, barely clinging to the recognition herself, but feeling different nonetheless, feeling clearheaded, feeling well.

He said something else but she wasn't listening, something about his life, something about leaving. "Yes," she said. "You should go."

"No, I meant Claire," he said. "She came to my house asking me to say some ridiculous stuff." He was tucking in his shirt, buttoning his jeans. "You'd better be wary of her. She's trying to pin her trouble on you, so she can get her job back."

Finally she realized who he was talking about. "I'd forgotten about her," she said, and she immediately let her name slip again from her mind. She walked back to her desk, stared at the receiver for only a moment before flipping the toggle. Its green lights immediately shone.

"Is Rita . . ." Denny's face darkened as his voice drifted off. "Is she going to be . . ."

"I don't know," Gay said. "She may starve herself. She may die."

"Jesus," he said. "I don't understand it. I can't figure it out."

"I do," Gay said, "but I can't explain it."

"She must hate herself, blame herself, feel—"

"She's fallen in love with . . ." She felt the answer rushing into her aware-ness, a powerful rush, as if the room were suddenly filling with water. "She's fallen in love with purity," Gay said. Then, because he still looked confused, she added, "Women love . . ." But she could not finish because it was fin-ished, so she said it again, "Women love."

He nodded at her vaguely. She could see that he was worried. She could see that he was a mostly good man. She could also see that they were fin-ished, that it was over. She did not feel any anger toward him or bad senti-ment, but he had been part of a long experiment and all of it was over now. She knew her daughter's declining health—her dying, she would no longer pretend—was not the product of her parents' manner of living, but for the moment how they lived was less important than Rita's health. Sander needed to be near his daughter, and Gay needed a constant partner in this terror, one to be strong when she was weak, one to be weak when she needed to be strong.

Perhaps there were other reasons that she had let Sander move back in, superstition, a groundless guilt, economics, convention—the pressure to conform could not be resisted in the face of her daughter's dying. The rea-sons did not matter.

Her unconventional life had not damaged her daughter. This was clear to her now, as it had not been before. She had felt obligated to blame herself, but now she saw the situation more clearly. This understanding led her to the next thought. When this was over, whether it ended in Rita's recovery or Rita's death, Gay would reinvent her own life once again. It would mean continuing to love the people she had to love, but in the manner *she* chose. She would own her life once more, would own the love that owned her.

"Should I call you," Denny began, "or would it be better—"

"Don't call me," she said. She thought for several long seconds, but she had nothing else to offer him, except a good-bye, and that was what she said.

Rudy rode shotgun, his elbow out the window, the sky refusing to go dark. A ratty Mexican flag pulled taut over the front seat of the Nova irritated his arms, made him scratch and twitch, like there were insects crawling over him. The gun weighed down his right hand, which hung below the window. He was headed to Persimmon to execute Enrique Calzado.

To the other members of *La Verdad*, he had simply said it was unfinished business. They agreed to drive him to Persimmon, drop him off in the neighborhood where Calzado lived, then wait for him at the diner. This would be their alibi. In the event of his arrest, they would claim to know nothing of his plans, say he had asked for a ride to Persimmon in order to get laid. Rudy had even given them Marcia's name. But he had no intention of sticking to this plan. He intended to shoot Calzado from the car and then force the others to take him to the border.

Billy, who drove the car, pulled off the highway outside of town. "We got our heads straight on this?" he asked. "You ready, *vato*?"

Rudy removed his shades and looked up into the dimming sky. Constellations he could neither name nor locate began appearing as he looked, patterns of light separated by distances too great to imagine. He punched the cassette player to stop the noise. Rap music. He had come to loathe these people who had saved him from the streets. He hated them for acting tough, for their relentless talk. They did things they did not want to do, not because one of them was persuasive, but because collectively they each intimidated the others into actions none of them desired.

Billy turned the music back on. "Don't be fooling with my tunes," he said. Liz sat in the back. She alone he did not loathe. Rudy could see her in the side mirror while pretending to still look at the stars. She smoked a mentholated cigarette and smiled when their eyes met in the mirror. Beside her sat a skinny guy with skin dark enough to pass for a black, a nervous kid who chewed incessantly on a leather key chain.

Liz said, "I still don't get why you got to do this guy."

Billy said, "Less we know, the better."

"Get us into Persimmon," Rudy said.

Billy nodded at him, then extended his arm into the backseat. Liz put her face to his knuckles, kissed them, her elaborately lipsticked mouth leaving marks on Billy's fingers. He started the Nova again.

Rudy wanted to take Liz with him across the border, where they could both act like Mexicans or like tourists or like anyone but who they were. He could not figure a way to do it without killing Billy, in which case she would not come with him.

"Where the fuck I go, *cabrón*?" Billy said.

They passed the Tumbleweed trailer park, the new Stop-'n'-Go by the old radiator shop, the Safeway, and they approached the diner. The Yugo sat in the back of the lot, and Rudy felt himself smile. Near the sidewalk, a shiny motorcycle reflected back the headlights. It was parked at an angle for better display to the street, fire painted across its gas tank, across the shiny thorax of the vehicle, as well as the words FREEDOM OR DEATH. Embraced by the chrome handlebars, a black plastic sign read FOR SALE.

"That's the diner." Rudy pointed, turned to look at Liz, who was staring at her own reflection in the rearview mirror, buttering her lips with lipstick.

He didn't have to do this. He could have them drop him downtown. He could spend an hour or two at Gil Drugs, then walk to the diner and tell them the Calzado house was dark, newspapers on the lawn, and he had grown tired of waiting. "Too many people saw me." He could hear himself say it. Then he'd take some time, develop a plan, a way to get Liz away from Billy.

But another part of him had made a different decision, argued that it was enough he wanted to shuck his responsibilities for this girl. Better, really, as she would undoubtedly let him down later on, and he would do the same, would betray her, forget to love her, smack her. There was a world of things he could do to her, and loving her was only one of those things. It was ridiculously outnumbered.

He directed them downtown, then up the street where the Calzados lived. Liz's fist popped him on the shoulder. "Don't get your ugly butt caught," she said, then surreptitiously slipped her fingers around his shoulder, a squeeze meant to convey tenderness even though it was too quick and forceful to actually be tender. Rudy's eyes burned, and he coughed to hide the stinging tears.

"Up there," he said coarsely. As he spoke, he saw the lawn, that green spectacle that fueled his rage. His doubts left him. The tears evaporated. He put his elbow out the window, took off the dark glasses, tossed them onto the dash. The boy was in the yard. He was climbing into the family car. The Shopper suddenly stepped into view, behind the screen door, calling something to the boy, then turning to speak to someone else in the house. When the Nova pulled even with the house, Rudy turned his head away and ducked slightly. Cecilia Calzado was getting in on the other side of the car. The boy had his driver's license, evidently, or learner's permit. Was he fifteen already? "Pull into that driveway and turn around," Rudy said.

"This where you want us to drop you?" Billy asked.

"I've got to get a better look at that car," he said. "Go back by and pass it again."

The car, an old Ford Fairlane, had just backed into the street. Billy accelerated to catch them. Rudy watched the back of Cecilia Calzado's head, the bounce in her hair. Her brother's head, from the rear, seemed identical to hers, except for the length of his dark hair. The Shopper had not joined them, but stepped now out of the house, and Rudy glared at her, wanting her to see him, to have a second to realize what was going to happen. But it was Rudy who flinched. She had become a skeleton, blinking into the sun. She looked like the living dead.

He turned from her, determined not to be distracted, swallowing hard to keep something rising inside him down. The moment that would measure his integrity had arrived. The heft of the gun in his hand became profound. "Pass it," Rudy said. Billy guided the car to the left side of the street and advanced on the Fairlane, the two cars side by side, taking up the whole road. Cecilia Calzado looked in their direction, her hand flying to her mouth like a winged thing, a squeal spewed from her lips. Rudy raised the gun. Liz shouted from the rear seat, and Billy threw an arm against Rudy's chest, just as the cars pulled even, just as boy's head turned, a foot away from Rudy's raised pistol, the barrel level with his eyes. Oh, that smile, that wickedly beautiful smile, the boy's mouth a greeting, a gift. He was happy to see Rudy, and Rudy, at the last second, recognized in himself that same happiness, as he discerned in the boy his true identity.

Tito Tafoya was driving the Calzados' car. Rudy's heart filled with love for him at the same moment his obedient finger pulled the trigger, and launched the bullet into the tender, smiling face.

Border

28

People brought folding chairs, situated them in the soft sand between the wall of cane and the rising river, and settled in, beer or soda in hand, some with burgers in a paper sack from Wendy's, some with homemade sandwiches in large Ziploc bags. One ambitious group brought a festive beach umbrella, a huge canvas thing, blue with white fringe, BUD LITE emblazoned in garish red lettering. A matching blue cooler filled with beer rested beneath the umbrella.

In contrast, a handful of sober-looking men and women carried handmade placards tacked onto two-by-fours reading APURO VIVE/VIVA APURO. Apuro Lives/Long Live Apuro. These people had the best seats, down at the water's edge, directly across the river from Apuro, having camped there through the night, holding a candlelight vigil, as if seeking a stay of execution for a condemned man. Cold wax in oblong puddles dotted the sand along the river's border.

Across river, beside the hodgepodge of houses and shacks, a mammoth bulldozer idled, smoke rising from its upright muffler. Its blade, worn free of paint, shone silver and reflected the morning sunlight, a brilliant slash of naked steel.

Gay came with Sander. They wove among the mulberry trees hand in hand. She could not help but think of the night she had met Denny, how they had taken the identical walk, but the memory carried no power for her now, was merely a curiosity. The path through the cane had been widened by the crowd, the trampled stalks of cane leaning broken against the survivors like victims at a scene of violence. Gay speculated that it would soon be completely removed, that grass would be planted, a sprinkler system laid, a city park installed to take advantage of the trees and the river—as soon as Apuro was gone.

She and Sander emerged from the path and stood behind the earlier arrivals, peering over the crowd at the river and the houses on the other side. They continued to hold hands.

The shooting, one Apuro boy firing on another within the city limits of Persimmon, had accomplished what Ron Morrison's editorials had not. The city had taken action to raze Apuro, and the state had responded. They had acted with such haste that residents of the *colonia*, mourning the shooting of Tito Tafoya, most of them living in the U.S. illegally, had not organized any opposition. Apuro had been condemned, notices posted in two languages explaining that the dwellings would be leveled in forty-eight hours.

Gay felt a peculiar mix of emotions. A sadness that innocent people were losing their homes, that people already damaged by violence would now suffer institutional violence. And that other feeling, that grim, secret glee, that ugly resolve that at least something was being done. She did not like feeling this, but she would not deny the fact of it. She understood why so many people wanted Apuro destroyed, but she condemned them for indulging that easy selfishness. However, there was no fighting them. The new popular political rant focused on blaming the poor for all the evils of the country, as if they were the powerful, and the wealthy were their helpless captives.

The Tafoya boy, the one who had been shot, had not died. The bullet had shattered the bones about one cheek. Fragments of bone had lodged in his brain. His coma lasted almost three days, but then he had emerged, blind in one eye, suffering strange gaps in his memory and personality, but alive. The prognosis for his recovery was good, although it would not take place in the United States. He and his family were being deported following his release from the hospital.

Rita had witnessed the shooting, as had Cecilia, who had actually been spattered with the boy's blood and bone. How had her daughter's world turned on its head so quickly and so thoroughly? For Gay, this was the most urgent question. She had worked to make for herself and her daughter a life of their own design, but all her work had been undone. Rudy Salazar was responsible, she thought, but even as the words formed in her head, she could sense their inadequacy. He was merely the agent of the violence, like a hired gun whose employers remained invisible.

Rita's reaction to the shooting had been so calm as to suggest to Gay that her daughter was insane. "Tito won't die," she had said to Cecilia. "It doesn't make sense for him to die." They had been in the hospital waiting area, an ugly cubbyhole where the carpet and walls reflected each other, and terror dwelt in the face of each inhabitant. Except Rita's.

Cecilia, by this time, had been sedated. She sat between her mother and older brother, nodding when Rita talked but not really listening. Gay had been listening. "What do you mean it doesn't make sense for him to die?" she asked Rita. For the first time in a long while, she did not tiptoe around her daughter's strange behavior. Rita had not improved, but this night she was not the one at greatest risk. "How does any of this make *sense*?"

Rita turned to face her with excruciating slowness. Enrique leapt up from the floor to stand beside her, as if he thought Gay might attack her. "Mother," Rita said, "there are patterns in our lives that we can't see, but I can . . . *feel* them. I can sense them. Tito will live." Her head teetered as she smiled, as if that small act overtaxed it, but her eyes carried the kind of certainty Gay had only seen in born-again Christians, people freshly in love, or the hopelessly mad.

Tito lived, which permitted Gay to entertain the notion that her daughter was exchanging her body for the gift of clairvoyance. This, evidently, was what Rita herself believed, or something like it. But being right about the Tafoya boy didn't make Rita any less mad.

Heart suddenly emerged from the crowd of people on the sandy shore. She tugged on the sleeve of Gay's blouse. "I didn't think you were going to witness this," she said. Denny trailed behind her. He gave Gay a brief hug, then shook hands with Sander, his expression glum, maybe angry, Gay couldn't tell. "Margaret's here, too," Heart said, "but she's stuck talking to that Claire woman."

"It's funny," Gay said, "that you and Margaret have become friends."

Heart made her toothy smile and nodded in agreement. "At first she struck me as the kind of person who lured salesmen into her basement and locked them in there to starve," she said, coloring as she said "starve," and speeding up the flow of words, "but I've since realized she doesn't have a basement. She just likes to pretend she does."

Gay slipped her arm around Heart's bony shoulders. "You don't have to watch what you say."

"Of course I do," she said. "Everyone does."

To Gay, Denny said, "Long time no see." Then he shrugged. "Seems like a long time, anyway. Seems like . . ." He squinted, trying to think of something clever or maybe something honest, but his wit failed him.

Before the silence between them could become awkward, the engine of the bulldozer revved, an almost prehistoric rattle. A collective gasp escaped the crowd. Black smoke rose from the little metal chimney in the bulldozer's nose.

"They're going to do it, aren't they?" Gay said.

"Looks that way," Sander said.

Denny spoke to Sander. "This is a good place to swim." He cast a quick glance at Gay, his wit evidently recovering. "You ever swim in this part of the river?"

"I'm more of a pool man," Sander said.

"I like it right here," Denny said.

The bulldozer raised its metal girder and addressed an adobe building, pausing for the driver to shift gears, for the crowd to take a breath. The dozer moved forward. It struck the house, a crack immediately fingering its way across the broad mud wall. A corner of the edifice toppled. A cheer went up from a section of the crowd, followed immediately by an equally loud chorus of boos.

It was awful, Gay thought, but there was something about it that was also thrilling. Here it played out on a scale that was visible, the ancient struggle between the powerful and the poor. Here were no abstractions, but physical buildings of slumping mud versus the heavy steel of the righteous diesel. Undeniably, in this brute and shorthand depiction of their culture, there was a terrible radiance, a patriotic beauty that these people, even those booing, could not help but love. It was the most sincere expression of a specific kind of love that Gay had ever witnessed, the naked spectacle of American Owned Love.

Her mind turned then, as it inevitably did, to her daughter. She understood there was a connection between her daughter's ravaged body and the violence taking place across river, not the literal connection of people and events but a larger connection, one she couldn't quite name, could barely cling to at all. Her daughter's body seemed at this moment an emblem of possession, a perverse expression of love, a love her daughter had no control over, as if she had starved herself out of principle, as if she had sacrificed herself for her country. Like the people cheering for the destruction of Apuro, Rita took pleasure in the ruination of her own body because it meant something to her, because it permitted her to be true to what it meant to be American. People could make themselves believe that you were a bad American if you were overweight, just as they believed you were a bad citizen if you were poor. And so you deserved to suffer. Only by suffering could you redeem yourself. The poor could redeem themselves by becoming wealthy, or by behaving in a fashion that befitted their degraded status. While Rita could redeem herself only by wasting finally away. Vanishing.

The bulldozer punched at another adobe wall and something besides dust flew up into the air, something slight and papery, a slip of something, a scrap of color. It caught everyone's attention as it lingered in the patch of sky over the river before rocking downward on invisible currents, and landing on the water. It floated for a moment, an image, a face, a lovely face, which then dipped beneath the surface and disappeared.

"What *was* that?" Sander asked.

"I think it was from an icon," Gay said. "I think it was the Virgin Mary."

"What a beautiful face," Heart said.

Denny worked his way forward into the crowd and talked to some of his students who had been among those camping near the water's edge. He pushed his way back to report to them. "Part of a poster," he said. "Michael Jackson."

"The singer," Heart said, as if there might be someone living on the planet who didn't know who he was.

The rubble of old brick and splintered beam grew before the blade of the dozer. Gay continued to hold Sander's hand, squeezing it with each push against the old house. He leaned down and spoke in her ear. "I've seen enough. How about you?"

"I don't know," she said.

"It's no contest," he said. "I thought—" His breath caught, and Gay looked up at his concerned face, and then followed his gaze. Claire Brownlee was pushing her way through the gawkers, intent on Gay. Margaret trailed, calling to her, "Now you wait!"

The first house fell, an expulsive push of dust and air preceding the thunder of the heavy adobes striking the ground.

Amid another round of applause and jeers, Claire stepped into Gay's line of vision, her head displacing the drama across river. She appeared before Gay suddenly large and tender, like a jack o' lantern that had begun to spoil.

"Didn't expect to see me here, did you?" she said.

"Hi, Claire." Gay searched the woman's face, the heavy layer of makeup around her eyes and over her cheeks, the stubble of eyebrow above and below the thin arches, the slight blond down on her lip. She no longer felt hatred for this woman, perhaps because she no longer thought she might lose her mind as Claire had lost hers. That option no longer existed, which, Gay realized, made her that much less free.

"I know—and you know—what you've done to me," Claire said. Her lipstick failed to cover her mouth but created a thin stripe, a perfect ruby line bordered above and below by unpainted lip. "Don't try to blame my husband."

Gay had failed this woman somehow. She felt both responsible and bored with it. "What do you suppose has happened to the people who lived in those houses?" Gay asked her. She wondered whether Claire could be distracted. "Where do you think they've gone?"

Claire's jaw jutted and her mouth shut. Her eyes grew narrow. She began grinding her teeth. She might have been considering the question, but she looked more suspicious than thoughtful.

"Were they deported?" Gay asked her. "Were they simply driven to the border and—"

"Everyone thinks I'm a fool," Claire said, her voice almost wistful. "Even the people who hate me."

"I don't think you're a fool," Gay said.

Heart crowded in to touch Claire's arm. "We really don't," she said. The sincerity in Heart's voice made Gay realize she herself had lied. Claire was a fool. One of the protesters by the river's edge waved her sign high in the air. It read: SOMETIMES TO SAVE A VILLAGE, YOU MUST DESTROY IT. It was a quotation, apparently, but Gay could not see to whom it was attributed.

"Yes, you do," Claire said, "and I can prove it. Knock, knock." She shoved Gay's shoulder. Her wrist was immediately encircled by Denny's hand. Gay sighed and glanced from Denny to Sander. Sander only raised his brows.

"Calm down," Denny instructed Claire.

"We're not angry with you," Heart said to her.

Claire jerked her hand free. "I'm not going to break her collarbone," she said angrily. "It's a joke, and she knows it. Knock, knock."

"Okay," Gay said. "Who's there?"

Claire smiled. "Aladdin."

"Aladdin who?"

"A lad in the water fucked your daughter." Her jaw dropped, as if by saying this she had shocked herself. Then she added, "In the mouth."

Tears erupted from Gay's eyes, and she slapped Claire across the cheek, hard enough to make her head turn, to make the cheek redden, hard enough to make her own palm burn.

"Welcome to the club," Claire said, touching her cheek. "You can be secretary or treasurer. But not president." Bubbles of saliva formed at the corners of her mouth as she began laughing. "I made you cry. Your daughter's become a scarecrow, but you're crying because of me."

"That's enough," Denny said. He stepped between Gay and Claire, glaring all the while at Sander. "Get her home, will you?"

"I'm not sure she's ready to go," Sander said.

"When the hell you going to be sure, pal?" Denny demanded.

"When we're on our way, I guess," Sander said. He offered his hand to Gay. She wiped the sudden tears from her face, then took his hand. Margaret's voice came out of the crowd, but Gay's eyes had clouded again, and she could not see her.

"Help me," Margaret demanded. "Grab her arm." It was not clear to whom she was speaking. "I don't care. Grab her arm."

Claire's laughter erupted again. "You bitch!" she screamed at Gay. "You traitor bitch!" Meanwhile, behind her, across river, another house made of mud tumbled down.

Standing in her kitchen, Gay poured gin into her husband's glass. Heart entered from the dining room while Gay could see Margaret at the back door, wiping her feet.

"What a day," Margaret called. "Days like this cause wrinkles. I don't need wrinkles."

"We're drinking," Gay said. "You have to join us."

"Whatever you've got," Margaret said.

Sander sat calmly at the table. "Some guy told me there's already a scramble for the land. Since there are no deeds to it, the state's thinking about auctioning off lots. The irony is, once people have paid money for the land, they'll get utilities and a bridge, the whole works. Great investment opportunity, this guy said."

"Oh, it really is for the best," Margaret said. "It's just hard to have to witness it. I know none of you agree with me, but those people are better off out of there. We all are. They just went about it in such a dreadful fashion." She started to say something more but stopped. She took a deep breath instead. Rita had entered the room. Her hair had begun to thin and looked fleecy now. Her eyes had slipped deep within her skull. She wore the green velvet Heart dress. "Rita," Margaret said softly, not a greeting but an act of identification.

"I'm going out," Rita said. "A group of us are going to the hospital to see Tito." She turned her back to them and headed through the living room and out the door.

Margaret touched the corners of her eyes with her fingers.

Gay studied the blue floor. It needed another coat of paint, she thought. Lighter paint showed through in places, and beneath the table, streaks of bare blond wood floated in the deep blue.

Heart said, "I feel I'm to blame for part of this."

"Part of what?" Margaret said. "You mean for Apuro?" She nodded fiercely at Heart, wanting, Gay could see, to make Heart agree, to keep Heart from talking about Rita.

"I mean Rita," Heart said.

"Nonsense," Margaret said. "That murdering bastard is the perpetrator. Don't you—"

"I know that," Heart said, "but I can't help thinking . . ." Her voice trailed off, but she looked to be concentrating, her mouth crooked and filled with teeth—the same shape of mouth she gave when smiling—but her brows were deeply furrowed and her eyes were serious and sad.

"What do you mean?" Gay asked her.

"She went to Mr. Gene's," Heart said. "And I've never heard a satisfactory explanation for that. And she was wearing one of the dresses I made for her when she went. And, well, I heard what that Claire woman said to you. But if anyone's a scarecrow, we all know it's me."

"I'd like to believe it's your fault," Gay said. "I'd like to hate you for it, to have somebody right here to hate. But I don't believe it."

"You know if I . . ." Heart's voice broke, and she put a hand to her mouth, as if to hold in her anguish.

Behind Heart, just beyond the kitchen doorway, stood Cecilia Calzado. She had been listening, or perhaps her expression suggested some larger embarrassment, some deeper guilt than eavesdropping. She seemed to be waiting to be recognized.

Heart said, "If there were some way I could trade with Rita . . ."

"I'd let you," Gay said. She nodded at Cecilia, but the girl didn't respond. She looked tired, Gay decided. She looked as if she might fall asleep, as if she might still be sedated.

Heart was not through. "But why Mr. Gene? What was she . . . Why him?"

"Do you know?" Gay asked Cecilia. The others turned then.

Their eyes on her made Cecilia shrink and look longingly at the door that led outside. "I was supposed to meet Rita," she said.

"Do you know?" Gay repeated.

Cecilia nodded. She touched her cheek, as if to wipe off a tear, but she wasn't crying. Sander turned back to Gay. He said, "I was thinking—"

Gay cut him off. "Why Mr. Gene?" she asked. "Why him?"

"Oh, that." Cecilia spoke weakly without looking up, but her voice carried across the room. She said, "Why not him?"

Gay waited to be certain she was finished, but, really, what else was there to say? "Rita's already gone," she told Cecilia. "You just missed her."

Cecilia nodded again, turned, and walked away. She had trouble opening the door, then waved sadly to Gay before she left.

"There's your answer," Gay said to Heart.

Sander had finished his drink, and he set it on the table. "You know what occurred to me? If we go from underneath, we could get in without scarring anything."

Gay had an instant to think he had lost his mind. He had slipped, like Claire, off the edge. Steady Sander, finally unhinged. Why she had chosen to love him, she did not know. She could have, all those years ago, named Miguel as Rita's father. She could have picked Denny. For that matter, she could have chosen Heart, chosen to remain with Heart and build a life around their friendship. But she had selected Sander. Why not Sander? The heart has a secret itinerary, she thought, and private destinations. Simultaneous with these thoughts she came to an understanding—if Sander were mad she would care for him, nurse him through whatever afflicted him. Which was how Heart must have felt, all those years ago, when Gay had been sick. They were all connected by the powers of love and betrayal, and by the emaciated body that had slipped in and out of the room like a specter.

Sander pointed above Gay's head to the cabinet that was nailed shut. Gay turned, raising her eyes to the nailed door. She said, "We need a saw."

"What are you talking about?" Margaret asked.

"Find me a saw and I'll tell you," Gay said.

They raided Randall Lamb's store of power tools, selecting a circular saw and a heavy-duty extension cord. Gay climbed up on the counter and emptied the shelves directly below the mystery cabinet. Sander joined her. He turned the saw upside down, pulling back the safety, placing the round blade up against the ceiling of the cupboard Gay had emptied. "Plug me in," he said.

Sawdust flew in his face and he spat. Gay stepped down from the counter to mix them all new drinks. Dust and tiny chips of wood floated in her gin.

"Did you see that Geraldo show where they dynamited open some vault that had once belonged to Dillinger?" Margaret asked.

"I heard about that," Gay said, then to Sander she added, "Careful. Hurry."

Heart said, "What did they find?"

"I didn't actually see the show. I hate that gossip TV," Margaret said. "But the vault was empty. A big flop."

Sander executed a cut along the near border, and a parallel cut as close to the wall as he could make it. He turned the saw and made an incision that linked the previous two. "One more," he said. "Any ceremonial statements before it comes down?"

No one spoke, but Gay suddenly recalled something strange she had heard at the riverside, a stray comment that had floated within earshot just as the bulldozer made its attack on the first adobe hut. "Here comes the beaver shot," the voice had said.

Sander pressed the saw to the board, which cracked before the cut was complete. He released the trigger and pushed up on the now loose board, which made it crack more. He worked his fingers into the opening and pulled down on the cut board. It creaked and then broke, the board flinging free of Sander's hand, the contents of the cupboard erupting from their hiding place, ricocheting off the shelf below, separating into a dozen shiny forms, flying out into the light. Margaret leaped back, her drink sloshing to the floor. Sander slipped on the counter and threw out a hand to steady himself. Heart lifted her arms and spread her fingers protectively. Gay let out a tiny cry, before her breath caught in her throat.

The freed stuff whirled through the sunlit space, glinting like loosed demons, then struck the sink, the countertop, skidded to the floor: a dozen packages of cigarettes. Lucky Strikes.

Gay regained her composure first. "Somebody quit smoking," she said. Sander returned to the hole he had cut. He raised his arm into the cavity to be certain it was empty. Gay lifted a package from the floor and tore off the cellophane wrapping. The filterless cigarettes in the package waited like soldiers in their paper uniforms, the tobacco so old it hardly had an odor.

29

The dark glasses curled around his face, the lenses bulbous and black like the amphibious eyes of certain reptiles. The cheap straw cowboy hat had a blue ribbon around the crown and settled low across his forehead, just above the top rim of the glasses and resting heavily on his ears. The saleswoman had commented on the smallness of Rudy's head, sticking to her poor English, assuming he was from the U.S., a tourist despite the pallor of his skin. What gave him away? He had wanted to ask her, but hadn't. He had been born in Mexico. Legally, he had been Mexican all his life. But he had lived his life in the United States, and that still held sway, something the saleswoman could tell by his manner.

His hair grew wet beneath the hat, and sweat seeped out and down his face to the stubble of his scant beard. The striped serape in this heat made him a ridiculous figure, he knew, but he needed it, and he had purchased one made of cotton, the lightest material he could find. It circled his neck loosely and draped his arms to the elbow with alternating blue and yellow stripes. Beneath the serape, the T-shirt that he had stolen from a clothesline and which advertised a basketball dribbling camp in El Paso blotted sweat from his chest and back, moons of perspiration so large and dense that patches of moisture showed through the serape.

His pants he had also stolen, an ill-fitting pair of brown slacks, flaccid at the waist and bunching in the crotch, creating a pouch about his groin as if he suffered from a disease that inflamed his testes. Clothesline substituted for a belt.

His socks were new and white, never before worn, a compromise occasioned by the sink full of still-wet socks in his hotel room. He had bought them in the *mercado*, the cheapest pair he could find, a plastic quality to them that seemed to encourage his feet to sweat in his leather Nikes, his basketball shoes, which had survived the metamorphosis, had moved with him from one country to another, one life to another, while everything else had fallen away.

Even his body had abandoned him. He had lost twenty pounds since fleeing the U.S. Food poisoning had started the decline, three days of sweating in his hotel bed, consuming nothing but white crackers, warm sodas, and bottled water. Now the daily stalking in serape and hat, the sunbaked strolls across the sweltering streets, kept his weight off. He had trouble adjusting to the food. The sauces on the meat and beans seemed textured with sawdust, and the hard rolls made his gums bleed. Every afternoon and evening he sat hunched on the toilet while shit dribbled out of him as if from a perforated sack.

Although he held a folded Juárez newspaper in his hands and bent his head over it, leaning against the shady wall of a tile store just off the busy sidewalk, his stance still seemed predatory, as if one could tell that the paper was several days old, as if the sideways glance behind the black lenses showed. He no longer called himself by his given name. He chose Carlos as a first name because it was the most common Mexican name he could think of. He picked the surname of Camacho, after a boxer that Antonio Nieves admired. He hadn't yet figured out how to get false ID in this name, didn't even know how necessary it was to have identification. So far, no one had bothered him. Except for the occasional clerk or waitress, no one even spoke to him.

The two Anglo women he was following emerged from the tile shop chatting about an elevated hot tub, about grout and clashing colors. Their children followed, five of them, none taller than a woman's waist. The woman who most interested Rudy had a large, puffy hairdo with sunglasses nestled just above the hairline as if she had a second pair of eyes. She wore a T-shirt that read TANTALIZING LOINS on one side and had the name of a steakhouse on the back. Her shorts were the blue of children's toys and their brevity seemed to deny the beefiness of her thighs, the dimpled flesh that appeared beneath their neat hems. A leather purse tethered to her shoulder by a long and thin strap bounced against her hip when she walked. Rudy had followed them down the tourist boulevard for the past hour and a half. Except for her teeth, which had slightly yellowed, Rudy thought the woman looked healthy.

The other woman had darker hair with a red tint, and her thin face was full of tension, little ropes beneath the skin connecting the base of her nose to the corners of her mouth. Her gray T-shirt read CAUTION: ZERO TO BITCH IN 30 SECONDS. The children had grown bored with Juárez, their pale skin the pink of a coming burn.

At the next corner they would either retrace their steps or veer left and head for the *mercado*. If they turned around, Rudy would forget about them. He had learned to be patient, cautious. If they pursued the *mercado*, he would cut through the alley and be waiting for them behind the Nuñez Bakery. The few blocks they had to cover between this tourist-crowded boulevard and the *mercado* were relatively quiet.

The women paused at the corner, looking in one direction and then the other before turning toward the *mercado*. Rudy rolled up the newspaper as he strode down the alley, which cut a diagonal to the bakery. His quick pace and the shorter distance would give him time to check the street for *policía*.

He lived now at the Hotel del Sur, a dilapidated building twenty blocks from the border, two dollars a night. He had become shrewd with money, spending only what he absolutely had to, even eating the scraps left on others' plates at the café he frequented, using the lessons Antonio Nieves had given him. Everything was cheap here if you went to the right places, away from the tourists.

At night he lay on his bed on the third floor and looked through the window, watching the lights in the nearby buildings go dark, the world blinking off, quieting, shutting down. One night, from the vantage of his room, he had seen two women running through the street carrying flaming boxes in their hands, their clothing so loose that Rudy had at first thought they were wearing blankets. Another night he had heard people fucking in the next room, and he had masturbated while listening to them. The man who lived there was tiny and sleek, his skin like a boy's. The next morning Rudy saw his neighbor with his lover in the hallway. They were both men. Later that same week he would spot the tiny man near the *mercado* wearing a dress. He looked good as a woman, while he was a shrimp of a man. This transformation made sense, Rudy acknowledged. Having a homosexual in the next room made Rudy squeamish but not angry. He imagined this man holding hands with Humberto Douglas, and he couldn't work up anger.

His first weeks in hiding had been sponsored by *La Verdad*, whom Rudy had ripped off before leaving. Close to one hundred dollars, including the wallets of Billy Valdez and the other kid who had been in the car. Rudy had forced them at gunpoint to drive him to the border. He had waded across the Rio Grande and disappeared into the city, their roll of cash in his pocket, his pants wet and dark to the knee. But now he had to work for a living, and he waited in the alley at the corner of the bakery to ply his trade.

He opened the paper again and pretended to read. The women would not be able to see him from the sidewalk. He tucked one hand beneath the serape and removed a knife from his pocket. By hooking the butt of the knife in a belt loop, he could pry open the blade with one hand in the secrecy of the serape.

No sooner had he opened the blade than he heard their trudging patter on the sidewalk, the children whining for ice cream. He tossed the paper to the ground, checked again for *policía*. One of the women threatened to leave the children home next time, while the other promised ice cream once they were back in El Paso. A little girl appeared first, walking ahead blindly, her hands twirling the tip of her ponytail. A little sunburned boy followed, and then the women, walking side by side, recounting the bartering they had done for a bullwhip that another child now studied as he walked.

Rudy leapt into the sun and fell in step just behind Tantalizing Loins, the knife slicing through the air, his other hand gripping the swinging purse, the leather strap digging into the soft meat of her shoulder, the blade digging into leather. He stepped in closer, his bent knee burrowing into the back of her fleshy one, causing it to buckle, the same maneuver that had buckled opponents' knees on the basketball court. Her weight, as she fell, pulled the strap down the final centimeters of blade and the strap snapped. The limp band slithered through her armpit, and Rudy sprinted down the alley, leaving the fallen woman squealing on the sidewalk and the other pointing, staring, too startled to move. One of the children had begun crying.

The alley intersected another, and Rudy veered into it, tucking the purse down inside his baggy pants. He ducked into a doorway. From his pants pocket he tugged a plastic bag, then pulled the serape over his head, the hat and glasses coming off with it. He jammed it all into the bag. He withdrew a clean shirt from his other pants pocket, snapping it once to make it unfold. After looking down the alley again, he peeled off his T-shirt and buttoned up the wrinkled shirt. He carried the bag like a tourist carrying a new purchase. The tail of the clean shirt hid the rope belt and waistline stuffed with purse. He trotted down the alley, then stepped into the street and began his stroll home.

No door separated his bedroom from the bathroom, just a rusted set of hinges hanging loosely from the jamb. There was no hot water, and the tub drained so slowly it had to be cleaned after every bath. But summer weather made hot water unnecessary, and Rudy took pleasure in the routine of wiping down the tub. He had almost nothing else to do.

The mattress bed had a crease in the middle as deep as the one in his cowboy hat. Rudy had tugged the mattress off the box springs and put it on the floor to correct its sag. He had dismantled the bed and shoved it and the box springs into the corridor, where it all still leaned against the wall. He placed mousetraps in each corner and tossed the little bodies out the bathroom window into the tidy yard of the tenement house below.

Ciudad Juárez was a huge city, a patchwork of neighborhoods and industrial strips, business centers and grassy parks. Rudy knew this and knew that he had found one of the filthiest neighborhoods in which to reside. He didn't care. He needed to conserve money. He stole metal door handles from the rear of an empty building and screwed them into the wall on either side of his door with a screwdriver he borrowed from the desk clerk. Then he took a two-by-four from a construction site and trimmed it with his knife until it would slide through the handles and bolt shut the door. No one could get in while he was there. He left the place open while he was gone, nothing for anyone to take but his folded pants and shirts in the dresser, his soaking socks in the sink.

He tossed his bag onto the mattress, then took the two by four and shoved it through the handles, before pulling the purse out of his pants. He dropped it onto the bed beside the plastic bag and headed for the toilet to let his insides drain.

If people knew that he was stealing purses, they would say he had learned nothing from shooting his friend, that he was unchanged, but Rudy understood that was untrue. The steel band was gone, was finally satisfied. He could become another kind of man if he could only figure out how. And he had a plan. One that required money. One thousand dollars. At first he had thought two thousand, but money was hard to come by, and living in Mexico was cheap. A thousand would do.

He would go to Mexico City, the largest city in the world. There he would find work. He would become respectable. He would give up his past entirely. He would become a Mexican.

He would give up Carlos Camacho, as well. No sense in bringing a purse snatcher with him. He would become a new man. He was working on the name. He was considering becoming Tito Tafoya. The one friend who had visited Rudy at the hospital. The boy he had shot.

He wiped himself and threw the dirty paper in the trash beside the bowl. The pipes here could not handle toilet paper, a fact that he found hard to believe, the strangest thing of all about living in Mexico, to have a real toilet instead of an outhouse, but to be forced to collect his filthy paper in a wastebasket.

He took the purse from the bed and walked to the window. The sky in Juárez was different from the sky in Apuro. It held more color at sunset, but seemed lower and less honest. At times it felt like a lid. Some nights he studied the stars. He had taken an interest in them because so few in the city were visible. They seemed more valuable.

He wanted to return to El Paso for Liz. He thought she might go with him. But he had found an El Paso paper outside the Kentucky Bar and read that Billy and Liz and the other boy in the car were all being held without bond for the shooting. He read also that Apuro had been torn down. Erased. Disafuckingpeared.

At first this combined news had sent him into a slough of despair, but it had turned on him. It had made clear to him that he had only one choice, to go far away and remake his life. The article said that Tito had lived, that he would be deported when he was released from the hospital. Rudy imagined himself running into Tito, apologizing, explaining his mistake. He imagined them friends again. He knew this was fantasy, but he could not help himself.

He unsnapped the purse and began picking at the contents. Kleenex, a colorful comb with wavy teeth, keys, a child's pacifier, scraps of paper, an uncapped pen, and a wallet. In the wallet, forty-eight dollars, credit cards, and a driver's license. Sandra Madeleine Taylor-Smith of 1542 Canton Drive, Tulsa, Oklahoma. A picture of her children, another of herself with a man and a black dog. The man had dark circles beneath his eyes and a hollowed-out face. Among the credit cards, Rudy found an ID card for the cancer ward of an Oklahoma hospital.

He returned everything but the cash to the purse. He tied the severed ends of the strap together. He tried to think of a way of returning all but the money to her, but he could think of nothing that wouldn't endanger himself. He wondered then whether the Shopper had cancer. It bothered him that he could no longer remember her real name. No matter the diagnosis, he knew her wasted body was his doing. It had been what he had wanted all along. Now, though, her emaciated body haunted him.

He fell into an uneasy and dreamless sleep, waking to find his window dark. In the next room, two men worked feverishly at loving each other. Their noise had brought Rudy back from sleep. He listened, imagining Liz, imagining himself with her, but he could not help but see the little man with another man on top of him. Nevertheless, he got hard. He wanted to complain to someone. At least speak to someone. He felt obliged to inform somebody about the circumstances of his life. He pictured the little man pulling up his dress to reveal his penis. Another man touching it. As if to prove to himself that his metamorphosis was complete, Rudy Salazar masturbated to this scene. He came before his neighbors were through. Then he cleaned himself up and returned to sleep.

30

By phone, Enrique's cousin Don, the nurse in L.A., told him that anything anybody could ever want was in California. What was it Enrique wanted him to get? "Something my girlfriend will eat," Enrique said. "There has to be something, right?" His cousin's tone changed then, became solicitous and careful.

"That kind of problem," Don said, "doesn't really have to do with the flavor of food." He told Enrique about patients he worked with in the hospital who would not eat or who ate but threw up their food. "It's not that their taste buds have gone bad," he said. "It's more like they're punishing themselves."

"I think Rita's different," Enrique said. The phone was in the kitchen, and he sat at the table and wrapped the cord around his finger. No one else was home. He was not supposed to make long-distance calls without permission, but he did not think he had a choice. "I can't explain it," he said, "but, see, to start with, she wasn't skinny at all. Then she got kind of attacked by this guy."

"Your mom told me about that," Don said. "I think maybe that made her feel bad about herself."

"It's not that so much as she thinks there was a reason for it." Enrique tried to relate what he barely understood. "Like she had to be attacked so this guy who did it could get better, you know, quit hitting people and stuff. She poked him with her earring, and thought that maybe straightened him up. So the next thing she knows, she isn't eating so much, and she thinks there must be a reason for that, too. Then everyone starts telling her how good she looks. You ever seen that actress Winona Ryder?"

"Was she in *Dracula*?"

"Probably. Anyway, Rita, for a while, started looking like Winona Ryder—not that she looked like her really, but she looked like what Winona Ryder would look like if she looked like Rita. She had that movie kind of thinness, and everybody knew she was beautiful."

"Not just you," Don said.

"Yeah." Enrique had seen it in the eyes of others, and he had known he was supposed to see it, but he hadn't found her any more beautiful than before. He understood that this was a failing of his, and he didn't want to admit it to his cousin. "So since everybody liked her skinny, she decided that this not eating, that there must be a reason for it. That it meant something."

"How thin is she now?"

"She doesn't look like Winona Ryder anymore," Enrique said. Her face had darkened beneath her eyes and even in the hollows of her cheeks, a darkness, like a shadow, like the beginning of a bruise. Her body—Enrique did not know how to say this—her body no longer looked like the body of a human. Instead it had become the body of a foreign creature, one from another planet, repulsive to all humans—all except Enrique. He could tell that in the alien world, she was beautiful. He could see the beauty and the not-beauty, the shadows of something not human. He could not say himself what this not-human quality was, but he could see in the reactions of others what it must be.

"My dad lost a lot of weight before he died," Enrique said. "Not as much as Rita, but a whole lot."

"I'm sorry about your dad," Don said. "He was okay in my book. I always liked him."

"Me too," Enrique said, and he lost track of the conversation. Every moment of his waking life, he thought about either Rita or Cecilia. He dreamed of them as he had once dreamed of Apuro. In one dream, his job was simply to hold on to their arms so they wouldn't drift away on a current of air. Obsessively, he worked on ways to keep them alive. He had already tried board games, making cards that required eating an apple to get out of jail or to send someone back to Go. But Rita had decided to linger in jail, and Cecilia had fallen asleep waiting for her turn.

His nights had a pattern his days lacked. He would begin in his bed, in his top bunk, but he would climb down from it during the night while still asleep and make his way out to the car, where he would sleep in the front seat, his head lolling over the floorboard, until Cecilia would appear in her nightgown at the car window and wake him. She no longer had to explain. He would follow her inside and sleep on the floor beside her bed. For some reason she needed him there. But the days had no routine. He missed the order that school provided, the distraction. If he was thinking about history, he might not be worried about his sister or considering ways to get Rita to eat.

"So this guy who attacked Rita," Enrique went on, "he shot a friend of ours. I guess Mom told you that?"

"I didn't know it was the same guy."

"Yeah, so I thought maybe Rita would see then that he wasn't all better, but she keeps turning everything around so it still makes into some kind of meaning. And her parents are back together, like that was all connected to her not eating." He wondered then if Rita felt responsible for the destruction of Apuro, as well. Did she see herself at the center of that? It was hard for Enrique to believe Apuro was gone. One day it was there, and then there was rubble, and then there was not even that. Enrique had waded across river yesterday morning. Cecilia had been asleep and Rita was on her way with her mother to see the counselor in El Paso. With the morning free, Enrique had hiked to the crossing spot, taken off his shoes, and walked across. But there had been nothing to see. Just the upturned earth, a curving scar alongside the river.

"You there?" Don asked.

"Yeah, sorry."

"Is your girlfriend Catholic?"

"No," Enrique said. "Why?"

"Just a thought."

"So I was thinking if I could find some food that has *meaning*, you know what I'm talking about? That she would eat it."

"Oh, Enrique, I wish I could help you with this one."

"I have to do something," he said, and then the line went quiet, a silence that seemed quieter than just the absence of sound. Which is how it had sounded across river in the place that had once been Apuro, a strange, loud silence.

His mind was wandering, and he needed to concentrate. He got up from the kitchen table, the phone tucked between shoulder and cheek. He leaned against the refrigerator to make it stop the noise it was making. He said, "I hate Winona Ryder now."

"I'll help you if I can," Don said. "Anything. Anything I can do. You name it."

"She's in this group. Once a week she goes and sees these other girls who won't eat. It's like a club. The counselor keeps telling them that they're great and stuff, but I don't think that's going to make her eat. She already thinks she's doing good things. She thinks not eating is the best thing she's doing."

"Did you want me to try and find some treatment for her here?" Don asked. "I could talk to this doctor at the hospital who's really smart about this kind of thing."

"I know she won't eat anything you can find in a school cafeteria," Enrique said. "And there aren't that many restaurants here. But I started thinking, you know, and I came up with this idea maybe you could help me with."

"I'll help you."

"I have to do something."

"I understand."

The cardboard pallet of persimmons arrived a few days later. They were small, each about the size of a hackey sack, the color of a peach but without the fuzz, the skin paper thin. A note from Don said that these were very ripe and to eat them quickly. Enrique called Rita and they agreed on a hike. He had wanted to suggest a picnic, but he was afraid she wouldn't come if food was involved. A hike, he called it, but he knew it couldn't be more than a walk. She tired quickly.

He woke his sister to see if she would come along. Since Tito's blood had spattered her dress, she slept a lot. Enrique kept looking for signs that she was going to quit eating or start acting strange. But she just slept a lot and watched television with their mother.

"A hike?" Cecilia said. "It's a hundred degrees out." She had slept in her clothes, a button-up blouse and denim shorts that didn't look comfortable.

"I have a surprise," he said, raising the backpack he had loaded with persimmons. "Rita's coming."

Cecilia sat up in her bunk and stretched. "She won't eat it," she said, "whatever it is." She slipped to the floor and began running her hands over her blouse, as if to erase the wrinkles.

Enrique left her room. His mother and brother were both out working. He should probably get a summer job, too, but there was no time for it. He sat at the kitchen table and tapped his fingers while Cecilia got ready. He believed his sister would be okay. She just had to wait it out, like waiting for a lingering cold to leave your lungs. It didn't seem it would ever be gone, but one day you felt not so bad and you realized you were recovering. He wanted Rita to see Cecilia recover. He wanted her to see that it was possible.

The shooting of Tito had not upset Rita the way Enrique had thought it would. She had started talking about angels, how she thought there were angels that lived in the spaces between sunlight and air. Somehow she had known that Tito wasn't going to die. Just known it. She never exactly connected it with the angels, but the shooting hadn't upset her. Nothing had surprised her.

Enrique had been happy, at first, that she didn't freak out, but then he worried about her reaction, worried that she was seeing herself in the car, taking the bullet, joining the angels. She thought she was making some kind of sacrifice for the good of everybody else, a sacrifice so obscure that only she could recognize its meaning, which made it impossible to talk her out of it. She told him that she had been baptized in the river of darkness, and everything that followed had occurred because of the three women who had stepped into the black water. Of the three, only she had been pure of heart. Now she was pure of mind, and pure of body as well. "I don't have a period anymore," she whispered proudly into his ear. "My body has cleansed itself. I used to be black inside, like the river that night, but now I'm pure."

Enrique, when he finally figured out what she was talking about, told her that he had seen the black river, too. She had smiled at him. "That makes it perfect, doesn't it? You saw it from the car, while I sank into it and was purified." She had leaned close then and said, "Don't worry. I've taken your darkness from you. I've burned it as if it were my own. You're cured." After that, he had been careful not to bring up the subject.

Cecilia finally entered the kitchen, having changed into different shorts and a clean shirt. Her hair stood up on one side, and her lids were puffy, but she was ready to go. "Do I have to do anything on this hike?" she asked him.

"Just have fun," he said, touching his own hair, which was growing out again—all of it the same dumb-looking length, but he didn't have time to think about hairstyle. "It's a fun hike."

"Okay," she said glumly. "Fun. I'll do my best."

Rita climbed the stairs to be certain, although she twice had to stop and rest on a step. She'd had a vision. A dream, really, but the dream had wakened her to a new understanding. Something very specific. In the dream, she had been on Mr. Gene's ranch, walking naked among the horses, whose loose mouths kissed her bare shoulders, whose long tongues caressed her neck. Mr. Gene stood on the other side of a corral, the wooden bars of the fence breaking up his body, his hand held high to block out the sun. She glanced at the sun as she worked her way toward him, and the intensity of the light played tricks on her eyes, turning everything black and white, as if she had entered an old movie. A breeze lifted the hat from Mr. Gene's head, and he stared at her bareheaded.

When she woke, the black-and-white image of him from the dream merged with the black-and-white photo she had seen in Heart's closet. She waited all morning until finally her parents and Heart left to get ice cream.

She had told them she would eat it if they would all three go and bring it home to her. Then she climbed the stairs. She wanted to confirm what her vision had revealed. That Mr. Gene was the boy in the photo. That Mr. Gene was Heart's brother.

The bed in Heart's room was perfectly made. The floor was swept and free of clothing or debris. Sunlight poured through the windows. The swamp cooler pumped in moist air by means of a metal vent. Rita dragged the chair from the sewing machine to the closet and climbed upon it. She took the shoebox from the top shelf.

Heart had taken advantage of him, Rita thought as she stepped down from the chair. She had blinded him. It was child molestation. It was sexual abuse.

The photo lay on the top of the pile. The boy stood closest to the camera, one arm raised, his squinting eyes creating the lines about his eyes that revealed the man. Heart stood behind him with another sister. They were in his shadow. It was unmistakably him. Mr. Gene. Brother Gene. Rita felt suddenly dizzy and leaned over the mattress. She had fainted a few times. The strangest feeling. Like floating. She held the photograph to her chest and let the feeling pass. Heart, in the picture, trampled his shadow. In real life, Heart had trampled his soul. Rita saw it all clearly.

She replaced the box on the high shelf above Heart's few dresses, but she kept the photograph. She dragged the chair back to the sewing machine, which Heart had situated before one of the dormer windows. There, through the glass, Rita saw Enrique and Cecilia up the street, standing together on the asphalt, talking through the window of her father's truck. Her father was driving the truck. Her mother sat in the middle on the hump. Heart sat by the passenger window.

Rita knew her new power had brought her parents back together. Now she would cast out Heart. She would reveal Heart in order to rescue Mr. Gene. It saddened Rita to bear this responsibility, but she owed it not only to Mr. Gene but also to the gift she had been given. She had been mistaken to think that Mr. Gene would love her once Heart was gone. That had been the corrupt thought of the earlier girl she had been. She must be selfless. Giving and not taking. She had thought she had a crush on Mr. Gene, but that had never been it. He had come to her attention so that she could save him.

As she descended the stairs, another piece of the human puzzle fell into place—the reason the photograph was black and white. All the pictures in the pornographic magazine she had taken from Heart's store were black and white. The photographs of sex had spoken to her, had told her that this other black-and-white photo, the boy and his sister, Mr. Gene and Heart—this, too, was a photograph of sex. She accepted the secret and profound workings of her gift, how mysterious threads wove together to reveal the very fabric of life. She rushed into her room to retrieve the magazine, jerking it from beneath the dollhouse, tipping the house over. The miniature family tumbled out onto the floor.

The truck pulled up to the curb just as she opened the front door. Her father had been attempting to reclaim the yard and had left the hose running. Water lapped up against the buckling sidewalk on either side. Enrique and Cecilia climbed from the bed of the truck, first him and then her. Enrique carried a backpack. They were going for a hike, she recalled.

Heart's door was next to the curb. She was the first to step from the cab, cups of ice cream in her hands, pink plastic spoons sticking up from the mounds. She approached, head down, looking at her feet. Rita understood that she would attack her, that she would shove her into the water, that she would stand above her and point, that she would reveal the truth to everyone. "You're fucking your brother," she would say. Or "Your lover is your brother." Or "Incest is a sin." No, not "sin," and it was not simply that it was against the law, against the rules that people had agreed to, it was something else, something beating within Rita, some dark thing with wings thrashing inside her.

She recalled the stories her parents had told about Heart, her head like a coconut, and the bet that had ultimately severed the marriage of Sander and Gay. Now she, Rita, had brought them back together. All along it had been herself versus Heart, a struggle she had waged blindly until now.

A surge of energy came to her, a rush of power. She charged forward over the uneven sidewalk, the photograph in one hand, the magazine rolled up in the other. Her feet slapped the concrete. Little streams of water crossed the walk, and she jumped over them as she ran.

Heart looked up, the corners of her grotesque mouth lifting at the sight of Rita's rapid approach. Incest was *unnatural*, but that word left Rita queasy, which must have shown, she could see it in Heart's eyes and Enrique's too. He followed Heart up the walk. His head, covered with the odd length of hair, quivered, as if he had a palsy. If she had not known him, she might have thought him as ugly as Heart.

Just before reaching Heart and heaving her off the walk, Rita stumbled, falling forward, the dark water rushing up to her. But Heart caught her first. Heart's arms wrapped tightly around her and pulled her close, the weight of the fall knocking Heart to her knees, ice cream tumbling down her dress. But she held Rita up, unharmed.

"You okay?" Heart said. One of Heart's knees slid off the walk and into the water. The other people were running now, approaching, their footsteps on the concrete like drumbeats.

"I just tripped," Rita said, pulling herself from Heart's arms. "I'm all right. Don't everybody gather."

No one spoke. Heart's mouth crinkled up in anger, as if she understood Rita's intentions. No, she was about to cry, and Rita could see the dead woman inside the living one, the Heart with cancer who inhabited the other Heart. Then Heart began weeping, while at the same time trying not to, her face contorting from the combined efforts. She got up, her knee muddy, her shoe—the hideous man's shoe—filled with water, the hem of her dress soaked. As she rose, Rita noticed the photo floating on the water. It had slipped from of her hand and slid beneath Heart's body, landing in the puddle, the black-and-white photo, Mr. Gene's bent arm, Heart's crooked smile, brother and sister standing on a sloping yard, and behind them a clothesline or it could have been a distant power line—some kind of wire showing discontinuously, disappearing behind the smiling boy, behind the smiling girl, linking them in this shared past. As she studied the photo, Heart—the real Heart—placed her hands on Rita's shoulders, planted a kiss on Rita's cheek, and the characters in the photo began to move, one toward the other, each pulling at the wire that connected them. The boy wasn't smiling after all. His lips were thin with fear, and the girl—Heart—was working to reach him.

Then the illusion passed. It was not the figures that had moved but the photo, slipping beneath the surface of the muddy water, a dirty film covering the image, as the photograph faded and then disappeared into the sludge.

"Rita?" her mother said. "Honey?"

"I'm fine," Rita said. "I ate," she added as she stood, anticipating the inevitable question, heading it off with a white lie. She held herself still until a momentary dizziness passed. "We're going on a walk," she said. "Enrique and I. And Cecilia."

Her father turned off the hose. Heart and Gay dawdled on the walk a while, but they stepped inside soon enough. The picture had vanished. What remained, for Rita, was another image. For a moment, when the crying had made Heart's face twist, the two halves had matched, Heart's eyes level, her mouth no longer crooked, the contortions of sadness making her features temporarily symmetrical. And even then, even with this fleeting gift, Heart had remained ugly.

Seeing this affected Rita. The anger she had held evaporated. She could feel its vapor rising from her skin.

They didn't hike far. They walked along the river to the trees, where Enrique picked a shady spot. He had brought a blanket, which he spread over the sandy ground. His sister had begun crying, a silent weeping that none of them acknowledged, except by his saying, "This is a good place. We can take a break here."

Cecilia turned to hide her eyes, then let herself down onto the blanket, saying softly, "I'm sleepy." She closed her eyes.

Already Enrique's plans were going askew. They hadn't walked far enough to work up an appetite, and now Cecilia would be too sad to talk. Had he done something to make her sad? He didn't think so, but how could he know? The world had become treacherous. If he smiled at the wrong time, his sister might start crying and his girlfriend might faint. He swept dirt from the blanket and scrambled up, taking Rita's arm.

She said, "If I die, you could marry Cecilia."

Enrique bent back over to grab the pack. His sister opened her eyes and made the same expression he was making, a *What's happening to her?* look, but she let go of it and pretended again to sleep.

Enrique straightened, the pack in hand. Rita stood before him, staring up at the trees—thinking, he could tell, or whatever it was she did now that substituted for thinking. "She's my sister," he said. "I couldn't marry her."

Rita lifted her brows in a funny way. "You could if you wanted to," she said.

In a whisper, he added, "You're not going to die."

She pretended not to hear. "Let's walk more," she said, extending her free hand to him. In the other hand she still held the magazine. There had to be a reason she had brought it with her, but she did not know what it was. She had come to believe that they lived in the shadows of angels, that the shifting patterns of light and dark had beauty and meaning, but it was a beauty that was beyond their reckoning, and a meaning that she could at best only glimpse. Some of the angels were forced to walk the earth. How awkward and slow they must be, she thought, their huge wings causing them to stumble and list.

Enrique suddenly fell against her, his chin bumping her shoulder. He had tripped over a root. "Whoa," he said. "Heavy pack." He held it up before her, but she had no interest.

"Take my hand," she said, offering it again, unable to recall the moment she had withdrawn it. She wondered if the people in the magazine—the people having sex in black and white for others to look at—she wondered if these people were angels themselves. Sex, they seemed to be saying, was just this and just that, precisely this with exactly that. Sex could be reduced to almost nothing of importance, even if it was between brother and sister, even if it was something you were forced to do. Once you understood as much, you could concentrate on the other things, the things between people that were less tangible, the things that could not be made explicit.

She turned to Enrique and said, "Let's take off our clothes."

"We'd get scratched," Enrique said.

"Don't you want to see me naked?" She felt a rush of blood to her head. It was not the same as when she felt desire, more like when she was about to faint, but she let herself pretend it was desire. She wanted to do something with Enrique. She wanted to lie next to him in the river mud and find that other thing that was not sex.

But the thought of the river brought to mind the soiled hem of Heart's dress, the shoe filled with dirty water, the photograph disappearing in the sludge. There was something she had not understood, still did not understand.

She lifted the hem of her Heart dress and pulled it over her head. Her panties were too large for her, and slid down her legs with ease. Her body, unveiled in sunlight, appeared to her to be perfect, her breasts flattened, absent, her ribs like ripples in the river, the beauty of her skeleton, that fragile human framework—God's architecture—exquisitely revealed.

She began undressing Enrique, unbuttoning his shirt, unclasping his belt. "We could get a sunburn," he pointed out, but he did not resist as she pulled off his shirt. She tugged at the waist of his pants, her fingers cold against his skin, although it was a hot day. She bent to study the clasp at the waist of his jeans. Her hair had grown thin, and Enrique could see the pale skin covering her skull. "You brought a catalog?" he asked when the magazine rolled in her fist knocked against him.

She did not answer, finally getting his pants undone. As she tugged them down, he examined her spine, how it showed through the skin. He could see every vertebra. Her skin had become nothing but a gown for her bones.

She yanked his pants down to his knees, smiled at him, then turned and faced the river. She was a delicate being, Enrique thought. Her legs, little more than stalks, brought to mind the wading birds he had seen at the El Paso zoo. As if she could hear his thoughts, she stepped off the bank and waded into the water, which looked to be deep, covering her to her thighs.

Enrique plopped down on the grass to struggle with his clothing. He tried to remove his pants without first taking off his shoes. Then he had to run a hand up the reversed pantlegs to untie the shoes. He had not planned for the river to be part of the hike. He did not know what she might do in water.

His shoes finally untied, he pulled his pants and underwear off. He stood on the grass and called her name. His voice sounded funny, he thought, as if he had been running and was winded. Rita thought otherwise. His voice sounded to her like something had been stripped away from it, as if his voice, like his body, were naked. She did not find his body attractive, but she liked looking at it. So much flesh.

"I want to show you something," he said, naked but evidently still with something unexposed. He knelt and began fiddling with his pack, the cleft in his buttocks widening slightly as he bent. She uncurled the magazine and paged to a picture of a naked man standing near a woman, as Enrique had just stood near her, but this man had an erection and Enrique had not. In the next frame, the man was having sex with the woman's mouth. Rita had examined these pictures often. The woman's face contorted. A lump showed through the skin like a bone, and then it disappeared inside her. Rita studied the woman's face, the glint in her eyes, the lines in her forehead. She wanted to see precisely what the woman was going through. She felt the pain in her own mouth, the slight tearing, the saline taste of blood.

In the final frames, the woman was smiling, perhaps from pleasure, or from having it conclude, or maybe because she knew that her expressions were being recorded. Rita liked the photograph and disliked it at the same time. Precisely this with exactly that. It excited her, and it made her sad.

Enrique still squatted over his pack, his bare shoulders revealing movement beneath the skin. She could see his genitals swinging beneath. Finally he stood again. He stepped off the bank and into the river. He had something for her.

"What is it?" she asked.

"A persimmon," he said.

Her breath caught. The magazine slipped from her hand and fluttered to the water. A small thing and delicate, but the persimmon felt heavy in her palm. "Which tree did it come from?" she asked him. "I thought they were all gone. I thought that was all dead."

Enrique put his hand on her back. He raised her arm, the hand that held the persimmon rising to her mouth. "It's sweet," he said.

The smooth skin of the persimmon parted her lips. Her tongue pressed against the flesh. Her teeth punctured it, the casing giving way to the sweet, rich fruit. Juice erupted from it. A slow, thick stream coursed through her mouth, down her throat, warming her from the inside. She offered a bite to Enrique. He shook his head. "It's for you," he said.

Sunlight illuminated the surface of the water. Though the river had appeared brown from the shore, up close the water was both clear and muddy. She could see her knees, but nothing below. A breeze lifted her hair and moved the face of the water. She imagined the man and woman who had founded the persimmon groves standing as she and Enrique were standing, naked in moving water. But their faces changed, and she saw instead Heart and Mr. Gene standing together long ago in a river such as this, as children together, as brother and sister all those years past, living in a part of the country Rita had never seen, during a time that preceded her own existence. Then she pictured Heart and Mr. Gene as they looked now, at the ranch, touching each other, one leaning into the other just as one had been leaning into the other for longer than Rita had been alive.

She had been foolish to believe she could save Mr. Gene. This awareness pressed itself upon her so resolutely she became embarrassed. She felt she might be blushing, but the intense heat of the sun on her face made it impossible to tell. It was likely that Heart was attempting to save him. It was possible that she took care for her brother simply because he needed her help. Rita did not really know that Heart and Mr. Gene were lovers. They could be. They might not be. It was conceivable that Heart did not need a man at all.

Rita held the persimmon to her nose. It smelled like something she knew, like the wet earth of a field recently irrigated. She put the persimmon to her mouth again but paused, hunching forward and smiling. Enrique immediately looked around, thinking she had seen something.

"You lost your catalog," he said and began wading after the magazine, which was floating downstream, beginning to sink, leaving a black trail in the water as the ink washed out. She grabbed his arm to stop him. "What?" he asked. "I can swim and get it. Don't you want your whatever-it-is? It looks like the catalog my brother orders his hair stuff from. He rubs this stuff in to make his hair stand up. Don't ask me why."

She put her hand on his shoulder, touched his chest, let her fingers run down to his belly button. And she knew she had not cured Enrique of anything. He had the talent for love. If he had not loved her, he would have loved someone else. Even her parents, whom she had brought back together, had also—she could see it—never entirely been apart.

Understanding these things sent a vibration through her, which she could see reflected in the movement of the water. She had saved no one.

"What is it?" he asked her.

"We're naked," she said and she laughed.

They waded back to the grassy patch. She gathered their clothes into her arms. Enrique slung the pack over his shoulder. Their walk back through the trees she found strangely exhilarating, an electric charge ranging over her skin. They returned to the blanket, where Cecilia slept, her knees bent, her hair and clothing dappled by the shadows of trees, her mouth open like a child's. Rita piled the clothes at Cecilia's feet, then sat beside her. Her skin would not stop tingling, a sensation she could not describe except to compare it to rain, the feel of rain on an overheated body.

Enrique revealed that his pack was full of persimmons. He held it in front of him, as if to hide his nakedness, but then he upended it. The persimmons tumbled out onto the blanket, rolling into a square of sunlight. Some were bruised. Some had burst open and were glazed with juice, which reflected the sun and made them golden.

Rita still held the first persimmon. She took another bite, the strange sensation shifting from her skin to her stomach, changing as it shifted, a peculiar feeling. She thought she might vomit, but that feeling passed while the strange one remained. No longer faint, no longer feigning desire, she felt a specific and powerful urge she could not name.

Enrique leaned toward her. Raising his hand, he offered her another persimmon. She recognized then the sensation she felt. It was hunger.

And she understood that he was saving her. It was his turn.

She could swallow no more, but she let her tongue rest on the wounded flesh of the persimmon, the flavor like a current of light in her body. Enrique sat cross-legged on the blanket. His skin painted by the sun. "It's good to eat," he said, selecting one of the persimmons from the blanket for himself. She smiled at him.

They ate.

A Note About the Author

Robert Boswell lives with his wife, the writer Antonya Nelson, and their children in Las Cruces, New Mexico, and Telluride, Colorado. He is an associate professor of English at New Mexico State University and is on the faculty of the Warren Wilson M.F.A. program for writers. He has been the recipient of two National Endowment for the Arts fellowships, a Guggenheim fellowship, the PEN West Award for fiction, the Evil Companions Prize, and the Iowa School of Letters Award for short fiction.

A Note on the Type

This book was set in Janson, a typeface long thought to have been made by the Dutchman Anton Janson, who was a practicing typefounder in Leipzig during the years 1668–1687. However, it has been conclusively demonstrated that these types are actually the work of Nicholas Kis (1650–1702), a Hungarian, who most probably learned his trade from the master Dutch typefounder Dirk Voskens. The type is an excellent example of the influential and sturdy Dutch types that prevailed in England up to the time William Caslon (1692–1766) developed his own incomparable designs from them.

Composed by PennSet, Bloomsburg, Pennsylvania
Printed and bound by Quebecor Printing,
Fairfield, Pennsylvania
Designed by Peter A. Andersen